DRAMATIS THINGUMMY

Matthew Edward Farrell	A very small but very important human.
Dr Maxwell	Chief Operations Officer. Not having a good year. Not having a good year at all.
Leon Farrell	Chief Technical Officer. Racing up and down the timeline. Again. Can he save the day? Again?
Tim Peterson	Not in a good place.
Mr Markham	Unexpectedly in charge of the Security Section.
Dr Bairstow	Director of St Mary's. Holding them all together.
Mrs Partridge	PA to Dr Bairstow and Muse of History.

HISTORY DEPARTMENT

Mr Clerk	Senior Historian.
Miss Prentiss	Senior Historian.
Mr Atherton Mr Bashford Miss North Miss Sykes	Normal historians – where the word normal has a different meaning from in the real world.
Miss Grey	Very unenthusiastic historian.

TECHNICAL SECTION

Mr Dieter	Second Chief Technical Officer.
Mr Lindstrom	Technical Officer.
	Terrified of women. He's not going to fare well at St Mary's, is he?

MEDICAL SECTION

Dr Helen Foster	Chief Medical Officer.
	Will now never be without a packet of cigarettes.
Nurse Fortunata	Junior Nurse.
Nurse Hunter	If she is married to Markham then not surprisingly she's keeping very quiet about it.
Dr Nathaniel Stone	Can't quite believe what's going on around him. Possesses a degree in advanced deviousness.
	Cocoa drinker.

RESEARCH AND DEVELOPMENT

Professor Rapson	Head of R&D
	One of the tossers.
Miss Lingoss	Multi-coloured member of R&D.
	The other tosser.
Dr Dowson	Librarian and Archivist.
	Surprisingly subdued this time around.

OTHERS

Mrs Mack	Kitchen Supremo, former urban guerrilla and maker of extremely good cakes.
Mrs Enderby	Head of Wardrobe. Unexpectedly good with a croquet mallet.
Miss Lee	Supposedly Max's PA. Not yet up to speed with telephone answering techniques.

THE TIME POLICE

(Managing to be both the baddies and the goodies depending at which point in the story you are.)

Marietta Hay	Commander of Time Police.
Captain Charlie Farenden	Her adjutant.
Captain Matthew Ellis	A familiar face.
A doctor	With his hands full.
Officers Trent and Parrish	Pizza bringers.
Officer Van Owen	An old friend.
Sundry Time Police Officers	Whose main purpose seems to be to stand around in corridors fighting with Max.

Adrian and Mikey	Time Travellers from the future and proud teapot builders. Slowly dying of radiation sickness.
Turk	An alleged horse. Possesses strong opinions concerning personal space.
Lisa Dottle	Not anywhere near as wet as she used to be. Only slightly damp these days and getting drier all the time. Fancies Peterson.
Colin	A dead dog currently residing on top of Max's wardrobe.
Rushfordshire Stinking Henry	A rather large piece of radioactive cheese.
Clive Ronan	Yep. He's back again.

HISTORICAL FIGURES

Harold Godwinson	Earl of Wessex and later King of England.
Duke William of Normandy	The Bastard.
Count Guy of Ponthieu	Proud possessor of Harold Godwinson and determined to cash in.
Odo of Conteville	Battling Bishop of Bayeux.
King Harald Hardrada	Earns his seven feet of English soil.
Tostig of Northumberland	An opportunist.
Eystein Orri	Unsuccessfully bringing reinforcements.

Giant Viking	Holding the bridge.
Edith Swanneschals	King Harold's mistress and body snatcher.

PLUS A CAST OF THOUSANDS...

The Lost Army of Cambyses	All fifty thousand of them.
The citizens of Beaurain	All of them probably suffering from some dreadful lung disease.
The citizens of Bayeux	All under their bishop's watchful eye.
The Viking army of Harald and Tostig	Meeting their end at Stamford Bridge. *Not* the boring football ground! The other one.
The Saxon Fyrd	Making its final appearance. Never to be seen again.
The Norman Army	Including mercenaries, adventurers and anyone else looking to make a quick buck.
The citizens of Constantinople	Not having a good day.
Crusaders	On their way to the Holy Land and inexplicably stopping off in Constantinople. Pillage and plunder almost certainly have something to do with it.

PROLOGUE

I was back at St Mary's. I was safe. My baby, Matthew, was safe. Leon was safe. Statements I'd once never thought I'd be able to make. These days, the three of us were a contented family unit. I loved Matthew. Matthew loved me. And Leon loved both of us.

Despite his dramatic entry into this world, Matthew was a happy, friendly, normal little baby, who would gurgle contentedly as he was passed from person to person and spoiled rotten, but mostly – he was mine. I was the one to whom he held out his arms first. He always held out his arms to me. I could hardly believe it. Leon laughed and called him 'Mummy's Boy', but the two of us had a special relationship. For me, it was a time of quiet happiness, because none of this was something I ever thought would happen to me.

True, Leon and I were still at St Mary's. After Clive Ronan's attempt to kidnap me, Dr Bairstow had requested that, for our own protection, we remain at St Mary's, and so we had. We had a suite of rooms up under the roof in the main part of the building, which, as Peterson said, were along so many narrow corridors and up so many crooked stairways, that any passing homicidal psychopath would never be able to find us.

He was a happy bunny these days, as well. No one knew what methods he'd used to persuade Dr Foster to marry him, but whatever he'd done had worked. He was regarded around the building with equal amounts of awe, admiration, respect and sympathy.

'About bloody time,' I'd said, grinning at him, and Markham had made a rude noise, which was a mistake on his part because attention immediately shifted his way.

'So what about you?' demanded Peterson, moving his chair slightly so Markham couldn't escape.

'What about me?' he said, innocence oozing from every pore.

'Are you married?'

'Me?' he said in astonishment.

'Yes, you.'

'Whatever gave you that idea?'

'You did.'

'Did I? When?'

A few days after Matthew's somewhat unconventional entry into the world, Markham had let slip he was married. To Hunter. They'd been married for years he'd said, and then nipped out of the door while we were too gobsmacked to stop him. Peterson and I had been attempting to get to the bottom of this ever since, but as teachers, employers, policemen, magistrates, army officers and Dr Bairstow had discovered, Markham can be a slippery little sod when it comes to prising information out of him. He was being one now, grinning at us over his mug of tea. We'd tried every possible approach and were still none the wiser, and neither of us had the nerve to approach Nurse Hunter, the terror of St Mary's.

We all work at St Mary's. Or, to give it the correct title, the Institute of Historical Research at St Mary's Priory. Our job is to investigate major historical events in contemporary time. It's not time travel because, as Dr Bairstow never fails to point out, we are not living in the pages of a sci-fi/fantasy novel, and no one argues with him, because our lives are hazardous enough without deliberately asking for trouble. So we never mention time travel. Although that's what we do.

We're located just outside Rushford at the end of a country lane that goes nowhere, because the Government thought we couldn't do much damage in this remote corner of a quiet county. That assumption was about as correct as government assumptions usually are. Surely the law of averages dictates that one day they must get at least one right.

Anyway, my name is Maxwell. I'm Chief Operations Officer and returning from maternity leave to a crowded schedule. We had a lot on these days. There were important anniversaries coming up and Thirsk University, our nominal employers, had commissioned an in-depth study of the events culminating in the Battle of Hastings. We were to witness the aftermath of Harold Godwinson's shipwreck – the one that placed him in the power of William of Normandy, followed by that critically important oath-taking ceremony at Bayeux. Then on to Stamford Bridge – that's the battle, not the much less interesting football ground – when Harold defeated the forces of Tostig and Harold Hardrada and then, nineteen days later, the struggle at Hastings itself and the end of Saxon life in England. If time and finances permitted, there would be a jump to William's coronation on Christmas Day, 1066. Something which I wouldn't be able to attend. We'd had a go at that jump a couple of years ago, allowed ourselves to be distracted and missed it.

The last few months at St Mary's hadn't been without incident, either. Only a few months ago, to worldwide excitement, the Sword of Tristram and a crown from the Holy Roman Empire had been discovered in our woods. I was on maternity leave but I wandered up a couple of times, parked baby Matthew under a tree and helped out. The sword and crown were exactly where we'd left them although, as Peterson said at the subsequent piss-up, they were hardly likely to get up and move, were they? There wasn't much of the sword left – only the pommel and a sliver of metal with a fragment of that all-important verse remaining. The rest was just a dark shape in the soil, but the crown, being mostly of gold, had fared much better.

Dr Chalfont, who had headed the dig, had been reinstated as Chancellor of Thirsk University just in time for them to take credit for the find. Which had been the whole point of us burying the stuff for her in the first place. She had returned to Thirsk in triumph and, according to rumour, the Night of the Long Knives had been nothing in comparison. The panelled corridors of the stately and venerable University of Thirsk had run red with academic blood. Metaphorically speaking. It had been, said the Chancellor, the light of battle still in her eye, an invigorating experience and an excellent opportunity for a great deal of dead wood removal, but she would be grateful if we would we never put her in such a position again. We had nodded and promised.

So here we all were and everything was fine.

I was a member of a happy family – somewhat to my surprise.

Peterson was training to be Dr Bairstow's deputy.

Markham had been reinstated as Major Guthrie's number two. And yes, all the bad jokes had been made.

St Mary's was relatively stable and solvent.

Everything was absolutely fine.

It began as a day just like any other. I awoke to a crisp, frosty morning and decided to go for a run. You can't use giving birth as an excuse forever. I've never been what you might call toned, but even I could see it was time to get into some sort of shape. Yes, I'd been on maternity leave, but I wanted to hit the ground running, so to speak, and therefore a little time spent running now might mean a lot less time hitting the ground later on.

I left Leon and Matthew in the bath, playing Attack of the Deadly Flannels. I'm not sure what the game entails, but there's always a lot of splashing and shrieking – and that's just Leon. Followed by massive mopping up afterwards, of course.

I blew them both a kiss, ignored Leon's invitation to join them, and shot off to pick up a bottle of water, bumping into Miss Dottle on the stairs.

Dottle wasn't actually a member of St Mary's. She and her boss, the idiot Halcombe, were from Thirsk University, and had been foisted on us last year. That had been my fault – we did something really bad, but no one talks about it so neither will I. Anyway, he'd tried to sabotage an assignment and Dr Foster had diagnosed him with leprosy – as you do – which had got rid of him

1

nicely, leaving us with the much more likeable Miss Dottle.

'Sorry,' I said, as she bounced off the banisters.

'That's quite all right.' She peered at me.

'Off for a run,' I said. 'Need to get back into shape before taking on the 1066 assignments. A couple of times around the lake should do it.'

As always, she looked over my shoulder for Peterson. She's a quiet girl and, even though she's Thirsk's representative here at St Mary's, people do quite like her. Besides, as Peterson pointed out, we'd sent them Kalinda Black – or that six-foot blonde psychopath, as Leon always refers to her – so they had rather got the worst of the deal. Miss Dottle was actually quite sweet. True, she had an enormous crush on Peterson, blushing like a sunset whenever he appeared over the horizon but, let's face it, if you're going to have a crush on anyone, you could do worse than Peterson. A lot worse.

It could be Markham, for instance, who was the next person to get between me and fresh air.

'Where do you think you're going?' he demanded.

'Honestly, I get kidnapped just once…'

'Exactly,' he said, 'and I've been tasked by Dr B to make sure it doesn't happen again.'

'You've been what?'

'Well, actually, he said, "Mr Markham, should anything happen to Dr Maxwell, I will hold you personally responsible and the consequences will be commensurate with my displeasure."'

I winced. 'Ouch.'

'Exactly,' he said. 'So, to repeat myself – where

are you off to?'

'A couple of times around the lake,' I said, patting my midriff. It rippled in a disconcerting manner.

Markham stepped back. 'The sooner the better I'd say. Got your thingy?'

My thingy – as the Security Section refers to it, because they have to keep things simple otherwise they can't cope – was the personal attack alarm, hanging around my neck. For further security, they'd increased the number of my tags. In addition to the normal one in my arm, they'd inserted another in my thigh. 'In case your arm gets chopped off,' said Helen, comfortingly, and a third under my shoulder blade.

'In case *all* your arms and legs get chopped off,' said Markham.

It's good to have friends.

Sighing and rolling my eyes, I presented my thingy for inspection, was instructed to wave as I passed the windows, not to overdo things, to remember my water, to try not to fall over my own feet, or get lost.

Since he showed signs of wanting to come with me, I asked him if he really was married, which always shifts him faster than one of Helen's constipation cures goes through a short historian, and eventually I made it out into the fresh air.

Bloody hell, half the morning gone already.

I wandered over to the lake, stretched out a few non-existent muscles and set off.

I have my own formula. A hundred yard's jog. Hundred yard's brisk walk. Hundred yard's sprint. Hundred yard's jog again. It covers the ground

3

surprisingly quickly. Although not as quickly as having a pack of enraged villagers coming at you waving pitchforks and torches and shouting about burning the witch. Then watch me really move.

It wasn't as bad as I thought it would be. Things wobbled a bit, but casting my mind back to pre-pregnancy days, things had always wobbled a bit, so I didn't take a lot of notice.

The day was lovely, with blue skies, fluffy clouds, and cool enough to keep me comfortable. The swans, always as far away from St Mary's as they could possibly manage, floated serenely on the lake or stamped around the reed beds muttering to themselves. We all gave each other a wide berth.

I completed one circuit, chugged back some water and, encouraged to find I was still alive, decided to give it another go.

I set off again, anti-clockwise this time, rather enjoying myself and, just as I was at the very furthest point from St Mary's, just where the reed beds hid me from sight, I came upon Clive Ronan, sitting on a fallen tree trunk, and apparently waiting for me.

Remembering the last occasion on which I'd seen him, the time when he'd kidnapped me and left me to give birth alone and lost in time, I screeched to a halt and began to grope for my thingy. Sadly, it was under my T-shirt to stop it bumping around so was not, therefore, immediately accessible.

'It's all right,' he said. 'I mean you no harm. I'm not armed. Look.'

His gun was on the ground some feet away. 'Pick it up

4

if it makes you feel safer.'

I did pick it up. As I'd suspected, it was empty but I could always use it to club him to death.

He stood up very slowly. 'I'm not armed,' he said again, arms in the air, rotating slowly. He wore a black T-shirt and jeans and I could see he had no gun.

'No ankle holster,' he said pulling up his jeans. 'And no knives either. No hostile intentions of any kind.' He sat back down again. 'I can understand that after our last encounter you might have a few … issues … with me, but since you apparently made it back safe and sound, I hope you'll be able to set those aside for a few minutes and talk. How is the young lad by the way? Does he look like his dad?'

I ignored the questions. He wasn't going to get any information out of me.

He gestured to another log. 'Please sit down.'

I ignored that too.

He seated himself again slowly and carefully. 'I have something to say to you and…'

I finally located my thingy and pulled it out. Carefully, because I'd once set it off accidentally and birds had erupted from the trees, glass had shattered, every dog for miles around had begun to howl, and Dr Bairstow had blamed me for stopping his clock. You get the picture. It's loud.

I've been dealing with Ronan for years now. He's a killer without conscience. He's ruthless. A complete bastard. He couldn't possibly have anything to say to me. Activating my alarm would have the entire Security Section here in moments. And Leon, probably, dripping

5

wet, baby in one hand, Glock 9mm in the other. And the History Department, of course, all wanting to see what was happening, and keen to make a bad situation worse.

'I want to stop.'

There was a silence, while my brain struggled with what was actually quite a simple sentence.

'What?'

'I want to stop.'

I stared at him.

He sighed and leaned forward, his forearms on his knees. 'I want to stop running. I want ... I don't want to...'

He stopped talking and stared at his feet.

I wasn't altogether surprised. I think I've said before that living outside one's own time is not easy. Today's society is much more fragmented than in the past – people are no longer linked in the traditional groupings of family, tribe, guild, or village, but even today, without a NI number, a credit rating, or an ID card, there's little chance of being accepted into society. Life on the outside is never easy. Everyone belongs somewhere. They may not like their life but it fits them exactly. It's where they're meant to be. Leave it for any length of time and History reacts by making things as difficult as it knows how.

Ronan had been running for years, damaging himself and everyone around him. His trail was littered with corpses and the wreckage of other people's lives. I could understand that he would want to stop running. Especially now that the Time Police were on his case. The question was – would he be allowed to? Should he be allowed to?

I thought of Mary Schiller. Killed and left in a box for

four hundred years. And Jamie Cameron. Killed to make a point. And Big Dave Murdoch who died saving me. I thought of what Ronan had done to Bashford and Grey. And to me.

I said nothing because silence is the best way to get people to talk.

Not looking at me, he said, 'I want to stop running all the time. I've found somewhere … I want to settle down with … I want to stop all this. Sooner or later, Max, one or both of us is going to be dead. And that doesn't have to happen. I now know the … the value of what *you* have, and I want it too. So I'm saying – you back off – I back off – and we both of us get on with the rest of our lives.'

I found a voice. 'That's it? That's what you want? A decade and more of killing everyone in your path and now you just want to close the door and walk away?'

'Yes,' he said quietly. 'A new beginning.'

'What about all the people you ended?'

'I can't do anything about the past. But I can do something about the future. People who might die in the future now might not. If we can agree to stop this.'

'I can't agree. I mean, it's not my decision. Dr Bairstow, Director Pinkerton, The Time Police, Leon – I can't begin to count the number of people who want to take you down.'

He squinted up at me. 'Have you ever heard of MAD?'

'Mutually assured destruction? Yes, of course. Are you saying…?'

'It hasn't happened yet, but you don't have to be a genius to work out where this is leading. We're all caught up in this deadly, downward spiral of violence and

7

revenge and it's going to end badly, Max, for all of us. You have a son now. You have responsibilities. Surely you want to keep yourself and Farrell alive for him. You want to watch him grow up, don't you?'

I lifted my thingy. 'I can do all that by having you arrested. Now.'

'I'll be gone long before they get here.'

'After you've killed me, I suppose.'

'No. I'll just step into my pod, which is only just over there and disappear again, leaving you to reflect on a wasted opportunity which could have changed everything.'

'Why me?'

Something in his face changed. Even his voice was different. Softer, but somehow more compelling.

'Because, my dear Max, you dance on the edge of darkness. You always have, and I don't think it would take very much for you to dance my way. I can't think of anyone I would rather have to speak for me.'

'I told you, I don't have the authority.'

'Your word carries weight. A great deal of weight. What do you have to lose? Love what you did to Halcombe, by the way.'

'I'm sure had you been in my position you would have done something similar.'

'Indeed I would. Why didn't you shove him into a real leper colony?'

I said in exasperation, 'Again – he doesn't actually have leprosy.'

'No, but he soon would have if you'd done that, wouldn't he?'

8

'I don't think I dance quite as close to the edge of darkness as you sometimes imagine.'

'No? Well, if you say so.'

I stared at him, shocked.

'Oh come on, Max. We both think the same way. The only difference is that you only think about these things and I actually do them.'

He stood up slowly.

'You're leaving?'

'I've planted the seed, which is all I came to do. Talk to Edward, Max. Tell him what I've said.'

'I can tell you now what he'll say.'

'Can you?' He smiled. 'Ask him what Annie would have wanted him to do? May I have my gun back please?'

I turned, took a few steps, and threw it into the lake. When I turned back, he was gone.

I whirled around a couple of times, but he really was gone. A sudden hot wind rustled the dead, dry reeds as his pod jumped away.

I could see something white on the log where he'd been sitting. An unsealed envelope with my name on it. Inside was a sheet of paper.

Thank you for listening. If Edward wants to take this further – and I hope he does – then meet me at the coordinates below. A little remote, I know, but excellent all round visibility, which makes it a good place for neither of us to be ambushed.

Au revoir.

I folded the paper, put it back in the envelope, and jogged back to St Mary's.

'He's in a meeting,' said Mrs Partridge, not looking up from her desk.

'Please interrupt him.'

She looked at me for a moment and then disappeared back into his office. I could hear the murmur of voices and then she reappeared.

'Come in, please.'

Dr Bairstow and Miss Dottle were seated at his briefing table, teleconferencing with the Chancellor. She smiled. 'Good morning, Max.'

'Good morning, Madam Chancellor. My apologies, but I must speak to Dr Bairstow at once.' I turned to him. 'Something has happened, sir.'

He nodded. 'Madam Chancellor, Miss Dottle, my apologies. We shall resume as soon as I am able.'

The screen went blank. Dottle picked up her papers and her scratchpad and scurried from the room.

'Well, Dr Maxwell?'

I gave him the details and sat quietly while he sat quietly. His face, as usual, gave no clue to his thoughts and, believe me, I was looking. Eventually, he said, 'Did you believe him?'

I didn't make the mistake of replying instantly. I sat and ran through everything. What Ronan had said. How he had said it. His body language. His facial expressions. I sifted through my thoughts and impressions and then said, 'If I had not known who he was, then yes, I would have believed him.'

'So, as far as you can tell, based solely on this morning's events, he was telling the truth.'

'I think so sir, yes.'

I waited while he picked up the note again.

'You have, of course, checked these coordinates.'

'I have, sir. They translate to a location in the Egyptian desert, around 525BC.'

'He's being cautious, Max. It would be very difficult to arrange an ambush in the middle of the desert. There would be little cover for miles around.'

'That would work to the advantage of both of us, sir.'

'Yes, indeed. He appears to have given this arrangement some thought.'

Silence again as he sat and stared out of the window. 'If I asked you to, would you go?'

'Like a shot, sir.'

'Why?'

'If he's genuine, then this is an opportunity we cannot afford to miss. If he's not, then I can shoot the bastard, and that's an opportunity *I* can't afford to miss.'

He stirred in his chair. 'If I alert the Time Police, they'll want to be there.'

'Yes, sir.'

'And if I don't alert them and he escapes or attacks you – then they will have a legitimate grievance, and the fault will be solely mine.'

'Yes, sir.'

'Go and have some lunch, Max. Come back in an hour. Not a word of this to anyone.'

'Yes sir. And no sir.'

*

I sat with Markham and Peterson at our usual table. They chatted away. I sat and listened with half an ear, busy with my own thoughts.

'You all right, Max?' said Peterson. 'Don't tell me this morning's gentle trot has knackered you completely.'

'Of course not,' I said with dignity. 'If you don't want your sandwich, can I have it?' and he was so busy defending his lunch that he forgot to ask any more questions, and Markham was playing fish finger Jenga and not listening anyway.

It was only as I was leaving that I noticed Leon wasn't there. Slightly concerned as to the whereabouts of the male members of my family, I went to look for them, eventually running them to earth in our room where Leon, covered in a protective sheet, was feeding Matthew. The way he eats – Matthew, I mean – it's the feeder rather than the feedee who needs to wear the bib. One mashed banana can cover every available surface for miles around and has frequently done so.

'There you are,' he said. 'How did your run go?'

'Unexpectedly,' I said, wondering whether to say anything or not. Leon's not always very balanced on the subject of Clive Ronan. I hesitated, remembered Dr Bairstow's instructions, and said nothing. If he wanted to, he could brief Leon himself.

I set off that evening. It was that funny time of day when people have finished eating and are wondering what to do next. Have a drink in the bar? Wander down to the pub in the village? Pile into someone's car and go into Rushford? Whatever they decided to do, they wouldn't be doing it in Hawking Hangar, which should be deserted.

Dr Bairstow limped along beside me. 'You have your instructions, Dr Maxwell.'

'I do, sir.'

'Take no risks.'

'No, sir.'

In accordance with instructions, Dieter had sent his people away. Only he remained. The hangar was empty and echoing. Two rows of pods sat quietly on their plinths. There was no tinny radio playing music, no tinkle of dropped tools, no bad language, no hum of power drills. I almost didn't recognise the place.

'I've checked the coordinates and laid them in for you,' he said.

'Ta very muchly.'

I dumped my bag in a locker and turned to check over the console.

Pods are our centres of operations. They're small,

cramped, smell of cabbage and the toilet rarely works properly. I was in Number Eight, my favourite pod. We'd seen some adventures together and it would be hard to say which of us looked the most battered. The console was to the right of the door, with the wall-mounted screen over. I scanned the various readouts – everything looked normal – and seated myself in the uncomfortable seat, wriggling my bum to try to iron out the lumps.

'Don't tell me you've got worms as well,' said Dieter, watching me squirm as he bashed away at his scratchpad.

I stopped wriggling. 'As well as whom?'

'As well as Markham.'

'Oh God, really? I've just eaten with him.'

'More fool you.'

'And it's not as if it's the first time. Or even the third. How does he do it?'

He shrugged. 'He's Markham – home to every passing parasite looking for somewhere dark and moist. Everything's set here. You OK?'

I nodded.

'Good luck, Max.'

I wondered how much Dr Bairstow had told him. 'Thanks. See you soon.'

The door closed behind him.

I felt suddenly nervous and took a deep breath to steady myself. Peering at the screen, I could see Dr Bairstow standing behind the safety line. As I watched, he was joined by Dieter and the two of them stood together.

I wiped my hands on my desert-camouflage combats. We weren't bothering with historically accurate costumes. It was the middle of the Egyptian desert, for God's sake.

Apart from Ronan and me, there would be nothing and no one for hundreds and hundreds of miles around.

I said, 'Computer, initiate jump.'

'Jump initiated.'

The world went white.

I landed in the middle of nowhere. A great, grim plain, shimmering in the heat, and broken only by an occasional rocky outcrop. Ronan had chosen well. Apart from a large rock about two hundred yards away, there was nothing. The sun hammered down from a sky from which the heat had drained all colour. There were no traditional golden sand dunes – this landscape was harsh and dry, with coarse brown sand blowing around in little eddies. I checked the temperature readings and groaned. Ronan really was a complete bastard. He could perfectly easily have selected a small tropical island somewhere and we could have dangled our feet in turquoise waters and eaten coconuts.

I panned the cameras. There was no sign of him anywhere, but that didn't mean he wasn't around and I wasn't going out in the blistering heat until I knew he was definitely here somewhere.

I sat for a while until it dawned on me that if he was here, he might be doing exactly the same thing. Leon's pod has a camouflage device which enables it to be almost invisible in most landscapes, and I was willing to bet Ronan's had something similar. He might be less than ten feet away. One of us had to make the first move and my guess was that it was going to have to be me.

I sighed, reached for my hat, and wrapped a scarf

around my neck to keep out the sand. Donning sunglasses, I pulled out a small backpack, stuffed it with a water flask, a pair of binoculars and a compass, and heaved it over my shoulder.

I took one last look at the console. I'd activated the proximity alerts and nothing had gone off. As far as I knew, I was the only person around for a thousand miles. Possibly a slight exaggeration, but that was how it felt. Time to earn my very inadequate pay.

I opened the door, flinched in the bright, white heat, and stepped outside. Careful to stand in the shade of the pod, I looked around. The landscape remained empty. Hot and still. I waited. An occasional stiff wind would gust sand in my face, and then subside, and we would be back to hot and still again.

I contemplated climbing onto the roof for a better look around, but it occurred to me that the lone rock over there would make a better vantage point. It was only a couple of hundred yards away. Even I couldn't get lost. Ramming down my hat, I set off, listening to the sound of my feet crunch on coarse sand as I trudged towards the outcrop, the only thing worth looking at in this dreary landscape.

I scrambled up the hot rock and rotated slowly, feeling sweat run down my back as the sun beat down on me. On the face of it, he wasn't here. No one was here. Except me, of course. I rotated back the other way, just for something to do. The only movement was loose sand scudding across the ground, blown this way and that by the intermittent wind. The landscape was empty. He hadn't come.

'Good afternoon,' called Ronan, looking up at me from ground level.

I spun around. Where the hell had he come from?

He stood, unmoving, as if we were both waiting for my heartbeat to return to normal. He wore the same black T-shirt and jeans but with a bandana tied around his head against the sun. I noticed that this time, however, there were no reassurances about not being armed.

'Well,' he said, 'isn't this nice? A little hot, of course. Would you like to climb down so we can sit in the shade?'

I slid down and we squatted in the deep shade at the foot of the rock. He politely offered me some water. Equally politely, I declined. Drug me once – shame on you. Drug me twice – not bloody likely.

'I don't want to keep you hanging around in this heat,' he said, a sentiment I would have found so much more sincere if he hadn't spent the last twenty minutes keeping me hanging around in this heat until he could confirm I was alone.

We looked at each other. Dr Bairstow had given me his decision and a message for Ronan, but I had discretion to act on my own initiative should the situation require it.

'Well?' he said, casually, although his voice was not quite steady. 'Is there a response?'

'Yes, there is. I've spoken to Dr Bairstow. In fact, we discussed it all afternoon.'

I stopped, remembering pacing the carpet in front of his desk, waving my arms, arguing … Because what we were proposing was not without risk. Strictly speaking, we should report immediately to the Time Police and await instructions. Let them handle it. Yeah, like that was ever going to happen. The Time Police are not noted for their lightness of touch. We had a chance here – a real chance – to end this now. Once and for all.

'Yes,' he said, impatiently. 'And?'

'Dr Bairstow completely…'

And that was as far as I got.

I stood up, staring over his shoulder. Over on the horizon, far over to my right, a tiny flash of light. And then another one.

I spun around to face him.

Whatever it was, it was too far away to be an immediate threat. A caravan, maybe, on its way to … I racked my brains. I'd studied maps of the area before setting out. The oasis at Siwa was too far north, and anyway, the traditional route was off to the east via the Dakhla and Farafra oases. I turned to Ronan in sudden suspicion. 'These were your coordinates. Is this a trap? What's over there?'

He was staring too. 'How should I know? It could be anyone.'

'Out here? In the middle of nowhere? Caravans travel to the east.' I gestured vaguely in what I hoped was an eastwards direction. 'There's nothing here except us.'

Except me.

Dr Bairstow and I had discussed the possibility of an ambush. Or kidnapping. Or even murder. I was armed and equipped for anything. I was certain he would be as well. So much for detente.

I opened my com and he pushed me back against the rock, a gun appearing from nowhere. 'Who are you talking to?'

I pushed his hand away. 'My computer, of course. Computer.'

It gave that irritating little trill.

'Computer, using current coordinates, speculate on approaching traffic.'

There was a slight pause as, presumably, it gave the matter some thought.

'There is no evidence of any major trade routes in this area. Subjects may be lost. Or...' It does this. I think it likes to build up the suspense. One of these days, I'm going to rip it out by its peripherals and show it who's the boss around here.

'Excavations in this area have revealed a considerable number of human bones and some artefacts, which date back to approximately two and a half thousand years ago. Some theorise they are the remains of an Egyptian army, believed to have been lost in a possible sandstorm, as it made its way to the Oracle of Amun at Siwa, resulting in the deaths of fifty thousand men.'

It stopped, presumably to give me some time to digest this.

'Oh my God,' I said, feeling the slow burn of excitement. 'The lost army of Cambyses.' I stood on tip-toe – as if that would make any difference – and squinted. Ronan, his gun, his offer of peace, the current location of his pod – everything was completely forgotten, because I'm an historian and my priorities may sometimes be a little different from everyone else's. Not my fault.

He turned to me, bristling with a suspicion equal to my own. 'Who are they? Did you alert someone?'

I squinted into the harsh sunlight. 'Yes, of course I did.

Knowing how you can be, I alerted the Pharaoh himself and he's sent his entire army just to take you down. Impressive levels of paranoia, Ronan. Well done.'

He looked down at me. 'Surely I can't be the only person in the world who wants to murder you.'

'God, no. Sorry to puncture your massive ego, but you're only one of many. Half the human race is ahead of you.'

As I spoke, I tried to push my way past him and he pushed me back again, demanding to know where the hell I thought I was going.

I regarded him with exasperation. 'Back to my pod for recorders, cameras, and the solution to a two and a half thousand-year-old mystery.'

'Are you insane?'

'Is that a serious question?'

He still had hold of my arm. 'And while you're gallivanting around wasting time, do you expect me to just wait?'

I took an enormous chance. 'No, Mr Ronan, I expect you to assist.'

He dropped my arm and we stared at each other. I became conscious that the wind was getting up. I could feel loose hair whipping around my face.

He shook his head. 'I think you're forgetting the key word here.'

'What key word?'

'*Sandstorm*?'

'*Possible* sandstorm.'

'If it can bury fifty thousand elite Egyptian troops, what the hell is it going to do to us?'

'We'll be fine,' I said, with massively misplaced confidence.

'Fine?'

'Oh come on, Clive. When did you last do anything just for fun?'

He seemed a little surprised by my use of the f word and while he was still gathering his wits, I set off across the sand.

He caught up. 'Just a minute…'

'Look, this might be just an ordinary caravan. In which case, we wait for them to pass and continue our discussion. Or it might – it just might – be Cambyses's boys, and I can't let this opportunity go. And don't worry about the sandstorm. It might come today, but it might equally be tomorrow or next week.' I patted his arm reassuringly. 'Don't worry, Clive. I'll look after you.'

He stood thoughtfully. 'It does occur to me to murder you now, bury your body, return to St Mary's and collect a small reward from your no doubt grateful colleagues.'

I looked at him. 'You were an historian once. Be one again. Just for one day.'

Ronan waited outside my pod, squatting in the shade. He wouldn't come in and I didn't want to push things at this stage. Once inside, I brought up everything I could find on the Pharaoh Cambyses and his army. It's actually quite a famous story.

In 525BC, Egypt was part of the Persian Empire, after being conquered by Cyrus the Great. On his death, his son, Cambyses, having failed to persuade the powerful priests of Amun to acknowledge his right to the throne of Egypt, assembled a massive army, some fifty thousand strong, and sent them off to the Oracle at Siwa to show them the error of their ways.

None of those fifty thousand men would ever be seen again.

There had been a theory that instead of following the traditional eastern route, they'd travelled west, before striking out for Siwa, and the entire army had been enveloped in a massive sandstorm and completely buried. Recent archaeological discoveries had given some credence to that theory, although they remain controversial and nothing has been proved.

'According to Herodotus,' I said – and don't get me started on that two-faced, conniving little git – 'the sandstorm comes from the south.' I stood in the doorway, gazing around. 'Which way is south?'

'How do you ever survive?' Ronan pointed in the direction of the approaching whatever it was.

'Right, so they're overwhelmed from behind which means…'

'Which means they'll be running like mad in this direction. Towards us.'

'Not necessarily. I mean – there's nothing to say the sandstorm will occur today. We can hide on top of that rock over there and get some fantastic footage as they go past. Marching to their date with destiny.'

'Their what with what?'

I stared again. Another flash. And another. And a blurring of the horizon which would be the dust kicked up by men, horses, chariots, all on their way to sort out the Oracle of Amun and its obstinate occupants.

'What about this pod?' he demanded. 'Are you just going to leave it here?'

'Well, it's a tiny pod in the middle of a vast desert. And they can't get in and it's too heavy to be towed, so apart from chucking a few spears at it, there's not a lot they can do. What about yours?' I said cunningly, hoping he would give me the location.

'It's fine. They'll never find it.'

Aha! Camouflage device. I knew it. Bugger. That could cause me some problems.

'Then let's go.'

The rock was mostly one giant, solid piece, but towards the southern end, it had fragmented into five or six smaller pieces. One leaned slightly, making a shallow cave, some twenty feet up, which gave us some welcome shade and a small degree of cover. We scrambled up, checked carefully for scorpions and snakes, and made ourselves comfortable. Ronan picked up a recorder and examined it.

'Point and press,' I said. 'It's quite simple.'

He looked at me. 'It would have to be.'

'You're very grumpy.'

'It's the company I'm keeping.'

Careful to remain in the shelter of the rock and not expose himself – because armies can sometimes be quite unkind to anyone they think might be spying on them – he stood up and stared thoughtfully. 'Please remind me never to listen to any future predictions you might make concerning armies, sandstorms, or indeed, anything at all.'

I stood beside him. 'What?'

He pointed at the horizon. Or rather, where the horizon had been. A dark yellow murky cloud obscured everything and was growing larger. Desert dust. I crossed my fingers that it was being kicked up by a marching army rather than the beginnings of a sandstorm.

'Oh.'

'Oh? Is that all you can say?'

'What else did you want?'

'Oh, I don't know. How about "I'm so sorry, Clive. I'm a complete idiot who shouldn't be allowed out on her own and, worse than that, I've risked your life for a few snapshots of a bunch of people who died two and a half thousand years ago when I could have been doing something much more important regarding world peace.'

'Hey, grumpy, they weren't my coordinates. Didn't

you check them at all?'

Silence. Well, that answered that question.

At this point, he could have gone back to his pod and left me to it. I wouldn't have been the slightest bit surprised if he'd said, 'You're on your own with this one, Maxwell. See you around,' and pushed off. Possibly pausing to shoot me on the way out if he was feeling really miffed. But he didn't. He fiddled with his recorder, panned around for practice, and then settled himself down.

I was aware that I was pushing my luck. On the one hand, I couldn't afford to let Ronan disappear with the situation he'd created still unresolved, but obviously, I wanted to see what might be the lost army of Cambyses as well. When I'd suggested Ronan remember his historian roots and assist, I'd never for one moment actually thought he would. But he was right – an approaching army was not a good thing. And an approaching army being pursued by a sandstorm was even worse. And a sandstorm that could bury said desert-hardened army was worst of all. If it all came our way, I would be trapped with a psychotic killer who had done me nothing but harm in the past. A sensible and prudent historian would pull out now.

Ah well…

'Heads up,' said Ronan softly.

Two chariots were heading our way.

Well, that settled one thing. Whatever was coming our way, it wasn't a harmless caravan. I don't know why I ever thought it would be.

'Scouts,' I said, drawing back into the cover of the

rock and activating my recorder.

A heavy sigh on my left indicated that Ronan was, at least for the moment, resigned to the situation.

We crouched and watched.

They approached at some speed. Each chariot contained two men, both balancing easily as the light vehicles bounced over the rough ground. The drivers concentrated on their horses, but the soldiers called to each other and gestured. They were checking out our rock.

'I have plans for the rest of my life,' said Ronan quietly. 'I would be greatly obliged if you could refrain from doing anything stupid. Although I'm not tremendously optimistic.'

We cowered back in our little patch of shade and watched them circle the rock. I was confident my desert camouflage would merge with the surrounding rock, and Ronan's dark clothing was almost invisible in the deep shadow.

Each chariot was pulled by two horses. I was surprised by the plainness of the harness. Contemporary pictures always show ornately dressed soldiers and drivers, in highly decorated chariots. Sometimes, even the horses wore headdresses. Not on a march through the desert, however. Perhaps they kept the good stuff for the victory parade. Or even for the battle itself. To dazzle the opposition with the wealth and power of the Egyptian empire. On this occasion, horses, men and chariots were smothered in desert dust and everything was a dirty brown.

Both soldiers had bows at the ready, arrows nocked,

covering every inch of the terrain. They circled our rock several times, shouting to each other as they went.

'They're very thorough,' I whispered.

'So would I be,' said Ronan.

'Not thorough enough to ensure no passing army would casually wander past when choosing your coordinates.'

'A moment ago you were full of girlish glee at this opportunity. Make up your mind.'

Apparently satisfied, the two chariots broke away and returned back the way they'd come, soon to be lost in the dust again.

'Happy now?' he said. 'Shall we go?'

'Go? Why would we go?'

'Temperature over a hundred degrees? Fifty thousand approaching Egyptians. Sandstorm?'

I did hesitate. This was not why I was here. I was here to deal with Ronan. And when I'd done that, I could easily pass the coordinates to the History Department and we could mount a proper expedition and do the job properly.

'OK,' I said, reluctantly. 'Your pod or mine?'

'Neither,' he said, staring at the horizon. 'It's too late.'

It was too.

Over to our right, a cloud of sand was approaching and even as I stared, tiny figures began to emerge. More chariots burst out of the dust. They were clearing the way for the oncoming army. Which would pass only a quarter of a mile away.

I said to Ronan, 'Any chance of getting back to your pod?'

'No,' he said curtly.

And my pod, although not in the army's path, was squatting several hundred yards away on the other side of the rock. No chance then. We'd have to wait it out here. I drew back into the shelter of the rock and waited.

Actually, if this was the legendary sandstorm then it wasn't too bad.

Yes, dust swirled madly, first kicked up by hooves, wheels and marching feet and then being blown around by the wind. I could feel it everywhere, getting down inside my clothes, in my hair, despite my hat, in my mouth, everywhere, but I could still see. They were about a quarter of a mile away. I set for extreme close-up and began to record.

First came what I assumed to be the Pharaoh's crack troops, all on foot, tramping solidly through the sand. Being at the front, they were more visible than the poor sods coughing their way along at the back.

They wore tunics, helmets and sandals. No one wore armour in this heat. Their helmets dangled from their belts. In their right hands, they carried the sickle-shaped khopesh, and in their left, a wood and leather shield with a short spear secured to its back. Quick, neat and easily accessible. They marched fast – almost at a trot. Every now and then, one of them would look back over his shoulder. They knew what was coming. What was behind them.

Following them was a single chariot, drawn by two horses. This would be the commander. The general. I had no idea of his name. I wished I was better prepped for this, but I could always check it out on my return. I tried to wriggle forwards for a better view and Clive Ronan pulled me back by my T-shirt.

'I really don't care about you, and if Cambyses's crew want to break you on a chariot wheel then trust me, I'll be cheering them on, but I do care about me, so stay quiet or I'll thump you with a rock and leave you to the vultures.'

The general's chariot was a good way back from his advance guard, so he wasn't choking in the dust like them. I could make out his leather and bronze tunic, but he also was looking back over his shoulder, possibly checking out the oncoming storm, and not looking our way at all. Sometimes, my job is so frustrating. His driver said something and he turned to look ahead. In my viewfinder, I caught a quick glimpse of a prominent nose and thickly kohled eyes and then he resumed his scan of the horizon. Our rock didn't even merit a glance.

He was followed by the archers, again wearing linen kilts and with the padded sporrans to protect their vital bits. I made a verbal note to check whether the Egyptians were familiar with linothorax, and whether it could turn back an arrow or spear thrust. Ronan rolled his eyes.

There were three companies of archers, and these were followed by the infantry. Row upon row of them, almost completely enveloped in dust and sand. They weren't quite running – not in this heat – but they weren't hanging around either. They knew something was behind them and they were pushing along at a brisk trot. Were they hoping to outrun it? There were no signs of panic or of physical distress. These were desert troops and accustomed to desert conditions, but imagine the size of a sandstorm that could bury an army so completely that no trace of it has ever been found.

They made no pretence at marching in neat lines. They had cloths tied around the lower part of their faces and, heads down, were eating up the miles. Several chariots broke ranks to check out our rock. Ronan and I lowered our heads and kept very, very still, but the check was cursory. It had already been cleared and everyone out there in the heat had other things to worry about anyway.

It took the army nearly two hours to pass by, and towards the end, we didn't even bother trying to record. Visibility was almost zero and the dust wasn't doing my equipment any good at all. The ground was shaking as they passed, and dust, grit, tiny pebbles and the odd stinging insect kept dropping from the stone roof over our heads.

Finally, the last of them marched out of view and silence fell. We sat up, drank some water, and literally waited for the dust to settle.

'Well,' Ronan said, handing me back the recorder he'd been using. 'That brought back unpleasant memories. I had honestly forgotten how tedious History is.'

Which might well be true, but looking at his power levels, he'd nearly drained the battery, so he'd been recording solidly for at least two hours. I refrained from pointing this out.

We sat back to take a moment. The sun had moved around behind us and our patch of shade was a little larger. I eased my cramped position, groaned, and tried to stretch out my aching legs.

Ronan stood up stiffly and rubbed his back. 'Do you

think, after that unwelcome interlude, we could resume our negotiations?'

'Good idea,' I said. 'Let's go back to my pod. I'm desperate for a cup of tea. And I want to see what we've managed to record.'

I made to stand up but my legs had gone to sleep. He hesitated and then offered me his hand. 'Here.'

We both looked at each other for a very long moment, then I took it and he hauled me to my feet. Sadly, my legs still weren't doing their job properly and I collapsed against him. He staggered before regaining his footing.

'Bloody hell, isn't it about time you lost some of that baby weight?'

I flexed my aching knees. 'Well, I did make a start this morning but some dozy pillock put a stop to that, didn't he?'

He made no response.

'Anyway,' I said, stuffing the recorders back into my pack. 'If that was the famous sandstorm then I have to say that as sandstorms go, it wasn't too bad, was it?'

'Far be it from me to rain on your ill-informed parade, but I don't think that was it.' He pointed over my shoulder.

I turned slowly. 'Oh.'

We all say stupid things from time to time.

'Peace in our time.'

'I did not have sex with that woman.'

'Britain will never rejoin the EU.'

'As sandstorms go that wasn't too bad.'

The entire horizon – the shimmering heat haze – everything had gone. Completely vanished. Disappeared. In its place, a huge, vast billowing cloud of brown was storming towards us. Not the horizon-blurring dust kicked up by a passing army. This cloud had to be hundreds and hundreds of feet high and it was solid dust and sand. Soon, it would swallow the sun. Already, the day was darker and colder. I could see intermittent flashes within the swirling mass. Lightning. And it was moving fast, sucking up everything in its path, whirling it around and then spitting it back out again.

This was what the army had been running from.

My pod was several hundred yards away. I had no idea where Ronan's was, and he wasn't saying. I would have made a run for mine, but last year I'd been at Stonehenge and we were caught in a snowstorm. Within only a very few yards, we'd become completely lost. If Leon – husband and hero – hadn't arrived, then we would have frozen to death.

This would not be dissimilar. Once down at ground level, poor visibility and buffeting winds meant we would soon lose our sense of direction. We probably wouldn't even be able to keep our feet. This rock would give us some protection. We should stay put.

The same thought had obviously occurred to him.

'Here,' I said, 'give me your bandana and water flask.'

He ripped off his bandana and handed it over, together with his flask. I spread it out together with my scarf and gave them both a good soaking of water.

He looked around. 'We don't want to be caught up here. We'll take shelter in the lee of this rock.'

We wrapped our wet scarves around our faces and clambered down to ground level.

'Here,' he said, pointing to a large outcrop jutting at right angles from the main rock. We crawled in as close in as we could possibly get, facing towards the rock itself.

He pushed me down on the sand. 'Get down on your hands and knees.'

'What?'

'Don't be alarmed. If you were a camel, I would shelter behind you. Sadly, you're only a small and very irritating historian, but I am, for reasons which escape me at the moment, doing my best to ensure your survival. Get down and make yourself as small as you can.'

He was giving good advice. I crawled as close against the rock as I could get. It would, to some extent, protect us from the wind, but nothing would save us from the sand.

I nodded to his arms. 'Pull your sleeves right down. In

34

a very short while your skin's going to feel as if it's been sandpapered.'

We knelt, side by side, making ourselves as small as possible. Already the sand was whipping itself into stinging little dust devils. Not long now. We huddled together, protected our faces and braced ourselves.

There was no gentle build-up.

The world grew cold and dark.

I could hear the usual sighing hiss of sand and then, suddenly, the wind came roaring across the desert, changing its note to a shriek as the storm hit our very inadequate rock, head on.

I turned my head to look. Lightning flashed somewhere, illuminating the dirty clouds with an inner glow. Ronan reached out and pushed my head down and suddenly the whole world contracted into just this tiny space.

Around us, the desert thundered. Like many people, I've used the expression sandblasted without any idea of what it truly means. Even through my clothes I could feel a thousand-thousand tiny pinpricks as wind-driven sand hit us from all directions. Keeping low was no help at all. The bloody stuff bounces. It flays you alive as it comes down and then does it again on the way back up.

And it gets everywhere. Inside your clothing. Inside your boots. In your hair. Up your nose. In your mouth. Under your eyelids. I tried squeezing my eyes tighter and that only made things worse. I could feel tiny grains of sand caught under my eyelids, grating painfully across my eyeballs.

My wet scarf dried out almost instantly. The mucus in

35

my nose dried out. With that and the sand, every breath became first just painful, and then as time dragged by, searingly agonising. Sand was beginning to build up around us. Every now and then, one of us would try to shrug our shoulders or shake ourselves, and I would feel it cascading off me. Without the shelter of our rock, we would have been buried alive. I no longer doubted that Cambyses's army had been lost in this sandstorm.

I lost all sense of time. My knees were on fire. I ached to stand up. Every muscle was screaming in protest. I could feel the sand scraping away at my back. I was convinced my T-shirt had been torn from my body. I hunched my shoulders even higher to protect my ears, which felt as if they were on fire, and just tried to hang on. After a while, I wasn't even sure I was the right way up. I had no idea if Ronan was even still with me. Had he taken advantage of the storm to push off back to his own pod and abandon me here?

That was just plain ridiculous. There was no way anyone could stand up in this lot, let alone navigate their way back to a small pod. Besides, he wouldn't leave me alone in all this. Would he?

Of course he would, said the voice in my head. How do you know he didn't lure you to this here and now for precisely that purpose? It won't take long for the sand to cover you completely. And your pod as well. No one will ever find you. No one will ever know what became of you. They never found Cambyses's army and there were fifty thousand of them, so you're not going to stand much of a chance, are you?

Unbelievably, I actually toyed with the idea of

staggering to my feet and making a run for it. Of straightening my aching legs. Of getting away somehow. Of returning to the cool, damp silence of St Mary's. I could feel sand piling up again. How long before I was buried completely? It was stupid to remain here. I should go and go now. Before I couldn't go at all.

I shifted my weight slightly, feeling sand move around me, and an arm as rigid as an iron bar shot out, pushed me down, and held me there. I heard him shout something but the words were torn away in the wind.

I subsided, tried to close my mind to everything going on around me, and endure. It was all I could do. Occasionally, I would shake my head fractionally, dislodging sand and grit, trying to protect my face as best as could.

Unbelievably, the noise of the wind increased. A sudden buffet caught us both unawares. I heard Ronan shout something and suddenly, he wasn't there. I didn't stop to think – I just automatically grabbed at him. I felt some kind of cloth – his T-shirt, I think. I seized whatever it was and hung on, but now we'd both changed our position slightly and the tiny, but vitally important shelter we'd had from our rock was gone.

I felt Ronan shift in the wind. I reached out blindly with my other hand. I couldn't see a thing. I found his arm. I hung on to him and he to me. Together, we were too heavy to blow away. Ladies – before heading to the gym you might want to consider hanging on to that baby weight. Very useful in preventing you being blown away in an unexpected desert sandstorm. Just saying.

More sand started to pile up around us. We crouched

together, hanging on to each other for grim death – and a grim death it was likely to be if this didn't let up soon.

I lost all track of time. Every breath hurt. My arms felt as if they were being pulled from their sockets. Wind, sand, and sound tore at us. Our skin was on fire. Well, mine definitely was and it seemed safe to assume Ronan didn't have some special dispensation. I was suffocating. I kept trying to lift my head out of the sand. It was coming down faster than I could clear it. It was in my mouth. I started to cough which didn't help at all. Ronan wrapped both arms around me and pulled me close. The shelter of his body helped a little. Huge amounts of sand were whirling around us. It was as if the entire desert was trying to pick itself up and take itself off somewhere else. I buried my head in his chest. He was sheltering me so I wrapped my arms around his head to try to give him what protection I could and we just endured.

It ended as abruptly as it had begun. It wasn't exactly that one moment there was shrieking wind and sand and the next moment the sun came out, but we were both aware that the storm was passing.

There was no sun – the air was still full of dirty brown grit and sand – but the wind had moved on. Chasing and catching a Pharaoh's army who, almost certainly, were breathing their last at this very moment.

I found myself lying on my side, half buried. If it hadn't been for the protection of the rock, we would have been completely covered. I twisted my head out of the sand and slowly unwrapped my arms from around

Ronan's head. He rolled off me with a groan and lay very still.

I coughed, spat sand, and coughed some more. 'So – not dead then?'

He began to cough, as I had done. 'No thanks to you. You're a bloody madwoman. You do know that, don't you?'

'It's been mentioned, once or twice.'

I lay back and concentrated just on not breathing in great lumps of desert.

I'd saved him. He'd saved me. God, this was embarrassing.

I sat up, shedding sand everywhere and looked around me. Clouds of fine dust still swirled around us, but I could see the sun trying to break through. It would be hot again soon.

I dug around and located a strap, pulled at it and my backpack came free. I shook off the sand, opened it up, and pulled out my flask of water. The way I felt, there wasn't enough water in the entire world to quench my thirst, but he'd saved me, and you have to pay your debts.

He looked surprised.

'Age before beauty,' I said, just in case he thought I harboured kindly feelings towards him.

He grinned, cracking the sand that had settled on his face and in his hair. He meticulously took only two swigs and passed it back. I appreciated the thought, took my own two swigs, and passed it back again.

We leaned back against the rock, passing the flask between us, and saying nothing. Time passed, but I don't think either of us was in any rush.

I don't know when I first noticed it. I was absently staring out across the desert when I realised there was a problem with the sand. It was still blowing everywhere – sadly, that's what sand does – but there was a small patch, slightly more than a hundred yards away, where it wasn't blowing quite right. As if it was blowing around something. Something I couldn't see.

There were two possibilities and both were good.

The first was that this was Ronan's pod and that, finally, I had its location. The second was that this was Leon's pod. As I mentioned, his pod has a camouflage device. High-def cameras feed info to the computer, which projects an image back again, making the pod virtually invisible. It sometimes has a bit of a problem with complicated backgrounds like leafy jungles, but a simple desert background would cause it no problems at all.

We have, occasionally, considered fitting similar devices to our own pods, but there are a number of arguments against this, not least because we often need to make a hasty exit. Imagine a group of historians – not the clearest thinkers at the best of times – racing in ever expanding circles shouting, 'Where the bloody hell is the pod?' as sundry armies, severe meteorological conditions, horrendous seismic activities and other catastrophes rain down upon them. To say nothing of a couple of harmless contemporaries walking smack into the side of an invisible pod after a night in the pub. So, on balance, we reckon we're safer without it.

I tried not to smile. I should have guessed. Of course Dr Bairstow would send back-up. He hadn't told me and that was fair enough. But I wasn't alone. Leon – and, I suspected, Major Guthrie too, were out here with me, keeping an eye on things. I didn't need them, but it was good to know they were here.

Not wanting Ronan to see where I was looking, I leaned back and closed my eyes. I was here at his invitation. I would leave him to take the initiative. And so, like an idiot, I sat in the desert and did nothing as the seconds counted down to disaster.

Finally, he handed me back the empty canteen. 'Appreciated.'

'You're welcome. So – what now?'

He turned to face me. 'I have two plans, actually. The first entails…' He broke off to stare past me. 'Who…?'

I twisted around.

From nowhere, I could see hazy black figures running towards us through the dust. I felt my mouth fall open with shock. No. No, no, no. This was so wrong. This wasn't supposed to happen. They weren't supposed to be here. This would ruin everything.

That patch of anomalous sand hadn't been Ronan's pod. It hadn't been Leon's either. It had been the Time Police. Waiting until it was safe to emerge and arrest us both.

I opened my mouth to warn him.

At the same time, I saw the realisation cross his face. He had been betrayed.

I stretched out a hand and said quickly, 'No – it wasn't St Mary's,' but it was too late. Too late to explain. Too late for everything.

He wrenched out his gun. His face was white. I could

41

see the blue veins at his temples. His eyes were dark and empty and terrifying in a way I cannot describe. My stomach turned over. Suddenly, I was very, very afraid.

He said quietly and far more chillingly than screaming threats could ever be, 'You traitorous ----' using a really bad word. Hauling me to my feet, he raised his gun, jamming the barrel against my right eye.

I couldn't move. Couldn't speak. I was going to die. I could feel my heart beating in my throat and the blood pounding in my head. I was going to die. Out here. In this blistering heat and emptiness. I was going to die.

And then, apparently he had second thoughts, because he lowered the gun again.

'No, Maxwell. You're going to live. Everyone else in your world will die, but you'll live on. You'll look back on today and wish I had killed you.'

Now that it was far too late, I knew beyond doubt that his offer had been genuine, because this was the face of a man who had revealed his inner self, in all its vulnerability. A man who had taken a step forwards if not towards friendship then at least towards peace. A man who had trusted me to do the right thing and now thought I'd betrayed him. There would never now be any sort of a deal. Any chance we might have had was gone for ever.

Voices were shouting to us to get down on our knees. To put our hands in the air. I shouted, 'St Mary's,' and scrabbled for my pocket, but too late. I felt a familiar pain in my chest. The world swayed around me. The ground tilted. I couldn't see. Couldn't hear. They had sonic weapons and they'd used them on us.

I began to run towards the Time Police, my legs

feeling as if I was running through porridge. I had no control over them at all. I staggered a few steps sideways, tried again in a different direction, then another, and bumped into something hard that wasn't rock. I remember thinking, *now* I find his bloody pod. I fumbled again for my pocket, but my arm wasn't doing what I wanted it to. My last chance was fading and there wasn't anything I could do about it. I tried to speak, to call out, but those sonic weapons are bastards and I couldn't get any part of me to do as it was told.

He managed to say, 'Door.' I caught a glimpse of a familiar-looking interior. He staggered inside. I tried to shout to him. To tell him to wait, but the door closed on my words. Hot sand and air blasted into my face as his pod jumped away. I was just outside the danger zone. The whole thing had taken only a few seconds. Far less time than it takes to describe. And then rough hands seized me and forced me face down into the sand.

I didn't resist. This was the Time Police. They'd shoot me as soon as look at me.

They rolled me over on to my back. I spat more mouthfuls of sand and tried to blink my eyes clear.

I was crying. Crying with rage and frustration and despair. Crying for that last, lost chance of peace. And in that hot, dry, dust-filled landscape, as the Time Police pointed their guns and shouted at me, I think a small part of me was already crying for all the grief I knew was to come.

I shouted, 'You stupid, stupid bastards,' saw something swinging towards me, and closed my eyes.

I half hoped they would drag me away to their pod because it would be less of a walk in this still furnace-like heat. I was assuming they had a snug spot awaiting me in the Time Police dungeons, where I could languish until Dr Bairstow turned up and made them wish they'd never been born. But two of them peeled off, presumably to their own pod, and the rest of us trooped back to mine. I don't remember much about the trek, two of them had hold of my arms and kept me upright. Someone did plonk my hat back on my head, for which I was grateful.

Actually, it was a good job they were there. Sand had piled up against one side of the pod – the side with the door, obviously, and it took them a good half an hour to clear it away. I sat in the pod's shade and let them get on with it. Just for once, they were doing something useful.

When they'd finished, they heaved me to my still very unsteady feet and demanded entrance and I was happy to comply.

I said, 'Door,' and wobbled my way into the blessed cool of Number Eight. I took the left-hand seat and tried to pull myself together.

They started poking around the console and I told them to pack it in before they broke something. They demanded I return to St Mary's. I said I had no intention of going anywhere else and told them to get out of my way.

I made them wait. I washed my face and hands, found an icepack in the med-kit, clapped it to my eye and took a good long glug of water before eventually coming back to the console.

The return coordinates were already laid in. I didn't bother warning them, saying, 'Computer, initiate jump,' before most of them were ready. No one actually fell over, but one or two staggered. No one does petty revenge better than me.

I made them decontaminate, refusing to open the door until the cold, blue light had done its business. I couldn't see any sign of their own pod, but that might be because even for the Time Police, it's considered very bad manners to appear uninvited. I guessed theirs would be outside Hawking somewhere. Protocol says to park outside and then wait to be identified and invited inside.

Dieter had gone and his place had been taken by Guthrie. Leon stood beside him. I touched my swollen eye said, 'Wouldn't want to be you guys,' and without waiting for permission to exit, opened the door. Still a little white and wobbly, I stepped out.

They shouldered me aside, weapons raised, shouting that confused babble that's supposed to be so intimidating. At one and the same time we were ordered to get on the floor, put our hands in the air, put them behind our heads, get on our knees and so on.

I ignored them all, saying wearily, 'Good evening, Dr Bairstow.'

He limped forwards. 'It's morning, Dr Maxwell,' and I realised they'd waited all night for me to come back. 'You appear to be injured.'

'Yet another Time Police-related injury, sir. One of oh-so-many over the years.'

He turned to whomever he had decided was in charge.

'Explain.'

'Dr Bairstow, you and all St Mary's personnel are under arrest for…'

'Shut up,' said Leon. He stepped forward and tilted up my chin. 'Which one of them did this?'

Some time ago, Leon had led the rebellion against the Time Police. He'd travelled up and down the timeline, engaging them where and whenever possible. They might not fear me – I imagine I'm about as intimidating as cold rice pudding – but Leon was another matter altogether.

'Not sure,' I said. 'I was on the ground at the time.'

He looked around. 'Six Time Police to subdue one small historian. Yes, that sounds about right.'

'I'm not all that small.'

'In the execution of our duties…'

'You … will …be … silent,' said Dr Bairstow and the suppressed fury in his voice frightened even me.

Everyone shut up. I could hear the silence echoing around the hangar.

'Dr Maxwell, report.'

Just by looking at him, I could see he was more furious than I could ever remember. Even more furious than the time we stole Arthur's sword back from Thirsk. Deadly, stone-cold furious.

'As per your instructions, sir…'

I gave him my report in full, ignoring the twitching Time Police around me. Leon never took his eyes off them and I could see he was making them nervous. Guthrie stood well back in the shadows. I wondered if the rest of the Security team was there as well.

When I'd finished, I shut up and waited.

They tried again. 'You are under arrest for…'

Dr Bairstow spoke quietly, but no one had any difficulty hearing his words.

'Your clumsiness has jeopardised the safety of St Mary's and everyone within it. It is my unit that will bear the brunt of your failure today. My unit that will be the focus of his revenge. My unit that will have to deal with the consequences of your unsuccessful and disastrous interference. That Dr Maxwell is not dead is no thanks to you. That Ronan has escaped *is* thanks to you. That he will now have no other purpose other than to damage my unit and my people is also thanks to you. I congratulate you – this day you have effortlessly restored the reputation for heavy-handed bungling for which the Time Police are so renowned.'

Unwisely, their officer tried to make his voice heard. 'Dr Maxwell here was caught, red-handed…'

Dr Bairstow interrupted him with ease.

'Dr Maxwell would you be so kind as to reveal the contents of your pocket. Please do it slowly. Our colleagues in the Time Police are not noted for their rapid and accurate assessments of ongoing situations.'

I put down the icepack with which I had been attempting, unsuccessfully, to prevent another black eye and very slowly pulled out a small EMP device.

The officer's face paled as he took in the implications. He took half a step backwards, but the Boss hadn't finished with him yet.

'Dr Maxwell's instructions were to advise Ronan of my complete refusal to accept the terms he had presented, but my willingness to embark on a dialogue that would be beneficial to all. There was never, at any point, any thought of allowing him to walk away from his past crimes, but a hope that a way forward could be found. To reinforce this point, and to prevent his escape, at a moment she judged appropriate, Dr Maxwell was to disable his pod, leaving him with no choice other than to return with her to St Mary's. Chief Farrell and Major Guthrie are here awaiting their arrival. If you please, Major.'

Guthrie made a small signal and the entire Security Section stepped out from the shadows. Armoured, armed, ready for anything.

'At this point, having apprehended Clive Ronan, and when it was no longer possible even for the Time Police to … Well, at this point, your commander would have been informed. Once we had him safely in custody. As it is, thanks to the Time Police, the only thing we have now is an escaped and angry Clive Ronan who is, no doubt, out there now, plotting new ways to injure my unit and its personnel.'

'By the powers vested in the Time Police…'

'No one from my unit is under arrest. Nor will they be. You will leave now and count yourselves fortunate. You will report to your commander on your return. Please advise her I am available to discuss your professional behaviour with her at her earliest convenience.' He gestured towards the hangar door. 'Do not allow us to detain you.'

The Security Section escorted them to their pod. No one suffered a 'fall' on the way out, which I thought was particularly restrained of them, and a few seconds later, they'd gone.

I drew a deep breath and turned to Leon. We're in trouble now, aren't we?'

He nodded grimly. 'We are. Listen to me, Max. From this moment on, you never set foot outside unless you have someone with you. Matthew is never to be left alone, not even for one moment. If one of us can't be with him, then he goes to Sick Bay where he'll be safe.'

I nodded. 'Is that where he is now?'

He nodded and reapplied my icepack.

'Leon, we had a chance…'

'I know, love. But there might be others.'

'You know there won't be. If he didn't hate us before, he does now.' I shivered. 'Especially me.'

He smiled. 'Go and get Matthew. Have a long hot bath. I'll see you in a minute.'

I left Leon and Guthrie talking to Dr Bairstow and made my way to Sick Bay. I would collect Matthew, get my eye looked at, swill down a couple of mugs of tea, have a bath and soak away ten tons of desert sand from all my nooks and crannies. The inside of my clothes felt like sandpaper. As did my throat.

Sick Bay was deserted so it was a good job I wasn't spouting blood or hadn't a limb hanging off. I had no idea where Hunter was, and Helen, I guessed, was in her office with her feet up, enjoying a peaceful cigarette.

Isaac Newton says that time is like an arrow – always moving steadily in one direction. Einstein says time is like a river, with currents and swirls and eddies, moving faster in some places and slower in others.

It was doing that now.

I let the door swing behind me and time began to slow.

I started across the reception area with its empty

nurses' station and it slowed some more.

I turned towards Helen's office to tell her I was here, and it slowed even more.

The door to Helen's office opened and Clive Ronan stepped out, still in the same sand-covered clothes in which I'd last seen him, and carrying Matthew in one arm and a gun in the other.

Time ... stopped.

He hadn't waited even one day to make good his threat. Always unpredictable, he had come straight from there to here. While I had been downstairs, distracted by the Time Police, he had been upstairs. With Matthew. I remembered his words.

'No Maxwell. You're going to live. Everyone else in your world will die but you'll live on. You'll look back on today and wish I had killed you.'

We stared at each other. Nothing happened. Neither of us moved.

And then, all at once, time started up again.

Another door – the one to the ladies' toilets opened – and Helen stepped out, drying her hands on a paper towel.

Seeing me, she opened her mouth to say something. I'll never know what it was.

A fraction of a second later, she caught sight of Clive Ronan standing in the doorway of her office, gun in one hand, Matthew in the other.

She stopped dead, staring, her mouth still open.

He swung his gun, covering first Helen, then me, then back to Helen again.

I couldn't speak. Couldn't think. I took one step forward. Just one.

The gun swung my way. At the same time, Matthew caught sight of me and smiled. The gun was pointing straight at me.

I closed my eyes and held my breath, waiting for the sound of the gunshot that would end my life. The last sound I would ever hear.

Nothing happened. I opened my eyes again.

He smiled at me. He actually smiled at me. 'No. Not today, Maxwell. I promised I'd make you suffer. Today is just Day One. Get used to it.'

He swung the gun towards Helen and fired.

A small black circle appeared over one eye. She stood for one moment, blank faced and then she crumpled to the ground.

Sound came back into the world. Matthew jumped at the noise of the shot fired only inches from his ear. He screamed in fear and began to cry. Tears of terror ran down his little face. He held his arms out to me. Just as he always did whenever he saw me. He held his little arms out to me. For me to save him. And I let him down.

I couldn't move. The most important moment of my life and I couldn't move. Couldn't cry out. Couldn't do anything. Couldn't save Helen, for whom it was already too late. Couldn't save Matthew. Useless, pathetic Maxwell.

The slam of a door and the sudden sharp smell of cordite brought me back. He'd gone out the fire door. I was blocking the only exit from Sick Bay so it had to have been the fire door.

The sound of the slamming door broke the spell. Now, suddenly, I could move. I had to raise the alarm. I opened my com and for a moment, nothing happened. The most important message of my life and I couldn't barely utter even a word. I took a deep breath, leaned against the wall for support, and desperately tried not to gabble.

'This is Maxwell. Code Red. Code Red. Code Red.'

I didn't recognise my own voice.

I stopped for another breath.

'Intruder alert. Clive Ronan is here. He's…'

My throat closed. I swallowed hard and forced myself on. 'He's taken Matthew from Sick Bay. He's outside. Lock everything down. Cover all exits. I repeat – he's got Matthew. Medics to Sick Bay. Man down.'

And then I was moving. He had twenty, maybe thirty seconds start on me.

A lifetime for Matthew.

I burst through the fire door, travelling far too fast for my own safety, slipping on the metal steps, and rolling from top to bottom. I landed, sprawling, on the gravel.

I heaved myself to my feet, looking wildly around. No one was in sight anywhere. I could hear shouting in the distance but I didn't stop.

I ran. I ran all around the outside of the building, screaming for Matthew all the time. I ran along the terrace, around the building, through the car park, past the Staff Block, past the Library windows, around Hawking and back to where I'd started.

No Ronan. No Matthew. Convinced I'd missed them somewhere, I set off again. People shouted to me as I ran past but I ignored them. Catching Ronan and getting Matthew back were more important than anything else in the whole world.

And then I thought he might be hiding. I ran in and out of the shrubbery, thrusting bushes and branches aside, scratching my face badly. He wasn't there. He wasn't anywhere.

And then I thought – stupid Maxwell. He's doubled back inside. He'll hide until the coast is clear and then make his escape.

I crashed in through the front door. There were people everywhere.

Someone said, 'Max…'

I saw Mrs Enderby, white and frightened. She was crying. I ran straight past her. No time to lose. I had to find Matthew.

They said afterwards that I went berserk. I wrenched open door after door. I tossed things all over the place. I pulled stuff off shelves. God knows why. Some of it fell on top of me. I had no method. I searched the same areas twice and some not at all. I ran into walls. I hurt myself and never noticed. I was frenzied. Beyond panic. Beyond reason. Not thinking at all. No one tried to stop me. I'm not sure anyone could have. I would have killed them.

Matthew held out his arms to me. That's all I remember. There must be other memories hiding in there somewhere, but that's all I ever remember. Matthew holding his arms out to me as that bastard Ronan stole him away and I never saw my baby again.

I have no idea for how long I was lost to the world. I might even now still be tearing around St Mary's, frightening everyone around me if I hadn't blindly collided with something warm and solid. Someone put his arms around me, holding me close, and Leon's voice said quietly, 'Max. Stop. You must stop. You're hurting yourself. Be still. Please, just ... be ... still.'

I struggled, but he held me tightly, his face close to mine, saying, 'Hush, now. Be still. Be still,' over and over again, until I suddenly realised that I was exhausted. My legs trembled. I could barely stand up. I hurt all over. My heart was hammering fit to burst. I honestly thought I might die.

He held me for a lifetime as slowly, very slowly, everything subsided within me. I laid my head on his chest and clutched at him as if my life depended upon it. The sounds of St Mary's receded and there were only the two of us in the whole world.

He broke the spell first, saying softly, 'Look at me, Max. Look at me.'

I lifted my head to look around me.

It was dark. All the lights were on. When had that happened? Where had the time gone?

He looked terrible. Ten years older. Grey-faced. Haggard. His own eyes red-rimmed and swollen. I put my hand to his face. He turned his head and kissed my palm.

I wiped my nose on his orange jumpsuit. He found me an oily handkerchief, saying shakily, 'Not your most attractive habit, Lucy.'

I made an enormous effort to pull myself together. Leon needed me to function.

'Can you go and see Dr Bairstow?' he said, and I nodded. 'He wants to talk to you. To find out exactly what happened. I have to find Ian Guthrie and join the search again. Will you be all right on your own for a little while?'

I nodded again. 'Please don't be too long.'

'I won't. I promise.'

The stairs seemed endless. I saw no one but I could hear sounds of searching. Doors opening and closing. People calling to each other. They must have been at it for hours. It was useless. I knew it was useless. Ronan was long gone.

With that thought, I felt my chest clench and everything swayed around me. I leaned on the banisters and struggled on.

Mrs Partridge was waiting for me.

'He's on the telephone at the moment,' she said. 'He won't be a minute. Please come and sit down.'

Not a moment too soon. My legs folded of their own accord and I sat down with a bump.

'I've made you some tea,' she said, passing me a steaming mug and I suddenly realised I hadn't eaten or drunk anything for hours.

I don't know what was in that mug but it wasn't tea. She'd done this once before – brewed me some sort of ancient corpse-reviver from the groves of Mount Ida. I'd been dying and it had certainly put me back on my feet again. Tonight was no different. I felt new strength course through my body. The sudden surge of heat only emphasised how cold I'd been. I sat up straight and looked around me.

'Finish your drink,' she said and I didn't need to be told twice, upending the mug and draining every last drop.

My lips felt stiff and dry. 'Thank you.'

'How are you feeling?'

'Much better, thank you.' I nodded at the door. 'Is there any news?'

'Not so far, but please be assured everything possible is being done. Dr Bairstow has put everyone on full alert. He's calling in favours. We'll find him Max. Wherever Ronan goes, they'll track him down.'

It wasn't Ronan I wanted to find, but I appreciated what she was saying.

Her intercom buzzed. 'You can go in now.'

Dr Bairstow stood up as I entered. 'Max, my dear.'

'Good evening, sir,' I said, struggling a little with kindness, as I always do.

'Sit down, please. You must be eager to know what progress has been made.'

I nodded, hardly daring to hope.

He sighed. 'I'm sorry, Max, not a lot. We can say, definitely, that your son…' I made a gesture. '…that Ronan is not anywhere here at St Mary's or in the grounds. I've spoken to the Chief Constable. Road blocks have been set up around the county – although I think it very unlikely he used conventional transportation to get in and out.'

He paused. 'I have, therefore, contacted the Time Police and formally requested their assistance.'

I swallowed everything down, made myself stay silent, and we looked at each other over his desk.

He said quietly, 'May I have your thoughts on this particular course of action.'

Half of me wanted to rise up in fury and demand he call them off. The other half thought it was a good idea because they had tech and resources far beyond anything we possessed. And actually, if it meant I got Matthew back then I'd do a deal with the devil.

The silence was still there. He was watching me closely. He'd done the right thing. Never mind that all this was their fault. The Time Police were absolutely the right way to go.

I swallowed everything down again. Mrs Partridge's potion must be working overtime to keep me this calm. As if I had summoned her by the power of thought alone, she entered. With real tea this time. I waited until she had poured and then said, 'An excellent idea, sir.' I paused. 'Will they come, do you think?'

'I think so,' he said, and now he paused. I knew what he was going to say. I sat back with my tea and let him say it anyway.

He cleared his throat. 'I think it would be helpful if today's events were not ... flung at them as soon as they walk through the door. And even more helpful if you could refrain from shooting them as well.'

'Certainly not, sir. Not until they've found…' I found I still couldn't say Matthew's name.

He held out his little arms to me.

'…Not until they've completed the mission, anyway. After that … I can make no promises.'

He nodded gravely. 'That seems eminently fair. Let us hope I remember to warn them of their peril.' He was unsmiling. 'I can make no promises either.'

He put down his tea. 'Now then, Max. What happened after you left us in Hawking? And in as much detail as you can manage. Please bear in mind you will probably have to repeat your story several times tonight. The first time will be the most difficult for you and so it is probably best to do it now, among friends.'

I closed my eyes and relived the scene. The doors. The empty nurses' station. Ronan. Matthew. Helen. Oh my God. Helen. I'd … No, I hadn't forgotten. I'd just pushed it to the back of my mind and now the images burst forth. Helen was dead. I saw again that neat little black hole just above her right eyebrow. Saw her crumple. Dead before she hit the floor.

'Drink this.' Mrs Partridge was at my side, offering me a small glass with another half an inch of corpse-reviver in the bottom. I chugged it back in one go and waited for the explosion of warmth again.

No good would come of being emotional. I'd seen friends and colleagues die before this. Dr Bairstow needed facts and he needed them quickly.

I closed my eyes again because for some reason that made things easier and described, as unemotionally as I could, the events in Sick Bay.

Corpse-reviver or not, I couldn't control my voice or stop the tears from running down my face. And nothing in the world could overcome my all-consuming fear for Matthew. What might Ronan be doing to him at this very moment? I remembered the Spartans who threw unwanted children off a mountain. Child sacrifice was widespread throughout the ancient world. And it wasn't as if Ronan actually had to do anything. He could just land – anywhere – anytime – open the door and just pitch him out. To be carried away by predators. Or die slowly in the pitiless glare of the desert sun. Or freeze to death in a snow bank somewhere. Or…

A strong, cool hand was laid on mine and I felt calmness and strength run through me. My mind cleared. Thoughts of death and suffering melted away. I opened my eyes, turned to Mrs Partridge and nodded my thanks.

She smiled slightly and then resumed her traditional seat behind Dr Bairstow.

I cleared my throat. 'Sir, if you've finished with me, I'd like to go to Dr Peterson. He shouldn't be alone.'

'Nor is he. Mr Markham is under instructions not to leave him.'

There was the sound of voices from Mrs Partridge's office. She slipped from the room.

Dr Bairstow looked at me.

'The Time Police are here.'

I stood up, gave a thought to what I must look like, decided it wasn't important, and turned to face the door.

First through was Leon, who looked immediately for me. I was relieved to see he seemed immeasurably better than the last time I'd seen him. He was pale, but that awful grey colour had gone. He looked tired, but calmer.

We have a self-imposed rule about never touching each other if we're in uniform. I kicked that into touch and held his hand. If anyone wanted to object, we could take it outside. I was just in the mood.

Next in was Ian Guthrie, himself looking tired. He saw me and nodded.

And here they came. The bloody Time Police. The cause of all the trouble. Despite all my good intentions, I stiffened. Leon tightened his grip on my hand.

First in was Commander Hay. We'd met before. After the battle of St Mary's, we'd all sat down and thrashed out a workable treaty. They hadn't stuck to it but then, neither had we, so probably enough said.

She was a few inches taller than me – so still not tall – and probably a few years older, although, with her, it was hard to tell. She'd fought in the Time Wars – that period when the Time Police had struggled against political and personal time travel. They'd fought to defend the timeline and for a while it had been touch and go. Make no mistake, we all owe the fact that we're still here and more or less intact to the Time Police. Anyway, there'd been some sort of temporal accident. One half of her face was older than the other. Rumours abounded, but I'd heard that during an emergency evacuation, the door had been blown off in mid-jump and she'd been exposed to whatever was out there. She'd been the lucky one. Everyone else in the pod had died. And it hadn't been pretty.

She was followed by two officers. One I knew – Captain Matthew Ellis, after whom Matthew was named.

The other I hadn't met before, but she introduced him as her adjutant, Captain Charles Farenden. He was a long, lanky man with brown hair who walked with a slight limp. And that was it. No soldiers. No weapons. Just Commander Hay herself, her adjutant, and an old acquaintance, making the point that this was not a punitive visit. We moved towards the briefing table.

Just as we were about to sit down, however, there was a tap at the door and Dottle entered. Bloody Thirsk shoving their oar in again. This was nothing to do with them. I think she might have had similar feelings because, without looking at me, she scuttled to a seat at the bottom of the table and pulled out her scratchpad.

Dr Bairstow began. 'Dr Maxwell, your report, please.'

Keeping my eyes on the table so I wouldn't have to look at Leon, I described the morning's events in Sick Bay. Dr Bairstow had been right. It was easier the second time around.

Guthrie reported no success with the search for either Ronan or Matthew. No one thought there would be, but he was a thorough man.

Leon reported he'd picked up a very slight trace of radioactivity behind the stables, presumably where Ronan had left his pod. He handed a printout to the adjutant. They could use this to help track Ronan. Every pod has an individual signature and it would give them something to focus upon.

And that was it. That was all we had.

Commander Hay spoke into the silence.

'Max, it's a long time since we last spoke. I'm sorry it's under these circumstances. I'm sorry too that the events of today probably arise from our failed attempt to capture Clive Ronan. I think the greater part of the blame must lie with us and I hope we shall be able to work together to put things right.'

Well – from the Time Police, who never apologise for anything – this was a gesture. And a generous one. I found a voice.

'Thank you, Commander. I hope so too.'

She nodded and looked around the table. 'I think we are all agreed – this cannot go on any longer. The man is out of all control. No one and nothing is safe. I have instructed Captain Ellis to put together a team to capture Clive Ronan as quickly as possible. Dr Bairstow, from this moment on, all the manpower, pods, equipment we can spare from our normal duties will be diverted towards apprehending this man. And Matthew Farrell, of course.'

Dr Bairstow inclined his head. 'Thank you. Your offer is greatly appreciated. You should not bear this burden alone, however. As a gesture of support and friendship, St Mary's will call for volunteers. There will be many, I am sure, but you will understand that I can't and won't leave St Mary's undefended. Particularly after today.'

'Of course.'

'I'll go,' I said, suddenly. 'I want to volunteer.'

No one looked at anyone else.

Leon stood up. 'I wonder if you would excuse us for a moment.'

Still no one looked at me. I found myself out on the gallery with no memory of how I got there.

'Max, I don't want you to go.'

'Leon!'

'No. I know you think nothing can go right unless you do it yourself, but I'm begging you. I don't want to bring Matthew back only to find something has happened to you. I lost my first family. I can't lose this one as well. I'm going after Matthew and you're going to stay here. No, please just listen for a moment. We're all going after Ronan in a big way. The Time Police are with us. Ian Guthrie's going as well – he has a score to settle too – and I expect one or two others will want to volunteer. There's no need for you to go, and what I need more than anything, Max, is to know that when I bring Matthew back – and I will bring him back, I promise you – that I'll find you here, safe and sound. I'm going to give this everything I've got, and to do that I must know that you're safe here at St Mary's.'

I opened my mouth to protest. How could he even think of leaving me behind? How could I possibly remain here knowing that somewhere out there my baby needed me?

'No, Max. Think about it. Helen's dead. Peterson is going to need you. And Markham will be Head of Security in Guthrie's absence. They'll both need you. St Mary's will look to you. You must appear to be carrying on as best you can. You can't leave now.'

'But Leon, I must go.'

'You can't. You're compromised.'

I stepped back from him. 'And you're not?'

'I understand how you feel, Max…'

'No, you don't.'

'He's my son too.'

'I know, I know. I didn't mean…'

'I know what you meant.'

'Leon – he's torn the heart out of my chest. I can't breathe. I can't think. I'll never be whole again. Matthew held out his arms to me and I didn't save him.'

'Listen to me,' he said softly. 'I've been thinking about this. I know it's unreasonable and unfair to expect you to wait here quietly while I could be gone for weeks – maybe even months, so I'll do you a deal. You stay here and I promise you faithfully that no matter how long it takes *me*, I will bring Matthew back to you next Friday. That's just a few days away for you.' He took my hands. 'Will you do it? Will you promise me?'

I nodded.

'Say it.'

I don't break my promises to Leon. They're too important. I took a moment to consider, then I looked up and nodded again. 'I promise.'

He smiled and cupped my face in his hands, saying, 'I will bring him back. You promised me and now I'm promising you. I will find him and bring him back to you.'

My eyes were so full of tears that I couldn't see him clearly. Any moment now, they were going to spill down my cheeks and I was going to disgrace myself in public.

'It's just two days,' he said, softly. 'I will bring him back to you in two days. That's Friday, Max. All you have to do is hold it together for two days and then, on Friday, you'll see him again. Whatever it takes, I will do this. Understood?'

I said reluctantly, 'Yes.'

'I'll find him Max. I'll get our little boy back.'

I looked around. No one was in sight. 'Promise me ... promise me, Leon. When you find Ronan – and I know you will – there'll be none of this bringing him to justice crap. No more worrying about any impact on the future. I don't care what everyone else says – just shoot the bastard dead.'

'I promise.' He bent, kissed my hand and then my cheek and before I could say another word, he was gone.

I wanted nothing more than to be alone for a few minutes. Just to pull myself together. To find a brave face to put on for the rest of the world.

Matthew, holding out his arms to me.

I rubbed my sleeve across my eyes, wiping away the tears. He'd wanted me to save him. To make everything all right again and I hadn't. I'd been useless.

But, perhaps there was some good I could do. I made my way to Peterson's room, tapping on the door. Markham opened it, stepped out, and pulled it to behind him. 'What's happening?'

I gave it to him in a few words and we looked at each other.

'I'd volunteer if I could, Max.'

'I know you would, but if Guthrie goes then you can't. How's Tim?'

He shook his head. 'Not good.'

'Does he know exactly what happened? In Sick Bay?'

'Dr Bairstow's spoken to him, yes. Look, I'm glad you're here. Can you stay for a few minutes while I get us both something to eat and have a quick word with the Major?'

'Of course.'

He disappeared and I stepped inside.

It was a mistake. Perhaps I should have taken those few minutes to step back from everything that had happened. Perhaps I should have given us both a little time and space. Perhaps I should have … I don't know what I should have done, but I know what I shouldn't have done. I shouldn't have gone in.

The room was dark.

I said, 'Tim?' but there was no response.

I tried again. 'Tim?' and brushed my hand against the wall, feeling for the light switch.

His voice came out of the dark. 'What do you want?'

'I came to see how you are. Can I do anything?'

'I would have thought you'd done enough damage today.'

I thought I'd misheard him. This wasn't Tim. This couldn't be Tim Peterson. I groped along the wall again for the light.

'Tim?'

The voice came out of the dark, flat and deadly. 'You were there and you didn't save her.'

The shock took my breath away. I felt as if he'd slapped me in the face. He was angry with me. Tim, who was never angry with anyone, was angry with me.

'You let her die. I don't understand you. Why would you do that? I thought she was your friend. She would have fought to the death for you. And you did nothing for her.'

I wanted to run. To run and run, and not have to hear

67

his voice, loaded with all the blame and recrimination I knew I deserved. Because he was right. I'd done nothing. When Helen – my friend – needed me, I'd done nothing. When Matthew – my baby – needed me, I'd done nothing. I deserved all the things he was saying to me.

'You really are the kiss of death, aren't you? People die all around you all the time and you just carry blithely on as if nothing has happened. It's taken me a long time to realise the truth, but you don't actually care for anyone but yourself, do you? You don't care for anyone or anything as long as you get what you want. The rest of us just drop by the wayside, broken and unwanted, while you just clamber over the ruins of people's lives without even noticing.'

I wanted to run. I couldn't run. I had to stay. He shouldn't be alone and Markham wasn't back yet. Tim himself shouldn't be here. He should be in Sick Bay, being tended to, except that was the very last place he should be. Because that was the place with so many memories of Helen.

I leaned back against the wall and stayed silent. He was right. I should have done something and I hadn't and this was my punishment. To stand in the dark and listen as my best friend said things that, in my heart, I knew were true.

I heard the door open and Markham came in.

The voice stopped. Silence dripped.

'Shall we have some light?' said Markham. I heard a click and, suddenly, light filled the room. I blinked.

Tim stood with his back to us, staring out through the window into the dark beyond.

Markham looked from him to me and said uncertainly, 'Max?'

I pushed past him to get to the door.

'Max, wait.'

He followed me into the corridor. 'Whatever he said, he didn't mean it.'

'Yes, he did.'

'He doesn't know what he's saying just at the moment.'

'Yes, he does.'

'He's in no fit state to talk sensibly and you're in no fit state to listen. I don't know what he said, but give him twenty-four hours and...'

I shook my head. 'He's right. Every word was true. He didn't say anything I haven't already said to myself. Several times over. It was just a bit of a shock that he should be the one to say it out loud.'

I walked away.

And that was the end of the worst day of my life.

Leon and I were up most of the night, packing up his gear, and drawing his kit and weapons from stores. Well, he packed – I sat on the bed and watched him and tried to come to terms with everything that had happened in the last twenty-four hours.

Matthew held out his little arms to me.

When he was finished, we sat and talked a little, heads close together, holding hands, taking and giving comfort. I struggled hard to appear calm and positive, because Leon needed to concentrate on the job in hand and not be distracted by me going to pieces.

Just before dawn, he went off to see Guthrie, and I, finding the silence of our empty room quite unbearable, went down to my office.

I stared out of the window and watched the pre-dawn glow as the sun had a think about putting in an appearance, and then someone tapped at the door. I had just one quick moment to wonder if, somehow, it could be Peterson, when Miss Grey walked in.

Even in my state of self-absorbed misery, I could see there was something different about her.

Elspeth Grey was yet another victim of Clive Ronan. He'd snatched her and her partner, Tom Bashford, and then dropped them into Roman Colchester, only one hour before Boudicca and her hordes swept down upon the town, leaving nothing standing, and no one alive. She'd struggled ever since, unable to rid herself of the fear that it would happen again, and that this time there would be no one to save her. To give her her due, she'd tried really hard to overcome her fears, but her one and only subsequent assignment had been a bit of a disaster and I was pretty sure this would be the final straw. For her, today's events had come too close to home and she was here to give in her notice. Now, of all times.

I braced myself.

'Max, how are you?'

'Absolutely fine,' I said, the traditional St Mary's response to any sort of catastrophe. 'What can I do for you?'

'Chief Farrell sent me. I want to volunteer and he said that as you're Head of the History Department, I had to clear it with you.'

Whatever I'd been expecting, it wasn't that. To cover my confusion, I sat at my desk and invited her to sit down as well.

She was different. Everything about her was different. She sat straight in her chair. Her grey eyes were clear and direct. Given recent events, she seemed surprisingly calm.

'Say that again.'

'I want to volunteer to join Major Guthrie's team. To hunt down Ronan and bring back Matthew.'

I was at a loss. She'd done everything she could to avoid getting back into a pod and now, here she was, volunteering not only to do that very thing, but to go after the man who'd abandoned her to a nasty death as well.

My confusion must have shown because she smiled sadly.

'I don't blame you Max, but this is something I must do. I've been mooning about, frightening myself to death, thinking about what could happen to me, and it never once occurred to me that it could happen to someone else. This bastard is a danger and a menace and he must be stopped. I want to help stop him. I must do this. I must go with Chief Farrell and Major Guthrie. I must get him out of my life. And everyone else's as well. You've kept me on here and I appreciate it; you've given me every chance to be an historian again, but we both know I'm not making any sort of contribution. Now though, I think I can. May I have your permission to go with Guthrie and Farrell?'

I couldn't think of anything to say except, 'Subject to Dr Bairstow's approval, yes. Thank you.'

She smiled and got up to go. 'We'll get him, Max. You just wait and see.'

Leon's goodbye was brief. We stood outside Hawking in the early morning sunshine. Two black pods stood at the edge of the pan, doors open, ramps down. Waiting for our people.

He took my hand. 'I hate to go off and leave you looking so broken.'

'Bring him back. And stay safe yourself. That's all I ask.'

'Two days Max. Just two days.'

'I know. Take care.'

He kissed my hand and my cheek. 'See you Friday.'

'I'll be waiting.'

I stood with everyone else as they set off. I watched Leon, Guthrie and Grey walk across the pan together, and enter the nearest pod. Leon turned briefly and raised a hand to me. Then the ramp came up behind them, the pods blinked out of existence, and they were gone.

All around me, people were dispersing. Getting on with their day. I looked down at my feet and wondered what to do with myself now.

He held out his little arms to me.

Turning to go, I saw Peterson standing some little distance away, staring at the spot where the Time Police pods had been. He looked around, saw me watching, and turned away.

I know that in popular romances, the suffering heroine is always too distraught to eat, thus arriving at the end of the book having not only triumphed over adversity, but gained the hero and a stunning figure as well. I'd never believed it myself. How could anyone ever forget to eat? But now I realised I couldn't remember the last time I had eaten anything. Lunchtime yesterday, I think. Before jumping to the Egyptian desert. This time yesterday. When I still had a family.

I had a sudden memory of Leon, years ago, telling me how he'd lost his first family. 'I started the week with a happy, healthy family, and by the end of it, I was the only one left.' Tragedy is that sudden. That unexpected. This time yesterday, I too had had a happy, healthy family. And now they were both gone.

He held out his arms to me...

I went for some food.

When I returned, Miss Lee was in my office, head down, working away. I stood in the doorway and looked at her. She was actually working, but this was not the moment for sarky comments.

She looked up. 'Max? Any news?'

I shook my head. 'Not yet. They've only just left.'

'There will be, I'm sure. What can I do?'

'Actually, I don't know. Nothing, I suppose. I can't do anything. Not at the moment, anyway. Thank you for coming in so early.'

'I can stay late, as well, if you need me. David is taking care of Benjamin.'

David Sands was a former historian with whom she lived and Benjamin was her son. Who must be doubly precious after yesterday's events.

I sat at my desk and pulled out a mission folder, centred it carefully on my desk, took a breath and opened it.

Two days. Just two days. I could do that.

I don't know about anyone else, but when confronted with personal tragedy, I'm always slightly affronted that the world seems to carry on as if nothing has happened. I never know whether this is a good or bad thing. True, it can sometimes help to keep things in perspective, but it doesn't make things easy. The world didn't stop for me and it certainly didn't stop for Peterson who remained alone in his room, seeing no one except Markham.

Dr Bairstow sent for me.

'Good morning, Dr Maxwell.'

'Good morning, sir.'

'Thank you for coming.'

'No choice, sir. In the absence of any other senior staff, we seem to be stuck with each other.'

'A burden,' he said gravely. 'I wonder which of us will crumble first.'

I knew who my money was on.

'I've sent for a new Chief Medical Officer.'

I caught my breath and experienced, once again, the shock of Helen's loss.

He was watching me carefully. 'It seems callous, I know, but we cannot afford to be without full medical support.' He laid a file in front of me. I opened it. The photo was on the inside cover.

A twelve-year-old boy with a bony face, large ears and heavy eyebrows stared back at me. I know I was at the age when policemen and doctors were beginning to look young, but even so ... Was he some sort of infant prodigy?

'Dr Nathaniel Stone,' he said. 'He will be with us possibly later today or, more probably, tomorrow. He will certainly be in place before our next assignment.' He paused expectantly.

'1064, sir. The shipwreck of Harold Godwinson.'

He knew that. He was just giving me the opportunity to ease myself back in gently and I was grateful.

'I would appreciate your reassurance that none of you intend actually to participate either in the shipwreck or the rescue.'

'Happy to give it, sir. Observe and document only.'

'Excellent. Let us hope then that it is some time before

we need to put our new doctor's skills to the test.'

He paused again and began to align the files on his desk. 'Dr Peterson…'

I kept myself calm. 'Yes, sir?'

'I am grieved to hear that you and Dr Peterson do not find yourselves able to support each other during this time.'

'Yes, sir.'

Without looking at me he said, 'I would not, if I were you, assign any importance to anything Dr Peterson does or says over the next week or so. He is, naturally, very shocked and distressed. He has not yet even begun to grieve. There are, I believe, certain stages to be worked through. I am certain that he will prevail, and when he returns to us – as I am sure he will – it will be good for him to find his colleagues ready and willing to offer him the support and understanding he will certainly need. I always think that true friends should never allow a few words, hastily uttered, to sever the ties of strong and longstanding friendships.'

I don't know how he knows these things. I honestly wouldn't be surprised if he had the entire building bugged. But then, if he did, he would have seen what was happening in Sick Bay. In time to prevent…

He held out his arms…

'And you, Max, how are you?'

'Absolutely fine, sir.'

'I'm very pleased to hear that. How are you really?'

I hesitated.

'How are you, Max?'

'I…'

He waited.

'I keep seeing … that moment … replaying it in my head…' Time for the truth. 'Sir, I froze. I did nothing.'

He started with the files again. 'Traditionally, in a crisis, there has always been the choice of fight or flight. I have always maintained that there is a third option. Freeze. I believe that in such circumstances as you found yourself yesterday, when there is no time for rational thought, a person follows their instinct. Your instinct was to freeze. The alternatives were either to run away – and I don't suppose that thought even entered your head – or to fight. I'm sorry to say this, Max, but Helen Foster was doomed the moment she stepped out of that door. Nothing you could have said or done could have saved her. And had you, at that moment, made any sort of move, then he would have shot you as well. Which means that, at the end of the day, Matthew would still have been carried off, and Leon would be mourning the loss of his wife as well as that of his son. You may not have thought it through, but you did exactly the right thing.'

'Sir…'

'Dr Peterson, when he is able to think more calmly, will realise this. It is unreasonable to expect that degree of clarity from him at this moment.'

I nodded, aligned a few files myself, and then said, 'Will there be anything else, sir.'

'Not at the moment. You are, at present, my only functioning senior officer and so I shall be leaning on you quite heavily over the next few days.'

I nodded. He was keeping me busy. Not giving me any time to fret.

'My next task is personally to inform Dr Peterson about our new member of staff. I would not like him to hear it from anyone else.'

'Will he leave us, do you think?'

'I hope not. Thank you, Dr Maxwell, that will be all.'

As I passed through Mrs Partridge's office, she said, 'Please let me know if there is anything I can do, Max.'

'Thank you, Mrs Partridge. That's very kind.'

Just as I was opening the door, she smiled and said, 'You are not alone.'

Miss Lee and I worked quietly in my office for the rest of the morning. I clung to the familiar routines like a drowning man to a lifebelt. I was beginning to think that my two days of waiting might go more quickly and more easily than I had thought, when Markham stuck his head around the door.

'Come in,' I said.

He looked tired. 'I thought I'd come and see how you're doing.'

'I'm fine. How's Peterson?'

'Sleeping. Evans is with him at the moment. Listen, I know it's a bit of a bolting the stable door thingy, but Dr Bairstow has asked me to do a survey and look at upgrading our security measures. Can I have a quick squint out of your window? You know, lines of sight and whatnot.'

'Go ahead.'

I don't know whether there was some sort of unseen message, but Rosie Lee casually picked up her bag and said if it was all right with me she'd go for an early lunch.

Since she normally didn't bother to ask, I was too gobsmacked to answer.

Markham closed the door behind her.

'What?' I said, alarmed. I really didn't need any more bad news.

'Nothing,' he said hastily. 'I have a message from Hunter.'

I felt guilty. She'd been Helen's head nurse, ally, and long-time friend, and I hadn't given her a thought.

'You can't do everything,' said Markham, always disconcertingly cleverer than he looked. 'You've got other stuff on at the moment. I'm looking after Hunter.'

'She's a lucky girl.'

'You wouldn't like to tell her that, would you? She never believes me when I say it. Anyway…'

He looked uncomfortable.

'What?'

'She has Matthew's stuff. From when he was … in Sick Bay. His blanket. His teddy bear. Other things. She asked me to mention it because she's not thinking very clearly at the moment, and she doesn't want to do the wrong thing and make everything worse. Do you want them back or should she keep them there? Until Matthew comes back.'

I had a sudden heart-searing picture of Matthew's little teddy bear. Made for him by Miss Dottle. Last year, on the day I'd departed on maternity leave, she'd shyly handed me a little, pale blue teddy she'd made herself. Matthew loved it and it went everywhere with him. I really wasn't sure I could handle seeing it now. Or the beautiful, soft lemon-yellow blanket that

Helen herself had knitted…

'It's OK,' said Markham, getting up to look out of the window again while I pulled myself together. 'I'll get her to hang on to them until Matthew comes back.'

I nodded, even though he had his back to me.

He turned back. 'I wish I could do something for you, Max.'

'You are. You're making the building safe. So that when we get him back it can never happen again.'

'Yeah. Well, I must crack on. I just dropped in … you know.'

'I do know. Thank you.'

He headed towards the door and as he passed me, he put his hand on my shoulder, just for a moment. Then he was gone.

Rosie Lee brought me some sandwiches. Another first. She plonked them down in front of me with her 'Don't get used to this' expression and I responded with the corresponding 'Don't worry, I won't' look.

After lunch, desperate to keep myself occupied and remembering I had departmental responsibilities, I called a meeting of the History Department. Normally, I'd hear them coming long before they arrived, clattering down the corridor and bickering about something or other. Today, they entered quietly, seated themselves around the briefing table, and looked at me expectantly.

I had a moment when I wasn't sure about my voice. The first few words were very wobbly and everyone had the good manners to pretend not to notice.

'Good afternoon, everyone. Thank you for coming.

Situation update. I am expecting Chief Farrell to return with Matthew sometime tomorrow, and Dr Bairstow has advised me that our new doctor, Dr Stone, will be arriving very soon. Either today or tomorrow. Please give him time to become acclimatised before presenting him with the traditional St Mary's medical mayhem.'

Helen, crumpling to the floor…

My voice still wasn't quite steady. I took a moment to rummage through my files, carefully laying what I needed in front of me.

'So – our forthcoming assignments. Miss North, I believe you have prepared a briefing?'

She nodded and rose to her feet. If she was disappointed at not being able to preside over the entire briefing herself, she was hiding it well and, to do her justice, I don't think such a thought had entered her head. She was ambitious and single-minded, but she wasn't completely heartless.

Sykes sat back and stifled a yawn. I frowned at her and she shrugged. They really didn't like each other. These days, I was rather well endowed with historians and it had been easy either to keep them apart or include them in a group so large that they could safely ignore each other, but the day would inevitably come when they would have to work closely together. Sometimes I wondered whether to get it over with and just despatch the two of them to somewhere, and wait to see which, if either of them, came back. But not just now. There was enough trauma around the place at the moment without adding the Sykes/North conflict as well.

I underestimated North. I always do. She briefs better

than anyone. Alone out of all the History Department, she never allows herself to get bogged down in unnecessary details, or distracted by passing comments, or lost in her notes.

'Four assignments altogether,' she said, 'and two months in which to complete them, which shouldn't be a problem.'

Yes, typical North. Grieving colleagues, murder and kidnap weren't even a blip on her radar. On the other hand, bracing unsentimentality was just what we needed.

'The first is the shipwreck of Harold Godwinson and his house arrest under Duke William of Normandy. The second will be the oath-taking ceremony at Bayeux when he swears to support William's claim to the throne in order to gain his freedom. The third is the Battle of Stamford Bridge against Tostig and Harald Hardrada, and the last is the big finish at Hastings.

She began to bring up images on the screen.

'There are two main players. Harold Godwinson, Earl of Wessex, and Duke William of Normandy – William the Conqueror...'

'William the Bastard,' murmured Sykes.

North swept on unheeding. 'Edward the Confessor, King of England, has no son. William and his fellow Normans firmly believe that Edward, notoriously pro-Norman after his time there in exile, has promised William the throne after his death. Whether he has or not is immaterial because the succession is not his to control. Primogeniture does not yet exist and under Saxon law, the next king is selected by the Witan – the council of leading nobles.

'Anyway, in 1064, Harold, for reasons which have never been entirely clear, embarks on a sea voyage. Norman chroniclers – from their position as victors, of course – claim that Harold was sent by Edward to do fealty to William, thus confirming William would be king after his death. This is generally considered to be unlikely. Some say the purpose of his journey was to secure the release of members of his family held hostage after Earl Godwin's revolt in 1051. The Saxons will maintain he was simply on a fishing expedition and the boat was blown off course.

'Whatever the reason, we do know he left from Bosham and was shipwrecked off Ponthieu. According to the law at the time, any victims of shipwreck were the property of the Count of Ponthieu, Guy I. It might be that initially, Guy was unaware of the status of his prisoner but, somehow, word gets to William – his overlord. Guy is subject to William's commands and William, probably unable to believe his good luck, makes his commands known immediately. Harold is carted off to Guy's castle at Beaurain; William arrives to claim him. And that's where we come in. Back to you, Max.'

She sat down.

'Thank you, Miss North. We'll take two pods – Numbers Eight and Five. There will be three members of Security to accompany us, one of whom will be Mr Markham. You have a week or so to get yourselves off to Mrs Enderby to be kitted out. Tunics, hose and cloaks for the men. Longer tunics and cloaks for the women. Hair in long braids please, ladies, and covered with a veil. Doctor Dowson will provide background briefing and language

84

tapes. A few words of Old French will be useful.'

'What's the weather?' enquired Bashford.

'No idea. At the moment we only know that the shipwreck took place in spring or early summer. Mr Atherton and Miss Prentiss have volunteered to act as Pathfinders. They'll hop about until they find the date and report back to us. Remember that whatever the season, Norman halls are dark, draughty and smoky and dress accordingly.

'Once we have the coordinates, We'll land at Beaurain and mingle with the crowds. This is an important day for Guy – he has something William wants. And it's a more than important day for William – his enemy has been delivered into his hands. Justice is a public affair – the actual details of the deal will be thrashed out in private, but handing over Harold to William will be done in public. Very politely and with a great deal of ceremony, and there won't be even a hint that he's a prisoner and a hostage to his own fortune. Everyone will smile. Hands will be clasped and wine will be drunk, but make no mistake, this is the day that Harold – and ultimately England – are stitched up for all time. With luck, right in front of our eyes.

'Are there any questions?'

People shook their heads. Our briefings weren't normally this subdued.

'I propose,' I said, 'that since we have two main protagonists, namely William of Normandy and Harold Godwinson, we divide ourselves into two teams for these assignments. One team will focus on Harold's part in these events and the other on William's. In-depth observations, please – appearance, clothes, mannerisms, actions, motives, policies, everything you can think of. It will, I think, be interesting to observe the same events from two opposing points of view. Does anyone have any particular favourite?'

North immediately volunteered for William – not least, I suspected, because she was always telling us one of her ancestors had been at Hastings. On the winning side, obviously. Sykes signed up for Harold. Bashford went with Sykes – no surprise there. Clerk wanted William as well, and Prentiss and Atherton were the Pathfinders.

'Excellent,' I said, and it was. I always hesitate to use the expression *well-balanced* to describe anything related to the History Department, but they were two good teams and with a senior historian on each. I was, of course, ignoring Peterson's absence. He could join us if he wished. I wondered if he would wish to. What would I do if he left? And what would I do if he never forgave me?

I pushed that thought out of my head and returned to the well-trodden path of procedure.

'Right, Team William will wait outside, get shots of his arrival – numbers, horses, the grand entrance, and then follow him into the hall. I'm optimistic about it being open to the public. Count Guy is doing his overlord a favour and he'll want everyone to know that.

Team Harold will be inside. I'll want shots of the Hall layout and those present – Count Guy, his clothes, his entourage, others present. You all know what to do. If, for some reason, Team William can't get in, Team Harold will split. Bashford and Sykes will stay on Harold and I'll take William myself. I particularly want details of

William and Harold's first meeting. How they react to each other. Will they leave at once or is there a feast? Does William treat Harold as an equal? When they leave, how is he mounted? Is he a guest or a prisoner? Remember people, we're witnessing the opening stages of events that still impact on us today. Any questions? OK, that's it. Thank you, everyone.'

I dismissed them all, sent Rosie Lee home early, worked quietly for a couple of hours, and then went back to my silent room. I closed the door behind me, crossed to Matthew's bedroom, and opened the door. The very emptiness of the room leaped out at me. There was his cot. Empty. His giraffe quilt was neatly folded at the bottom. There was the small chest of drawers with his clothes. His brush and comb sat on top. I picked up the brush. I could see dark hairs twisted among the bristles. I replaced it carefully. His ball lay on the rug. I picked it up. It was made of some soft, furry material, warm and brightly coloured. And slightly sucked. He loved his ball. I put it next to his brush. The room smelled of baby powder. It was very quiet in here. I switched out the light and closed the door.

I took a shower, pulled on one of Leon's T-shirts and went to bed, where I lay and watched the moon travel past the window, and refused to give way.

And that was the end of the second day.

I was up at dawn the next morning, because Leon hadn't said what time on Friday and, as far as I was concerned, Friday was any time after midnight on Thursday.

The first thing that happened was that Dieter banned me not only from Hawking, from outside, as well. I'd bounded down there, bacon sandwich in one hand, mug of tea in the other, and stood around waiting. I was prepared to wait all day and night if necessary. I was determined that whenever Leon turned up, I would be here. I would be the first thing he and Matthew would see when they exited the pod.

I turned around to find Dieter standing behind me, his early morning coffee clutched in one hand.

'Max, go back to the main building.'

'But I...'

'There's no need for you to be here. We've no idea when Leon will be back. You can't stay here all day. It's freezing.'

'But...'

'No. You can't be here. Go back to your department. Find something to do. The time will go so much more quickly. You do yourself no good at all by waiting here. I promise you – as soon as the pod materialises, you'll get the word. I'll call you myself. They'll take a minute or two to shut things down and decontaminate and then, when they open the door, you'll be waiting for them.'

'Dieter…'

'Max, I'm doing you a favour. Don't make me call Dr Bairstow.'

I trailed back down the long corridor. He was right. It was barely dawn. The security shifts were changing. I looked for Markham but couldn't see him. Perhaps he was still with Peterson.

I went to my office, pulled my in-tray towards me, and lost myself in the comforting routine of work.

Dr Bairstow bombarded me with emails – all demanding instant responses, and when I next had time to look up, it was past noon. The morning had gone and there was still no message from Hawking. I tried to pick up my work again, but my concentration had fled. I tidied my desk and then went back to my room. I would get Matthew's things ready for him. His clothes would be dirty. He would need clean stuff. I hesitated a long time over whether to lay out a blue babysuit or an orange one. It should be orange, surely, in honour of Leon who had brought him back safely. I laid out his clean clothes, changed my mind, chose blue instead, and then thought, idiot – he'll have to stay in Sick Bay for a major check-up, so I put away the babysuits and pulled out his pyjamas. Unable to choose between Superman or Mr Happy, and in the end, gripped by a sudden panic that Leon would return and I wouldn't be there, I unzipped my old sports bag and shoved in nearly everything Matthew owned. I would choose properly when he was safely in

Sick Bay. When I could hold him again. Feel him wriggling on my lap. Feel his strong little back.

He held out his arms to me...

Shouldering the bag, I went downstairs again, walking around the gallery, looking down into the Great Hall.

We were planning our four assignments more or less simultaneously. The Hall – the traditional historians' working area – was crowded with untidy, paper-strewn tables. There were whiteboards covered in scribbled notes in different colours, with maps, diagrams, and flowcharts pinned to the walls. On the face of it, there was chaos everywhere, but I could see a clear division between assignments. Everything relating to the shipwreck was over by the stairs; the oath-taking ceremony was in the corner by the library; Stamford Bridge was down the middle and Hastings over against the wall. We were very busy and in a week's time, we were going to be even busier.

I put down the bag and sat on the stairs, watching the History Department trail back from lunch, every one of them clutching a large mug of tea to see them through the rigours of the afternoon. Or until the next official tea break, anyway.

The minutes inched by. I kept checking my com, terrified it had suddenly developed a fault. I imagined Dieter trying to contact me and giving up. Suppose Leon and Matthew arrived and I wasn't there. I gripped my hands together and tried to remain calm.

Clerk looked up, saw me, and said something to Sykes. She trotted off, returning a minute later with a mug of tea for me. I thanked her because it was a kind thought, and I was a bag of nerves.

She sat down beside me. She didn't say anything; she just sat beside me. After a minute or so, Atherton put down his file and joined us. North looked up, hesitated a moment, and then she too climbed the stairs and sat in front of Atherton.

One by one, they all stopped working and came to join us. As their department head, I should have something to say about this lack of productivity. As Max, I was grateful for their silent support.

It wasn't just the History Department. Dr Dowson, with much groaning and assistance from Miss Lingoss, lowered himself and sat down. He was joined a second later by Professor Rapson and his entire team. Astonishingly, none of them were on fire.

Mrs Enderby appeared, trailing the Wardrobe Department behind her. They all joined us and now the stairs were completely blocked. I was surrounded by St Mary's.

Dr Bairstow, limping around the gallery, contemplated us.

'Please reassure me you are not all about to start grooming each other.'

It was exactly the right thing to say. I felt my heart lift a little.

And then we all sat in silence and watched the clock.

The afternoon wore on. My focus changed. As the hours passed, I thought of Friday as any time *before* midnight. Half of me knew that Leon would return. He had said he would bring back Matthew and he would. Leon was a man who kept his word. I knew that. But there was no sign of him and there should be. He was in a pod. He could choose to return at any time he chose. Why was he making me wait? I looked at the clock. Three o'clock. A good time to appear. Three o'clock was exactly the time I myself would have chosen. Lunch over and done with. It was the middle of the afternoon. If anyone ever has an afternoon appointment, three o'clock is always the time of choice. Now would be the perfect time for him to return.

No call from Dieter. I checked my com. It was working perfectly. I looked at the clock. The minute hand moved inexorably on.

I was running through the contents of Matthew's bag again and wondering if I'd forgotten anything, when Dieter spoke in my ear.

'Max. They're outside Hawking.'

I was up and running.

They were already exiting the pod when I arrived. I skidded to a halt and watched as, exhausted and dirty, the Time Police clambered out of their pod, followed by Guthrie and Grey. Dieter had everything organised. They were whisked away to Sick Bay where our new doctor would be waiting.

No one was looking at me. The last of them trickled away and not one of them had looked at me. Not one. Not even Guthrie or Grey. They hadn't found him. I could see it in their faces. Even worse, there was no sign of Leon.

I stood outside Hawking on the frosty pan, my breath puffing around me and clutching my stupid sports bag.

Was it possible…? Was it possible that in addition to losing Matthew I had now lost Leon as well? I stared at the big, black pod. It had been designed to put the fear of God into people and it was certainly having that effect on me.

I could see Dieter waving his people away, leaving me standing alone. I heard the last footsteps. A door banged somewhere. No one had said a word. Why had they left me here?

Of course. My brain was really not functioning today. Leon would wait inside so we could have a few minute's privacy. To be together again.

I climbed inside.

Leon stood in the middle of the pod, facing the ramp. Facing me.

Alone.

Leon stood alone. No Matthew in his arms. It wasn't until that moment that I realised how completely I'd believed in him. He'd promised he would bring Matthew back. And now – despite everything he'd said, despite all the promises he'd made – he'd come back without him.

I made myself look at him. He looked terrible. Dirty, grim-faced, worn out.

I wanted to say 'Where is he?' but no words would come.

I remember I looked all around the pod. I don't know why. It wasn't likely Leon would have left him lying under the console or put him away in one of the lockers.

Still we looked at each other, and then, slowly, he stepped to one side and I saw he'd been standing in front of a small boy.

I stared, first at Leon and then at the boy. Who the hell was this? I don't know what I thought. That Leon, unable to find Matthew, had brought back some stray kid as a kind of consolation prize?

I saw a very little boy. Not attractive in any way. Leon had wrapped him in a blanket, but enough of him was exposed for me to see he was filthy, with badly grazed knees and elbows. His feet were blue with cold and badly burned in places. Sullen eyes peered out at me from underneath thickly matted hair. There was an overwhelming aroma of wet soot and urine. I put his age at around five or six years old. If called upon to hazard a guess, I would have said he was a chimney sweep's boy from sometime in the early 19th century.

We stared at each other. I took in his stick-like limbs, the calluses on his hands, feet, knees and elbows. His left arm looked oddly bent. From the way he was cradling it, I wondered if it was broken. Even from here I could see he had lice. And fleas. His skin was rubbed red-raw in some places and flaking away in others.

The silence rolled on and on as the two of us stared suspiciously at each other, and then Leon said quietly, 'Max, this is Matthew.'

I dragged my gaze from the filth-encrusted boy in front of me and croaked, 'What did you say?'

'This is Matthew. This is our son.'

I'm not proud of what I did next. I suppose I could say I didn't believe him, but that wouldn't be true. My own eyes glared back at me from under that shock of matted hair so dark with dirt and soot that I couldn't have told you what colour it was. Deep down, I knew Leon would

95

never lie about anything so important to both of us, but I couldn't accept it. I didn't want to accept it. My Matthew was a baby. He could barely sit up on his own. He smiled and blew bubbles. He held out his arms to me. He always held out his arms to me. He was his Mummy's Boy. He wasn't this … this…

I became aware I was still holding his bag, full of little vests and babysuits and Mr Happy pyjamas and nappies and a dozen other useless items that would never be needed again. Leon had brought Matthew back, but my baby was gone for ever.

Leon said, 'Max…'

I jerked back to him, tried to speak, and failed. I let the bag drop to the floor where it landed with a thump. The noise broke the spell. For the first time in my life, I deliberately ran away. I bolted.

Someone shouted something behind me. I didn't stop. I was desperate for time and space to think. I was out of that pod like a whippet, gasping in the cold air. I didn't get far, which was just as well because I had no idea where I was going. I couldn't seem to catch my breath. I ran to the lake and sought the shelter of the densely planted willows, their hanging branches just beginning to show green. I pushed my way through them into the soft, filtered light and away from the real world and the ugly things happening there. I hung on to a trunk, feeling my world reel around me.

My baby was gone.

There are fairy stories about this sort of thing. About babies being stolen by fairies or by elves, about ugly substitutes left in their place while the human child is spirited away to the hollow hills and never seen again. Except that this ugly boy *was* my child. This was Matthew. This stranger was my son. I would now never see his first steps, or hear his first words, or…

Someone was pushing their way through the hanging branches. I looked around, seeking a way out. I didn't want to see anyone. I didn't want to have to talk about this nightmare. I didn't want to have to force myself to come to terms with what had happened. To force myself to care for that ugly changeling…

I kept very quiet, hoping they would push their way past and miss me altogether. That I could have a few quiet moments just to think.

The nearest branches parted and Peterson appeared.

I braced myself. If he was going to have a go at me again then this time I was ready for him. And this time he might find he'd bitten off more than he could chew. This time I was in no mood to stand quietly while he vented his anger. I became aware I was sucking in great lungfuls of air. The world spun around me.

He caught my arm. 'Sit down. Quickly.'

I slid down the trunk, closed my eyes, and laid my head back against the tree. I don't know for how long I sat there before the dizziness passed.

'Max.'

I kept my eyes closed, waiting for him to go away, but he didn't.

'What do you want?'

'You have to go back.'

'It's not him.'

'Yes, it is. You know it is. He has your eyes.'

97

I opened my eyes. 'Why should I believe *you*?'

There was a very long silence and then he said, very simply, 'I'm so very sorry.'

I felt the tears prick. I couldn't speak for the lump in my throat.

I think he mistook my silence. 'Please, if you can, forget what I said before. I wasn't thinking properly. I'd just lost Helen. I forgot you'd lost Matthew as well. Of course he was your first priority. Of course he was your first concern. I understand. Now. So please, listen to me just this once. You can go back to hating me tomorrow if you want to – but listen to me today, because I'm giving you good advice.'

I could hear the intensity in his voice.

'You should be overjoyed. You have Matthew back. What does it matter if he's older than when he left? It's still the same Matthew. Do you think I wouldn't give anything to have Helen back again – at any age? But she's gone for ever and nothing can ever bring her back. Max, Leon has brought you back your son. And nearly killed himself doing it, by the look of him. *You* won't wake every morning to face each day alone. *You* won't have to think about how to spend the rest of your life without him. So stop pissing about, get back in there, and sort it out before it's too late.'

We contemplated each other for a while. There was no doubting his sincerity. Even in the short time since I had last see him, he looked older. His face was thin and white and he was regarding me through pain-filled eyes.

I looked away. 'I don't hate you.'

'Then I'm luckier than I deserve to be.'

'I'm sorry, too. You were right. I should have done something. Anything.'

'No, you couldn't. He would have killed you too, and about the only good thing in all of this is that you're still alive. Come on.' He stood up and reached out his hand. 'They're in Sick Bay. I'll walk you there.'

I thought about what that would mean for him. 'You don't have to do that.'

'I have to do it sometime and I might as well combine it with my good deed for the day. Up you get.'

He pulled me to my feet and we stood for a moment, hands clasped.

He looked at me. 'All right?' and I knew he wasn't asking me how I felt.

'Yes,' I said. 'Always.'

We pushed through the Sick Bay doors to the sound of screaming. Ear-splitting, glass-shattering screaming.

I flagged down a hot and flustered Nurse Fortunata. 'What the hell's going on?'

'Your son is having a bath and he's not happy.'

'I'll be off then,' said Tim, hastily. 'Happy parenting.'

Just for a moment, a glimmer of the old Tim shone through, and then he was walking away.

The screaming stopped.

'A mild sedative, probably,' said Fortunata. 'Before the windows shattered and our ear drums burst.'

'Is Leon with him?'

She nodded. 'Do you want to go in?'

'I think I'll wait. This strikes me as an excellent opportunity for father-son bonding.'

She grinned. 'Take a seat. The doctor wants to see you anyway.'

'Oh? Do we know why?'

'Morbid curiosity, I think. He's been reading your file.'

Ten minutes later, Hunter appeared. Another one shocked and grieving. She and Helen had worked together for years. She was carrying a medical-waste bag – at arm's length – which she handed to Fortunata.

'For immediate incineration.'

'Was this his blanket?'

'Yes. He only had it on an hour or so and already it contains a variety of wildlife that even Markham could never achieve.'

Fortunata took the bag, nodded towards me, and disappeared.

Hunter came over.

'Hey, Max.'

'Hi. How is he?

'They're both exhausted and struggling to keep their eyes open. Our new doctor is here and he wants a quick word with you.'

I nodded. 'Will you tell Leon I'm here if he needs me?'

'Will do. Did I see you with Peterson?'

I didn't want to talk about that. 'Yes.'

'I know he turned on you, but he's suffering, Max.'

'I know. How about you?'

'Oh, I'm fine. I think Markham is planning to contract something appalling just so I can yell at him. He thinks it will make me feel better.'

'And will it?'

'No, but it's the thought that counts. We're all pretending these days.'

I heard a door open behind me and turned for my first glimpse of our new doctor.

He looked even younger than in his photograph. His ears stuck out even further than in his photograph. His eyebrows were even more wayward than in his photograph. He was taller and thinner than in his photograph. And in the photograph, he hadn't been wearing the traditional expression of one encountering St Mary's for the first time and wondering what he's got himself into. Apart from all that though, the photo was spot on.

'Your husband's having a shower,' he said. 'Why don't you come into my office?'

Said the spider to the fly.

'I'll bring you some tea,' said Hunter.

'Thank you.'

'For the patient.'

'Ah. Right you are.'

I shook my head. To eat or drink anything would make me sick.

'No thanks.'

She left and he fussed around with some paperwork.

'She scares me.'

'She scares everyone,' I said. 'Don't take it personally.'

We stared at each other over his desk.

I couldn't help myself. 'How old are you?' and waited for him to say twelve.

He blinked. 'I'm twenty-eight. Is that a problem?'

'Are you sure? You don't look it. Did you lie about your age?'

'No, of course not. Why does everyone keep asking me that? I never had this problem in the Army. They laughed at how old I was there. Called me granddad.'

'What did you do in the Army?'

'I'm a doctor. Didn't you know?'

'Yes, but what's your experience?'

'Gunshot wounds. Shrapnel. Explosives trauma. Burns. Exposure. Oh – and radiation. Which I can't talk about because it's Top Secret.'

'Seriously? There's something out there that's more secret than us?' I think I was slightly miffed. No one likes to come second.

'You'd be surprised what's going on out there.'

'No, I wouldn't. I know all about the underground aliens in Saffron Walden.'

'Everyone knows about the underground aliens in Saffron Walden. Do you know about the tunnel to the centre of the earth? Starts under Shepton Mallet.'

'No.'

'True as I'm sitting here.'

'Well, for God's sake don't tell Professor Rapson.'

'Who do you think told me? Is he for real, by the way?'

I said with the smoothness of long practice, 'Professor Rapson is a valued and highly regarded member of this establishment.'

'Dear God, whatever must the others be like?'

I was a little annoyed by this unwarranted criticism of

my unit. And by a complete stranger, too.

'You surely didn't take this job without checking us out first?'

'Well, I did several times mention the possibility of a preliminary visit before I committed myself, but I don't think Dr Bairstow heard me.'

'And that wasn't your first clue?'

He was frowning at his scratchpad. 'According to this, your records show you're down for an eye test. And have been for quite some time.'

I closed my eyes. So that I wouldn't wear them out, presumably.

'Not ... now.'

'Of course not now. Whenever you have a moment.'

I nodded. That moment was never going to come. I'd see to that.

'So, how are you feeling?'

I stared at him, bewildered.

He became aware of the silence and looked up. 'What's the matter?'

'I'm confused by the question.'

'Didn't you understand it?'

'Yes, but I've never actually heard it asked in this room before.'

He looked around. 'This is the medical section?'

I nodded. 'Yes, but the previous incumbent ... Helen...' I stumbled. 'Dr Foster's policy was to tell *us* how we felt, hold us entirely to blame for whatever had befallen us, outline the treatment we were to receive in gruesome detail, and describe the consequences should we fail to respond.'

My words seemed to drop into some sort of dark hole, because that was the moment I realised I'd never see her again. Never hear her voice again. Never watch her puffing her cigarette smoke out of the window. She was gone for ever.

My voice failed me. My eyes filled up with tears. I struggled.

He pushed a box of tissues across the desk.

I pushed it back again.

He smiled. 'It's all right to let go, you know.'

I shook my head. 'Not in front of a member of the medical profession. They can smell fear.'

'Very wise. Let me make you some cocoa.'

'What?'

'Cocoa. Magic stuff. Heals all wounds.'

'I thought that was time.'

'No, it's cocoa.'

He passed me a mug of frothy brown stuff and I sipped suspiciously. It was gorgeous.

He sat back with his own mug. 'When I was a med student' – last Wednesday, presumably – 'it was part of my seduction routine. I have a theory that you can overcome resistance and induce feelings of goodwill and cooperation in the opposite sex by feeding them hot sweet drinks. I scored my highest success rate with cocoa.'

'How high?'

'Oh. Um…' He looked like a shifty twelve-year-old caught shoplifting.

'How often did it work?'

'Once.'

Out of how many attempts?

'Several hundred. I think.'

'Perhaps you could favour me with your definition of the words "success rate".'

He sagged with dejection. Or possibly rejection. Whatever it was, his shoulders dropped. Even his sticky-out ears drooped.

I hardened my heart. 'I hate to add to your catalogue of failures, but I don't want to sleep with you either. Cocoa or no cocoa.'

He drooped even further. I began to feel like a bit of a monster. 'Look, I'm sorry, I didn't mean to be rude. I'm just not very good at handling sympathy.'

He sat back. 'Well, not handling sympathy is nothing to be proud of, is it? It's like proudly announcing you bite your fingernails. You know – a bad habit. Harmless but not pleasant.'

'But something to be proud of if you've just weaned yourself off heroin.'

Now he stared at *me*. 'What?'

'Well, if your previous bad habit was drugs and you've downsized to fingernail biting, then don't you think that's something to be proud of?'

'Tell me,' he said carefully. 'Are you a glass half full or a glass half empty person?'

I said, 'Well, it depends where you are at the time. The Technical Section will say never mind whether it's half empty or half full, the glass was obviously too big in the first place. Dr Dowson will tell you it's not contemporary to the time period and you should be using a goblet. The History Department will enquire what bloody glass? The Security Section will be gloomily surveying the broken shards on the floor, and Mrs Mack will just tell you to get out of her kitchen.

He blinked, but at that moment, Hunter stuck her head around the door to tell me Leon was asking for me.

They'd put the sleeping Matthew in the isolation ward. I stared through the window at the skinny form under the bedclothes.

'The plan is that the three of you spend the next few days here,' said Dr Stone. 'To give you an opportunity to get to know each other again. Tonight, however, I suggest you and Chief Farrell take some time together. Have a talk. Get some rest. The next few days aren't going to be easy for any of you.'

The two of us walked silently back to our room. Leon closed the door behind us. We stood and looked at each other. What now?

Foremost in my mind was the thought that I had run away. I couldn't look at him.

'Leon, I'm sorry I ran away.'

He put his arms around me. 'It was a shock. I know. It was a shock when I first saw him and I knew what to expect.'

'Tell me. It is him, isn't it. There's no possibility of a mistake.'

My little baby holding out his arms to me...

'None. The Time Police tested his DNA. It's him.'

I was very, very careful to prevent any hint of criticism

creeping into my voice. 'How did this happen?'

He sat on the sofa and pulled me down beside him.

'It was hard, Max. Even with all their technical equipment, we just couldn't get close. Every time we landed, we had to spend hours searching the entire area because there was always the fear that he'd just abandoned Matthew somewhere. We had to be thorough so, of course, it meant we were getting further and further behind with each jump. Nobody actually said it, but there was a real feeling we were never going to get him back. And our power reserves were way down and the pod was beginning to drift. You know, the way they do.'

I nodded. Pods need regular servicing otherwise they begin to drift. A decade in one direction – one hundred miles in another. Four or five jumps are usually about the limit before they need some care and attention. That's not usually a problem, because after four or five consecutive jumps, the pod is not in half such bad condition as the historians inside, who by this time are generally in need of care and attention themselves. To say nothing of a couple of stiff drinks.

'Anyway, one day, we had no choice but to stop and recharge the batteries. The pod's and ours. We made ourselves a decent meal, took the time to shower and shave and, in sheer desperation, we sat down and brainstormed. Nothing was discounted, because we had to think of some other way than just blindly trying to pursue Ronan up and down the timeline and only ever getting further behind. Ellis suggested we return to Time Police HQ and throw the problem at them and no one could come up with anything better, so we did. They have all sorts of resources there – most of which I'm not even allowed to think about, let alone tell you – but it seems they have a few whizz kids whose main purpose is just tinkering with the Time Map, and one of them had a bright idea. I don't know what she did – she did try to explain it to me but I lost her half way through the second sentence, which was embarrassing. Anyway, the upshot was that they modified the Time Map to show traffic, rather than actual historical events. They eliminated everything except pod movements. It took them a couple of days, and what they were left with was a tangled network of coloured lines. It was then just a case of filtering out all St Mary's jumps – they're blue, by the way, and there are a lot of them.'

He paused and chugged back more beer.

'The next step was to fade out their own traffic – their jumps are purple. That left a mish-mash of tiny jumps; mostly illegal – homemade pods trailing radiation, amateur catastrophes – all that sort of thing. All in varying shades of red and brown. They took all that out and that just left a tangled maze of green stuff. They matched it with the radiation signature I'd given them and said most of it was probably Ronan's pod. It should have taken weeks, but apparently the whizz kids put their phones away, plugged in their personal soundtracks and got stuck in. I've no idea how they were able to disentangle things, but they did. They took a close look at the patterns and...' He stopped.

I felt myself grow cold. 'And what?'

'They superimposed our jumps over the top and

confirmed we were slipping further and further behind. We were never going to catch them. Commander Hay held a conference, and they said they'd identified what they were convinced was Ronan's latest jump. To 19th-century London. They concluded that either Ronan was still there – or...' He very put his beer down very carefully and spent some time turning it around and around, not looking at me, '... or that both of them had remained there for some reason.'

'Or died,' I said.

'Or died there before we could catch up with them. To cut a long story short, it was decided we would take a chance, stop following them, and jump directly to those coordinates. Even though it meant...'

Even though it meant that Matthew would no longer be a baby when they found him.

'We landed in the East End. Once we were there, it took us three days to track him through the worst slums imaginable. We questioned, we bribed, we threatened. Sometimes we ... I ... got physical, but we found him in the end.

There's an alleyway – Grit Lane. With a courtyard at the end. Tall narrow houses, one of which was occupied by Jeremiah Scrope and his wife, the very unlovely Ma Scrope. They lived in the downstairs rooms. I've no idea who was above them.'

He stopped talking. I offered him another beer. He took it but set it down unopened.

'You didn't find Ronan then. Wasn't he still there?'

'We don't know. And there was no time to look for him. You saw the state Matthew was in. We had to bring

110

him straight back. Max…' He stopped, unable to go on.

I said, 'I understand, Leon. You did exactly the right thing,' and rubbed his arm.

'As soon as they've had a breather, Ellis and his team, and probably Guthrie and Grey are going back to find Ronan.'

I nodded, still rubbing his arm.

'Max, I'm sorry. Please believe we did everything we could to catch him as soon as possible. We'd chased them day and night. I'd done what I could to keep the pods aligned. I worked non-stop, and every day they were even more jumps ahead of us.

'Leon, I understand.'

'It was a calculated gamble. To jump ahead to a place where we knew he'd definitely be. And then, when we got there, he was eight years old.'

My heart sank. 'Eight? He's eight years old? I thought he was about five or six. Why is he so small?'

He shook his head. 'Well, malnutrition, of course. I don't think he's had a decent meal in his entire life. And let's face it, his parents aren't that tall. The doctor thinks he's about seven or eight years old.'

I couldn't believe it, saying stupidly, 'Matthew is eight?'

'Probably. There's another thing, Max…'

'What?'

He took my hands. 'That's not his name any longer.'

I was bewildered. 'What isn't his name?'

'Matthew. He was just a baby when he was taken. If he ever knew that name, he's long since forgotten it. He's never known his name was Matthew.'

It was all too much to take in. Just one hammer blow after another.

I said, 'What's his name now?' and my voice wasn't steady. That bastard Ronan had not only stolen him, but he'd stolen his identity too.

'He doesn't have one. As far as I can see, Ronan has been jumping around with him, selling him, returning a year later to steal him back, and then selling him on again. Some of his owners didn't bother to give him a name. Scrope called him Joseph. He doesn't respond to it. He doesn't respond to anything very much.'

I remembered his silent watchfulness. With closed throat I said, 'Can he talk?'

'A little. I think he understands more than he shows, but over the years he's learned it's safer to keep quiet.'

He fell silent again.

'Leon, what is it?'

'There's something else you should know.'

'There's more? What else could there possibly be? Isn't all this enough?'

'Yes, you're right.' He stood up. 'Let's get something to eat. I want to hear what's been happening here.

I pulled him back down again. 'Tell me.'

He didn't look at me. 'The thing is, Max. He hasn't been well-treated.'

'Yes, I can see that. I'm assuming he's been a climbing boy.'

'Yes, Ronan sold him to Scrope. For about seven shillings from what I could gather. His wife demanded two guineas to give him back to us however, because he'd been properly indentured and strictly speaking, we were

112

breaking the law by taking him away, but Guthrie presented her with a couple of bottles of gin and a hard look, so she was induced to let him go. Eventually.'

I was silent. Most children from poor families worked from the age of seven onwards. In the factories, in the mills, on the land. None of it was pleasant and climbing boys had the worst of bad conditions. Their masters were paid to teach them the trade so that one day they could be master sweeps themselves, but most never made it that far.

Scrambling naked up the inside of a chimney that was sometimes no more than fourteen inches by nine and caked in creosote and soot, those that survived being trapped, suffocated or burned to death frequently fell victim to chimney sweeps' cancer.

The boys – and sometimes girls – would sweep four to five chimneys a day, their elbows and knees scrubbed with brine to harden them. The sweep would light fires to make them climb faster until that dreadful moment when the climbing boy, weak with hunger and exhaustion, choking in the smoke and soot, allowed his centre of gravity to drop. And once his bottom dropped below the level of his knees, he was – as the official trade name defined it – 'stuck'.

Whatever it was called, positional asphyxia would kill him. Alone. In the dark. Unable to move up or down. Knowing that if he survived this, his master would beat him severely for losing him his fee, because sometimes the only way to retrieve the child was to demolish the chimney. Only by then it was usually too late.

This had been my little boy's life for…?

'How long?' I said to Leon.

'About eighteen months.'

'That long?'

'Yes. He was one of three owned by old Scrope, who was a nasty piece of work, especially when he'd had a drink or two, but the real cruelty came from his wife. I never learned her name. She was just Ma Scrope and they feared her. Everyone feared her – including her husband.'

He stopped again. 'He's learned to be afraid of women, Max. You're going to find that he's not as … affectionate as you might wish. He's all right with me. And with Guthrie, a little. And Ellis. But he doesn't like women. I'm sorry, love.'

I said quietly, 'He won't remember me at all, will he?'

'No.'

'Or his life here?'

'No.'

'Does he think Clive Ronan was his father?'

'I don't know. I'm not sure he's familiar with the concept of parents. Just owners. He's been a climbing boy for as long as he can remember, which isn't very long. I think he's naturally small and skinny so he's ideal and, of course, they'd want to keep him that way for as long as possible, so they fed him just enough to keep him on his feet. He was a business asset so they stopped short of punishing him enough to stop him working. Although his arm's been broken at one time.'

He stopped and we both struggled for a moment.

I drew a breath and said firmly, 'It's probably best if we don't think too much about that at the moment. We'll need to divide this into manageable lumps – like a big

114

assignment. We'll get him fit first. We'll feed and clothe him and hope that somewhere along the way he learns to trust us enough to … to…'

I had no idea what would come next. We were the parents of an eight-year-old child who had no memory of his life in this time. Who had only ever known brutality and hardship. Everything would be strange and new and frightening. And that was just for us. Heaven knew what it would be like for Matthew.

Absolutely nothing went according to plan.

We saw Dr Stone early the next morning.

'He's still asleep, which is a good thing. He'll need breakfast when he wakes. I've only been here two days but as far as I can see, the St Mary's idea of a balanced meal is not to put all their food on one side of the plate. I've seen no evidence of any kind that anyone in this unit is familiar with the concept of healthy eating in any way, so we in Sick Bay will set his menu. Let's start with you all eating together as a family.'

Chance would have been a fine thing.

I've heard the expression 'feeding frenzy'. I've even witnessed it a couple of times – St Mary's falling on a platter of sausages on their return from a long assignment springs to mind – but we're amateurs.

It took him less than four and a half seconds to clear his plate.

'Well,' said Leon, bending down to pick up an unused spoon as I wiped a splodge of scrambled egg off the wall. 'A bit of work needed there, I think.'

It wasn't just his eating habits we had to contend with.

He had no concept of bathrooms and certainly not the individual components therein.

'Your son has just peed in the washbasin again,' complained Leon.

I put down my book. 'Why does he keep doing that?'

'Well, I've shown him the toilet and how it works, but I think it's because he always leaves things until the last moment. He races in, does a quick appraisal of the equipment provided, chooses the wrong one, and lets rip.'

I picked up my book again because this was one problem I felt I could safely leave to Leon to sort out. I'd been lumbered with the other end, so to speak. Because, not content with peeing in the wrong receptacle, he would, unless restrained, drink water from the toilet. He didn't understand taps and from his point of view it was perfectly simple. There was water available in the bottom of the toilet bowl, so why not?

We had a long road to travel said Leon, as we sank, exhausted, into bed that night.

We buried Helen the next afternoon.

It was a horrible day. The sky was dark. Rain fell persistently, drumming on the ground and people's umbrellas.

Kal had driven down from Thirsk. She stood beside me throughout. I knew she'd had a few words with Peterson before the service. They had been partners once and I know he always listened to her. I wondered what she'd said to him. With Kal, it could have been anything.

Leon, Markham, Guthrie, Atherton, Bashford and Dieter carried her coffin. Not Tim. I don't think he could have. Dr Bairstow stood beside him at the graveside. There was no sound but that of trickling water.

I looked at Tim's white face. Would he leave St Mary's? He shouldn't go. Not now, anyway. Maybe give it a month or two and then decide. I hoped that had been Kal's advice. And what of him and me? The two of us. What was our relationship these days? He hadn't spoken to me since he'd come to the lake.

Cold, we huddled together as the words were read. I could still hear her voice. Somewhere in my memories she was thumping Leon for operating on the wrong bloody arm. Telling Markham his ringworm would eat his eyeballs from the inside out. Holding Tim's hands just before the Battle of St Mary's. She and Tim should have had a long and happy life together. Neither of them deserved this.

The words ended.

They lowered her coffin into the ground.

Resting on the top was a single red rose, a packet of cigarettes and a box of matches. I knew Peterson had kept her lighter.

For the first time in my life, I didn't want to go out on assignment.

'You should go,' said Leon.

'But...'

'You should go,' he said again, and stopped.

I knew why. He was a good man. He didn't want to say that Matthew didn't like me. That he distrusted and feared women and I was a woman. He didn't want to tell me that, initially at least, they'd probably make more progress if I wasn't around.

I tried not to feel unwanted, because I wasn't, but it was hard. I took a deep breath and lifted my chin. Going out on assignment would be good. It would clear my head. I'd only be gone for one day. Two at the most.

'We'll have a little party when you get back,' said Leon. 'So he learns to look forward to seeing you.'

I swallowed a big lump and nodded. 'Good idea.'

We assembled outside our respective pods. I was in Number Eight, with Bashford, Sykes and Markham. North, Clerk, Evans and Keller were in Number Five.

'All set?' said Dieter, scanning the console one last time.

'Of course.'

I peered at the screen. Leon stood on the gantry. He'd taken a few minutes to come down and see us off. Matthew was still in Sick Bay. Dr Bairstow had made it very, very clear that Matthew was never to be allowed in Hawking. Whether he thought he'd stow away or break something, I had no idea, but it was fine with me. An additional safeguard for someone who was, at the moment, possibly the most guarded kid in the world. With all the additional security there was no way Ronan could ever get back inside St Mary's, but no one was inclined to take any chances.

I'd waved at Leon, who'd smiled for me alone, stowed my gear, counted heads and now we were ready to go.

'Good luck,' said Dieter. 'Try not to incur any damage.'

'Observe and document only,' I said, reassuringly. 'We can't possibly get into any trouble.'

'I was talking about the pods.'

'The rectangular thing behind you is called a door. Would you like Miss Sykes to show you how it works?'

'Just saying,' he said, grinning.

'Go away and wind the motor, or whatever it is the Technical Section does do to make these things work.'

'Ignorance – thy name is Maxwell.'

He closed the door behind him.

I checked everything over one last time, watched Number Five blink out of existence, and said, 'Computer. Initiate jump.'

'Jump initiated.'

The world went white.

*

We landed on the outskirts of a small wood. Judging by the number of broken branches lying around, there had been a recent storm. The one that shipwrecked Harold, presumably. Certainly the wind was still strong enough to stream my flimsy veil across my face. I had to keep pulling it out of my mouth. I could tell it was going to get on my nerves.

I opened my com. 'Miss North, report.'

'Here and safe. We're a hundred yards to your left. I can see you.'

I turned and there she was, picking her way delicately through the trees. Her veil streamed gracefully behind her and did not, in any way, wrap itself around her face and try to strangle her, or become entangled in passing trees. It probably wouldn't dare. Sykes had tamed her veil by tying it in a knot under her chin.

You watch these movies and holos about medieval times and the heroine is always wafting her way around the landscape with what looks like a traffic cone on her head, flowy sleeves and a dragging train and she is never, ever, up to her knees in piss, shit, ordure, offal, dead rats, whatever. If I ever make a movie – and stranger things have happened, to me, usually – my heroine will be cursing buckets as she struggles to move with twelve and a half yards of wet wool wrapped around her legs and stinking like a fish factory on a hot day.

At least when we left the wood, the wind was blowing into our faces, so, for the time being, at least, I could see.

We stood on a slight rise. The river Canche twisted away from us, a glittering ribbon of light as the sun played hide and seek in the scudding clouds. Below, a small town nestled along its banks, the wind shredding the smoke that curled from a hundred and more roofs. We could smell the tang from all the way up here.

'Must have been a hell of a storm,' said Clerk. 'And it hasn't blown itself out yet.'

'OK, everyone,' I said. 'We all know what to do. Head to the gates and split into the two teams. Team Harold goes through and heads towards the castle. Team William hangs around looking innocent and non-threatening until William turns up. If he hasn't arrived by sundown, it's everyone back to the pods and try again tomorrow. But I think it will be today. He won't want Guy getting any ideas about indulging in a little private enterprise himself.'

Beaurain was a bustling little place, clustered around the usual gloomy Norman donjon. There were many people on the streets. Whether this was normal or the result of recent events, we had no way of knowing.

We picked our way carefully through streets cluttered with debris from the storm. In some places, there was more waterlogged thatch in the streets than on the roofs. Shattered tiles lay strewn across the cobbles.

We stuck tightly together and headed for the castle. The gatehouse was guarded, but people were passing in and out quite freely. We were dressed as richly as we dared. The colours were dark but the material was good. Usually I carry a basket or pack of some kind, but today I had servants to do that. Bashford walked beside me, and I rested my hand lightly on his arm. Sykes followed behind, with Markham bringing up the rear.

The secret is to walk slowly and not to gawp around. I bent my head attentively as Bashford spoke quietly to me. Actually, he was reciting 'The Rime of the Ancient Mariner' in Latin, but if the guards wanted to assume he was imparting words of wisdom they weren't important enough to understand, then that was fine by me. Above all, we exuded confidence. As if we had every right to be here.

Markham opened his com to inform Keller we were approaching the castle now.

'Communal link,' I said and he nodded. It makes me nervous when we split up. I like my people herded together so I can keep an eye on them. If I can't have that then we're all on the communal link so I know exactly what's going on at all times. Control freak? Moi?

We tucked ourselves behind what looked like a party of local merchants, all in their best clothes and talking loudly so people could see how important they were. They were obviously known to the guards who waved them through. For one moment, I thought we might be that lucky too, but we're St Mary's. Luck only happens to other people.

We halted, apparently in surprise that we should be challenged in this way. Bashford broke off what he was saying to frown. I gave them my best haughty Norman matron stare. Which is, actually, exactly the same as my haughty medieval matron stare. And my haughty Elizabethan matron stare. And my haughty Roman matron stare. Behind me, I could sense Markham moving to my shoulder. Just in case.

He wasn't needed. They were just going through the

motions. This was the day Duke William came to Count Guy, and Count Guy wanted as many people as possible to witness this important event. They were packing them in.

We had no chance to look around us. I had a vague impression of a courtyard and dark, towering walls, and then we were hustled through a disappointingly small door and into the Hall itself. Of course, the Hall was built for defence. It made sense to have a small, narrow door through which only one person could enter at a time.

I had an impression of echoing vastness, although the exact dimensions were difficult to ascertain. Despite any number of wildly flickering candles impaled on tripods, and torches thrust into sconces, the corners of the room were near invisible. A few shafts of light filtered through the louvered lantern in the roof high above us, but were lost in the prevailing gloom. And it was gloomy. A large fire burned in the centre from which the smoke curled optimistically up towards the louvres, but the wind outside was so strong that it was immediately blown straight back inside again. Occasionally, a man would appear and fiddle with the long strings that opened and closed the vents, but to no avail. No one seemed particularly bothered, so I could only assume that near-asphyxiation was an accepted hazard in these times. My eyes were stinging. Many people were coughing.

The floor was cold, hard stone; its discomfort only mitigated by the thick layer of crushed rushes spread over the top. They looked fairly fresh – maybe laid down especially for today, but I knew that if I kicked aside the top layer I would find old bones, grease, dog shit, spilled beer – and worse. I left the top layer where it was.

A raised dais stood at the far end, on which stood two ornately carved chairs of equal height and importance, because although William was Guy's overlord, every man is a lord in his own hall. They'd resolved the problem of who took precedence over whom by moving Guy's chair from its central and commanding position under the canopy and setting it a little to one side, with William's chair a meticulously measured equal distance to the other. I suspected that, behind the scenes, a chamberlain or steward was going quietly insane.

The chairs were the only furniture in the place. The eating tables were temporary trestles and had been removed, so today was obviously all about business, not pleasure.

The far wall behind the two chairs was covered by a tapestry, subject unknown in all this gloom, and probably almost completely obscured by layers of smoke and soot anyway.

Two rows of hefty stone pillars marched down the hall, supporting equally hefty smoke-blackened timbers that, in turn, held up the roof – although frankly the whole place was so murky that the roof could have been supported by four elephants standing on the back of a giant turtle and no one would ever know.

We started off near the door, but such was the crush of people still fighting to get in, that without any effort on our part, we found ourselves pushed to the front, our backs to a pillar. We couldn't have asked for a better position. We stood closely together and refused to budge. People streamed around us. There was a little muttered cursing, but we stood our ground and people left us alone.

Looking around, although the company was predominantly male, there were some women present. About one in five were female. And we were definitely among the better dressed, which made a pleasant change and was probably why, strangers though we were, people were leaving us alone.

We palmed our recorders and got what discreet footage we could. And then we waited.

Two hours. Two bloody hours.

I know the greater part of our job is to stand and wait. Wait for the charge, the fire, the battle, the murder, whatever, and then observe and document. And then we usually to have to run like hell afterwards, of course, so you think we'd be used to it. Sometimes it's not too bad, but here in this smoke-filled cave – there really was no other word to describe it – the usual standing quietly and waiting was a bit of a bloody ordeal.

According to Markham, there's a knack. Apparently, you don't just stand there. That's the wrong way to do it, according to the Security Section – famed for complicating simple situations since the beginning of time. You don't stand with your weight on one foot, then the other, then shift it back again, and so on, because that makes at least one leg ache and after a while, your hips and shoulders as well. You should stand straight but relaxed, weight equally on both feet, hands hanging loosely. Then you ease your weight forwards onto the balls of your feet for a few moments and then rock backwards onto your heels. You're not actually moving but you are – says Markham. Keeps the blood flowing, prevents cramp, aching ankles and knees, sore feet, blood clots and possibly cellulite as well. And for all I know he's right. Anyway, we stood there, swaying back and forth like a thicket in a strong wind and no one fainted, so we must have been doing something right. Sadly, it does nothing to alleviate boredom. I began to wish I'd stuck with Team William. At least they were out in the fresh air. There were some nasty, wet, hacking coughs in here and a great deal of sputum was being propelled around the place. It really was a miracle anyone made it past the age of twenty.

Two bloody hours.

We heard them coming. Horns sounded above a clatter of hooves in the courtyard outside. Unseen men shouted orders.

'They're here,' said North in my ear, presumably in case I wasn't paying attention, and I stifled my usual urge to set fire to her.

'OK, everyone,' I said. 'Heads up.'

And then it all went quiet.

'They've gone in through another door,' reported North. 'Through to the count's private quarters, I guess.'

'Get yourselves in here if you can. We're on the left as you come in, and near the front, so try for somewhere on the other side of the fire. Security to remain outside in case we need rescuing.'

'Copy that.'

The link closed.

There was another long pause. Although not two hours long. Around us, people stood on tiptoe and craned their necks in anticipation. As, I admit, did I. We were going to see William, Duke of Normandy and Harold Godwinson, Earl of Wessex. The two great players of their age. Either would have been remarkable but for the two of them to share the same time period … and to be together … here … today … I realised with a shock that I hadn't thought about Matthew for a couple of hours, realised why Leon had insisted I go on this assignment, and then shoved everything out of my head, because they were coming.

I think we could have been forgiven for not noticing the two doors either side of the tapestry; we could barely see the tapestry itself. The one on the left opened, however, and a man – a steward, I guessed from his dress – strode forwards onto the dais. Lifting his staff, he solemnly pounded the boards three times. For silence, presumably, although he'd had that from the moment he made his first appearance.

He made a ringing announcement, not one word of which I caught, but I think the gist was pretty obvious to everyone there. A stir of anticipation ran through the crowd. Well, our part of it, certainly. Bashford caught my eye and grinned. And then it was full attention on what was happening now.

The same door opened and we held our breath. What were we going to see? Who would be first through the door?

They did it beautifully.

As the lord in his own hall, Guy was first through the door. My first impression was that he looked like a fox. He was a thin-faced man of medium height in a russet red tunic. His cloak had been dyed to match and was trimmed with vair. Look it up.

Entering, he paused for one moment, gathering all eyes on himself, and then stepped to one side, allowing his overlord to make his entrance.

There are no images of William. Contemporary reports say he was dark, burly – he would be extremely fat, later in life – that he enjoyed excellent health, was a good fighter, and a tireless huntsman. They also said he was fierce and unforgiving, that he had no pretensions to intellect, and managed at the same time to be both pious and cruel. A not uncommon combination in any age.

With courtesy, but not a huge amount of deference, Guy attended William to his chair and took up his own position. Around us, everyone bowed. Even the women. At this time, there was very little difference between the bow and the curtsey. Women spread their skirts a little in what might be the ancestor of the formal female curtsey, which wouldn't make its appearance until sometime in the 17th century, but otherwise, everyone bowed. Including us.

Their entourages followed on behind and arranged themselves behind the appropriate chairs. Count Guy's men were dressed in similar though less colourful robes. Under their cloaks, William's men wore their famous knee-length chainmail hauberks with the loose, elbow-length sleeves and carried their conical helmets with the noseguards. Whether they wore mail because they didn't trust the Count Guy, or simply because they'd been riding, was not clear.

William himself wore a tunic of purple and gold, his lack of armour signifying he wasn't here to fight. His mailed escort signified he would if he had to. Apart from a huge golden brooch securing his cloak, he wore no jewellery of any kind. He didn't need to. He could have worn an old sack and still commanded the room.

He was invited to sit and wine was brought. The two men sat and sipped. Their escorts eyed each other. No one seemed to be armed although I wondered how many daggers were tucked into sleeves, or hidden in the folds of a thick cloak.

There was polite conversation. Both men smiled with their mouths. Count Guy politely offered a refill, which was as politely refused. You could have cut the air with a knife, and such was the tension that if they didn't get a move on then someone probably would.

There was no doubt who was in command here. William, obviously considering he'd more than fulfilled polite convention, stirred impatiently in his chair, and at once Guy beckoned a man forwards and whispered in his ear. The man left immediately.

William and Guy sat quietly in their seats. No one was moving anywhere. One of the most fateful encounters in History was about to kick off. The silence was so complete I dared not even whisper to North. I just had to hope she and Clerk were here, somewhere, and recording their bloody socks off.

As we had done, Harold and the remaining survivors of the shipwreck had to make their way through the tradesman's entrance. They'd been found dry clothes from somewhere, but Harold, as if to underline his position here, was significantly less magnificently dressed than his hosts. Or gaolers, if you like. He himself seemed more or less intact. One of his men had a bandage around his forehead and could walk only with assistance. Another seemed to have a broken arm. There were only eight of them altogether. There were no other survivors.

A path was cleared for them and Harold led his party to the foot of the dais, paused some six feet away, and stood waiting. He was making them come to him. Power games.

Both William and Guy rose, and Guy stepped down to greet him formally. Harold answered him politely enough, inclining his head to what I guessed was an enquiry as to his health.

I had a fat stone pillar on my left and Markham on my right, shielding me from view. To an uninterested observer, it must have seemed as if I was holding my cupped hand to my face. With the exception of Markham, who never allowed what was going on in front of him to blind him to what was going on around him, we were all recording like madmen.

Finally, Count Guy stepped aside. William, who had waited and watched, now stepped down and for the first time ever, Harold and William were face to face.

Harold was the taller of the two. In his chronicles, Ordalis Vitalis describes him as very tall and handsome, and he was. His hair was light, but not blond, worn longer than the Norman fashion, and with one of those huge, droopy moustaches that Saxon men so mistakenly thought were a good look. His cool blue eyes met William's heavily lidded, dark ones. William stretched out his hand and they stood together, hands clasped, for a very long moment, eye to eye, each appraising the other. Polite.

Smiling. Affable. Wearing their public faces. And neither of them giving any clue as to their inner thoughts.

It is possible, I suppose, that both Harold and William were aware of the importance of this moment. Of the implications for the future. They were on a collision course. Only one of them could survive. They wouldn't know that it would all end in savage and bloody slaughter at Hastings, of course, but they might have been aware there was only room in this world for one of them.

Guy coughed discreetly and both men moved apart. William to proffer a goblet of wine, filled with his own hands, and Harold to accept a hastily found chair. The three of them sat on the dais, and now William had the dominant position in centre, with Guy on his one hand, and Harold on the other. They drank and talked and laughed as if not one of them had a care in the world.

We recorded until our arms ached.

At last, Guy rose from his chair and gestured to his steward again. William set down his goblet and rose without haste. Harold did the same. The room bowed, again in silence, and Guy escorted them back through the door in the tapestry. For a private meal was my guess.

I looked up at the louvre. The sky was darkening. Shafts of light no longer illuminated the clouds of swirling smoke. The day was over. We would return to the pod and then tomorrow, we'd hang around the gates to catch a glimpse of them riding to William's castle at Rouen. There was no real need – we had what we needed – but a glimpse of the size of the party and Harold's position within it would round things off nicely. There was no doubt he was a prisoner, but would he ride at

William's side as all accounts seemed to say, or at the rear, under guard?

I imagined them riding through the crisp, sparkling afternoon air, experienced a moment's unexpected claustrophobia, and was suddenly desperate to get out of this dark and smoky Hall. The great men and their entourages had disappeared. Time for us to go as well.

The greater mass of people was heading for the tiny door. The more intelligent were holding back, giving the crowd time to disperse. I caught a glimpse of North and Clerk standing by the central fire, looking around them. Clerk caught my eye, gave no sign of recognition, took North's arm, and began to lead her to the door.

We met up outside the gatehouse. The sun was sinking and the still strong wind had turned cold. Dark purple clouds were moving up from the horizon. I became aware I was parched, starving and desperate for a pee. Definitely time to get back to the pods.

We nearly missed them the next morning. They must have been up well before dawn. It was eighty miles and more to Rouen and they obviously wanted an early start. We weren't able to get to the town in time, but we stood on the small rise and watched them canter out through the gates and away.

William's banner, the golden lions of Normandy, led the way, with William himself a few yards behind. Earl Harold rode alongside him. On a good horse. There was no sign of any of the other members of his group. I wondered what became of them. Had William left them with Guy as compensation for the bigger prize he had snatched from him?

We watched them down the road, pennant fluttering in the still strong wind. They breasted a small hill and then disappeared into the distance.

'Time to go,' I said.

'What went wrong?' said Dieter as we exited the pod.

I looked around. 'Nothing. Why do you ask?'

'No one's injured. No one's bleeding. Nothing important is hanging off. Either from you or the pod. There's no smoke. No alarms. Are you sure you actually left the hangar?'

'I know it's difficult for the Technical Section to keep up with the rest of us, but we do occasionally have assignments that go without a hitch, you know.'

'We could take an axe to the console,' said Sykes helpfully. 'Knock it about a bit if that will make you happy.'

'Actually, I think I may have broken one of the cupholders,' said Markham, holding some sad remains in his hand. 'Sorry.'

'Don't apologise,' I said. 'You've made his day. Fixing this will keep his entire section busy for weeks and even then they'll probably have to call in specialist help.'

Dieter silently relieved him of the broken cupholder and indicated we should leave as quickly as possible. Clerk's team were already heading for Sick Bay. We followed on behind. Half of me was eager to see Leon and Matthew again. The other half wasn't quite so sure.

It seemed strange to crash through Sick Bay doors and find a strange doctor waiting for us. We'd all been gabbling away and suddenly silence fell. We looked at him. He looked at us. I felt a little sorry for him. It wasn't his fault he wasn't Helen Foster.

'Dr Maxwell, would you like to come this way? I expect you're eager to see your family again. Anyone else in a rush?'

They shook their heads. Normally, there would be a kind of human surge, with each of us demanding priority because everyone hates hanging around after an assignment. We're often dirty, wet, cold, tired and still terrified. Helen would repel each request with scorn and harsh language but, in some mysterious fashion, when everyone stopped arguing and pushing, everything would have been done and we'd been scanned, shoved into the appropriate wards, showered, fed and, where appropriate, put to bed.

Now, everyone shuffled their feet and said nothing. There wasn't anything I could do. He was going to have to work things out for himself.

Pronounced fit for human consumption, I made my way to the isolation ward. Hunter let me in. I barely recognised the place. The central table was covered in building bricks and half-completed jigsaws. I had no idea what they were constructing out of Lego, but whatever it was it was huge. Books, papers and crayons littered every horizontal surface. Matthew's pale blue teddy sat on his pillow.

The two of them were crouched over something as I entered. Leon looked up and smiled. 'Hi. How did it go?'

'Perfectly,' I said.

'Oh, that's disappointing. I thought you could regale us with tall tales over dinner.'

'I can still do that, if you like. How's everything here?'

'Absolutely fine,' he said, which is St Mary's speak for absolutely bloody awful but don't ask.

'Jolly good,' I said carefully, and dropped my gear on a bed.

Matthew had barely glanced at me, keeping his distance.

Leon looked from me to him and back again.

'Well, I can see you're busy,' I said, 'and so am I. Reports to write, historians to chase. Don't let me interrupt you.'

I sat at the other end of the ward, making sure to keep out of their way. I dictated my report, harried the others for theirs, viewed their footage, signed and initialled everything and packed it all off to Dr Bairstow.

By the time I'd finished, it was dinner-time. We sat around a small table. Leon had made some small progress with Matthew's table manners and at least we didn't have to duck low flying cutlery this time, although he still fell on his food like Theodosius's troops fell on Thessalonika.

I turned away to say something to Leon and when I turned back, from the corner of my eye, I saw Matthew stuff a bread roll into his dressing-gown pocket. He was hoarding food. Because he couldn't believe that this would last. He was hiding food against the day when, for whatever reason, there wouldn't be any. I bet if I looked in his locker, there would be any amount of foodstuff stashed away there. Slowly going stale or bad. But he couldn't help himself.

I could say something or I could let it go. I let it go. For the time being.

Since it seemed to make very little difference to Matthew whether I stayed or went – I went. The very next morning, as soon as Dr Stone discharged me. I said goodbye to Leon and promised to be back for lunch. I said goodbye to Matthew, ignored him ignoring me, and set off for the Boss. Who was pleased. We both took a moment to savour this phenomenon.

'Satisfactory work,' he said, so he was actually very pleased. 'I see the two teams will remain the same throughout the assignments.'

'Yes, sir. I thought each team could become an expert on their particular protagonist, which will make it easier to spot anomalous behaviour or predict how their subject will react to events around them.'

I thought he looked at me strangely for a moment before he nodded.

'If you are certain, then very well. When is your next assignment?'

'Next Wednesday, sir. The oath taking at Bayeux.'

He paused and shuffled a few files. He does this when he has something difficult to say. About Peterson, I guessed.

'Dr Peterson has indicated his eagerness to return to work. On Monday, he will take up the position of Deputy Director. You will still report to me regarding assignments, but for admin and personnel matters, you will now report to Dr Peterson. Do you anticipate any difficulties with this arrangement?'

I didn't give myself time to think about it. 'None, sir.'

'Very well. There will be an all-staff briefing tomorrow to announce this.'

He paused again.

'And how is your son?'

'Very well, thank you, sir. I've just come from Sick Bay. His injuries are healing. He looks considerably cleaner, although some of the dirt is so ingrained there's still some way to go. And there is absolutely nothing wrong with his appetite.'

'Excellent news. Max. I appreciate you are, at the moment, more concerned with his physical condition, but I have been speaking with Dr Stone about the future. Matthew is, apparently, around seven or eight years old.'

He paused again. I waited.

'This is difficult to say, Max. I had not anticipated having this conversation with you for a few years yet. When Matthew was a baby, this was of no concern. And, of course, you planned to live in the village so security concerns might never have arisen. But, we now find ourselves in a position where a young boy will be running around the building and possibly seeing all sorts of things he should not be seeing. And then going on to tell others. At school – at play – whenever. The opportunities for him to say something unfortunate will be enormous.'

'Are you asking for my resignation, sir?'

'Most definitely not. I regard you as one of the key members of this unit. And with Clive Ronan out there, I cannot allow anyone to leave, anyway. For how long this situation will continue, I don't know. But Matthew is growing. He has needs now and these needs must be met. I am consulting Dr Stone and Dr Dowson, and together with you and Leon, we will put together a learning programme for him. He must learn about this world and the people in it. He must learn basic maths and to read and write. He can learn all that here, together with a little history and geography. We can handle this. What we cannot provide is the company of his contemporaries. I am sure you do not wish him to have a solitary existence with no friends or contact of any kind with other children.'

He paused yet again. I still said nothing.

'At my request, Dr Dowson has been researching educational establishments. There is a special school – not too far away – especially for children whose early years have been difficult. Trauma, severe illness, any reason why a normal education has proved impossible. Dr Dowson has all the information, which I would like you and Leon to study. There is no possibility of him attending any outside establishment while Clive Ronan is still at large, but with Captain Ellis and Major Guthrie on his tail, I hope that problem will resolve itself soon. When it does, with luck, Matthew will be able to avail himself of their quite exceptional facilities.'

I still said nothing.

'I should say, Max, that even if Ronan were not in the picture, there would be no question of sending him away to any sort of school until you and Leon have established a happy family relationship, and he has become accustomed to our world and can operate easily within it. I mention all this only for you and Leon to consider.

Please be reassured that all decisions will be made by you and Leon – and to some extent, Matthew – alone. I and other staff members are happy to advise and discuss, but every decision will be yours.'

He paused again. I couldn't have said anything to save my life.

'This silence is concerning me. I shall, of course, deny this in any future conversations, but I always feel much happier when you are waving your arms around and arguing with me. Please reassure me by uttering at least one small sentence. Shall I ask Mrs Partridge to bring in some tea?'

I nodded. 'Yes, please sir.'

'That will do nicely.'

I divided my time between Sick Bay and the History Department. My personal life and my professional life. I'd never had to do that before.

Peterson was duly installed as Deputy Director. He stood beside Dr Bairstow as the announcement was made. Like the Boss, he now wore the formal black uniform instead of his usual blue jumpsuit. He looked pale, remote, and unfamiliar. And he'd gone back to wearing his arm in a sling. The dreadful wound to his upper arm was healed, but some of the muscle damage was permanent, and whenever he was tired or unwell the old ache would return, and he would be back to the sling again.

Mrs Shaw would continue to be his assistant and he would keep his old office, which meant he was almost next door to me. Well, we'd just have to wait and see how that worked out.

I turned up the next day with pod schedules and personnel rotas for his approval. He scanned them briefly and thanked me. I thanked him for thanking me and that was it.

Everything was just … awful. Even the weather was awful. It was spring, but every day was darker and windier than the last. The rain never stopped. I remember listening to it lashing against the windows throughout the entire Bayeux briefing. I turned up the heating, topped up my mug of tea – my talisman against everything unpleasant – and we got stuck in.

I'd asked Sykes to prepare the background briefing on this one.

She assumed what she fondly imagined to be an American accent. 'Previously on *William and Harold – The Road to Hastings*…'

North tutted and I frowned at the pair of them, but in a way, Sykes was right. Nothing happens in isolation. Everything is connected to everyone else. The build up to Hastings started some fifty years before the battle itself.

Sykes as usual, was bright and breezy, speaking without notes, and bringing up images as required.

'OK, people – the story so far. William has "rescued" Harold Godwinson from the clutches of Guy of Ponthieu. We last saw the two of them riding off together – not into the sunset as you might think, but off to another adventure. Conan II of Brittany has rebelled and at William's invitation, Harold joins William in putting down the rebellion.

She brought up an image of the Bayeux Tapestry. 'As you can see here, not only do William and Harold fight side by side – and no doubt sussing out each other's technique as they do so – but Harold wins a few hearts and minds by single-handedly rescuing two of William's soldiers from drowning in quicksand.

'They go on to chase Conan to Dinan, where he surrenders. William presents Harold with armour and weapons and knights him. A friendly gesture on the face of things, but actually binding Harold to him even more closely than ever.

Because nothing has changed. Harold is still under polite house arrest at William's court. And it's been made very clear that he's not going home unless he swears an oath relinquishing his own claim to the English throne and supporting William's.

'Harold's problem is that the king, Edward the Confessor, is ill and can't last much longer and if he, Harold, isn't in England when Edward dies, then he's probably lost all chance of the crown. Events are closing in around him. If he doesn't take the oath, then he'll never be released and never be king. If he does take the oath and keeps it, then he'll never be king. If he takes the oath and subsequently breaks it – as he will do – then he stands before Christendom, a perjured man.'

'But he would still be King of England,' said Bashford.

'Yes he would. He will claim the oath was extracted by trickery and therefore invalid. England stands with him. The rest of the world will not.'

She looked at me. 'Over to you, Max.'

143

'Thank you, Miss Sykes.' I stood up. 'Firstly, thanks again to our Pathfinders, Mr Atherton and Miss Prentiss, who have successfully located the time and place.'

'Yes,' said Prentiss. 'It's as the Bayeux Tapestry shows – the oath is taken in the cathedral. Not at Rouen. Or Bonneville. IT has the coordinates. We can go anytime you're ready.'

'Next Wednesday,' I said. 'The oath will be in Latin so brush up your linguistic skills. Same teams as before. Same pods as before. We will take opposite sides of the cathedral. In the event of any difficulties, Mr Markham and I will act as sweepers and go where needed. You all know the drill. Footage of the cathedral, inside and out; the people inside, who belongs to whom and stands where; the oath itself and, most importantly, what happens afterwards. Team William – I want close-ups of William as the oath is being taken. I doubt if even a flicker of emotion will cross his face, but if it does, I want it recorded. Team Harold – we all know that Harold is making what he, and the rest of the world, consider to be a very minor promise, but that actually William will trick him into making a much more serious oath. One that can't be broken. I want close-ups of his face as he realises he's been duped and that, whichever path he chooses, whether to keep the oath or break it, he's in very serious trouble. Any questions?'

People shook their heads, picked up their scratchpads and files, and slowly dispersed.

As the door closed, I turned to Rosie Lee. 'I need your help.'

She looked wary.

'I suddenly find myself the proud owner of a young lad very similar in age to yours. He can't run around in an old T-shirt and dressing-gown for much longer. Any recommendations?'

Measuring him wasn't much fun. He obviously didn't like me being so close but whatever old Ma Scrope had done to him had rendered him obedient, if not cooperative. I jotted down his measurements and opened up my laptop.

I've no idea what colour his original clothes had been. Leon said everything had been a kind of grimy grey. I suspected there had never been much colour in his life. And they'd been stiff with dirt and soot and dried urine, chafing wherever they touched and letting the cold in wherever they didn't. So warm, soft and colourful were my first priorities.

I ordered a red sweatshirt, half a dozen T-shirts, a couple of pairs of jeans, a blue hoodie, another green sweatshirt (just because I liked it), some new pjs, a blue dressing gown to replace his too large St Mary's one with the sleeves turned back, two or three bright and baggy shirts, a blue sweatshirt (because I liked it even better than the green one), underwear, and some brightly coloured socks. I chucked in a couple of pairs of slippers, a pair of yellow wellies, and a bright, warm coat.

And then I had a brilliant idea.

I entered the search terms, found what I wanted, and placed the order.

I paid a fortune for overnight delivery for all of it, and sat back to await arrival.

*

Mr Strong brought it all up the next morning.

I pulled everything out of the packaging and took it in to Matthew.

'I've brought you a present,' I said, laid it all out on his bed, winked at Leon, and went and sat at the table as if I wasn't interested.

Matthew's face was a picture. He'd only ever seen Leon and me in our jumpsuits, or me dressed as a Norman matron, and probably had no idea what modern clothes looked like. The medical team wore scrubs; Miss Lingoss in her Goth gear wasn't a good example to anyone; and yes, all right, Professor Rapson wore the right clothes, but usually in the wrong order. This was the first time Matthew had ever seen modern kids' clothing.

I could see he was entranced by the colours, but I think it was the softness that really held him spellbound. He kept stroking the red sweatshirt, and when he picked it up and held it to his cheek, I had to look out of the window.

Leon helped him with zips – which fascinated him – and all the fastenings, and then it was time for The Big Finish.

I held out a shoebox. I didn't take it to him. He had to come and get it. Inside was a pair of light-up trainers. I'd picked the best I could find. Not only did one flash red and the other green – which I thought would be useful teaching him right from left – but they had fluorescent laces as well. We drew the curtains and switched out the lights.

His face was a picture. His eyes brighter even than the flashing lights.

'If he hadn't been tongue-tied before,' said Leon,

amused, 'he certainly is now. Bet you didn't think to get me a pair.'

Dr Stone had warned us we might have some problems getting him to wear shoes. That he'd probably gone barefoot all his life and would refuse to wear them. We never had that problem. Our problem was getting him to take them off. We finally compromised with him agreeing to take them off to go to bed or have a bath. Otherwise, they were pretty much welded to his feet.

He slipped them on – Leon tied the laces for him – and we were good to go.

We packed up his stuff for him, pretending not to notice as he stumped up and down the ward in his new gear, admiring himself in the mirror. Leon took one hand – I took the other – and, at last, we were able to take him home.

11

Not that I was around for long. As part of my role as absent parent, I was off to Bayeux.

It was yet another dreary day in Normandy. Theoretically the sun had risen, although the sky was dark and overcast. The rain hammered down. Surely the sun must shine here sometimes. No wonder they all wanted to move to England. And it's not as if we're famous for our lack of rain.

Architecturally, the town had everything, from wattle and daub huts with scruffily thatched roofs, to the magnificent cathedral still under construction, and every type of building in between. The town was bigger than I had imagined and had spread out from beyond its walls in a series of small villages to the north-east.

Rainfall ran off the roofs and splashed into the streets below. Rivers of water gurgled along the gutters, such as they were, paused briefly to swirl around our feet – my hem was soaked in seconds and wet wool is very heavy – before running down to the river, itself swollen and brown with heavy rain.

People scurried along with us, heads down, heavily cloaked and hooded, all heading to the cathedral, that scaffolding-encased monster dominating the town. No one was working on the building itself today – nothing must distract from the approaching ceremony – but behind the scenes work had by no means ceased. Masons and their men swarmed everywhere. I could hear the incessant chink of metal tools on stone. Hefty horses were pulling great blocks of dressed stone.

As far as I could see, the building was intact – we wouldn't be dodging any leaks in the roof – but there was still a way to go before it was finished.

We'd turned up early to be sure of getting in and it wasn't much past dawn when we arrived outside the cathedral, but already the building was packed. I stared in dismay. No one ever mentions this in stories about time travel. You identify and locate your destination, defy the laws of physics to get there, somehow manage to avoid as many as possible of the huge number of hazards History has littered around the place, manage not to lose or break your very expensive equipment, you're poised to record the History-changing event of your choice, and then you find you can't bloody get in.

On the other hand, we have the Security Section who, just for once, could justify their presence. I said to Markham, 'Get us in, if you please, Mr Markham.'

He nodded and we formed the traditional St Mary's battering ram. Security at the front, historians at the rear, pushing. It works. People weren't happy but we were well dressed and, in those days, people were perfectly accustomed to being shoved aside for their betters. We did it as gently as we could – eventually arriving, breathless, a little dishevelled, and probably hugely unpopular, at the entrance.

There was no sort of crowd control inside. The important people stood at the front – that was a given – so we historians split into our two teams and used our elbows.

We were just in time. We'd only been inside a few minutes when I heard raised voices. They were turning people away now and, although it was traditional to leave the doors open so the crowds outside could hear what was going on, if we hadn't been able to get inside, we might as well have gone home and Dr Bairstow would not have been at all happy with us.

The place was huge. An echoing cavern. Huge and chilly. It smelled of damp stone, candle wax, incense and wet people. There were candles everywhere. In sconces, on tripods, impaled on what looked like wheels, hanging above our heads on chains that disappeared up into the gloom. The place was brilliant with light. It was vital that everyone present must see Harold perjure himself today. This was a very important occasion. Critical, you might say. From the moment he took the oath, Harold and William would be in direct conflict. From that moment on, only one could survive.

Unlike the gloomy hall at Beaurain, with its smoke-darkened tapestry, this place throbbed with colour. There were murals on the walls, their colours still fresh and sharp. Scenes from the Bible abounded. And there were images of the Virgin Mary in her blue robe everywhere. Every niche held a statue. Every corner had a full-sized representation of a saint, all exquisitely wrought and lovingly painted in glowing reds, blues, greens and gold. I thought I saw Saint Christopher, the patron saint of travellers, and always popular at St Mary's. And St Catherine, on her wheel. I counted over thirty figures visible from just where I was standing. This colour and vibrancy in the main part of the church contrasted sharply with the unfinished side chapels, still closed off and covered, where building work was still in progress.

There were large numbers of ecclesiastical figures around. William wanted to make very sure of the Pope's support. Quietly, in the background, I could hear chanting, but above all there was the murmur of people. The sounds of their movements echoed around this vast space. Pews hadn't yet been invented and there were no chairs. Everyone stood. The weak and feeble stood, sat or leaned around the walls – hence the expression 'the weak went to the wall'. Only one chair was visible – a magnificently ornate affair with carved arms, set under a canopy, bearing the lions of Duke William.

While I was keen to see him again – and Harold, of course, because they were becoming old friends to us – I was also eager to see the Bishop of Bayeux, William's half-brother, Odo of Conteville, who was in his own way at least as remarkable as William.

Odo supported his brother throughout his life. Not just a clergyman, he was a warrior and statesman as well. In addition to providing ships for the crossing to England, he would fight at Hastings, albeit only with a wooden club, since clergymen weren't supposed to wield a sword. Those who thought this might hold him back were wrong. Apparently he still managed to do a formidable amount of damage. It would be Odo who would commission the famous Bayeux Tapestry, and William, who valued personal loyalty above all things, would reward his war-like brother with enough land and property to make him the largest landowner in England – second only to William himself. In 1067, Odo would become Earl of Kent.

We spent an hour slowly working our way as far forward as we could get. Which wasn't that far. We were still quite a long way back, but that's what the close-up function is for.

And then, we waited. Because we're historians, and if we're not running – we're waiting. And vice versa, of course.

I whiled away the time by looking around me. They'd pulled out all the stops for this one. I could see the altar. Gold and silver plate and candlesticks winked in the candlelight. An enormous golden cross, encrusted with what I took to be rubies stood in the centre. The contrast between the pristine white cloth and the brilliance of the rubies was breath-taking.

The area in front of the altar, hitherto empty and guarded by soldiers was beginning to fill up with richly dressed men. These would be the movers and shakers of the day, and all of them invited so William could have impeccable witnesses to the events. My heart went out to Harold. Stitched up by a master.

In our game, it's always tempting to play 'What If?'. What if Harold had never been shipwrecked? What if – as the legitimate choice of the Witan – he had become king in the normal manner? Without the backing of the Pope, would William even have considered crossing the Channel? Would he have been able to assemble his enormous army if he had? If Harold had been a strong king, would Tostig and Harold Hardrada have dared to attack and draw him north at that vital time? And if William had never attacked and Harold remained king, if Anglo-Saxon culture had remained intact – where would England be today?

It's fashionable to say that at the time of the Conquest, England was a backwater – a tiny half-island off the coast of Europe and nothing more – and that William's invasion dragged it into mainstream Europe. Then there are those who say that England was doing very nicely thank you, and only became a backwater *after* the Conquest, because it was just a small part of the Norman holdings. That the Normans still looked to Normandy as their heartland and that was where their kings spent most of their time.

And what of our language? If the Saxon tongue had prevailed, then we would regard something as kingly rather than royal. Miss North would be fair rather than blonde. We would have selfhood cards rather than identity cards. We would sunder rather than sever. We would eat cu, not boeuf, swin, rather than porc, cicen rather than pouletrie, deor rather than venesoun.

Fortunately, before I became too entangled in the game of What If? – and it does happen – Markham nudged me, because the important people were beginning to arrive, and the first one up was Harold.

He entered from the side, emerging out of the gloom. Another man, slightly shorter but with a strong facial resemblance, stood at his elbow. I wondered if this was his brother, Wulfnoth, held hostage here for years, because he seemed to have become more Norman than Saxon.

Harold was politely escorted. Or guarded, if you want to give it the correct name. He wore a brilliant sky-blue tunic, heavily embroidered around the neck and hem, that fell to just past his knees. His hose were green. A jewelled belt hung on his hips and his cloak, a darker blue, was fastened at the right shoulder by a jewelled pin. His shoulder-length, fair hair was neatly trimmed and he'd retained his unfashionable and unflattering moustache. I didn't blame him. Everything he wore – everything he owned – had been given to him by William, the soul of generosity. The only thing he still possessed was the prospect of becoming King of England one day, and even that was about to be taken from him.

There was a huge air of expectation. No one knew what Harold would do. Maybe even Harold didn't know what Harold would do.

On the other hand, of course, no one knew what William was about to do, either. I had to remind myself again that apart from William, Odo and a few others, we were the only people here who knew what was about to happen today. As far as everyone else knew, Harold was about to take a simple oath of loyalty and then push off back to England.

William was making him wait, but Harold showed no signs of impatience or damaged ego. He stood, one hand on Wulfnoth's shoulder, head bent, apparently listening to an amusing story. I admired his composure.

William didn't make him wait long. Trumpets sounded, the chanting began again, louder this time, and here he came, entering from a door opposite that used by Harold. He wore a long, crimson tunic that suited his dark colouring well. An ornate golden chain hung around his neck. His belt was of soft leather, set with rubies. In contrast to Harold's bare head, he wore a small circlet of gold. It was as if everything had been contrived to isolate Harold. The predominant colour amongst William's supporters was crimson. Looking around, Harold was the only blue in a sea of red. Even Wulfnoth wore crimson.

William was followed by his coat of arms. A red banner with two golden lions. Or, if you had looked it up beforehand so as to be able to describe it accurately – gules, two lions passant or.

I looked around. Everything was crimson and gold. The hangings, the banners, the canopy over the chair. Everything was in William's colours. And reinforcing his position as the top dog here, William was accompanied by his half-brother, Bishop Odo. There was a strong family resemblance, which I'm sure both brothers cultivated.

An acolyte preceded them, bearing yet another ruby cross.

I whispered, 'Miss North, report.'

'We're in place. Everything's fine.'

Sykes was some little way off. I could just see the top of her head with Evans standing next to her.

'Miss Sykes, report.'

'We're good,' she said in my ear. They both sounded preoccupied so I left them to get on with it.

Bishop Odo was dressed to impress. As burly as his brother, he wore a long, snowy white tunic with sleeves, and his stola hung around his neck. His overgarment, the dalmatic, was made of some stiff material and slit up the sides. His chasuble continued the crimson silk motif, beautifully embroidered in light-catching gold thread. Everything was in crimson and gold to match William. Just in case anyone had failed to get the point.

His crozier, held in his left hand was heavily ornamented and inlaid with ivory, and his pectoral cross was – again – of gold and rubies.

William himself walked alongside, but a polite half pace behind. I was convinced he'd made a conscious effort to associate himself with the Church. And modern politicians think they invented spin, bless them.

William bowed to the altar and strode to his chair, paused for a moment and then, in complete silence, he seated himself. I stole a glimpse at Harold, who stood quietly nearby, politely attentive, as if attending a pleasant diversion Duke William had set up for his amusement. You couldn't fault his self-control.

The bishop was followed by a whole raft of chanting clerics who, in turn, were followed by two men carrying a box suspended between two long poles. I craned my neck. This was it.

With great care and reverence, the box was set up in front of the main altar. After a suitable pause to collect everyone's attention, the heavily embroidered cloth was removed. A stir ran through the crowd and as one, people knelt. It was another altar. A portable altar – the kind a household would carry with them as they travelled from one home to another.

Duke William was making doubly sure. One oath – two altars. Harold's wiggle room was getting smaller by the moment. Lying on top of the altar was a huge Bible, leather bound and already old even in this time. Under that was a blood red cloth, again embroidered with the lions of Normandy.

It would appear Harold had only to take a simple oath on the Bible. I looked for signs of relief in his face. To break a simple oath was not so serious. His face was expressionless, however. William was not the only one giving nothing away.

We rose to our feet, along with everyone else.

The bishop greeted the clerics who, in turn, bowed to William. No one spoke to Harold.

Even in this huge space, and even with all these hundreds of people around me, I could hear only silence. Complete silence. No one even coughed.

Stepping forwards, Bishop Odo respectfully guided Harold to the space between the two altars. I could hear his low murmur as he instructed Harold to place a hand on each altar. A minor cleric held a golden cross before him. Another spoke the oath which Harold was required to repeat.

He did so, loudly and clearly. In front of everyone present, he promised to support William, Duke of Normandy, in his claim to the throne of England, so help him God. His voice echoed around the huge stone vault of Bayeux Cathedral as he steadfastly held the bishop's gaze. His manner was solemn and dignified, as befitted a man taking an oath before God. There was nothing to suggest he had treachery in mind. All around us, people's heads were nodding in approval. Not more than ten feet away from Harold, William's face was expressionless.

The best thing about being a sweeper is that I was free to look around. With both teams concentrating on their particular target, I was able to stare about me. At the rapt faces all around. Everyone was craning forwards, desperate not to miss a moment of what was going on. I turned back to William, looking for some clue in his face. I was wasting my time. Adept at displaying only what he wanted to, William was showing nothing more than polite interest and respect for the occasion, and was, apparently, quite relaxed about the whole thing. It's no big deal, said his posture. We'll get through this, nip off for a quick drink and you could be home by this time next week. Trust me. He sat on his throne, calm and unperturbed, but when I looked closely, he was gripping the arms of his chair so hard that his fingers had turned white.

The ceremony was quite short. Only a few minutes and it was done. Once the oath was taken, there was no need to linger. Both William and Harold were now irrevocably set on the road to Hastings.

Harold finished speaking, lowered his arms to his sides, genuflected three times and bowed to the golden cross, which was taken away. The Bible was carefully removed.

Obviously thinking the ceremony was finished, Harold turned to William who stood up and made a slight gesture. I saw tension in those standing around him. The moment had come.

With a gesture similar to that of a modern conjuror, a minor cleric whipped the crimson cloth off the second altar.

Every historian in the place strained for a closer look.

Actually, everyone in the cathedral strained for a closer look.

The altar was actually a hollow box. The Bible on which Harold had sworn his oath concealed a small compartment which itself contained a small golden casket.

Bishop Odo himself stepped down from the main altar. Taking the casket from its hiding place, he reverently opened the lid and displayed the contents. Firstly to William, who nodded grimly. There was no sign now of the affable duke.

Turning, he showed the casket to Harold who stood, stiff as a board, exposed and alone, in the light of a thousand candles.

The casket contained three or four small bones, nestling in folds of rich, purple cloth.

A huge gasp ran around the cathedral.

Harold staggered backwards, somehow regained control of himself, and stood frozen. At no point did he meet William's eyes. The net had closed around him. He had sworn a public oath not merely on a Bible as he had thought, but upon the blessed bones of Normandy's saints. He had sworn a sacred, unbreakable oath. William had outwitted him.

Every eye, including that of William himself, was fixed on Harold. What would he do? What *could* he do?

He pulled himself together. I had no idea what the effort cost him. He must have known that from that moment on, he and William were on a collision course from which only one of them would emerge. He drew himself up, perfectly in command of himself. For all anyone knew, he might only have tripped on an uneven stone and temporarily lost his balance. William, of course, knew better. And so did we.

Harold turned to William who, with the same superb self-control, had not for one moment allowed any flicker of satisfaction to cross his face. Then Harold bowed his head slightly, turned on his heel, and strode from the cathedral, his blue cloak flying behind him. His entourage trailed uncertainly after him.

It was an insult, but William wisely let him go. He had what he wanted. There was no point in forcing a confrontation now.

No one could leave before William, and he was in no rush to depart. He spent some time talking to the ecclesiastical officials as the relics were carefully and reverently returned whence they came. From there, he took some time to speak to members of his own retinue, possibly issuing instructions to keep an eye on Harold, although there was no point now. Now that Harold had sworn away the crown, he could return to England any time he liked. Now that it was too late.

Eventually, he left as he came, with his half-brother the bishop, and everyone else was free to leave. I eased my aching back and legs, sighed with relief, and collected my teams.

It was late afternoon when we finally fought our way out of the cathedral. There were people everywhere. Notwithstanding the traditional Norman weather, the streets were full of families enjoying themselves. It was possible they feared their fierce duke, but they were proud of him as well. Barrels had been broached and somewhere, I could smell roast meat, reminding me that I was starving. William had spared no expense to ensure this day would be remembered by the people of Bayeux.

We meandered our way through chattering groups and I became aware that all was not well with my teams. Vigorous discussion was taking place. Actually, vigorous discussion is St Mary's speak for a bloody great argument.

The divisions were team based. Team Harold was having a go at Team William over his deception. Team William was giving as good as it got, claiming Harold was a perjurer and oath breaker. Team Harold was countering with the claim that the oath was worthless since it had been extracted under false pretences. Team William was maintaining that whether he meant to keep the oath or not, he did actually swear. It was binding. And how duplicitous was he, swearing an oath he never meant to keep in the first place?

'Not so,' countered Team Harold. 'The oath could not be valid because he was tricked into it.'

'He never meant to keep it,' shouted Team William. 'He's forsworn.'

'Not important,' argued Team Harold. 'The crown was never his to give away. The decision rests with the Witan.'

'He broke his word,' began Team William again, and were shouted down by Team Harold, informing us that politicians break their word all the time. Any politician will promise anything to anyone to get a vote. Everyone knows they have no intention of ever keeping their word.

Team William were maintaining their position on the moral high ground. 'You can't disregard an oath just because you don't like it.'

Team Harold were red-faced and waving their arms around. 'The oath is not valid. It was taken on Norman soil.'

They were face-to-face and about to come to blows. People were looking. I should intervene. Markham and I got between them before we were all arrested for being drunk and disorderly. Well, disorderly, anyway.

'Enough,' I said, sharply. 'For God's sake, don't we have enough trouble with things that could normally go wrong on assignment without starting on ourselves as well? Back to the pod all of you and behave yourselves.'

It was interesting though, to see that emotions could run so high even one thousand years after the events at Bayeux took place. What passions must they have raised at the time?

Dr Bairstow lost no time informing me that he'd told me so.

'I'm sorry sir?'

'I did wonder whether not varying the composition of the teams was a good idea. I was a little concerned that each team might become too involved with their own particular protagonist and lose the detachment necessary for effective observation and documentation.'

I nodded gloomily. He was right. On the other hand …

'I take your point, sir, but I do think that in our job we do require certain amount of passion. We're not accountants, sir, studying rows of figures and drawing conclusions. These are people we're observing. Real people, whose actions then are still impacting upon us today. The events at Bayeux were hotly disputed at the time and in many academic environments today, they still are. I think a little loss of professional detachment might be forgiven.'

'You misunderstand me, Dr Maxwell. It's not the loss of detachment I deplore, but the location of that loss of detachment. I have, over the years, grown perfectly accustomed to witnessing brawling in the corridors as historians seek to impose their points of view upon one another, but not when you are all … on the job … so to speak. I trust the venerable and picturesque town of Bayeux is undamaged?'

'Not a scratch, sir. It was all sound and fury, but you're right. I apologise and I'll speak to them about it.'

I thought he looked at me rather keenly. 'Oh, I think you'll find there's no need for that.' He began to rummage in his in-tray. I braced myself.

'Two things this morning, Dr Maxwell. Dr Stone has requested me to request you to present yourself for an eye test. Consider yourself requested.'

Dr Stone had grassed me up. The bastard.

'And Professor Rapson has presented me with an invoice for…' he peered artistically and I braced myself for fresh horrors. '… seven former dogs of mixed breeds, eleven former cats all designated DSH…' He frowned.

'Domestic short-haired, sir,' I said, glad of the opportunity to prove I wasn't completely useless.

'And a … *Gavialis gangeticus*.'

I know when to keep quiet.

'You are very quiet, Dr Maxwell.'

I refused to be tempted into unwise speech.

He frowned at me. 'Might I enquire…?'

I have an automatic response to this sort of thing. 'I believe Professor Rapson is in the early stages of a valuable and relevant experiment, sir, the details of which, unfortunately, cannot be revealed at this time. To avoid possible outside contamination. Sir.'

This was St Mary speak for – *I haven't got a clue what's going on there and even if I did, I don't want to tell you because you'll probably put a stop to it, and anyway you'll need plausible deniability with the Chief Constable when the Professor blows up most of south Rushfordshire.* Although surely even Professor Rapson couldn't do anything incendiary with twenty or so small mammals and a Gangly Thingummy. Could he?

I made my way back to my office, dropped my files on my desk, and stared in amazement at a large bouquet of yellow roses, stuffed into what appeared some kind of container designed to collect body fluids for medical analysis. Provided, no doubt by Miss Lee, to whom that sort of thing would be funny. There was more. Square in the middle of my blotter was an enormous box of the world's most expensive chocolate biscuits.

The accompanying note read, 'Sorry, Max. Promise to do better next time,' and was signed by Sykes, North, Bashford, and Clerk.

I read it again. There was definitely something wrong with my eyes after all, because the writing had gone all blurry.

Miss Lee was staring at me, so I bent hastily and rummaged for something in my bottom drawer until I was able to face the world again.

'You know you'll have to divvy them up at the Stamford Bridge briefing, don't you,' she said, referring, I hoped, to the biscuits.

'Of course. Although if you put the kettle on, I can have one now.'

'And what about me?'

'I'll let you look at the picture on the front.'

With Bayeux safely achieved, I had a week or so to take

off my historian hat, and replace it with my hitherto little used and very unfamiliar mother's hat. I went off to find my family. Another phrase to get used to. Still, I had managed to get my head around 'my husband', so 'my family' shouldn't cause me any trouble at all. I hoped.

According to Dr Stone, it was important to establish a routine. To give Matthew a framework for his day and make him feel secure. So we did.

The three of us would always breakfast together. Matthew was, at first, perfectly bewildered by the choice offered – he thought he had to eat everything– a challenge he appeared more than capable of rising to. Much of it was completely unfamiliar to him, so we always had the same. Scrambled eggs, bacon, toast, marmalade, and as much tea as I thought I needed to get me through the morning.

From there, Leon would take him to Mr Strong where he would spend the first part of the morning taking care of the horses. He was good with horses and they liked him. When he'd finished there, he went on to Dr Dowson in the library. Initially the books were read aloud to him as he looked at the pictures, and then he progressed to picking out letters and words.

At lunch, Leon would try to get him to talk about his day so far. He seemed to have a very small vocabulary. If he wanted something, he would just point, or if pushed, say, 'Want.' Leon and I would chat away together, epitomising – we hoped – familial bliss and harmony, and hoping he was picking up words along the way.

He spent his afternoons with Professor Rapson, ostensibly learning maths and science. In reality, the two of them would trot around the place, putting things together and then blowing them up again and, incidentally, getting unbelievably dirty. When the weather permitted, they would potter about outside. The professor was showing him how to excavate one of Mr Strong's many compost heaps.

At the end of most afternoons, the Security Section – who would stop work at the drop of a hat if there was a ball involved somewhere – would call on him for a kick-about around the back of Hawking Hangar – into which he was not allowed under any circumstances – then back for tea and a much-needed hose-down before bed.

We kept him busy and, I hoped, happily occupied, while he learned to cope with this strange new world in which he found himself.

He and I were outside one day, hidden away in the little sheltered area behind Hawking. The Security Section had kicked football into touch today – pun intended – and were having a game of cricket instead. Someone had made Matthew a small cricket bat, which he was wielding with an expression of immense concentration but very little success.

I was leaning against the wall with my mug of tea and rather enjoying this happy and peaceful scene, when Dr Bairstow walked around the corner.

He stopped dead. Everything stopped dead. The Security Section shuffled its feet. Evans paused in mid-run up. Matthew looked around to see why.

They'd met, of course. Dr Bairstow had formally shaken his hand and welcomed him to the unit. They'd stared at each other in mutual incomprehension and then

Dr Bairstow had moved on, heroically refraining from wiping his hand as he did so.

Anyway, here we all were, deserting our duties. And not for the first time, either.

On the other hand, Dr Bairstow likes cricket. I have no idea why. If asked, I would have said nothing could be more boring than football, but I was wrong. In what other game, I had once demanded, could two teams play for five days – five long days! – and not have a result at the end of it? Incidentally, there is no satisfactory answer to that question.

Once, long ago, during a particularly tedious assignment to Sogdiana, before Kalinda began her reign of terror at Thirsk, she and I had sat down and re-jigged the game a little. To make it a little more spectator friendly, we said. To rid it of its coma-inducing qualities. We'd called it Cage Cricket.

Picture the scene, if you will. One of those gladiator-style wire cages, bathed in a harsh light. A thick layer of sand on the floor to mop up the blood and guts. Flashing lights. Heavy-metal music blasting from speakers each the size of a bungalow. The huge crowd, unseen in the darkness, laying bets and baying for blood. The booming announcement, 'One batsman. One bowler. To … the … death.'

Enter the players – although we'd decided combatants would be a better word. There would be a bowler, a young man in his mid-twenties, we thought, with good musculature development, wearing rather a lot of baby oil and a small loincloth.

Peterson, listening in horror, had been moved to

protest at this point, but we'd overruled him.

Anyway, the bowler hurls his ball with maximum force at the batsman – who would be similarly dressed. Or undressed, depending from which direction you were approaching.

What about his box? had demanded Peterson, and been told to stop making difficulties. The batsman's job would be to whack the ball straight back at the bowler. Between the eyes if possible. They carry on like that, bowling and batting around the cage, scoring a four for a body hit and a six if they manage to render their opponent unconscious – at which point the body is dragged away, Coliseum-style, fresh sand put down, and replaced by another player – sorry, combatant – until both teams are dead, exhausted, hospitalised, or any combination thereof. Meanwhile, outside the cage, the music blares, the lights strobe, and the invisible frenzied mob screams for blood in the darkness.

It'll be great, we'd said to a speechless Peterson. Two contestants, stalking each other across the bloody sand. The crack of ball on willow. Or bone, possibly. Two men enter – only one will leave. And then at 3.30 everyone breaks for tea and fairy cakes.

Peterson, regaining the power of speech, had vetoed the whole thing as ridiculous, not least because, apparently, the MCC has a very strict dress code that, inexplicably, does not include either baby oil or loincloths. We replied that he might have put his finger on the very reason for cricket's lack of popularity with the thinking gender, and he had sulked for the rest of the assignment.

Anyway, here we were, and here was the Boss, limping unexpectedly around the building and catching his entire Security Section doing something they shouldn't. And, as I've already said – not for the first time.

He watched in silence, leaning on his stick. Evans, apparently emboldened by the lack of thunderbolts raining down from above, resumed his run up, arms windmilling, and delivered a neat little ball. Matthew swung wildly and missed.

No one spoke. I stepped into the breach. 'Good afternoon, sir. Matthew, you remember Dr Bairstow, who is in charge of us all.'

They regarded each other in silence and then Matthew made a quaint little bow from the waist. I'd never seen him do that before and I don't think it did him any harm at all. I think it's safe to say no one had ever bowed to Dr Bairstow before. I hoped it didn't catch on.

Markham beamed encouragingly at Matthew and said, 'Come on, mate, have another go. I think you've nearly got it.'

Matthew stumped his bat on the ground, squared his shoulders, and waited for the next ball.

Dr Bairstow spoke. 'Chin down, young man and watch the ball.'

He hit the next one straight through the toilet window. The tinkle of falling glass gradually died away. No one caught anyone's eye. I think Markham was already envisaging the latest Deduction from Wages to Pay for Damages Incurred form, neatly stapled to his next pay slip.

Matthew stared, first at the window, and then, discarding the rest of us as unimportant and irrelevant, at Dr Bairstow. He had gone very pale, his eyes huge with fear. He was ready to drop the bat and run. Anywhere. Away from whatever punishment he thought was coming his way. None of us moved. In just one second, all our good work had been completely undone.

I was about to go to him – for all the good that would do – when Dr Bairstow said calmly, 'A good shot, Matthew, but you should watch those elbows. Try again.'

Another ball was produced. Evans bowled him an easy one and he hit it straight into Markham's waiting hands. Markham fumbled artistically, dropped it, and then fell over for good measure.

There was a torrent of good-natured abuse.

Dr Bairstow shook his head and moved on. No Deductions form was ever received.

In the evenings, we would watch a little TV. In my role as bad cop, I wouldn't let him watch much because I didn't want to overload him. He did like doing jigsaw puzzles, though. We would all sit together at the table while he frowned over the pieces. He never smiled much, but I suspected he hadn't had much to smile about. He liked books and stories as well, and every night Leon would disappear for a tactful hour while I read to him in bed. I kept the stories simple, because his knowledge of our world wasn't great, and we would look at the pictures together.

We introduced women into his life very slowly.

First up was Mrs Mack. She let him help make jam tarts for us to eat in the evening as we read together. He

173

never greeted her with wild enthusiasm, but he tolerated her – I think he'd worked out that she was the source of all food. He politely avoided Mrs Enderby because of her tendency to cuddle, but the real breakthrough was Miss Lingoss.

He took one look at her blue-tipped hair and was her devoted slave. He trotted after her whenever she would allow him to. She was very good-natured about it all, promising faithfully not to engage in anything too hazardous when he was around. I was always catching glimpses of the pair of them disappearing around a corner somewhere, laden with dubious-looking equipment that could, in the wrong hands – i.e. Miss Lingoss's – lay waste to most of the surrounding countryside for miles around, cause near-earth satellites to drop from the sky, and possibly start a small pandemic as well. As a caring and concerned mother, I should probably investigate their activities. As a short and harassed historian, I would pretend I'd seen nothing.

With everyone else cherry-picking the good stuff, I seemed to be stuck with hair-washing, ear-cleaning and badgering him to eat broccoli. The three things he disliked most in the world. A mother's lot is not a happy one.

He didn't talk much but he wasn't unfriendly. Not even distrustful. He was just watchful.

I forced myself be patient and tried not to think about the little baby holding out his arms for me to save him. It was slow, but we were making progress and it was possible, said Dr Stone, that given a little time and patience, everything might be all right after all. And how

174

about that eye test while I was here?

'I'm very busy,' I said, backing away. 'Some other time, perhaps.'

'Of course,' he said. 'I quite understand. You've a lot on at the moment. Tell you what – how about a quick preliminary, and if you get through that then there's no need for the full test. It'll only take a few minutes and we could get it out of the way now.'

I indicated that this might be acceptable. It was beginning to dawn on me that this eye test thing wasn't going to go away.

'Won't take long,' he said cheerfully, sitting me at a table. Not a lightbox in sight. This might go well.

He handed me a sheet of paper and a pencil. 'Let's see how well you do at this easy test, shall we. Draw me a house.'

I drew a tiny house.

'Excellent,' he said. 'No problems there. Now, draw me a garden.'

I did a few scrappy flowers and a lollipop tree in front of the house.

'Yes, that seems OK. Last one – draw me a snake.'

I rather went to town on the snake. I drew a giant python, all curled around the outside of the picture, rather like a reptilian picture frame. I drew a dramatic diamond pattern on his body and coloured it in. I gave him a flickering, forked tongue, big eyes with huge curling eyelashes and a wicked expression, and a giant rattle on his tale. When I was satisfied, I handed the paper back.

He looked at it for some time.

I got up to go.

'Where are you going?'

'Well, I've passed, haven't I? Look at the detail on that snake. Nothing wrong with my eyes.'

'Yes,' he said, shifting in his chair. 'I might have ever so slightly misled you about the true purpose of the test.'

'In what way,' I said, moving ever so slightly into fighting stance.

'Well, let me show you. Firstly, the house represents your nesting instinct which, as we can see here, barely exists. The garden represents your desire for gentleness and peace which, as we can see, is no greater than your stunted nesting instinct.

I sighed. 'What has this to do with...'

'The snake, on the other hand – this easily three-hundred-feet-long, beautifully drawn, exquisitely detailed, all-encompassing snake, represents your sexual urges which, apparently, appear to be quite massive.'

I snatched up the paper, demanding to know what this had to do with an eye test.

'Oh, nothing. Nothing at all. But failure to make an appointment will almost certainly result in my posting the results of this test all over St Mary's. For people's own safety, of course.'

I crumpled the paper and threw it in the bin. 'What time do you want me?'

'I've already pencilled you in for 14:30 this afternoon. Don't be late.'

I began to see why Dr Bairstow had hired him.

I did turn up for the eye test. Something told me it wasn't wise to cross someone with an access all areas pass to my more private parts, together with a diploma in advanced deviousness.

I seated myself with a reasonable degree of confidence. I've long since memorised the letters in the light box. There are three options and I had them all down pat. The secret is to stumble on about the fourth line down, squint realistically, correct yourself and carry on, faultlessly, to the end.

He entered, we smiled engagingly at each other, and he switched on the light box.

I stared, speechless. This guy was a complete bastard. If there's one thing that really pisses me off, it's people who look as if butter wouldn't melt in their mouths and then cheat on an eye test. He'd changed the letters.

'Off you go,' he said encouragingly, while I tried not to squint. 'Start with the third row down.'

The first symbol was either the old sign for British Rail, the Greek letter omega, or two ladybirds humping each other.

'G,' I hazarded.

There was quite a long pause.

'I'm sorry, did I not make it clear? The whole row, please, Dr Maxwell.'

The next letter was a toss-up between the letter R, a floorplan of the Circus Maximus, the figure 8, the letter B, the German symbol for double S, or…

'R,' I said with confidence, because that's half the secret.

Actually the next was easy because there's no figure two on an eye chart.

'Z.' I stopped. It's always a good idea to end on a high.

'Continue.'

'Could I have a glass of water, please.'

'No.'

'I don't see well when I'm dehydrated.'

'I'm beginning to suspect you don't see well at all. You're short-sighted.'

I pointed out of the window. 'What's that?'

Now he squinted. 'The sky?'

'No, that big yellow ball of flaming gas.'

'You mean the sun?'

'It's ninety-three million miles away. How much further would you like me to be able to see?'

'Shut up and read the next letter.'

'B?'

'No, it's not.'

'Yes, it is.'

I went to get up so I could check personally – and possibly to have a quick gander at the rest of the chart as well – and he pushed me back into my seat.

'It's E,' he said.

'I was actually going to say that but you distracted me.'

'Continue.'

'How many more have I got to read?'

'It's taken you ten minutes to read three letters. At this rate, we'll be here until next Thursday.'

'Four letters actually.'

'The last one was wrong.'

'We could take an average.'

'We could just get on with it.'

I sighed. 'S. No Z. No S. Yes S. Or possibly Z.'

'Make up your mind.'

'I'm an historian. We like to keep our options open. But the next one's definitely a Z. Which makes the previous one an S.'

'It's not a logic test. Next letter.'

I couldn't decide whether it was a C or an O. 'Seeoh,' I said.

'That's not even a real letter.'

I decided to pass on that one and move on to the next.

'Z,' I said confidently, because we'd had that one before and I was beginning to recognise the blurry outline. 'Are you sure this chart's in English? Maybe that's why I can't read it. You've set up the Polish one by mistake. I can come back another day.'

'Just two more left.'

'And then I can go?'

'I doubt you'll be able to find the door on your own.'

I glared at the chart. What hadn't we had yet? Vowels. The law of averages said the next one would be a vowel. Or would it? Or maybe a semi vowel.

'Y,' I said hopefully, watching his face for a clue, but he was tapping at his scratchpad. 'What are you doing? I'm busting a gut here. The least you can do is pay attention.'

'Looking up the contact details for Guide Dogs for the Blind.'

'Dr Bairstow won't let us have a dog. He says that a) it would be the most intelligent thing in the place and b) he doesn't want the Security Section learning to cock their legs. Are we done?'

'One more left.'

'W. No – Y. No, we've had that. Not Z again, surely? No W. W. Definitely W.'

He sighed. 'It's K.'

'Well,' I said cheerfully, 'one out of ten's not bad.'

'How did you even find your way here?'

'Isn't this the dining room?'

He sighed. 'You know what I'm going to say, don't you?'

'I'm going to be making a spectacle of myself?'

His telephone rang and he picked it up. 'Yes, I'll tell her.' He looked at me. 'Dr Bairstow would like to see you in his office. It would seem the Time Police are here.'

This was not shaping up to be a good day.

It was a full senior officer meeting. Dr Bairstow sat at the head of his briefing table. Commander Hay on his right. On her right was her adjutant, Captain Farenden. Guthrie, still in Time Police gear, sat on the Boss's left, with Leon next to him. I sat opposite Leon with Captain Ellis on my other side and Markham beyond him. Peterson's place was empty. Mrs Partridge sat behind Dr Bairstow, scratchpad in hand. Dottle sat in her traditional place at the foot of the table. This looked serious. I felt a twist of unease, but Matthew was safely – if that word can be used to describe someone in Professor Rapson's care – ensconced in R&D, doing heaven knows what.

The rain hammered on the windows again. This was turning out to be a shit spring.

'Good afternoon, everyone. Thank you for coming. I think we all know each other here, so, Commander Hay, if would you like to begin.'

'Thank you, Director.' She looked around the table. 'We have, I'm afraid, been unable to locate and apprehend the renegade, Clive Ronan. I am now, therefore, designating this top priority. We are putting together a task force whose sole function will be his capture. This will be a long-term initiative. We simply cannot allow Clive Ronan to continue murdering his way through the timeline. Since we cannot spare as many people as I would like, we are calling on St Mary's, present and future, for volunteers. Director Pinkerton has released four historians to us and only regrets that she cannot spare more. Before you call for volunteers, however, I should warn you now that I have no idea how long this operation will take. We will not stop until we find him, but it could be some considerable time.'

Dr Bairstow said, 'I too, will not be able to release as many people as I suspect will want to volunteer. You will appreciate that after recent events, I cannot leave St Mary's unguarded. However, I shall hold an all-staff meeting first thing tomorrow morning and anyone who wishes to volunteer will be considered. Department heads will report to me this time tomorrow to discuss whom we can spare.'

Guthrie spoke. 'I'll go.'

From the corner of my eye, I saw Markham's shoulders slump. If Guthrie went, then he couldn't.

Leon said, 'I volunteer.'

Dr Bairstow nodded. 'I thought you might. Thank you.'

I said, 'Me too,' and from the way no one looked at me I knew what they were thinking. Leon had already been accepted. We couldn't both go. Leon was a soldier. He'd led the rebellion against the Time Police. If I forced a choice, then they would choose Leon. Of course they would. I would choose Leon. No matter how desperately I wanted to go – and I did desperately want to go – I couldn't. Shouldn't. I had to remain at St Mary's and hone my mothering skills.

Still no one was looking at me. No one would say it. I shouldn't make them.

'I withdraw my application, sir.'

He nodded. 'A wise decision, Max.'

I wasn't the only one not allowed to go. Clerk and Prentiss were both denied. As were all of the Security Section, but Dr Bairstow let them down gently.

'I thank you for your willingness to volunteer. However, this mission has no end date. I cannot do without two senior historians or the entire Security Section for however long it takes to bring in Clive Ronan. My refusal to accept your generous offer is based on the fact that you are, all of you, too valuable to be absent from St Mary's for so long. We must continue to function as normal or Ronan has won without even lifting a finger. If it in any way mitigates your disappointment, I would like to pass on my grateful thanks for your offer.'

So in the end, it was just Leon, Guthrie, and Grey. Again.

'The ones not making any sort of valuable contribution,' I said to Leon.

'That's us,' he said cheerfully. 'Always surplus to requirements.'

I felt a sudden wave of desolation wash over me. No

matter how cheerful a face we were putting on things, the future was not looking good. I tried again.

'Leon, it makes so much more sense for me to go. You're the one who has the connection with Matthew. Let me go in your stead.'

He stopped packing up his gear, pulled me down to sit on the bed beside him and took my hands.

'No. It has to be me. You know that. They don't want me just for my military abilities – considerable though they are,' he added modestly. 'I'm going as Chief Technical Officer. It's my job to keep the pods going. We can't afford to keep returning for routine maintenance, so it's going to have to be done on the hoof. That's why I have to go. And if I go, you can't. Markham has accepted it. You must too.'

I nodded drearily.

'I'm sorry, I don't have much comfort to offer. I don't even know how long we'll be gone, but I will try and get back to see you whenever I can.'

I nodded again. We both knew that wouldn't happen often. If at all.

'Listen,' he said softly, 'I've had a brilliant idea.'

'You?'

'And why not?'

'Let me count the ways.'

'Do you want to hear my brilliant idea or not?'

'Of course,' I said. 'What rarely happens is always worth waiting for.'

'Every night – when it's ten o'clock for me, I'm going to take five minutes to think about you. Where you are, what you're doing and so on. If you can do the same – at

183

your ten o'clock every night, you stop what you're doing and think of me – then just for five minutes every day, we can be together. What do you think?'

'For a bloke who spends his days up to his elbows in machinery and gunk, you're quite romantic, aren't you?'

He picked up his pack and threw it onto the floor.

'Speaking of romance.'

Once, we would have broken the furniture. Well, the bedside light, at least, but now he was gentle and loving and he made me laugh. I knew he was deliberately keeping things light. Because my heart was breaking.

They left at dawn. There was no reason for them to do so but as Leon said at the time, what was life without a little drama?

Two big black pods stood outside Hawking, their ramps down and waiting. I don't know about anyone else, but they put the fear of God into me. As, of course, they were designed to do. There's just something about their black, implacable immobility.

All of St Mary's turned out to watch them go. I stood at the back – Leon and I had said our goodbyes in private, but Captain Ellis sought me out.

'Max, would you like to walk to the pod with me. There's someone who wants to say hello.'

Slightly mystified as to who it could be, I followed him. As we approached, a small, slim figure walked down the ramp. She removed her helmet as I drew near. I stopped dead in surprise.

'Greta?'

It was indeed. Greta Van Owen. Former historian and

now, it would seem, a member of the Time Police. Ellis politely wandered off to supervise loading procedures. Which basically consisted of stowing bags in lockers, but I appreciated the thought.

'Max, how are you?' Her voice was quiet; her manner reserved. It was hard to believe she'd emptied a gun into Izzie Barclay. Just for a moment, I was back in the barn, lying in the dirt, watching the bullets shred flesh already dead.

'Fine, thanks to you. And you? How on earth did you of all people end up with the Time Police?'

She smiled a small, sad smile. I had the impression that was the best she could do these days. 'I was lost for a very long time. Not physically, but … you know.'

I nodded. I did know.

'And then the Time Police came for me. They made me an offer I couldn't refuse. Gave me a purpose at last.' She paused. 'It's so good to see you again.'

'And you. I'm so glad you've found somewhere to belong. I never felt I really thanked you enough…'

'Yes, you did. You thanked me more than enough. I'm sorry we're meeting again like this. Maybe one day we can sit down and talk properly. Catch up.'

'I'd like that.'

Captain Ellis appeared. 'Time to go.'

I shook his hand. 'Good luck, Captain.'

He nodded. 'We'll get him Max. I promise you.'

'I know you will.'

I nodded to Leon boarding the first pod. He waved and disappeared. I turned back to Ellis and Van Owen. 'Look after each other. And good luck.'

I turned away. There was no point in prolonging things. I joined the silent crowd standing outside Hawking.

The two pods just as silently disappeared. And that was it. Leon was gone.

And I was left with Matthew. We stared at each other. It had always been Leon he looked to. I wasn't sure how he would react to me on my own.

'Easy,' said Hunter, to whom I had confided my fears. 'Let him get him dirty, then clean him up at the end of the day. Give him something to eat and make sure he knows he's safe when he goes to bed. That's how I cope with Markham. Seems to work.'

It wasn't easy to begin with. We'd discovered he had no concept of family life. He had no idea what bedtime was. Or why it should apply to him when he was wide awake and enjoying himself. Equally, he saw no reason why he should have to get up in the morning when he was fast asleep. He wasn't yet brave enough to defy me, but there were a lot of hard looks. On the other hand, he'd almost stopped peeing in washbasins, so I had to be doing something right. In my darker moments, I wondered if that would be my sole contribution to his life.

We didn't speak much. I resisted the temptation to gabble away – anything to fill up the silence. We had our routine and we stuck to it.

And then the nightmares started.

I don't know if this sort of thing is hereditary. I had

bad dreams as a child. I still do, occasionally. And so, apparently, did Matthew. I would make him a milky drink and sit with him until he slept again, but it kept happening and I wondered whether to mention it to Dr Stone.

One night, however, I had a bit of a brilliant idea. Before Matthew had been born, Leon had made a holo of the Time Map and rigged it to project around his bedroom. Every night, Matthew had lain in his cot and watched, wide eyed, as a mosaic of silver lines and coloured points swirled around him until he finally fell asleep. When he was taken, I'd put it away and forgotten all about it. Now I firkled around in a drawer until I found the plug-in that Leon had made.

The Time Map is mesmerisingly beautiful. Two shining, iridescent cones of light and swirling colour. There's a vertical axis – the Timeline – and a horizontal axis which represents Space. The constantly changing point where they intersect is Here and Now. Everything above Now is the future, and below Now is the past. Lines radiate outwards from Now and these delineate the boundaries inside which we must work. This is how we plot historical events, their coordinates and their relationship with each other. Because, as I've already said, nothing happens in isolation. It was the prospect of working with the Time Map that had seduced Miss Lingoss away from the stern purpose of the History Department and straight into the clutches of those irresponsible catastrophe causers, Professor Rapson's R&D section. Now I hoped it would make enough of an impression on Matthew to distract him from his nightmares.

He was sitting, as usual, bolt upright in bed, clutching his mug to his chest, his eyes scanning the room for whatever it was that had woken him up. He would never talk about his dreams.

I said, 'Here, have a look at this,' and switched it on.

Immediately, the bed was enveloped in a swirling vortex of light, shot through with a network of silver lines. He stared in amazement. I gently took his mug off him before he dropped it.

'It's the Time Map,' I said casually, turning away. 'You used to look at it for hours when you were a baby. Of course, I can switch it off if you're too old for it now,' and bent over to do so.

He made a faint sound of protest and I smiled to myself.

'Shall I leave the door open in case you want me?'

I was talking to myself. He lay back on his pillows, quiet and still, all eyes.

I headed for the door, well pleased. Perhaps I wasn't such a bad mother after all.

From that day onwards, things got a little better. Slowly, the nightmares became less frequent. I thought that eventually I would show him a few basic moves so he could learn how to manipulate the Time Map for himself.

So much for my simple plans. When I went in one morning, the Time Map was whizzing around the room like an hysterical elephant on greased roller skates. Huge lumps of it were out of place, or rearranged, or just not there any longer. It wasn't a problem, this was only an old copy that Leon had put together to give our baby something to look at, but I hadn't taught him to do this.

189

He'd worked it out for himself.

I watched the conglomeration of silver lines and red blobs that had been our Troy assignment disassemble and reappear somewhere else. Surely he shouldn't be able to do that? This was amazing. This was a Good Thing. Wasn't it?

I felt some qualms at leaving him for our next assignment. Stamford Bridge. I know that if I'd gone to the Boss and asked to be excused boots for this one he would certainly have said yes, but Matthew had to get used to me disappearing at regular intervals. And, with luck, reappearing again.

I wasn't too sure about leaving him in Sick Bay – the place held no good memories – but Auntie Lingoss stepped into the breach.

'Auntie Lingoss?' I said, disbelieving. She just laughed at me. Today's hair was blue again. Apparently it was Matthew's favourite colour. I pushed aside the worry that she knew that and I hadn't.

'Yes, I'll keep an eye on him,' she said cheerfully. 'He's got his normal sessions with everyone else. All I'll have to do is make sure he eats his lunch.'

'That's not usually a problem.'

'No, the problem is when he wants to eat everyone else's. And all the furniture around him.'

'Are you sure about this?'

'Quite sure. If you're not back by the end of the day, then he can help me with the research on 17th-century animal sporting events I'm doing for the professor, so it will be educational as well.'

'Thank you for not saying it really doesn't matter whether I'm here or not.'

'Oh no, he does talk about you sometimes.'

'Really? What does he say?'

'Well, you gained huge Brownie points with the Time Map.'

I tried not to smirk.

'Oh, and he says you have good chimneys here.'

'Is that good or bad?'

'No idea.' She lowered her voice. 'Can I just ask – how's Peterson?'

'Not too bad, I think. Keeping busy. Why do you ask?'

'Dottle wanted to know.'

I wasn't sure how I felt about that.

As Leon had suggested, every night, after Matthew had gone to bed, at what was ten o'clock for me, I would switch off the light and the TV and sit on the windowsill to look out over the moonlit gardens and think of Leon. I would weave memories and plans together, making a tapestry of our life – what had been and what was to come. Escaping, for a short while, from the darkness of the here and now to make a bright new future that I hoped one day would come to pass. Although I wasn't optimistic.

And then I would take a deep breath and drag myself back into this world again.

Two days before the Stamford Bridge assignment, I had an appointment with Dr Bairstow in his office, to take him through the schedule and discuss the mission parameters.

It was an intensive session. I think it was all part of his 'Let's work Maxwell as hard as possible so she doesn't notice her life is falling apart' strategy. Anyway, I was bashing away at my scratchpad and completely immersed in what I was doing, so I don't know what made me look up.

Dr Bairstow's office is on the first floor. We were about twenty feet up. I mention that because the view through the window generally consists of a rectangle of sky – sometimes blue but usually grey, because this is England after all – together with a few clouds and the occasional passing bird.

A small dachshund cartwheeled past. For a moment, I sat rigid with surprise, then I shot a glance at Dr Bairstow, mercifully absorbed in a topographical representation of Stamford Bridge and the disposition of Hardrada's Viking forces.

Back at the window, another dog – breed unknown this time – sailed gracefully skywards, legs uppermost, and then disappeared again.

I just had time to thank the god of historians for ensuring Dr Bairstow usually sits with his back to the window when, with startling suddenness, a small Yorkshire terrier sailed through the open window, thudded onto his briefing table, bounced once and came to rest about two feet in front of him.

The two of them stared at each other, equally speechless. In Doctor Bairstow's case, justifiable surprise rendered him thunderstruck – in the Yorkie's case, I think death was the main contributing factor. It was very dead – its glassy eyes staring at Dr Bairstow in mute reproach.

Even Mrs Partridge seemed taken aback. Actually I was glad she was here because, traditionally, this sort of thing turns out to be my fault and, just for once, she could see I was absolutely blameless.

It takes a lot to shake Dr Bairstow. I think that being Director of St Mary's for all these years has caused his awareness of shock, horror, surprise and disbelief to shut down in self-defence. Although looking at his face now, they might simply have been in hibernation, and were emerging, blinking, into the sunlight, rather in the manner of an irritable and very hungry bear after a long winter's sleep. Seeking what they might devour, so to speak.

He turned to look at the window, just in time to see a small poodle describe a gentle parabola before disappearing from view.

Dr Bairstow and Mrs Partridge swivelled back in their chairs and fixed me with identical stares only slightly less reproachful than that of the dead dog lying on the briefing table in front of us.

I know my duty.

I sighed, stood up, and trudged towards the door.

Mrs Partridge cleared her throat, conveying a wordless world of menace.

I sighed again, trudged back and picked up the Yorkie, noticing, as I did so, that it had a tiny tartan collar with a sad little name disc attached. Colin. I tucked Colin under one arm, and went to investigate.

Markham was lurking in the gallery.

'There you are,' he said.

'Why are you lurking?'

'I'm waiting for you. I think I might be going mad.'

'Why would there be any doubt?'

You're not going to believe this, but I've just seen…'

'A small dog fly past your window.'

'Well, actually it was a cat, but thank God.'

'Why?'

'I thought I was becoming delusional.'

'What do you mean, "becoming"?'

'So I didn't imagine it?'

'No,' I said wearily.

'Seriously? Someone's throwing dead cats around?'

I held up Colin. 'Cats *and* dogs.'

He peered at me in puzzlement. 'Why are you walking around with a dead dog?'

'It's the latest craze. For people who want a dog but don't have the time to look after it properly. You get one of these instead.' I flourished Colin. 'You have all the benefits of a loving pet without it crapping on the kitchen floor and humping the furniture. Hunter wants one to replace you.'

He began to shuffle backwards. 'Well, since you obviously have everything in hand…'

'Well, since you've obviously just volunteered to assist me in my fact-finding assignment…'

He grinned and we set off to see what we could see.

Atherton and Sykes were running up the steps outside. Familiar pieces of the puzzle began to fall into place.

'Oh, hello Max,' said Sykes, cheerily. 'And Mr Markham, too. You'll never guess…'

'Well, let me have a go. We're in the middle of some dog- or cat-related catastrophe.'

She looked impressed. It never does any harm to

remind my department of my omnipotence.

'Yes,' she said. 'We were talking to Bashford and a dog dropped out of the sky and knocked him out cold.'

I held up Colin the Yorkie. 'Like this one?'

'Oh, poor thing. Is it dead?'

'It's just flown through the window and landed on Dr Bairstow's briefing table, so for its own sake, I hope so. Lead me to Mr Bashford.'

'This way,' said Sykes and we trotted off around the corner to find Bashford, lying like a stunned starfish beneath what looked like some sort of terrier.

Another dachshund and two tabby cats lay nearby.

'Oh my God,' said Markham in delight. 'It's raining cats and dogs.'

I ignored him because I'd wanted to say that.

'Should we do something, do you think?' said Sykes.

'Well, yes, probably,' said Markham.

They all looked at me.

I sighed and opened my com.

'Doctor. Yes. Good afternoon. I wonder if you could spare us a moment. Mr Bashford appears to have been involved in some sort of canine-related accident … No … As far as I can see he appears to be stunned rather than bitten … OK.'

I closed my com. 'On his way.'

He was with us almost immediately, accompanied by Nurse Hunter. Like us, they looked down at Bashford and then looked up at the sky.

'Where did that scruffy mongrel come from?'

'History Department,' said Markham, falling about at his own wit.

We ignored him again.

'I know I am going to regret asking this,' said Dr Stone, 'but what, why, and how could this happen?

'It was easy,' said Atherton. 'One minute he was talking to us and the next minute a dog fell on his head.'

'Let me be more specific. Why would a dog drop out of the sky onto Bashford?'

We looked at each other. 'Who else would it fall on?' said Markham, reasonably.

'What?'

'Well, isn't it obvious? If a dog is going to drop out of the sky and Bashford is even in the same county, then it's going to fall on him, isn't it?'

'But … why are dogs and cats falling out of the sky in the first place?'

Hunter rolled her eyes and began to examine both bodies for signs of life.

'One dead,' she reported. 'One not dead.'

Dr Stone dragged his eyes away, scanned the small crowd gathering around, presumably looking for the most intelligent person present and astonishingly picked me.

'Did the dog bite him and then die? Because I could believe that.'

'I don't think so.'

'Did it fall on him and then die?

'No, I think it was dead when it got here.'

Nurse Hunter poked the stiff corpse. 'Yes, it's been dead for some time.'

I began to feel she should be paying more attention to her current patient rather than the ex-dog.

'Is he all right?'

'God, no. Dead as a doornail.'

'I *meant* Mr Bashford.'

'Hard to say, really. Define all right.'

Dr Stone appeared to recall his medical responsibilities.

'Nurse, we'll get him inside and take a proper look.' He trailed away and looked up at the sky again, mystified.

I, on the other hand, was looking for the missing component I knew would be around here somewhere.

And here she came. Miss Lingoss trotted around the corner, peering left and right, obviously looking for something. She stopped when she saw us, and attempted unobtrusively to ooze back the way she had come. Given that today's hair was black and white, that she was wearing an enormous hooped purple dress of vaguely 17th-century European design, and was clutching what appeared to be a dead corgi under her arm, this seemed a fairly unrealistic ambition.

I beckoned her over.

'Ah,' she said, looking down at the two prone bodies. 'There he is.'

It was unclear to which of them she was referring.

At our feet, Bashford stirred faintly.

'He's coming round,' I said, prodding him gently with my foot. 'Well done, doctor.'

'I don't think it was anything I did,' he said. 'I get the impression he's done this sort of thing quite often. He's probably got some sort of recovery routine that automatically kicks in as required.'

He bent over Bashford who had opened his eyes. 'How are you feeling? Oh – no – sorry – old habits die hard. Let me try again. What the hell do you think you're playing at, you moron?'

'Much better,' said Markham. 'You're really getting the hang of this, doc.'

'Thank you.' He regarded Bashford, now struggling to sit up. 'Let's get you back to Sick Bay, shall we?'

Bashford nodded fuzzily.

'Do you know where you are?'

He nodded again, eyes rolling around like two marbles in a jar.

'Do you know your name?'

Bashford squinted down at his name, stencilled on his top pocket. 'Oh my God, I'm upside down.'

Dr Stone tried again. 'Who's the current Prime Minister?'

Silence.

'Can you not remember or don't you know?'

Bashford's eyes travelled vaguely around, seeking inspiration.

'Really? Not even the faintest idea?'

He shook his head. The doctor sighed. 'Does anyone here have any conception of the world around them?' He sat back on his heels. 'Who's the current PM? Anyone?'

There was a certain amount of foot shuffling.

'Oh for heaven's sake.'

'This dog is stuffed,' said Hunter, suddenly. 'And so is this cat. Where did you get them?'

She stared at Lingoss, who stared monochromatically back again and said, 'Job lot. Taxidermist selling up. Professor Rapson thought they might come in useful.'

'They?'

'Well, you know – he bought one or two things.'

'Such as?'

'Oh,' she stared vaguely at the sky. 'Um…'

Dr Stone began to repack his kit. 'Never mind that now. To return to my original question. Why?'

'Well,' said Atherton, slowly, 'and it's only a guess, of course, but I'm thinking Fuchsprellen.'

'Ah,' said Sykes, enlightened. 'Yes, of course.'

Mystery solved, she and Atherton began to move away.

'No, you don't,' said Dr Stone. 'No one goes anywhere until … What was that word again?'

'Fuchsprellen,' I said, pronouncing carefully, and remembering, far too late, that Lingoss had actually mentioned 17th-century sports to me a day or so ago when we were discussing arrangements for Matthew. Speaking of whom … I looked around. 'Where's Matthew?'

He stepped out from behind her skirts, a small, grubby satellite emerging from the dark side of a purple planet, gazing big-eyed around him. In the interests of historical accuracy, he was kitted out in a linen shirt and a pair of breeches that were far too big for him. In the interests of Health and Safety, he was wearing a Roundhead helmet, which again, was far too big for him and kept falling over his nose. 'Is Uncle Bashford all right?'

'There is no correct answer to that question,' said Sykes.

'Yes,' I said, frowning reprovingly at them all. 'Uncle Bashford is fine. Isn't he, doctor?'

'He's better than me, anyway,' said Dr Stone. 'What in heaven's name is…' he paused.

'Careful,' said Sykes, grinning. 'Youngsters present.'

'Fuchsprellen,' said Atherton, showing off, although to be fair, in a department that contains Sykes and Bashford – to say nothing of Miss North – he doesn't get many chances to hog the limelight.

Dr Stone looked bewildered.

'Animal tossing,' said Auntie Lingoss, who would be accounting for all this at some length later on. 'An aristocratic pastime of the 17th and 18th centuries, hence the costume.' She gestured at her only marginally accurate purple dress. 'Usually takes place in the courtyard of your average north European castle. You lay your sling on the ground. You and your partner grasp each end. Someone releases the animal – usually a fox – to run over your sling. At the appropriate moment, you jerk the ends and if you've done it properly, the unfortunate animal is propelled some twenty-five feet or more through the air. European aristocrats thought it was an hilarious way to pass an afternoon, so we thought we'd give it a go. It's actually more difficult than it looks and even though we made it easy by only using dead animals, it still took us a couple of goes to get it right.'

'Would the animal be alive?'

'When they did it – yes. Well, it was when it was tossed.'

'And when it came down?'

'Still alive. Until the moment of fatal impact, of course. Usually with the ground, but in this case, Mr Bashford.'

Too late, I remembered Professor Rapson's mysterious invoice. I really had to pull myself together. Warning bells should have been tolling the instant Dr Bairstow mentioned it. 'So you and Professor Rapson...?'

'We're the tossers, yes.'

'And that's why you and the professor wanted stuffed animals.'

She beamed at me. I felt as if I'd won a prize.

'So what other animals did the professor get?'

'Some cats. And a couple of dogs, and some ferrets. And ... um...'

Enlightenment struck me in much the same manner as a small dog had struck the unfortunate Mr Bashford. 'Aha, the Gangly Thingummy.'

'*Gavialis gangeticus*. Yes.'

Mystery solved.

Dr Stone, assisting a still shaky Bashford to his feet, looked up and said apprehensively, 'Wait, can we expect crocodiles to drop from the skies now?'

I was impressed he knew what a Gangly Thingummy was.

'No,' said Lingoss, pityingly. 'Of course not. They're about as aerodynamic as an oil tanker. We could barely get it off the ground.'

Time to break things up. 'Right,' I said. 'Mr Bashford off to Sick Bay, please, and everyone who has not incurred Dr Bairstow's extreme displeasure is dismissed – not so fast Miss Lingoss – to continue with your working day. Miss Lingoss, you wouldn't like to pop in and explain a few things to Dr Bairstow, would you?'

'Actually...'

'Actually, that wasn't a request.'

She sighed, picked up the terrier, tucked it under the

other arm, and jogged off, her purple skirt swaying around her. Matthew trotted faithfully behind.

The medical team took themselves off, supporting a still groggy Bashford. We watched them go.

'God,' I said, suddenly aware of a gaping hole in my afternoon. 'I need a drink.'

'Good idea,' said Markham.

So we went. And we took Colin with us.

Atherton briefed us on the Stamford Bridge assignment. He spoke with authority and to the point as he always did. Both Sykes and North sat quietly for him. The three of them had trained together. North was bossy and brilliant. Sykes was unconventional and brilliant, but he was their unofficial leader. I don't how he'd managed it. I don't think he consciously did anything. He was actually a very modest man, but somehow, the two of them deferred to his judgement. Their choice reflected credit on them as well. They could have done a lot worse.

'All right,' he said. 'King Edward has died. Harold Godwinson has been crowned King of England, breaking his oath to William, who immediately sets about building a fleet and assembling an army. He sends an envoy to the Pope for papal blessing, which he gains. In the eyes of all Europe, King Harold is a perjured man.

'However, Duke William is not the only one with his eyes fixed on the English crown. Tostig, brother to Harold, ex Earl of Northumbria, and brother-in-law to William, has allied with King Harald Hardrada of Norway. The two of them raise an army and sail for England. Three hundred ships sail up the River Ouse towards York. The northern earls meet them at the Battle of Fulford on 20th September and are soundly defeated. The entire northern army is scattered across Mercia, Northumbria and Yorkshire. This is a bit of a double whammy for our King Harold because it means none of them can be reorganised in time for Stamford Bridge or Hastings. People often wonder why Harold undertook the long march north to meet them when, if he'd stayed down south, there was a very good chance he would have beaten Duke William, because William was a foreigner in a foreign land and his back was to the sea, but King Harold has publicly stated that neither Tostig nor Hardrada will gain one foot of English soil, so he speeds north.'

'Yes, all of History could have been different,' said Sykes, 'but we could just as easily have had the same result but the other way around. Harold stays in the south and defeats William. Then races north to engage Tostig and is defeated at Stamford Bridge instead of at Hastings. We could be celebrating the Battle of Stamford Bridge, 1066. The last time the English were successfully invaded. Imagine if, instead of Europe, it was with Scandinavia that England had been linked.'

We took a moment to think about the implications.

'Anyway,' said Atherton, rousing himself. 'Here are the protagonists – Tostig and his ally, King Harald Hardrada. And King Harold Godwinson, whom we know quite well now. Since we have two Harolds and they're both kings, I shall refer to them as Hardrada and Godwinson. Everyone clear?

'Right. Godwinson, with little choice in the matter, sets off for the north. Tostig and Hardrada are passing the time with a little high-spirited pillaging and looting. The village of Scarborough has a particularly bad time of it. The Viking army thinks it has nothing to fear. Not only is the northern opposition scattered, but Godwinson is down south, hundreds of miles away and, they think, preoccupied with the Norman fleet heading his way. They've misjudged their man, however. Godwinson obviously decides that Hardrada and Tostig are a more immediate threat and he heads north to sort them out.'

'You can see his point of view,' said Clerk. 'If the Vikings get themselves established in the north and William arrives in the south, he could be caught in a very nasty pincer movement.'

'Indeed,' said Atherton. 'At this point, Godwinson's army consists only of housecarls or thegns. Three thousand mounted men. They're trained fighters and the backbone of his army, but he needs the fyrd. The men at arms. He sends the thegns to range ahead and recruit fighting men along the way. And they don't hang about, either. Godwinson and his army will march one hundred and eighty miles in four days.

'In the meantime, Tostig and Hardrada have negotiated a very lucrative peace deal with the terrified citizens of York. Stamford Bridge is to be the meeting place for an exchange of hostages and money. From the Viking point of view, what could possibly go wrong?'

He paused for a sip of water.

'There's always something, though. Some little fly in the ointment. This time, it's the weather. The 25th September is a very hot day. No doubt thinking the hardest part is over and done, Hardrada has left a large part of his army back with the ships back at Riccall guarding his plunder, together with the greater part of everyone's armour, because it's just too hot to wear it. Everyone else is relaxing twelve miles away on the banks of the River Derwent and having a 'me' day after their recent exertions. They think they're safe because their enemy is hundreds of miles away and are definitely not aware that he and around ten thousand slightly miffed Saxons are going to appear over the horizon any moment now. Max.'

He smiled at me.

'Thank you. As Mr Atherton has said, this is the point at which we will appear. Thanks to excellent contemporary sources, just for once, we know exactly where and when we want to be. We'll land, fairly early in the morning, on the outskirts of a small wood slightly to the north of the area now known as Battle Flats.'

I brought up a map of the area.

'The Vikings are camped on the east side of the River Derwent with a small force on the west side, holding the bridge itself. Godwinson and the Saxon army will approach from the west.

'Miss Sykes and Mr Bashford, please stick with Harold Godwinson. Miss North and Mr Clerk – William isn't around for this one so you've got the Vikings. I particularly want you to focus on the legend of the giant Viking who holds the bridge against the Saxons. Did it or did it not happen? Did he actually manage to kill forty men before being killed himself? You know the drill. At some point, Eystein Orri will arrive with Viking reinforcements. Mr Atherton, if you could cover him and his army, please. Miss North and Mr Clerk will remain with Tostig and Harald Hardrada.'

They both nodded.

I continued. 'We're all in Number Five for this one. We won't be venturing outside so there are no costumes involved. You've all read up on the background, battle strategies, the aftermath and the lead-up to Hastings. Report to Hawking 09:30 tomorrow morning. Any questions?'

We landed on the north side of what would be known as Battle Flats on the outskirts of a small deciduous wood. Although we were heading towards October, the warm weather meant the leaves had hardly begun to change at all and there was plenty of cover. And, as Atherton said, pretty soon everyone was going to have much more important things to worry about than us anyway.

We had a good position, sitting on a small rise above Stamford Bridge and the River Derwent. In fact, it couldn't be better. We would have an excellent view of Harold's army when it arrived – although I did feel that even we couldn't miss three thousand mounted men and around ten thousand men at arms.

It was a hot day. A very hot day. Down below us, the Vikings were relaxing in the sun, playing ball games, fishing, or wrestling. Many of them were having a nap. They were armed – I could see their swords thrust into the ground only an arm's reach away, but most of their armour was back at the boats, twelve miles away at Riccall.

He might have won the battle and scattered the northern army, but Harald Hardrada was making a huge mistake. He was far too complacent. We scanned backwards and forwards, but as far as we could see, there were no sentries. No scouts. They had invaded a foreign country; they were far from home and they hadn't posted lookouts of any kind. It was madness. And then he'd compounded his error by splitting his army into two. The very much smaller contingent was stationed on the western side of the bridge, with the bulk of his army sprawled on their backs on the east side.

We checked over our equipment, made ourselves a cup of tea, and sat down to await the arrival of Godwinson's Saxon army.

The first Hardrada knew about it – the first any of us knew about it – was when a massive roar could be heard and the ground shook. The Vikings leaped to their feet, dazed and sleepy, staring around themselves in bemusement just as Godwinson's army breasted the hill and came storming down upon them. In one moment all was peace and quiet and, in the next, thousands of Saxons were pouring down the hillside, axes in their hands and revenge in their hearts.

They completely engulfed the smaller army on the west bank of whom there were only about a thousand anyway. The Vikings snatched up their weapons – many of them had been swimming and were naked or nearly so – and setting their backs to the river, prepared to defend the bridgehead, to give Hardrada time to get his main force armed and ready. We could hear his chieftains shouting orders as they struggled to get the shield wall together. Without it they would be cut to pieces.

They *were* cut to pieces.

Nearly a thousand men died in the first fifteen minutes.

They had only swords or axes. No mail or armour. Blows that would be turned aside by armour, or even mail, cut deeply into unprotected flesh. Arms and heads flew through the air. Men fell, gutted from groin to gizzard. It was a slaughter. There seemed to be nothing to stop Godwinson and his men thundering across the bridge and laying into the main body of Hardrada's army, who themselves still seemed stunned by the swiftness of an attack from a man they had believed to be hundreds of miles away.

Hardrada, however, did not completely lose his head. From out of the milling turmoil of his army still desperately trying to form up, three riders emerged, galloping hell for leather away from the slaughter. He was sending a desperate appeal to his ships at Riccall. Three thousand of his men lay there, guarding not only the ships and the plunder gained so far, but all their armour and spare weapons as well.

I said quietly, 'Miss North…'

'I'm on it.' And indeed she was. Two of the screens showed close-ups of the riders galloping over the crest of a hill and disappearing from view.

I did some quick calculations. Ten miles away. On horseback. Unfamiliar countryside. Say an hour to get there. How long to assemble three thousand men and get them moving? And that was the easy bit, because even if every available man set off immediately, not only would they themselves be heavily armoured, but they would be carrying spare shields and armour for those who'd left them behind. And it was a very, very hot day. So say another hour to get themselves organised and moving. And then the ten miles back again. At a run. Heavily laden. In this heat. Two hours. Minimum. Harald Hardrada could not expect to see reinforcements in anything under four hours. Could he and his men last that long?

'There,' said Sykes suddenly. 'There. At the bridge. The Viking. There he is.'

And there he was indeed. Long-handled axe in one hand, giant shield in the other. A legend springing to life before our very eyes.

There's a story – well, a legend really, that the main part of the army was only saved from early annihilation by a giant Viking warrior, who planted himself on the bridge, and held it against Godwinson's attack, thus giving Hardrada the time he so desperately needed. The legend goes on to say that the Viking – his name sadly lost over time – killed over forty men that day, laying about him until the river ran red with the blood of his fallen foes and the bridge itself was littered with their limbs.

Well, it wasn't forty men, but it was close.

True, he had only his axe, but the bridge was narrow and could only be approached by a maximum of three men at a time and he was a ferocious fighter.

Accounts say that the battle stopped as everyone watched this modern day Horatio, but no, the battle didn't stop. On the western side the struggle continued until he stood almost alone, splattered with blood and gore, friends and enemies alike piled around him. Heads, limbs, and bodies lay everywhere.

He was unmoveable. The man was truly a hero, and today no one can even remember his name.

The forty men might have been an exaggeration, but not by much. The bridge was awash with blood which dripped into the river beneath. Ribbons of red trailed downstream. I don't know how long he could or would have lasted, but further upstream, an enterprising Saxon had climbed into half a barrel and, armed to the teeth, was floating downstream. We zoomed in on him being borne downstream, his spear ready in his grasp, and with two or three spares ready to hand. He had no shield with which to defend himself. The barrel was swirling madly in the current, uncontrollable. Its occupant could only hang on with his other hand and hope and pray he arrived at the right place at the right time.

It was hard to see how he could be a threat, but a group of Harold's men, seeing what he was doing, hurled themselves on what would turn out to be a suicide mission, engaging the Viking for as long as they could, sacrificing themselves to push him back across the bridge into the path of the oncoming barrel. He tore into them, but for every one that fell, another stepped up to take his place, and while the Viking was concentrating on the enemies before him, the soldier in the barrel reached his destination. Holding fast to the bridge with one hand, he stabbed upwards through the planking with the other. Once, twice, three times. He must have caught the Viking in the groin because a great gout of blood spurted into the faces of his attackers. Still he stood, however, and the soldier was forced to use a second and then a third spear. Still roaring, the giant yanked them out and fell to his knees. Panting Saxons stood back and watched as slowly, he slipped sideways into the water. Trailing ribbons of his own blood, he floated slowly away. Out of sight and out of History.

Roaring their triumph, the Saxon army streamed across the bloody bridge, took a moment to form their line, and advanced.

Hardrada had arranged his forces in some semblance of order, ready to receive them, but only just in time. Their long front line ranged from north to south. It had to be as long as they could make it so that the Saxons couldn't get around them, but they were stretched very thin. Too thin in places, it seemed to me. And not every fighter had a shield.

The two armies faced each other, ready to begin. A horn sounded. And again. Both sides seemed to pause.

'A parley?' said Sykes in disbelief.

'Yes, of course,' said Bashford in excitement. 'This must be where Godwinson tries to negotiate a deal with Tostig. And when Hardrada demands a piece of England for himself, Godwinson offers him seven feet of earth. Because he's tall. My God – that could actually have happened.'

Well, maybe it did and maybe it didn't – we had no way of knowing, but a parley was definitely taking place. It lasted only a few minutes – just long enough for an offer to be made and rejected. Both sides moved away from each other, and without waiting another minute, Godwinson advanced his men.

Still the sun beat down. The heat was almost unbearable and there wasn't a cloud in the sky to give either side any respite.

They went at each other like madmen. Both sides incurred heavy casualties, but the unarmoured Vikings were faring worse. Much worse. In a desperate effort to shore up his weakened shield wall, Harald Hardrada was moving groups of men from one point to another, but his men were falling faster than he could replace them.

Time passed – the sun wheeled across the sky. Hardrada must have been growing more desperate by the minute but there was still no sign of reinforcements. His line was ragged, his men exhausted.

And then…

'Listen,' said Atherton suddenly, and turned up the volume. We could hear horns blowing in the distance, faint but clear. 'Eystein Orri is here.'

Weary Vikings raised their heads and even managed a ragged cheer. Their own horns rang out in reply. As if in answer, a group of men breasted the hill, paused for a moment, silhouetted against the pitiless blue sky, and then swept down towards the battle.

There weren't anything like as many as Hardrada could have anticipated. If he had hoped for three thousand fully armed warriors ready to get stuck in then he was to be bitterly disappointed. I wondered how many had fallen by the wayside. Their exhaustion was apparent to everyone. Any hope they might have brought to the beleaguered Vikings was short-lived. The reinforcements were as fatigued as those they were relieving. They'd run more than ten miles, not only in full armour themselves, but carrying spare gear for their comrades. Many had died of heat exhaustion before even reaching the battlefield.

Godwinson's army, realising the newcomers were not likely to be a big threat to them, regrouped for a fresh attack.

The Saxons weren't big on archers. They relied mainly on their shield wall and their sword arms, but Godwinson took advantage of the lull to bring up the few he had. A hail of arrows darkened the sky. And then another. And another.

We knew Hardrada would be killed by an arrow in the throat. He would die in seconds.

I said to North, 'Make sure you don't miss it,'

'I won't,' she said shortly, so I left her to get on with it.

I didn't see it myself – I was focussing on another part of the battle, but we heard the roar that went up from both sides, announcing his death.

Even then the Vikings didn't give up. I could see Eystein Orri desperately trying to hold their forces together. Horns sounded again and, abandoning the wavering shield wall, he grouped his men into a solid mass, weapons bristling outwards, still formidable foes.

This stand is known in song as 'Orri's Storm', and they held for a while, beating back the Saxons time after time, but slowly and surely, as the sun began to drop in the sky, the Vikings were whittled away. The final straw was when, surrounded by half a dozen roaring Saxons, Tostig himself went down, bringing Hardrada's raven banner down with him. The Saxons closed in and that was the end. Leaderless, the Vikings scattered in every direction. Some would be chased all the way back to their ships at Riccall.

For the Vikings, the day had been so disastrous that of the three hundred ships that had brought them here, only twenty-four were needed to take the survivors home.

Of those fleeing the field, some ran uphill towards us, seeking refuge in the woods. Time for us to go, too.

I said, 'Start shutting things down, Mr Clerk, and let's go home.'

'Copy that,' he said, and he and North busied themselves at the console. Sykes and Atherton began to clear things away into the lockers.

I said, 'Everyone ready?' but before we could initiate the jump, a group of blood-splattered Vikings crashed through the undergrowth, closely followed by some half dozen Saxons, their swords and axes raised. They were seeking out the enemy, driving the exhausted men before them, mercilessly pursuing the final remnants of Hardrada's army.

With nowhere to go, the Vikings turned at bay, to make a stand. They were hacked down, one by one until, eventually, not one was left standing. The shouts and screams died away and only a handful of victorious Saxons remained, leaning on their swords, panting, surrounded by the wounded, dead, and dying.

I stared thoughtfully at the screen, wondering what to do next. We were still well concealed and even if someone should come across us, there was no way they could get in. We could risk a jump, but there were people all around us. There was a very real possibility they'd get sucked into the vacuum of our leaving. We have a safety line in Hawking for a reason.

'We'll stay a while,' I said. 'Let's see what happens next.'

All around the little glade, the green grass had turned red with blood. I wondered how long the wounded would be left here and the answer was – not very long at all. The standard of medical care depended upon whose side you were on. Saxons who could walk were helped to their feet and taken away. Those who couldn't were carried on makeshift litters made of cloaks and spears.

Those who weren't Saxons were despatched on the spot. Even a young lad who couldn't have been much more than fourteen or fifteen. He wasn't that badly hurt, but a wound in his leg prevented him running away. He saw his death approaching and began to cry. A blank-faced Saxon stood over him, said a few words – perhaps in consolation, or perhaps a prayer to the gods. The boy's final shriek was cut short. He spasmed once and then lay still.

And once again, we were watching people die. Real people. It's what we do. We wrap it up in all sorts of fancy phrases – investigating major historical events in contemporary time is our favourite, but, basically, we watch people die. We sell it to ourselves on the grounds they would have died anyway. That our being here makes very little difference – or shouldn't do. That in our time they've been dead for x-hundred years. That it's always important to have an accurate record of what really happened. Before those who write History – nearly always the victors – put their own particular spin on events. And all that's good, I know it is. But not when you're watching a young man, a boy even, white faced,

216

teeth clenched in agony, curled around a mortal wound and watching his own life's blood pump into the thirsty earth on a lovely summer's day, as the birds sing in the trees around him.

It takes a hell of a lot of getting used to. I haven't managed it yet. And actually, would that be a good thing? Do I want to be able to watch, dispassionately, as another life departs this world? I don't think I do. So I suppose I just have to put up with it.

I was putting up with it now.

Sykes drew in her breath with a hiss. I put a hand on her shoulder and said, 'Keep filming.'

She did, and it was worth it. Because someone shouted suddenly and, before we realised what was happening, Harold Godwinson himself strode through the trees.

We knew it was him, because he was preceded by his personal banner, the Fighting Man. He'd discarded his mail and wore only a sweaty and bloodstained tunic. His legs were bare and his hair dark with sweat. He stood in the centre of the glade, hands on his hips, staring about him. As far as I could see, he appeared unscathed. His mouth set in a grim line as he surveyed the two piles of dead bodies – Vikings on the far side of the clearing, and the Saxons, neatly laid out on the other.

North was nearly falling over herself trying to get all the cameras focused on him.

'He looks older,' said Bashford, zooming in.

'He looks ill,' said North.

I agreed. And I could hazard a guess as to the cause. Whatever brave face he was putting on for England, in his heart, Harold was a perjured man – an oath-breaker – and he knew it. It wasn't sitting easily on his conscience.

Kings are not supposed to have a conscience. It's not a luxury they could afford. Medieval kings had two simple tasks. To safeguard the realm and to ensure the succession. Nothing complicated, but failure to do one or both usually resulted in catastrophe.

The very unwar-like Edward II lost humiliatingly to the Scots at Bannockburn and was only just able to force himself to father an heir. He ended his days supposedly impaled upon a red-hot poker.

Richard II – son and grandson of mighty men – was weak, fickle and childless. Eventually it cost him his throne.

Henry VI was pious, mentally frail, lost most of the English possessions in France, and was very surprised to find he'd fathered an heir. Popular opinion reckoned that, actually, he hadn't. Henry too was overthrown. Twice, in fact.

And what about King Stephen? He wasn't the rightful heir – that was his cousin, Mathilda. Stephen had two excellent qualifications for the job – he wasn't a woman and his name wasn't Mathilda, but he foundered because he couldn't live up to the popular image of a medieval king which, basically, was to be the biggest bastard in the country. Stephen's problem was that he was just too nice, which was not what people looked for in their king. His ability to listen patiently and sensibly to other people's point of view all but wrecked the kingdom. His weakness and lack of resolution caused his uncle's system of administration, so patiently assembled over the previous reign, to fall apart in what is always known as 'The

Anarchy', and the country foundered. Not surprisingly, after his death, the crown went back to Mathilda's line. I personally always felt the country would have done much better to have stuck with Mathilda, who would cheerfully separate any man from his testicles as soon look at him, thus easily fulfilling one of the two requirements for the job of king – conscienceless brutality – but she was a woman and therefore not eligible.

Of course, you could go too far. Edward III overdid things slightly when it came to heirs and had too many sons. The family fragmented into the houses of York and Lancaster and gave us the Wars of the Roses.

Or what about Henry II's boys? Young Henry, Richard the Lionheart, Geoffrey and John happily schemed and betrayed their father and each other without a second thought.

So basically, all a king had to do was keep the realm safe and father an heir. Job done. Recent monarchs have added waving to the list, but let's face it – it's still not that difficult. The point I'm circumnavigating is that having a conscience is a luxury kings can't afford. As opposed to politicians and bankers who could do with having one inserted and yet appear to be complete strangers to the concept. From looking at him now, however, it would seem King Harold was having trouble with his.

His hair had darkened and it seemed to me there was less of it. Although that might simply have been helmet hair. He looked exhausted but, to be fair, he'd had a strenuous week. It was the look in his eyes that gave him away. He had the look of a man whose inner voices gave him no rest.

Sykes stirred and I was conscious that things were getting very hot and stuffy inside the pod. I wished they'd get a move on and leave.

'Suppose they decide to stay up here?' said Sykes, wiping sweat off her face with her sleeve. 'It's cool, shady and pleasant. That's why we we're here.'

'We could use the sonic scream,' suggested Bashford.

The sonic scream is brilliant. Some time ago it was discovered that if you broadcast at a low frequency, only teenagers can hear it. Normal people aren't affected. It induces feelings of discomfort and slight nausea. Not unnaturally, the teenagers don't like it, so they move on. They don't know why they're moving on – they just do. I believe this is now illegal, but Professor Rapson and the Technical Section never allow little things like that to stop them, so we have something similar installed in our pods. We usually keep it for hostile animals and suchlike, but it certainly works on humans, too.

Sadly, the effects can be a little unpredictable. On one occasion we'd caused a herd of Roman bullocks to stampede, causing massive damage to private property, and then, not content with that, we'd gone on to shatter every pane of glass in Hawking.

I was weighing up the pros and cons of activating it with so many seriously wounded people still around when Sykes said, 'Hang on, who's this? Look.'

A rider on a sweat-drenched horse was thundering up the hill towards us, shouting as he came. Every man turned to see what was happening. Most of them drew their swords. Two or three stepped in front of the king.

He reined in so hard his horse sat back on its haunches,

foam flying. Flinging himself from his horse before it had even stopped moving, he shouted again, looking wildly about him.

'What's going on?' said Sykes, adjusting the cameras and turning up the sound.

'No,' I said, in disbelief. 'We couldn't be that lucky.'

'Lucky?' said Bashford, and then realisation dawned. 'Oh my God. Oh my God. Quick, turn up the sound.'

The messenger was standing, hand on his knees, struggling for breath and trying to talk at the same time. Someone passed him a wineskin, but he waved it aside, grabbing a man by his arm and speaking urgently. The man pointed at Harold, standing quietly at one side of the clearing, hands still on hips. The messenger hastened over, flung himself on his knees in front of his king, speaking fast and gesturing south.

Yes, we really were that lucky. I couldn't believe it. He was gabbling so fast that we couldn't make out the words, but we didn't have to. We all knew what this was about. I was watching Harold's face. I was watching the face of a man feeling his kingdom tremble beneath his feet.

It couldn't have happened at a worse time.

Duke William had landed.

Every man here had only nineteen days to live.

It seemed strange to exit the pod and not find Leon waiting for me, but I pushed that thought aside. I was full of plans. We had three full weeks before the next assignment. Yes, there were reports to write and presentations to plan, but I had three weeks for me and Matthew to get to know each other a little better. Perhaps we could have some fun in the improving weather. I had been planning things out in my mind. I had to be careful. His life had been so narrow and miserable that almost anything was a treat, but I had to take care not to overwhelm him. Perhaps a trip to the zoo. Or we could go shopping and buy him some new clothes. I was surprised to find that the ones I'd bought him were already showing signs of wear and tear. And he seemed to be outgrowing his jeans. They were flapping around his ankles. I couldn't believe it. He'd only had them a little while. I made a mental note to instruct him to stop growing.

We decontaminated and, led by North, everyone left the pod and trailed through Hawking on their way to Sick Bay. I checked over the console, pulled my bag from the locker, and made to follow them.

Dieter entered, grinned at me, and began to shut things

down. 'Now then, Max. Everything OK?'

I smiled at him and woke up in Sick Bay.

Three birds with one stone.

This was a strange new world. No Helen. No Hunter. My head hurt. I couldn't focus properly. Shapes swam around, hurting my eyes until I gave up and closed them again.

And opened them. It was night-time. A night light burned above my head. Which still hurt, but now my body had joined the party as well. Peterson sat nearby. His face was in shadow but, even so, I'd never seen him look this bad. He hadn't shaved and deep lines had etched themselves across his face. And his arm was in a sling again.

Three birds with one stone.

I closed my eyes again.

And opened them again and now it was morning.

Peterson was still here. I turned my head on the pillow and was hit with a huge wave of nausea. I just had time to croak a warning. He seized a basin and saved us both.

Someone wiped my face and hands and I closed my eyes again.

And opened them again. This time for good. I felt much better although I suspected I owed a lot of that to chemical assistance.

Peterson was still here. He saw me looking at him, and grabbed for the bowl again.

I tried to utter a reassurance, and he put down the bowl and picked up a cup with a straw.

'Sip slowly.'

Obediently, I took two or three small sips of something sweet.

'Can you see me? Can you hear me?'

I nodded very carefully.

He disappeared. I assumed he'd gone for Hunter, but he returned with Dr Stone, who dropped into a chair beside the bed. 'Hello, Max. How are you feeling?'

I nodded again because talking was just too much effort.

He looked at Peterson, standing at the foot of my bed.

People laugh about scattered thoughts, but it's true. My thoughts were all over the place. Every time I tried to get a grip on something, it just sneered at me and slid away. Occasionally, something bubbled to the surface, popped and vanished again but mostly I had nothing.

The chair creaked as Dr Stone leaned forward. I heard the rustle of his clothing. He smelled of soap.

'Matthew is safe. He's with Professor Rapson and Miss Lingoss.'

I slurred, 'Jolly good,' and wondered if someone would tell me what was going on. It was too much effort to ask for myself.

'Max, do you remember anything? Anything at all?'

'Stamford Bridge,' I said slowly. 'Harald Hardrada's seven feet of earth.'

Three birds with one stone.

They looked at each other again and then moved away so I couldn't hear what they were saying. I caught only the words, 'No point in telling her now. We'll wait,' and Peterson nodding agreement.

And still no Hunter.

*

The next day I was better. I still had a head full of cotton wool but at least now I could string two or three coherent thoughts together and hang on to them. Unkind people might say that was an improvement on before.

Before … what?

Obviously something had happened … But Matthew was safe. I'd lost count of the number of times they'd told me Matthew was safe. Which was good news. I was really pleased for this Matthew. Whoever he was.

They brought breakfast. I nibbled on a piece of toast, because either eating something or opening your bowels is the quickest way of escaping from Sick Bay. Although not simultaneously, as I'd once discovered to my cost.

Peterson turned up again after breakfast. He'd shaved at last but, looking at him now, any peace he'd gained since Helen's death had been shattered. His eyes were shadowed and heavy.

We looked at each other for a while.

I had no idea what was happening. Why was he here? I sought for something to say and enquired why he had gone back to wearing his blues.

'I've got the History Department,' he said quietly, 'until you've recovered.'

Silence fell. I felt something was required of me, but what?

He took my hand. 'You haven't asked what happened. Why you're in here.'

Hadn't I? What was wrong with me? I tried to think. Nothing came to mind.

'Max, I'm sorry but we felt I was the best one to tell

226

you. They thought it would be easier it if came from me.'

Easier for whom was a good question.

Dr Stone interrupted. 'Max, do you know why you're in Sick Bay?'

'No, but my head hurts. And my back. And my shoulder.'

'I can give you something for that.'

Silence fell again

'All right,' I said. 'Why am I here?'

I thought they'd be pleased I was taking an interest but, again, they just looked at each other.

In the silence, I became aware of the sounds of heavy machinery outside, and men shouting.

'What's going on?'

Tim took my other hand. Whatever had happened between us was forgotten. He looked so distressed that I was distressed for him. 'Max, there's been an … explosion.'

My first thought was that Professor Rapson had finally taken out the entire R&D corridor but their faces were … wrong.

And then, something flickered at the back of my mind. I said, 'Say that again.'

'There has been an explosion.'

There it was again. Something. I began to claw my way through lumps of cotton wool that fought me every inch of the way.

A white flash. Tumbling. Dieter.

I opened my eyes. 'Dieter.'

'We've discharged him. He's fine. Just a sprained wrist and some bruising.'

They both watched me again. I shook my head. 'No. Sorry. Can't you just tell me?'

'The thing is, Max, it's not good news. I think your memory will return quite naturally in a couple of days and then we could take things from there.'

'No. Tell me now.'

'I'm offering you a period of – well, you could say, blissful ignorance, which…'

'Tell me.'

'All right. Dr Peterson? Would you like to begin?'

Tim hitched his chair a little closer. 'Max, think back. You're in Hawking. You've arrived back from Stamford Bridge. Do you remember?'

'Yes.'

'What happens next?'

I closed my eyes. 'Dieter comes in. He's shutting things down. I take my bag out of the locker. It's heavy. I heave it over my shoulder. Dieter's finished. He's asking me how things went. I turn to speak to him.'

I stopped, confronted by more giant lumps of cotton wool. 'That's it.'

'No, that's very good, Max. Now, you're in Hawking. What do you see? What can you smell?'

'The Hawking smell. Concrete. Dust. Metal. Hot electrics.'

'Good. What can you hear?'

'People shouting to one another. Echoes in a big space. An electric drill somewhere. The radio's playing the classics. Abba.'

And suddenly, without warning, I was there. In Hawking. And I remembered everything.

It all came crashing back. I remembered that last scene. Those final moments. My people up ahead, heading for the door. Techies dragging the thick black umbilicals across the floor towards Number Five. The big hangar doors slightly open, letting in light and a welcome shaft of rare sunlight. Hawking Hangar during a normal day.

Just before it was all gone for ever.

I jumped down off the plinth, dodged Mr Lindstrom's grinning attempts to trip me with an umbilical, and set off for the far door and Sick Bay. Ahead of me, Bashford and Sykes were just passing through. I remember he held the door open for her. They were arguing about something or other and then, without any sort of warning, every alarm went off. Every light flashed above every plinth. The blue emergency lights strobed overhead. The red alarms over the blast doors came on, hooting and shrieking. With a boom that made the building shudder, the big interlocking blast doors crashed together.

I stood like an idiot wondering what the hell was going on. I think I thought one of the pods was about to blow. Which wasn't so very wrong as things turned out. Dieter was shouting something but I couldn't hear over the noise of the alarms. People raced for the open hangar door. Major evacuation. I saw Polly Perkins urging people through.

And then, off to my right, an unknown pod materialised. I stared. It was in a hell of a state. The casing was scorched and twisted and in some places it had disappeared altogether. It shouldn't make any difference to the pod – the casing is purely cosmetic, but this level of damage outside gave every indication that all would not be well inside.

A fraction of a second later, another one appeared, directly opposite. This one I recognised. Squat and black and menacing. This was the Time Police. Which gave me a pretty good clue as to the occupant of the first pod.

I was right. The door slid open and Clive Ronan stood on the threshold. He was only about twenty feet away from me. He didn't look good. I could see the tears in his jeans, the mud on his boots, and the sweat stains in his armpits. He hadn't shaved in a very long time. He looked unkempt and exhausted. A wave of stale, foetid air billowed out of his pod. God knows what it must be like in there.

At that exact moment, the other pod's door opened and there stood Leon and Guthrie. They were heavily armoured and helmeted but I knew who it was. They carried heavy-duty blasters. The big ones. Even over the shrieking alarms, I could hear them whining on full charge.

I could hardly believe it. They'd got him. They'd got Clive Ronan at last. They'd chased him up and down the timeline, all the way back to St Mary's. How fitting that they should finally corner him here.

Ronan caught sight of me and smiled. He actually smiled, saying, 'Excellent. Three birds with one stone.'

Neither Leon nor Guthrie spared me a glance. All their attention was on Ronan. They brought up their weapons with a snap and slowly moved towards him, yelling at him to surrender. That there was no escape. To put his hands in the air. Now.

I should have guessed. We should all have guessed. Ronan was far too calm. He was even smiling. Slowly, obediently, he raised his hands, just as he'd been told to do, and they weren't empty. He held a small, round object in each hand. Occasionally, a small red light flickered ominously.

I had no idea what they could be, but they were enough to bring both Leon and Guthrie to a halt.

Someone must have switched off the alarms because sudden silence crashed down. Except for a tinny metallic voice.

'Sixteen. Fifteen. Fourteen…'

A countdown.

Leon, apparently noticing me for the first time yelled, 'Max, get out of here.'

Someone pushed me out of the way, and Markham, appearing out of nowhere, shouted, 'Max. Go,' and raced past me. He too was armed.

I flew back towards Dieter, still standing in the entrance to Number Five. 'Do something, Dieter. For God's sake. Help them.'

'I am helping them,' he said, grimly and grabbed my arm, dragging me into the pod.

He shouted, 'Door,' and then the world went white.

But for all the wrong reasons.

I faltered to a halt and looked at them. 'Tell me what happened next.'

Peterson stared at his lap for a moment and then said, 'Max, I'm so sorry.'

I said, 'No,' because I think I thought if I didn't accept it then it couldn't be true. I even wished I'd never said anything and continued in my happy state of cotton wool-filled ignorance. For the rest of my life. For ever.

He said again, 'I'm so sorry, Max, but yes.'

'No, you're wrong.'

'We're not wrong.'

'You must be. It's Leon – he always – he never... There's been a stupid mistake. You've missed something. Have you searched everywhere? Have you...?'

'Max, there's nothing left.'

'I don't understand. What do you mean, nothing left?'

'Ronan had explosives. They went off. They destroyed him and his pod. He's gone for ever.'

'And Leon?'

'They were too close, Max. Which we think was what Ronan intended. They were closing in. He probably had only one jump left and he couldn't get away and so he jumped here, fully intending to do as much damage as possible.'

Three birds with one stone.

'That's what he meant, isn't it? Three birds with one stone. Leon. Ian. And me.'

His face said there was more.

'Tell me.'

'Markham didn't escape the blast, either.'

Too late, I remembered Markham, pushing me back to safety and running towards Ronan, gun drawn. Doing his job. He was doing his job and he died for it. With Leon. And Ian. But, sadly, not me.

I couldn't take it in. 'All of them. All three of them? All dead?'

He nodded.

'And I lived,' I said, bitterly.

'Don't say that.'

'Why not?'

'Because … I know. I've been here and I know what you're thinking and you can't think that, Max. Not for one moment. You mustn't. You have a little boy. You have duties and responsibilities. Dr Bairstow is devastated. The unit is in pieces. We stand or fall with you. *I* stand or fall with you. If anything should happen to you … I know how you feel. Many things have ended. Gone for ever. And carrying on without them seems too heavy a burden to bear. But you must, Max. We both must. Neither of us has the luxury of falling apart at the moment.'

Nurse Fortunata came in. She was carrying a tray of tea. Now I knew why there was no Hunter.

Dr Stone looked from one to the other of us. 'If you

can truthfully assure me that both of you are as well as could be expected, then I'll leave you alone for an hour or so. Please use the time to talk to one another. Max, you need have no concerns over Matthew. He knows there's been an accident in Hawking, but no more. He has no reason to assume his father was ever here. He's happy and busy with Miss Lingoss. I advise you leave him with her for a day or so.'

Peterson nodded. 'He couldn't be in better hands, Max.'

I nodded. 'I know. And you're right. I will tell him. But not now.'

'No, definitely not now. Give it a day or so.'

Actually, I never told him. I just kept putting it off. I told myself I needed to get on grip on things myself first of all, so I could deal with his questions and emotions. Then I thought I'd put it off until after Hastings. Which made sense. And then after Hastings, summer was coming and he seemed happy and somehow the moment was never quite right and so on and so on.

He never asked what had happened in Hawking. It wasn't that he was incurious. He was very curious. Almost terminally so sometimes, according to Miss Lingoss, but I think, in his past life, he'd been discouraged from asking questions. Probably quite brutally discouraged. So he shut up, watched what was going on around him, took it all in and kept it all to himself. Occasionally I wondered about this, but he seemed happy, so I dodged the issue and told myself the right moment would present itself. One day.

They discharged me after a day or two. I collected Matthew from Miss Lingoss and made a pathetic stab at resuming a normal life. I kept us both busy. We had our daily routines and then in the evening there was television, his beloved jigsaws, a book at bedtime and his Time Map. I made sure there were little treats occasionally. I took him into town and we sat in the park and fed the ducks. At least, we did once I'd persuaded him to take out the bread he'd hidden in his pockets. The ducks were grateful and we had a Knickerbocker Glory afterwards, so everyone was a winner that day.

I've always been good at compartmentalising. You take the stuff you want and lay it out on the mantelpiece of your mind, all ready to be looked at and enjoyed in those quiet moments. The stuff you don't want – and doesn't that increase as the years go by? – gets shoved in a dark room somewhere at the back of your mind. To be forgotten. Slam the door. Turn the key. Walk away. It works for me.

I couldn't escape completely, of course. The day I left Sick Bay, Dr Bairstow sent for me.

He looked dreadful. Worse than me and I wasn't looking good these days. Leon had been his long-time friend. Ian Guthrie and Markham had both been with him on the day he first walked through the front doors of St Mary's.

'Good morning, sir.'

'Good morning, Max. How are you?'

'Absolutely fine, sir, thank you.'

He had the big screen set up at his briefing table.

Gesturing, he said, 'It's taken a while, but the technical

section has finally been able to restore a very little of the damaged footage from the cameras in Hawking. This is entirely your decision, of course, but we are now able to see exactly what happened. I've viewed the tapes. Several times, in fact. Do you wish to see them yourself? Please do not feel uncomfortable about saying no.'

I thought. Did I want to see them? Did I want to see Leon and Guthrie die? Or Markham, racing to help with no thought for his own safety. Did I want to see that?

Someone once asked me why I do this job. Why I – all of us – turn up at some of History's most gruesome moments and watch people die? I had replied that we should never turn away. That by turning away from those unpleasant events does not mean they cease to happen. These were three of the people I loved best in all the world. The least I could do was bear witness to their deaths. After all, didn't most of my job consist of watching people die?

'Yes, sir. I want to see.'

He gestured and we sat at his table. I remember how quiet his room was. All the familiar noises of St Mary's just seemed to fade away.

The screen blinked into life and, suddenly, I was back in Hawking, looking down from an unfamiliar angle.

The quality wasn't too bad. I clearly saw Number Five materialise. I saw my team depart, arguing. They passed out of shot.

I saw Dieter go in, and for a few minutes nothing happened. The picture jumped a couple of times and then I appeared in the doorway.

I saw myself look around, say something to Dieter,

heft my bag to a more comfortable position, and set off down the hangar towards the far doors and Sick Bay.

The image jumped again and suddenly, every light was flashing on and off in agitation. The soundtrack was crackly, but I could hear the alarms going off.

The picture jumped badly as the blast doors crashed together.

I saw Ronan's pod materialise from nowhere. Right slap bang in the central gangway between the pods. Between Number Three on the right and Number Four on the left. TB2 was behind him.

His door opened and there he stood, looking around.

Dr Bairstow adjusted the controls slightly, and everything slowed down.

I saw myself stand, frozen again. I was doing a lot of that recently.

I saw Leon's pod arrive, away to my left. The door slid open and there they were. Guthrie and Leon. Their visors were down, which I had forgotten. Such a simple detail, but I'd forgotten. Every time I had run the pictures through my memory, I'd been able to see their faces, even though I knew I hadn't – if you know what I mean. Just another example of my memory playing tricks on me.

I could see Ronan stand quite still. I peered closely at the screen and could swear he was smiling. Then he turned his head and saw me standing stock still a little way off.

'Excellent. Three birds with one stone.' I could hear the words quite distinctly.

The picture broke up and when it reassembled itself again, Markham was appearing from nowhere. I never did establish where he'd come from. He was just there, moving fast.

He tore past me, giving me a shove to get me moving. I couldn't make out his words, but that must have been when he was telling me to get out.

Leon and Guthrie stood as I'd last seen them, two or three steps away from their pod, thinking they had control of the situation. Until Ronan opened his hands and revealed his intentions.

The picture jumped again and then I was racing down the hangar towards Dieter, who grabbed my arm as I passed, and yanked me inside the pod. I saw the door close.

I saw Ronan say something. Sound quality was not so good now.

Ronan turned directly towards the cameras, smiled and bowed, his arms held wide. He kissed his hand to the camera.

And then – one after the other – like a juggler at the circus – he casually tossed the two blinking devices high into the air.

And now it was just a blur of motion. And then everything went black. For five or six seconds, this time, and when eventually it was restored, there was nothing like the clarity there had been before.

Actually, there wasn't anything there that had been before. The original camera must have been destroyed in the blast because this one had a different point of view. This was the one from Leon's office down at the other end of the hangar. The picture was very grainy, due, in no small part, to the swirling mass of dust and dirt inside the hangar.

But not all the dust and dirt in the world could conceal the damage. There was no sign anywhere of Leon's or Ronan's pods. Just a huge crater in the concrete floor. TB2 was a mangled wreck. A large lump of it was embedded in Number Seven. Number Eight had been blown off its plinth and slammed back into the hangar wall. As had Three. Four was completely destroyed. Shattered pieces of twisted metal lay everywhere. Number Five, still with me and Dieter inside, lay on its side, half on and half off its plinth.

Everything was gone. Nothing was left alive. The only movement was the clouds of dust and smoke swirling around the hangar before being sucked upwards through the gaping hole that had been the roof.

I swallowed. I was looking at the stuff of nightmares. Hawking was devastated. Just like me. Just like my life.

The whole roof was completely gone. Just like Leon. And Guthrie. And Markham.

I heard Ronan's voice. *'No Maxwell. You're going to live. Everyone else in your world will die but you'll live on. You'll look back on today and wish I had killed you.'*

Hawking had been built like a fireworks factory, with strong walls and a weak roof, so that in the event of any explosions, the blast wouldn't spread outwards, but would be channelled harmlessly up through the roof. Because roofs can be replaced. And electrics. And pods. And equipment. Everything could be replaced. Except for Guthrie. And Markham. And Leon. They were gone for ever. Blown out of existence.

'You'll look back on today and wish I had killed you.'

I blinked, trying to see through the cloud of brownish yellow dust and smoke swirling upwards, taking with it everything that was left of Leon. Somewhere in all that murk, his scattered atoms and molecules were about to begin a new journey. Making their lonely way around the universe. On their way to become something else. In the fullness of time they might become a tiny part of a new star. Or a new planet. Or a new mountain. Or a new person, even. But no matter how long they travelled and no matter how long the universe continued, they would never again assemble in the combination that had been Leon Farrell.

On that bright sunny morning, I stared at the blurred picture and finally accepted that, dead though he might be, Ronan had won.

I don't know for how long I sat there. I think it was some considerable time. At some point, Dr Bairstow had switched off the screen and was watching me.

I took a deep shuddering breath. Fortunately, he didn't seem to expect me to say anything.

'Listen to me Max. You and I have known each other for a very long time now. You may be wondering why I wanted you to watch that. You must understand that, no matter how painful it is to accept, Leon is dead. I know you well. Don't tell me that somewhere, deep down, you weren't convinced that somehow, against all the possibilities, Leon had not been killed. To continue to harbour such false hope is futile.'

He was right. I hadn't even realised I was doing it, but I hadn't accepted Leon was dead. A small part of me was still expecting the knock on the door that would tell me there had been some dreadful mistake and that they were all alive. Was that why I hadn't told Matthew his father was dead? Because, deep down, I hadn't really believed it?

He continued. 'It would have eaten away at you and prevented you continuing with your life. Sooner or later – and you know as well as I, Max, that sooner is usually better than later – you must accept the fact that Leon is dead. That they are all dead.'

I nodded. The silence in his room was very heavy.

I sighed. 'Ronan got them, sir.'

'I prefer to think that they got him.'

I shook my head. 'Too high a price.'

'They didn't think so. Neither did Mr Markham who died doing his duty.'

He sat in silence for a very long time. 'They were almost the last you know. There's only Mr Evans left.'

'The last, sir?'

'The last of those who walked through the front doors with me the day I opened St Mary's. Guthrie, Murdoch, Ritter, Randall, Weller, Evans and Markham. Good men all of them. But yes, Max, for once we find ourselves in complete agreement. Too high a price.'

He looked out of the window.

I was suddenly aware of why the silence was so … silent. 'Your clock has stopped, sir.'

'What?'

'Your clock, sir. It's stopped.'

'Oh yes, I'm afraid it has. It has been on its last legs for some time. I believe that the blast has dislodged or

242

damaged some vital part.'

I knew how it felt.

'You should fix it, sir.'

'Should I? Why is that?'

'Markham always said it gave him something to focus on when he was being … the object of your displeasure. It wasn't that he wasn't listening – although we both know he probably wasn't – it just took his mind off things. It's a kind of tradition with us, sir. We stand in your office, listen to your clock, accept our punishment, and survive to return another day.'

He smiled sadly. 'I have always been an advocate of tradition.'

I got up to go. I had a great need to be alone. 'Was there anything else, sir?'

'Not today, no. I understand you are off to Hastings next week.'

'Yes, sir.' I pulled out my scratchpad. 'Mr Dieter says we can use Pods Six and Eight.' He already knew this. Again, he was easing me back into the real world. 'It's cutting things a bit fine, but Mr Dieter has confirmed he can have both the pods and their plinths serviceable in time. After that, everything is on hold until permanent repairs can be effected.'

'If you feel you would rather not…'

'No, thank you, sir. I'd like to go.'

Because when everything else has gone; when everyone else has left you; when all you had is lost for ever – there is always duty. For me, the one certainty in this world that was without Leon.

'As you wish. By the way, at their request, I have

243

given a copy of the tape to the Time Police.'

'Why?'

'There was a third person in their pod. The driver.'

Oh God, I hadn't even thought.

'Sir, I'm so sorry. Please tell me it wasn't Captain Ellis. Or Miss Van Owen.'

'I'm sorry, Max, I can't do that.'

'Who?'

'Miss Van Owen was piloting the pod.'

Poor Greta Van Owen. Her life ruined once. And then taken from her too soon.

'They wish to conduct their own investigation and I welcomed the opportunity to be able to assist.' He sighed. 'Relations between us are good at the moment. I would be happy if they could remain that way, but our two organisations do seem fated to misunderstand each other.'

I nodded. We did, didn't we?

It had rained for Helen's funeral, but the day of Leon's, Guthrie's and Markham's service was fine and warm, with the sun shining on bright, fresh green leaves and shy spring flowers. The sort of day when it was good to be alive. A nice kick in the teeth from Mother Nature.

Lingoss had taken Matthew to the cinema in Rushford. Which he adored. They would be back in time for tea.

The Time Police had sent a delegation. Captain Ellis and Charlie Farenden escorted Elspeth Grey. She, I, and a white-faced Hunter sat together. It crossed my mind that it wasn't so very long since we'd sat here for Helen.

There were three coffins. I felt a dreadful laughter bubbling up inside me. An explosion that size wouldn't have left anything worth burying. Were we solemnly interring kitchen waste? Or builder's rubble? Or unwanted files? I pressed my mouth together and looked at my hands and struggled not to give way completely. I looked up at the Boards of Honour. At the three names, freshly inscribed underneath Helen's name. Our four top people gone in only a few months.

I thought of Leon – all he'd ever wanted was a family. I thought of Dr Bairstow and his lifelong unspoken grief for Annie Bessant. I thought of Helen Foster, and of Mary Schiller. Of Jamie Cameron and Big Dave Murdoch. Of Ian Guthrie, who had saved me at Troy. And of Markham – always just one surprise after another. They had, all of them, been good people. People who had left this world a better place. People who had died before their time.

I looked around. Sunshine streamed in through the stained-glass windows. Glorious pools of blue, green and red reflected off the walls and floor, contrasting with St Mary's – a solid mass of black in our formal uniforms. A few people were crying but most stood, stony-faced and still.

Outside in the cruel sunshine, the three of them were laid alongside each other. I was saying goodbye to Leon for ever. I couldn't get my head around it at all. Leon was gone. I stood quietly while something inside me howled like a wounded animal. I thought of the words of Henry Vaughan.

'They are all gone into the world of light. And I alone sit lingering here.'

After the service, people drifted away, leaving the three of us together. We stood, still and silent, like so many monoliths under a winter moon. I can only remember the disbelief. He was gone. Leon was gone. He was just – gone.

Grey stirred. 'I always thought it would be me,' she said.

I nodded. 'I always thought it would be me, too.'

Hunter sighed. 'I always knew it would be him.'

There was a small gathering afterwards. I can't begin to say how kind everyone was, and it really didn't help at all. The worst moment was when someone said, 'You've had a really shit year, Max.'

And someone else said, 'Yes, a real *annus horribilis*,' and we waited for Markham to make some comment about a horrible anus and there was a sad little silence, because the hole left by his death – all their deaths – was unfillable.

That evening, after the service, I was in my room with Matthew. I asked him to tell me about the movie he'd seen that afternoon and he managed to outline the entire plot in about four words. We'd done half an hour on the jigsaw, watched a programme about a boy who had adventures with his robot, which I suspected was giving him ideas I wasn't going to be able to cope with later on, and we'd had the book at bedtime. I'd told him to clean his teeth – something he couldn't see the point of at all, and he'd stumped into the bathroom in a bit of a mood.

He emerged from the bathroom. I wiped the foam off his mouth.

'Where's Daddy?'

'I'm not sure. Bed now.'

'Not sleepy.'

'You can have the Time Map for half an hour.'

He played for a while. I watched him whizzing great lumps of Time Map around the room while I put his clothes away. By the time I'd finished, he was asleep.

I had a long bath and decided against pouring myself a stiff drink because that wasn't a road I wanted to go down. I stood looking out of the window into the dark. It occurred to me that this was exactly what Peterson had done. I sighed, wondering whether I would be able to put my life back together this time. And actually, did I want to?

Someone knocked at the door. Initially, I ignored it, hoping whoever it was would take the hint and go away. Fat chance. This is St Mary's. Hint-taking is something that happens to other people. Whoever it was knocked again.

I opened the door. Peterson stood in front of me. He'd changed from his formal uniform and was wearing an old pair of jeans and a T-shirt.

I swallowed my surprise and held the door open for him.

He sat on the sofa. I softly closed Matthew's door and sat alongside.

'How are you, Max?'

I shrugged. 'I don't know.'

'Can I do anything?'

I looked at my lap. 'Does it ever go away?'

He said quietly, 'No, but it does become easier to bear.'

I nodded, still not looking at him.

'Max, this too will pass. You'll rebuild your life.'

'I'm not sure I want to. It seems to me that every time I build it up then someone knocks it right back down again. Every time. The moment comes when any sensible person says, "Enough. Leave it. It's just not worth it any longer."'

'You don't mean that.'

'I think I do. I'm lost and alone, and I'm not sure I have the strength to pick myself up again. And why would I want to? It's not as if I've ever…'

'That's not true. Listen. I wouldn't be here if it wasn't for you. Bashford and Grey would be dead in Colchester. You saved Dr Bairstow at the Crystal Palace. You gave young Hoyle something to die for. You're part of the framework on which this organisation hangs, Max, so don't try to tell me you're not worth anything. You're the most important person in my life, and it terrifies me to hear you say such things.' His voice wobbled. 'And what about that little boy next door? What will he do if anything happens to you? For God's sake, Max, you must stop thinking like this. You and I are the only ones left. Please don't you leave me, too.'

We were both crying now and perhaps it was what we both needed. I wondered if he'd cried over Helen, or had he kept it all deep inside. I buried my face in his shoulder. He put his arms around me. I could feel his tears in my hair.

After a long time, I pulled back, kissed his cheek and said quietly, 'Give me a minute.'

While I was in the bedroom, he'd put the kettle on.

When I came out, he somewhat shakily handed me a mug of tea. We sipped quietly together.

'I forgot to ask you, why have you come to see me?'

'What? Oh, no particular reason – I just came to see how you were and to say – well, if you don't want to be alone tonight then I'm happy to stay – on the sofa, obviously – not that I meant – I mean – will you stop looking at me like that.'

'Oh, Tim – smooth as a cheese grater. No wonder Helen was so drawn to you.'

I stopped. I hadn't meant to say that. I hadn't meant to bring up Helen. There was a long silence, and then he said, 'What do you think of our new doctor?'

I wondered if he wanted to change the subject.

I said cautiously, 'He seems OK. What do you think?'

'He wants to syringe my ears. I wasn't keen.'

I couldn't help laughing. 'What are you so afraid of?'

'That's what he said. He asked me if I'd had it done before and I said yes, but the way Helen did it, it was like waterboarding but with clean ears afterwards. And then he looked at me a long time and told me to talk to you about Helen.'

I suddenly realised our new doctor was a very clever young man. Because Tim wanted to talk about Helen. Finally, he wanted to talk about Helen.

We did. We talked about Helen for hours. And then we talked about Leon. We talked all night, sitting together, drinking tea, remembering, and watching the moon move across the sky, and when the sun came up the next morning, it was the beginning of a new day for both of us.

They slung tarpaulins over Hawking and we carried on. We'd get Hastings out of the way and then effect permanent repairs. We had no choice really. We had to keep going. We'd only just reinstated ourselves in Thirsk's good books and presentation dates were looming.

I took the Hastings briefing myself. I didn't want to. I wanted to sit quietly in my room, but I had to come out sometime, and the longer I left it, the harder it would be.

I decided to hold it in my office, rather than the Hall, requested refreshments from Miss Lee, made sure we had enough chairs, requested refreshments from Miss Lee, distributed briefing notes, and informed Miss Lee that if tea and biscuits were not forthcoming right now then I'd transfer her to Professor Rapson and see what she made of that. She crashed around for ten minutes but at the end of it we had tea and biscuits. I would have gloated, but she seated herself at her desk, ready to take notes with such a grumpy expression that I let it go. There was enough conflict in my life.

Present were Clerk, North, Sykes, Atherton, Bashford, Evans and Keller from Security, with Dieter and Lindstrom representing the Technical Section. Mr Lindstrom – for whom the word sapling could have been invented as a description – was famous for his nervousness around women. With both North and Sykes in the same room as him – equally terrifying in their own, separate ways – Dieter was acting as an enormous buffer zone and Mr Lindstrom was sheltering gratefully in his shadow.

I began. 'Good morning, everyone. Thank you for coming. Firstly – as you've guessed, notwithstanding recent events, we are proceeding with the Hastings assignment as normal. Mr Dieter informs me he can have Pods Eight and Six ready for next Monday. After the completion of this assignment, Hawking will be shut down while permanent repairs are effected and the pods rebuilt.'

'Do we have a completion date?' asked North, managing to sound critical as usual, but she was only a squashed insect on the windscreen of Dieter's good nature.

'Months,' he said, stretching his long legs in front of him.

'Can you be more specific?'

He thought for a while and then turned to consult Mr Lindstrom. The two of them held a whispered conversation, and then Dieter turned back again.

'Many months.'

Sykes coughed and I ploughed on.

'Right, situation update. The Pope has ruled that Harold is a perjurer and given William a consecrated banner as a token of papal support. The deal is that William will hold England as a fief of Rome and pay tribute to the Pope.'

'Always good to see an impartial decision,' muttered

Bashford.

'Because of this, England is in turmoil. In what many people see as a punishment from God, the northern army has been shattered. The Normans have landed in the south. Harold is racing down from Stamford Bridge, and just to make things even worse – Halley's Comet is back. This is a deeply superstitious age, and the Norman propaganda machine has swung into action, claiming the sighting is in their favour, although even William has been heard to mutter that in that case, it's pointing in the wrong direction.

'In England, the comet is widely regarded as a sign of God's anger at Harold the Oath Breaker and the Normans are quick to capitalise on this. William of Jumièges says it portends a change in kingdoms. And it will, one way or another because if William had failed at Hastings, then it would have been very unlikely he'd have found his dukedom waiting for him, even if he had survived the battle and returned home. Always willing to utilise the social media of the day, the Normans later incorporate the appearance of the comet into their version of Facebook, the Bayeux Tapestry.'

Sykes pulled out her scratchpad. 'Yes, everyone seems to feel it was a bad sign for the English. Elmer of Malmesbury seems to have taken the comet's appearance quite personally. He says, "You've come, have you? … Source of tears to many mothers, you evil. I hate you. It is long since I saw you, but as I see you now you are much more trouble, for I see you brandishing the downfall of my country. I hate you." Strong stuff.'

'It certainly is. Everyone knows this is a fateful time.

This is a key point in History. There are many of those, obviously, but this is one of the … key-est.'

It was only a very tiny joke, but people smiled, relaxed and reached for the biscuits. This was better.

'Right then, back to specifics. Harold has won at Stamford Bridge. His losses are heavy however and he's forced to march south to meet William, leaving the northern army behind to regroup under Earls Morcar and Edwin and follow on as best they can.

'He spends a few days in London, resting his men, recruiting, replenishing supplies, and repairing weapons. They finally set off, picking up the shire levies on the way, arriving at Caldbec Hill on the night of the 13th October. Eighteen days after Stamford Bridge. It's a good position – on a slight rise with good all-round visibility. And close to Duke William's forces camped only eight miles away.

'On to William now. He's been busy since we last saw him. He's sent out a call to anyone and everyone, offering land, money, or both, for their support. Adventurers and mercenaries have flocked to his banner. Reports say he was able to put together nearly seven hundred ships. They carried twelve thousand mounted men and twenty thousand men at arms.

'The fleet lands between Pevensey and Hastings, where William strengthens an existing Roman stronghold and then pushes on towards Hastings, where he builds the first of his trademark motte and bailey castles.

'Harold is still in London at this point, and would have done better to have waited there and drawn William further and further from the coast, but he's sworn an oath that William will not advance into England,'

'Oh,' said North, nastily. 'He's going to keep that one, is he?'

Sykes opened her mouth to respond and then jumped in the manner of one kicked under the table by Mr Bashford.

I moved hastily along. 'William has been at Hastings for two weeks. His troops are fresh and ready to go, but he has to move soon, because his supplies are running out and feeding his army is becoming a problem. Harold's arrival solves this for him. He cannot afford to be surrounded and starved into submission. He must close with Harold as soon as possible.

'The battle will take place the next day. No one knows why Harold allowed his hand to be forced in this way. He's known to be impetuous and impatient, however, and let's face it, politically and personally, these two have been at war for years. Perhaps they just can't wait to get at each other. Any questions so far?'

Nope. I pulled out a map of the battleground.

'Right. Mr Bashford, Miss Sykes and Mr Evans will be with me in Number Eight. I looked over at Dieter who gave me a confident thumbs up.

'Mr Clerk, Miss North, Mr Atherton and Mr Keller will be in Number Six…'

Again, I looked at Dieter, whose thumb was slightly less confident this time.

'Number Eight will be behind Harold's lines. We'll be a good way back with the Andredsweald Forest to protect our rear.

'By the way, you will have noticed that Mrs Enderby

is not present today. Hastings is a long and bloody struggle, people. The Saxon army will be almost obliterated. Even the Norman losses are not much less. This is a battle for a kingdom. To the death. Dr Bairstow has forbidden us to leave the pods, so no costumes will be required.'

'Why do we need security then?' enquired Atherton.

'Insurance,' said Evans with a grin, and whether they would be there to keep invaders out or us in was anybody's guess, and Evans certainly wasn't saying.

I was pleased with the way this briefing was going. We'd all suffered a huge personal loss – our hangar was wrecked, our pods destroyed or damaged, but we were still functioning.

'The other pod, Number Six, will be situated just north of the Hastings Road.' I pointed to the map. 'You'll be to the east of William's army, again on a slight rise. You should have an excellent view.

'Inside your mission folders you will find details of the composition of both armies, and a map of the battlefield and the surrounding area. Each team will focus on their own particular protagonists, while Mr Atherton will give us an overview of the whole battle. It's going to be a long day, people, so team leaders make sure both pods are well provisioned.

'Any questions?

There were none.

'Right, we meet in Hawking at 09:30 Monday morning. Thank you, everyone.'

We arrived an hour before dawn on the 14th October. I

called up Number Six. Clerk reported they were all present and correct. We wished each other good luck and closed the link.

Remembering the stuffiness at Stamford Bridge, we had the door open while we could, listening in the dark. In the distance we could hear the noises made by tens of thousands of men, their horses, the armourers, blacksmiths, cooks and so on. You can't keep an army quiet. We could see their cooking fires dotting the landscape. An occasional voice was raised in song.

'This time tomorrow it will all be over,' I said.

'It will all be gone,' said Bashford. 'A nation, a way of life, a culture, a language.'

'Not so,' said Atherton. 'Yes, it all disappears for a while, but it's the Normans who eventually vanish, don't they? Swallowed up, you could say. And what emerges three hundred years from today, is England and the English.'

We stood quietly, radiating Englishness. Except for Sykes, of course, proud daughter of Caledonia, stern and wild.

The sun rose and we got cracking.

Admittedly, we were a long way off, but it did seem to us that it was William who made the effort to avoid the conflict.

We watched his envoys leave the Norman lines, unarmoured, cantering easily up the hill. A small force detached themselves from the Saxon ranks and met them half way. Harold's personal banner, the Fighting Man, fluttered above them. His other emblem, the Red Dragon of Wessex, remained with his army.

If this was what we thought it was, then William was offering Harold all the land north of the Humber and promising to confirm him as Earl of Wessex. I suspected the Saxons would be informing the Normans that Harold already ruled over all the land north of the Humber, and was not only already Earl of Wessex, but King of England to boot.

The Normans would go on to remind them of Harold's oath – his very public oath – to support William's claim to the throne. They would go on to advise Harold that he was forsworn, a perjurer and that the Pope, Alexander II, had excommunicated him from the church.

This last was a big thing. The pronouncements of a pope a thousand miles away might seem unimportant to us today, but in this time, to be excommunicated was the worst thing that could happen to anyone. Worse even than death. Because if you died then your soul went unshriven and you couldn't get into heaven.

Harold would remind them the oath was extracted by trickery and therefore not valid. Neither side would budge from their points of view and the parley would fail.

The battle was about to begin.

We weren't sure what to expect. All the primary sources contradict each other. We knew the battle started around nine in the morning and would last until sunset. We knew that it took place seven miles north of Hastings. And we knew that William won. Apart from that...

We were crouched at the console, cameras rolling already so we could identify which banner belonged to whom on our return to St Mary's. We had the sound turned up, all ready to go. The uneasy calm dragged on. Both sides were contemplating the other. Horses stamped and snorted. Occasionally, one would rear up with impatience, unsettling those on either side of him. Their riders would haul them back under control again and the silence would resume. The Saxons were motionless, their banners hanging limply in the heat. If William though he could tempt them down from their advantageous position, then he was very much mistaken.

And advantageous it was. His men might be exhausted from their recent forced marches to and from Stamford Bridge, but Harold had commanded them to dig a ditch and embankment. Atop the embankment the Saxons had piled breastworks – a combination of thickly packed brushwood and outward-facing stakes to deter the cavalry.

259

They looked impregnable.

'Here we go,' said Bashford and at the same moment, trumpets sounded and to roars of encouragement from the Norman ranks and shouts of derision from the Saxons, William opened the batting with his archers – moving them up the hill until they were within range.

The Saxons hooted their contempt at this move and they were right.

William's archers might have proved their worth across the Channel, but here they were useless. They were shooting uphill and the angle was wrong. Many arrows overshot, flying uselessly over Saxon heads. Others thudded impotently into Saxon shields.

They were worse than useless, in fact. The Saxons didn't use bows in battle – axes and swords were their weapons of choice – and because there was no returning fire, the archers soon ran out of arrows, and suddenly, far from being an effective fighting force, they were alone, exposed and defenceless.

Even worse – for the archers, that is – the Saxons might not have had arrows, but they did have axes, stones, and excellent throwing arms. Missiles rained down upon William's unprotected men.

More trumpets sounded, and with a roar, William's infantry hurled itself up the hill. Shouts of '*Dex Aie*' – God Aid Us – filled the air.

Brandishing their spears and swords, they surged up the hill like the tide coming in, smashing their way through the breastworks. They negotiated the ditch only to run full tilt into the shield wall. The almighty crash was drowned out by the guttural Saxon, '*Ut! Ut! Ut!*'

In vain did the infantry strive to reach the enemy, safe behind their wall of shields. They crashed to the ground in their scores. The Saxon axes easily penetrated the Norman armour. The ditch was fast filling up with Norman dead and wounded and the Saxons hadn't given one single inch.

'Bloody hell,' said Bashford. 'They're going down like flies. However did William manage to win this?'

The answer being, of course, that William didn't win it – Harold lost it.

And now, William unleashed his cavalry. Slowly at first, the horses moved forwards – a sea of colour and pennants. The remains of the Norman infantry slipped back through the advancing cavalry. As soon as they were clear, the riders picked up the pace.

They thundered up the hill in two long, solid lines. We could feel the earth shake from all the way back here. There were no lances – the ground wasn't suitable – but the riders leaned forwards, swords raised, a solid mass of horseflesh bearing down on the Saxon front line, now only yards away.

The remains of the breastworks shattered on impact, but for William's knights, the ditch was not so easily overcome. The front rank of horses floundered and lost momentum. Some fell into the ditch, dragging their riders down with them. Some of the second rank went down as well, their horses crashing to their knees, and many, unable to stop, rode straight over the top of their fallen comrades.

The ditch was full of panicking horses, heads straining, their eyes rolling, forelegs scrabbling in panic as they struggled to escape, their massive iron-shod hooves trampling those around them. Their riders were scarcely less terrified, clambering over each other in their desperation to escape before another wave of horses crashed down on top of them.

We could hear the screaming and the war cries from those so far uninjured, but easily over everything we could hear the Saxons, still in place and still shouting their battle cry. 'Out! Out! *Ut! Ut!*' A terrifying sound, especially when they clashed their axes on their shields in time with the words.

With his archers out of the game, his spearmen in retreat and much of his cavalry down, things really weren't going well for William, who showed his true valour at this crucial moment. Love or loathe the man, he was a leader to his fingertips. He led the next charge, making himself an easy target as his personal banner followed along behind him. The now familiar golden lions of Normandy rose above the chaos of the battlefield. We still have lions on our flag today.

His huge white destrier galloped towards the Saxon lines, foam flying from his bit, with William seemingly dragging his Norman knights behind him by brute strength alone. His horse soared over the ditch, still filled with struggling horses and men. He met the shield wall with a roar, his sword arm rising and falling as he hacked at those standing between him and his kingdom.

It was a disaster. His presence made no difference at all. The shield wall never wavered. The Saxons repelled this attack as they had the others and stood firm, their lines unbroken.

For William, catastrophe beckoned. His left wing, led by Alain the Red and consisting mainly of Bretons, Poitevins and Rhine auxiliaries began to waver. Losses on this wing were particularly heavy. Beaten back by swords, stones, axes, javelins, and anything else that could be picked up and thrown at them, the entire left wing broke and fled. Men and horses turned tail and ran. The whole left side of William's army was collapsing. Fleeing for their lives. And worse, the centre and right wing began to give way as well.

It was so very, very nearly the turning point of the battle for William, and as if things couldn't get any worse, it was at this crucial moment that his standard bearer's horse was killed. I watched the lions waver and then, quite suddenly, they disappeared from view.

A huge groan went up from the Norman ranks. We could hear men shouting.

I couldn't make out the words over everything else happening at the time, but I guessed word was going out that the duke was dead. All across the Norman lines, men stopped. Swords fell. They looked ready to turn and run.

That's the one problem with a strong leader. This was William's army. They were William's men. Brought here on William's ships. To fulfil William's destiny. And without William, they might as well go home.

I think that was the thought uppermost in everyone's minds. Norman and Saxon alike. The Saxons clashed their shields, their guttural battle cries filled the air.

'There he is,' said Sykes suddenly, as a blood-splattered white horse broke free of the ranks, racing up and down in front of the Norman army. The rider pulled off his helmet and waved it above his head. It was William – still alive, still fighting, and obviously expecting everyone else to get on with it and do the bloody same.

His men recognised him. A shout went out. Slowly, ponderously, the Norman ranks began to reorganise themselves.

Not all of them were so easily recalled, however. The weak and wobbly left wing continued its headlong flight, as they thought, to safety. Sadly for them, they fell straight into the arms of the battling Bishop of Bayeux, William's half-brother Odo, last encountered at the oath-taking ceremony, and obviously determined not to let any of those inconvenient ecclesiastical vows of humility and forgiveness get in the way of a cracking good fight.

I knew the other team was focusing on William's army, and this was too good an opportunity to miss. 'There,' I said. 'Mr Bashford, focus on Odo, please.' Bashford nodded and angled a camera.

There has been some controversy recently about Odo's part in the battle. Whether he was, in fact, an early example of muscular Christianity. I can't speak for other occasions, but on this day it would be fair to say that Odo was a man who really knew how to encourage and inspire those suffering a temporary lack of bottle, and seeking the quickest exit from a bloody battlefield. I'm not sure whether, in our modern times, this skill is still listed as a 'must have' in a bishop's job spec – although I do know that when confronted with an egg-throwing critic outside her palace last year, the current Archbishop of Canterbury caught it neatly and threw it back. Apparently her popularity soared and even I have to say she damned near converted me on the spot when I saw it on TV that night.

Anyway, there was no doubt that Bishop Odo was a major factor in stemming the rout, laying about him with his own staff and driving the fleeing men back to face the Saxons. He was a big man, like his brother, and wearing an odd mixture of ecclesiastical robes and chain mail. Caught between a belligerent bishop on one side and savage Saxons on the other, the left wing opted – wisely, I think – for the Saxons.

The fortunes of war changed again.

While I'd been concentrating on Odo, a large number of Saxon men at arms, lacking the discipline of the thegns, had seen the fleeing Normans and wrongly assumed it was all over. They broke ranks, left the protection of the shield wall and streamed down the hillside after them. Now William's army showed its skill. A number of horsemen wheeled as one, reformed, and urged their horses back up the hill. Caught without protection, the Saxons were hopelessly exposed. Some tried to return to the safety of the Saxon lines and were cut down. Others tried to group together, to make a stand, and were ridden down by bloodstained horses. Only a small group remained intact and they were clustered around a body on the ground.

'Look,' said Sykes, leaning forwards and pointing at the screen.

Some five or six men had formed a defensive ring around someone who was very obviously dead and were endeavouring to hold off a small squadron of mounted knights.

'That must be Gyrth and Leofwine,' I said. 'Close ups, please.'

Gyrth and Leofwine were Harold's brothers and this was Leofwine's famous last stand. When his brother fell he refused to leave him, standing over his body until the end. Which wasn't far off. He shouted defiance, his two-handed axe whirling around his head. The Normans had learned to fear the Saxon axe. No one would engage him directly. They surrounded him with a wall of Norman knights, hiding him from view. We couldn't see what was happening. And then horses reared and plunged and snorted, trampling men and weapons into the earth, and when they rode away again, there was nothing left to see.

There are those who say that from that moment, after the loss of his two brothers, the fight went out of Harold. If it did, he hid it well.

I straightened my aching back and reached for some water. Sykes was concentrating on the Saxon lines, watching the gaps being plugged as reinforcements were brought up. That last manoeuvre had resulted in heavy losses on both sides.

It would have been a good moment for both sides to regroup, perhaps take a moment to readjust strategy or reform lines, but already, William was unleashing his cavalry again.

Again the cavalry thundered up the hill, sweeping away final remains of the breastworks. Again, the shield wall held. A long-handled Saxon axe was easily capable of cutting through both horse and rider. William was getting nowhere.

The fighting was vicious. Unhorsed knights fought

hand to hand with Saxon thegns who, shoulders to their shields, struggled to push them back. Those behind them joined in, like a giant rugby scrum, putting their backs into it, holding the front line firm and keeping the shields up, fulfilling their purpose, which was to stand firm, come what may. From behind them, long Saxon javelins stabbed over their shoulders, piercing Norman mail. Men screamed and fell backwards to be trampled by their fellows. Blood arced through the air. Horses reared and plunged and screamed. Axes cartwheeled to embed themselves into Norman skulls. And still the Saxon shield wall held.

There were bodies everywhere. Thousands of bodies. The Saxons were clearing their lines, carrying their dead and wounded back to the rear. The Normans had no such luxury, slipping and tripping over their fallen comrades. The pile of dead men and horses before the Saxon lines grew ever higher. The savagery was horrific. Even Agincourt hadn't been this bad.

I looked at the time. We were approaching noon. I could hardly believe three hours had passed already. The sun shone down from a cloudless sky on to the sweltering soldiers.

What was William thinking at this point? If he couldn't break the Saxon shields, then he couldn't possibly prevail. And if he couldn't prevail today then he had lost everything. The battle. His army. His chance at the throne. Probably his life.

There was blood everywhere. Every man was red with it. If not his then someone else's. Horses were bloodied up past their bellies. Everywhere lay limbs, heads, misshapen torsos, crippled and dead horses.

Still the missiles rained down upon the Normans, whose ferocity was slowing. Men and horses were exhausted in the heat. Some horses could barely stand, their eyes rolling white in exhaustion, their bits dripping blood flecked foam.

Now would be a good time to take a breather.

So now, of course, was the time William hurled his right wing into the fray. It was a mirror image of his actions only an hour or so ago. The right wing charged up the hill, banners flying, to hit the Saxons hard. Again the fighting was savage, each side pushing against the other but there was no way they could break the wall. Again, they fell back. And once again, the Saxon lines broke and a large part of the fyrd pursued them back down the hill.

'Why?' said Bashford puzzled at this Saxon stupidity. 'Why would they do that? Surely they saw what happened on the other wing?'

'No,' I said slowly, 'I don't think they did. Harold's forces are in a shallow U-shape. The right wing can't see the left wing. They have no knowledge of what happens to those who leave the shelter of the ditch and embankment.'

'They're about to find out,' said Sykes grimly.

Saxon figures poured down the hill, pursuing the fleeing Normans. Thousands of voices screamed in triumph.

'They think it's all over,' said Bashford.

'It is now,' said Sykes as once again the Norman centre crashed down upon them, surrounding them and cutting them off. Shouts of '*Dex Aie*' rose over the screams of the dying. There were no Saxon survivors.

And then, in a heartbeat, the fortunes of war again swung back the other way. As they do.

The Norman centre had gone too far too fast. Intent on returning to their own lines as quickly as possible, they fell victim to their unfamiliarity with the landscape. There was another reason why Harold had chosen this spot. The horses, plunging downhill back to their own lines, ran straight into a concealed ditch. None of them were able to stop in time. They fell, screaming, into the ditch and were crushed by those coming along behind.

We watched in silence, and then Sykes said, 'Was that the Malfosse incident?'

'I don't think so,' I said doubtfully, 'I think that occurred at the end of the battle and there's hours to go yet.'

She looked at the struggling men on the screen. 'Hard to believe they'll last that long.'

'Many of them won't.'

They had been fighting for hours and William had made no progress at all. The Saxons still stood around their two standards. Harold was making good on his promise not to cede one inch of English land. The ditches were full of bodies, lying in a tangle of bloody arms and legs. The breastworks had disintegrated. Absolutely nothing was left. Not even a few splinters to show where they had once been. The Saxon ranks were dreadfully thinned but the Fighting Man still stood, seemingly immoveable, and blocking William's path to the crown.

Presumably William thought so too, unleashing charge after charge up the hill. One after the other. Both sides met with a terrible impact and loss of life, but every time, the Normans were thrown back. Every time. The day was wearing on and still William was getting nowhere.

Around mid-afternoon, there was a lull. We all shot off to the bathroom – me first, because rank hath its privileges. I splashed water on my face and returned to my place at the console.

It would seem that William had used my absence to have a bit of a think. He desperately needed to rest his knights and their horses. New tactics were called for.

He recalled his archers. From somewhere they'd found or cut fresh arrows. It seemed a new strategy had been devised. Now the archers fired into the air, over the front ranks, their arrows falling on the largely unarmoured fyrd behind the shield wall. The Saxons could do nothing but stand and endure the storm of arrows that fell from the sky, blackening the sun, but those who had shields protected themselves and their comrades as best they could. Still they stood firm. It would seem that nothing William could do would ever shift them.

The sun was beginning to set, sitting over the horizon like a giant red ball in the sky, but no redder than the earth beneath. They'd been at it for hours and hours. William must be growing desperate. The longer the Saxons stood, the better the chance that the northern Earls, Morcar and Edwin, would turn up with the reinforcements and, on the hill in front of him, still the Saxons stood, greatly depleted but still obstinate and unbreakable.

Horns sounded again for yet another cavalry charge. Although a cavalry trot would have been more accurate. Some of the horses could barely get up the hill. They dashed themselves against the front ranks. The hand-to-hand fighting was ferocious. The Saxons were crowded together so tightly that there was no room for the dead to fall, but still the Normans couldn't break the line.

It seemed to me that the hail of Saxon missiles was thinning. Harold's army was running out of things to throw. Many of them were making do with simply clashing their axes against their shields and shouting, '*Ut! Ut! Ut!*' Well, why not? It had worked well for them so far.

The sun nearly gone. I could see mist rising from the marsh at the bottom of the hill. Where the day had been hot – now it was turning cold. If the Normans couldn't break them now…

William responded by hurling everything he had. The archers never let up, unleashing volley after volley, high into the air. The blood-splattered cavalry charged again. Spearmen ran up the slope, dodging through the horses. I'd never seen anything like it. The entire Norman army was hacking at the Saxon shield wall.

The Saxons took a weary grip on their weapons, steadied their shields against their shoulders and braced themselves through onslaught after onslaught.

The Normans were equally exhausted. Their knights were right up against the shield wall. Many were on foot. Both sides were slugging it out, face to face, so tired they could hardly raise their arms. Horses fell because they simply couldn't stand any longer.

It did the Normans no good at all. Horns sounded and William's forces disengaged and trailed slowly back down the hill again.

The light was nearly gone.

Thousands and thousands of men were dead. Brutally, horribly, bloodily dead. The fyrd was nearly gone. A few thegns still surrounded Harold. The Fighting Man and the Red Dragon still flew, but there were so few of them left.

The last light was fading. Surely it must be over. I knew how this ended but looking at the state of play now … I had no idea it had been so close. If William couldn't break the shield wall in the next few minutes, then he was finished. The northern levies would sweep down and between them and the survivors today, his exhausted army would be annihilated. I know – we all know – how Hastings ends, and yet I couldn't help wondering if I hadn't strayed into another universe somehow, and that in this one, Harold won. Or – always our main fear – by simply being here we had changed some tiny event which meant that William lost and Harold won. Which would be a bit of a bugger, not least because History would have something very terminal to say about that.

The sun was going. The Saxons were intact and the Normans finished. William would never get them up that hill again.

And then, unbelievably, a shout went up from the Saxon lines. A great groan of anguish and despair rippled outwards. The Fighting Man dipped.

Harold had fallen.

'What?' said Bashford in disbelief. 'When did that happen?'

'Close up,' I said. 'Find him. Quickly now.'

We focused on the milling confusion in the Saxon ranks.

'I can't find him,' said Bashford, panning back and forth.

'Me neither,' said Sykes.

'Concentrate on the area around the Fighting Man,' I said.

There was no time.

Horns were sounding and Norman heads lifting.

Weary men turned their horses around to confront a hill that must have seemed like a mountain. To give him his due, William was right up there at the front. Somewhere along the way he'd lost his white horse and now rode a black one. His tattered banner followed at his shoulder.

The horses could only advance at a walk. There was no more strength for thundering charges.

They walked up the hill, the men at arms following on behind them.

Orders rang out. Whether Harold lived or was dead already, the Saxons drew together. Both sides knew that these were the deciding moments. If the shield wall held then the Normans were beaten. Wiped out. After today none of them would survive to make the voyage home to Normandy.

If the shield wall crumbled then the Normans would swarm over the top of them, obliterating every last one of them, and that would mean the end of Saxon England for ever. It was make-or-break time.

The shield wall did not hold.

Men fell like trees. Holes began to open up that could not be filled. With roars of exultation and triumph, the Normans forced their horses through, trampling men too exhausted to crawl away. The foot soldiers followed. For a few minutes, the whole thing was just a massive mêlée and then, suddenly, the famous shield wall disintegrated. Odd pockets of resistance lingered, but the Normans had the scent of victory now. They were unstoppable.

We could barely make out what was happening and in this strange half-light our night vision wasn't much help.

I was simmering with frustration. Somehow, we'd missed Harold falling. I'd had every camera trained on that small area around the Fighting Man. If Sykes had got any closer she'd have been on the other side of the screen, but we'd missed it. And certainly no one was staggering around with an arrow poking out of their eye. Dusk was falling fast and there were just so many indistinguishable people – everyone was red with blood. All this time and effort and we were no nearer to establishing the cause of Harold's death. I could only hope that once we got all this lot downloaded and had a chance to go through it, frame by frame, that we would be able to establish, once and for all, how Harold died at Hastings.

The Fighting Man banner went first, slowly toppling sideways until it disappeared, never to rise again. A moment later, the Red Dragon of Wessex swayed violently as a group of knights hacked at it, and then it was cut down and lost.

His thegns fought. Dear God, did they fight. They grouped themselves into a tight bunch and fought like madmen. One by one they fell, gushing blood, limbs missing, pierced by many wounds. The survivors simply closed up, gritted their teeth and fought on.

They were massacred, almost to a man. None made

any effort to flee. They were Harold's men and their king had fallen – they saw no point in surviving him. Did they have some idea what was to happen to their nation? If they had fled and regrouped later, could they have mounted an effective resistance? Could they have tempered, somehow, William's brutal obliteration of Saxon culture? Useless to speculate. We could only watch as the Golden Lions of Normandy were raised up. Ten thousand Norman throats bellowed their victory.

We sat back in silence.

'Bloody hell,' said Bashford.

Lights sprang up as fires were lit. People took torches and began to move around the battlefield. I suspected Norman and Saxon alike were looking for Harold's body.

The whole area was a wreck. In some places, the bodies were piled three or four deep. Occasionally there was a movement as someone attempted to extricate themselves from underneath a corpse. Men tried to drag themselves away to safety, inching their way along on bleeding stumps. Horses stood among the corpses, heads down, exhausted or too injured to move.

The Norman wounded were being tended. Someone had put up a row of tents for William and his nobles. Someone somewhere was cooking something. I remembered William was famous for his hearty appetite.

Sykes put the kettle on and we sat down with a cup of tea. I called up the others. Their pod was closer to the battlefield than ours and I wanted to make sure there weren't any Normans trying to batter their way inside.

'We're fine,' reported North.

'Did you see Harold fall?'

'No – didn't you?' she said, with more than a hint of criticism. Sykes stiffened.

'Probably,' I said, loyal to my team. 'We covered

everything, so yes, almost certainly.'

I heard a muffled voice in the background and then she said, 'We have to go, Max – there's a procession of civilians arriving and there are women amongst them. I think this might be Harold's wife and mother, come to claim his body.'

These were the two most important women in the realm. Harold's mother, Gytha Thorkelsdóttir, would offer William Harold's own weight in gold in exchange for the body of her son. An offer William would refuse.

His handfasted wife, Edith the Swan Neck, or Edith Swanneschals, would identify Harold's body by certain marks apparently known only to her, and request permission to take the body away. Again, William would refuse. Wisely, I think. He wouldn't want Harold's resting place becoming a centre of resistance, although the legend persists that Harold received a Christian burial by the monks of Waltham Abbey.

This was an important moment. We might yet catch a glimpse of Harold's body and learn how he died.

I called up North. 'Can you see what's happening?'

'Of course not,' she said irritably. 'William's receiving them in his tent. Wait no, they're coming out. Hell and damnation!'

'What? What?'

'They're bringing up a body. It must be Harold. They've laid it on a bier. There's torches everywhere, but it's wrapped in a cloak and I can't see. I think the tall woman must be Edith. She's identifying the body and we can't bloody see it for everyone clustered around.'

Just for a moment, she sounded nearly human. And

exactly like a frustrated historian. I knew how she felt.

'What's happening? Tell me.'

'Well, he's treating both women with great respect. They don't seem to be subjected to any … jostling … They have an escort. Norman knights obviously. They seem to have been granted safe passage. They're talking. She's leaving now. Without the body. No – we've lost her in the crowd.'

'OK,' I said. 'Don't beat yourself up about it. We'll sort it all out when we get back. That's it people – start shutting things down. We'll jump back in thirty minutes.'

I sat back in my seat. This assignment hadn't been a complete success. Yes, we'd got the battle. We had some really good footage. Thirsk would be pleased. But unless we could identify Harold, we were no nearer to solving the mystery of his death. On the other hand, North had some shots of his mistress come to identify and claim the body, even if we didn't have any of the body itself.

I shifted my position and became aware my back was hot and sweaty. I realised we could really, really do with some fresh air.

I switched the internal lights to night mode and said to Evans, 'Can you cover the door?'

He nodded, took out a stun gun and took up position by the open door. Cool, damp air flooded in and we all breathed a sigh of relief.

It wasn't quiet out there. Apart from the ordinary noise made by thousands of men moving around or talking, we could still hear the cries of the wounded. A horse would neigh occasionally. Someone would shout an order or there would be a burst of laughter. I suspected the wine was going around.

I stepped to the door to look outside. It still wasn't completely dark. A glow of lighter sky hung over the horizon. I took a moment to take it all in. I was at Hastings. The Battle of Hastings had just been played out in front of us and we'd been there. We'd seen it. All of it. Except for Harold, of course. I was suddenly impatient to get back to St Mary's to view the footage and work out what was what.

I turned to step back into the pod and at the same moment, a proximity alert pinged and Evans pulled me inside.

Bashford said, 'Door,' because they were either fleeing Saxons who wouldn't let anyone or anything get in the way of their escape, or they were Normans, despatched to dispose of any survivors. Neither would be good for us.

'Two or three people,' said Bashford, studying the readouts. 'No, four or five. Maybe more. It's hard to say. They're not moving very quickly.'

'Men searching for cover? Looking to hide somewhere?'

'Even slower than that. I don't know.'

'Are they within range?'

'I think so. Just a minute.' He angled a camera.

I saw dark figures, perhaps six or seven of them. One man led a horse which appeared to be dragging some sort of litter. They were moving very slowly. Because the litter carried a wounded man. And one of the figures was a woman.

Every historian in the pod stiffened. Like a collection of gun dogs pointing at their quarry. All quivering noses, pricked ears and outstretched tails.

'No,' said Evans in alarm, moving in front of the door and blocking our way.

'It's only for a moment.'

'Out of the question.'

'It's our job.'

'And this is mine.'

I yanked open a locker and pulled out a blanket, tying it around me like a cloak.

'Then you can tell Dr Bairstow there's a possibility that Harold Godwinson passed within twenty feet of us and we didn't check it out.'

'Still preferable to telling Dr Bairstow I let three historians stumble around in the dark during the aftermath of a big battle.'

'Don't be silly,' I said. 'There's no way I'd let three historians stumble around in the dark during the aftermath of a big battle.'

He relaxed.

'I'll go by myself.'

There was a storm of protest from everyone else in the pod. Historians hate being left behind but, as I said, it was far too dangerous for them to go outside, and Bashford said that was kind of the point. Evans said he never thought he'd find himself in agreement with an historian, and while they were beaming at each other, I got the door open.

Evans sighed. 'You two stay put. You…' he looked at me … 'stay with me at all times. Mess me about in any way and I'll shoot you myself.'

'OK.'

We slipped out of the pod.

They were heading towards us so all we had to do was move towards them, step into deep shadow and wait. The horse plodded slowly, his head held low. This was no warhorse, but an old farm horse, watching where he put his feet.

We drew back further and waited. Waited to see whether this actually was Harold Godwinson being smuggled from the battlefield. And whether he was still alive.

How had they managed this? Had they had some sort of contingency plan, or was the idea hatched as Harold fell? It was vital to get him away to safety, so he'd been smuggled away and Edith Swan Neck, having waited nearby, goes to William and begs for his body. She identifies *a* body, mangled beyond recognition apparently, by marks conveniently known only to her, and while she's distracting everyone, the real king is sneaked away.

William would be desperate for confirmation that Harold was dead. Especially if, far from meeting a noble end on the battlefield, he was castrated and chopped to pieces by four knights, one of whom might have been William himself, viciously venting his frustration on a helpless enemy. He certainly wouldn't want that story getting around, so he supported the story of the arrow in the eye. A much more chivalrous and above all, politically acceptable story, than he and his knights hacking a helpless man to death.

And then, out of the darkness comes Harold's mistress, conveniently identifies Harold beyond doubt. requests his body, probably knowing the request will be refused, and disappears back into the night again. Everyone's problems are solved. William has an identified body and Edith is able to sneak the still living king away to safety. Because if William had even the slightest doubt that Harold was not dead, he would tear the country apart to get at him. So here they were, smuggling Harold Godwinson into the night and out of History.

The shadows were dark and we never made a sound but they found us, nevertheless. In an instant, we were surrounded by a ring of swords. The horse stood patiently with his burden.

'Don't move,' said Evans. I wasn't going to. We were in some deep shit here. Two sword thrusts and we were bleeding to death in the undergrowth while they vanished back into the dark. And they would kill us – no doubt of that – they would kill to keep their secret.

Still no one had spoken. I'm not sure why they were hesitating. We obviously weren't Norman knights – had they taken us for locals? Was it possible everyone felt enough Saxons had died today? Or was this just wishful thinking on my part?

I turned my head to look at the man on the litter. I might as well know the truth before I died. I had nothing to lose.

I wasn't the only one who was going to die tonight. I looked at the ruined and blood-soaked man in front of me. A bloody bandage covered one side of his face, including his eye. So no clue there. One leg was gone above the knee. And I was pretty sure he had been castrated, as well. I struggled to compare this broken man with the mighty figure I had seen at Beaurain. Or Stamford Bridge.

There are all sorts of stories, of course. Some say that Harold survived the battle and went abroad. Others that he remained in England but lived out his days as a hermit. Although looking at the state of him, my guess was that if he wasn't dead now then he very soon would be. I'd seen Harold Godwinson in his prime and I couldn't believe that, while he had breath in his body, he would not have come back to fight the usurper William every inch of the way. The crown of England would have sat very uneasily on William's head. My guess was that he would die this night.

On the other hand, there are those stories...

So now what?

We had an uncomfortably large number of swords pointing at us. They weren't going to run the risk of us giving them away. We were going to die.

The silence just dragged on. I could hear the horse breathing. I could certainly hear my own heart pounding away.

And then, not too far away, a horse neighed. Two men immediately muffled the farm horse with their cloaks. It shifted uneasily but remained calm. I could hear voices – Norman voices – and the sounds of undergrowth being beaten down.

The escort glanced nervously over their shoulders. The riders were very close. What could they do? Any attempt to move would be heard. Staying put would lead to their discovery. Someone should do something.

Yes, well, we all know who that's going to be, don't we?

I put out both my hands, palms outwards, in the

traditional 'Stay where you are,' gesture.

They stared but stayed.

I said to Evans, 'Get yourself back to the pod.'

His response was unrepeatable, but the gist was that that wasn't going to happen.

I made one final 'Stay here and stay quiet,' gesture and turned to run.

'This way,' said Evans.

Always run downhill. Especially when you're trying to get away from a bunch of men on horses. We fled down the hill, making as much noise as we could. Which was a lot. We crashed through the undergrowth, snapping twigs and small branches as we went.

I enquired where we were heading to.

'As far away as possible,' he panted. 'Australia, perhaps.'

Wherever we were going, it was working. I heard shouts behind us, and a second later, the sound of hooves. Evans picked up the pace.

As far as I could tell, we were heading in a south-westerly direction, with the Andredsweald Forest behind us and to our right, into which, I hoped, Edith Swanneschals and her entourage were now disappearing as fast as they could go. I knew there was a stream somewhere around here and a lot of boggy ground nearby. If we could get to that then we might yet escape the horsemen.

Fat chance. Another group of them where thundering up the hill towards us. We were pushed northwards. Uphill. And now it was dark. I could barely see a thing.

'Keep going,' panted Evans. 'We'll get back into the

woods and climb a tree.'

They were gaining on us. The hooves sounded very close now. I heard a shout. They'd seen us.

We veered off left again. It was uphill and hard work. I could feel my breath rasping in my throat. My lungs were on fire. This was all Clive Ronan's fault. If I'd completed my run that day – and the next day, and so on – instead of having him crash into my life and throw everything into chaos, then today I'd be lithe, svelte, fit, athletic, whatever.

I fell over. I know – such a cliché. In films, when running from peril, it's always the silly little heroine who trips over her own feet. Sadly, life imitates art and I went down with a bloody great crash.

Evans screeched to a halt, whispering, 'Max?'

'Keep going, you pillock,' I said, struggling to disentangle my foot from something or other. 'Don't stop.'

He completely ignored me, turning back to kneel beside me.

And suddenly there were horses everywhere.

I pulled him down beside me. They had torches, but there was a slight chance they might miss us in the dark. We lay in the long, coarse grass, breathing into our sleeves so they wouldn't hear us panting.

I heard shouts of recognition as the two groups caught sight of each other and they both turned towards us.

'Shit,' whispered Evans.

Spurring their horses, they moved uphill, strung out in a long line that left us nowhere to go, all ready to flush us out.

'Shit,' said Evans again.

Now what? Did we stand up and run? Where to? Did we stand and fight? With what? Did we crouch and hope they'd miss us in the dark? I've heard that horses won't willingly stand on a human being, but with our luck, these horses would be ancestors of the infamous Turk, the horse allocated to me for side-saddle training, whose relationship with his rider included biting, kicking, rolling on, crushing, attempted drowning – and trampling.

I could hear the horses snorting as they increased their speed. They couldn't see us. Yet

We began to inch our way backwards. The torches were less than twenty yards away. They would be on us in seconds.

We were concealed by long grass and some of the prickliest brambles in south-east England, but they didn't have to see us to run us down. Which was probably what they intended to do. Yes, we both had stun guns, but frankly, who wants a stunned horse and its rider crashing down on top of them in the dark?

'Come on,' said Evans. 'We have to make a run for it. Stay with me.'

Someone shouted.

I don't know what happened next. I was nearly blind. Their torches had ruined my night vision. My ears were full of the sound of thundering hooves. They were almost on top of us. And then, someone shouted a warning. And then someone else screamed. The sound of hooves became confused. A horse neighed – high pitched in fear. And then another. I could hear furiously scrabbling hooves. And then a series of crashes. Men shouted in warning and in fear. More men were screaming. And horses too. The torches began to disappear, one by one.

Some went out, but some lay on the ground, still burning and giving us flickering glimpses of a dreadful scene.

My first, admittedly slightly overwrought, thought was that the ground had opened up beneath our feet, illuminating a scene from hell. But it was true. The ground had indeed opened beneath our feet. Here, at last, was the Malfosse. The Evil Ditch.

The story goes that a small group from William's forces, responding to the taunts of a bunch of anonymous Saxons, were lured into an area where long grass concealed a number of steep-sided and very deep ditches. Oh my God – were we those taunting Saxons? My heart turned over. What had we done?

No time to think about that now. Unable to see in the near darkness, the Normans had run straight into one of the open ditches. And they didn't just stumble and fall. They had been galloping headlong when the ground ended and the earth gaped for them. Horses had fallen headfirst, somersaulting over each other. We had heard the crack of broken backs and legs. Their riders, flying through the air, had hit the ground with bone-shattering force and lay helpless as they were either trampled to death or crushed by those falling in after them.

Another wave of horses and riders were following them in – tumbling and cartwheeling, to land with hideous impact. Huge, heavy destriers flew through the air as if they weighed nothing. Broken men and horses lay in a mangled mess of bodies and limbs. Any survivors of the initial fall couldn't possibly be saved and were perishing either from their injuries or suffocation.

The dying screams of fatally injured horses and their riders echoed through the gathering night. Down below, in William's camp, horns sounded the alarm. Already, we could hear the sound of hooves as Duke William, possibly fearing another Saxon army falling on his camp from out of the dark, despatched forces to investigate.

I tried to look away, but there are some things you can't unsee. I saw a horse, one of the first to fall, I guessed, wedged vertically, head down, trapped and suffocating beneath a mass of bodies. Its back legs were clear, and it kicked and kicked, legs flailing violently in its frantic efforts to be free, injuring all those around it. Even as I looked, its struggles weakened and then ceased.

A solitary, riderless horse ran past us, almost knocking me over, its reins flying loose. I caught a glimpse of a wild, rolling eye, and then Evans grabbed my arm.

'Come on. Uphill and to the left. Get into the trees.'

'But this is the Malfosse incident. I have to …'

'Listen. Guthrie's gone. Markham's gone. I'm in charge and I'm not losing you on my very first assignment. Get into the trees or I'll stun you and drag you there myself.'

Fair enough, I suppose.

We made no attempt at concealment, running as fast as we could for the cover of the forest, finally collapsing and crawling, panting, into a patch of scratchy brambles.

I could see lights moving uphill. Part of William's army was coming to investigate.

We crawled deeper under cover and I called up Sykes.

'Oh, hello Max. Everything all right?'

'A bit busy here, but I know what happened after the battle. I've just seen Edith Swanneschals making away with Harold. *And* he's still alive. *And* I've just witnessed the Malfosse incident. *And* there's any number of Normans on their way to investigate. *And* I'm trapped in a bramble patch with our Head of Security.'

'Oh dear,' she actually sounded sympathetic. 'Well, if he gets a bit frisky, you should fetch him one with a rolled-up newspaper.'

Bashford intervened. 'Do you know if Edith got Harold away?'

'She must have. There's no report of him being captured after the battle and there were always rumours that he got away.'

'Do you think he survived?'

I thought of big, strong, vigorous Harold Godwinson. Then I thought of those wounds. 'No.'

'Why not?'

'Because if he had lived he would have fought William with every breath in his body. The country would have risen up and followed him. It didn't. So no, I'm sorry, Mr Bashford, but I don't think he did.'

Evans intervened. 'Far be it from me to interrupt this intellectual discussion, but I need to get your lost historian back to the pod. Watch out for us and be prepared to have the door open in a hurry.'

'We'll come and search for you.'

'No,' I said alarmed. 'We're quite safe where we are.' Evans rolled his eyes. 'We'll work our way back to you. No one leaves the pod. That's an order.'

We struggled back in the dark. We saw no one and no one saw us. We tumbled in through the door, where Sykes passed us some tea. I don't think mine even touched the sides. I gulped it down while Evans described what we'd seen. He had a bit of a job dissuading them from going to have a look for themselves.

Then we washed our face and hands, tidied ourselves up, because historians never go back looking scruffy, and, finally, we jumped away.

Normally, the return from an assignment as important as Hastings is a triumphant business. As many of the unit as can be prised away from their work – which is all of them – assembles on the gantry or behind the safety line and cheers us in. We wave and march to Sick Bay for them to pull us about in the name of medicine and then retire for a shower and a favourite meal. Reports are written, arguments settled, the odd margarita secretly imbibed and we sleep for twelve hours.

This wasn't anything like that.

We disembarked quietly. I don't know about anyone else, but I could still hear the ring of steel on steel, the thunder of hooves, the moans of the dying.

And then we stepped out of the pod into Hawking. Only a few emergency lights were on. The roof was covered with a giant tarpaulin that flapped and rustled occasionally. The giant space was almost completely empty, making it easy to see the great gouges in the walls where lumps of pod had been blown around like dandelion seeds.

Dieter appeared with a glow stick and in silence, guided us around the holes in the floor. In equal silence, we followed him. There were no dreadful jokes. No banter. There weren't even any arguments. The effects of what we'd just witnessed, together with disembarking to a wrecked Hawking … We'd had some tough times. It wasn't the first time St Mary's had blown up around us, but I thought at the time that this was our darkest hour.

We pulled everything together, viewed the footage, wrote our reports, and indulged in a bit of speculation just for the hell of it. I recommended Bashford and Sykes do the presentation to Thirsk and, since every technician was now working his socks off in Hawking, that they take Lingoss along for technical support. As I said to Dr Bairstow, it was time we gave the younger generation a chance to shine. There was a short pause as we both envisaged what Miss Sykes and the Senior Faculty would make of each other, and then he agreed.

He rearranged one or two things on his desk and then said, 'Our current schedule of assignments is ended. May I enquire as to your plans for the future?'

I hadn't been going to say anything, but this seemed a fortuitous coincidence, so I said, 'Well, sir, actually…' took a deep breath, and with some misgivings, admitted I was seriously thinking about taking Matthew away. Ronan was dead, I said. We could live quietly in Rushford. Perhaps we could stay with Mrs De Winter for a while. I would commute. Matthew could go to the school Dr Dowson had found, I said. We could say he'd been subject to some sort of trauma and evolved stories of living in another time as some sort of defence mechanism.

And living a normal life, with normal friends, doing normal things, would surely cause bad memories to fade and he would become a normal little boy with a favourite football team. He'd leave his stuff all over the house, become indescribably dirty at the drop of a hat, refuse to eat his vegetables, incubate new forms of life under his bed, sulk in his room when he couldn't get his own way, and just generally be normal.

I'd clean the house on Saturday mornings, I said, becoming quite carried away at this fantasy of another life. I'd shout at him about the state of his room, demand to know why one of his socks was always missing, force him to do his homework, moan about the cost of living, my job, my life. We would go to the cinema – but not on school nights. We'd have a week's holiday every year in Devon. He could have pizza on Saturday nights.

Eventually emerging from cloud-cuckoo land, I asked Dr Bairstow's opinion.

After a long silence, he said, 'I cannot take exception to any of your plans, Max, although I myself have never regarded pizza as nutritiously acceptable, but from a purely personal point of view I would feel much happier if you were to wait, say, six months. If you are still of the same mind then, it might be a good step for both of you – but I need to be sure you are taking it for the right reasons.'

'What would be the wrong reasons?'

He hesitated. 'If you are running away from bad memories, then your strategy won't work. Wherever you go, you will be taking your memories with you. It is always better to confront them. Furthermore, I think you underestimate how lonely and how difficult is the life of a single parent. Here, you have friends and their support. They tell me Matthew is settling well and I think it would be a shame to jeopardise the progress made so far. And from a personal, purely selfish point of view, I would like you to stay. You are a key member of this unit. I know you don't think so, but people look to you for guidance and example. If you were to leave, others might think of following your example. Obviously I cannot compel you to remain and nor would I wish to do so. All I ask is that you wait six months and if you are still of the same mind, then yes, we can make plans. Together.'

He was right. I nodded, rather glad of the excuse not to have to make any hard choices just yet.

The days dragged past. One after the other. As they do. People said I was handling things well and I was. No credit to me. I didn't do anything. The bits that loved and laughed and experienced emotions had all disappeared with Leon. Wherever he was, those parts of me were with him. What remained was some kind of shell or husk – empty and dry – that walked and talked and never felt a single thing.

I've never told anyone about this. I've never even mentioned it to Peterson. Even after it was over, I wasn't quite sure it hadn't all been a dream.

I'd put Matthew to bed, quietly closed his door and sat down to watch a little TV. When I awoke, hours later, cold, cramped and groggy, someone was outside, fumbling with the door knob.

I didn't make the mistake of leaping to my feet to challenge whoever it was. For a start, I'm not good when I wake up. I'm never sure where my feet are, and it's hard to be taken seriously when trying to challenge someone from ankle height because you've fallen flat on your face.

I checked Matthew's door was still closed and that I was between him and whoever was out there, and reached for my old walking stick which I still kept propped against the bookcase. The door finally opened and a dark figure slipped through, closing it noiselessly behind him.

I raised the stick, said, 'OK, buster, don't make a move unless you're really, really fond of hospital food,' and Leon said, 'Well, there's a fine welcome,' and I dropped the stick in shock.

'Leon? *Leon*?'

'You sound astonished. Perhaps we should take a moment to discuss who you *were* expecting? And why are you sitting in the dark?'

Quite automatically, I said, 'I fell asleep watching the TV.'

'Bad habit. Shall I put the light on?'

I nodded. In a dark room. There's no hope for me.

The light clicked on and I stared at him. It *was* Leon, dressed in battered Time Police armour. His hair was now almost completely silver and he was wearing it brushed back from his face, which was deeply lined with weariness. He had a fresh scar on one cheekbone and another on his chin.

He shrugged off his pack, dropped it to the floor and grinned at me. 'Don't I get a hug?'

I couldn't speak, but my feet moved of their own

accord and I nearly knocked him off his feet.

'That's my girl,' he said, wrapping his arms around me and burying his face in my hair. 'You smell so good. It's been a long time and I'm sorry I haven't been able to get back to see you before this. I've missed you so much. How's Matthew? How long have I been away?'

I didn't know what to do. What to say to him. I couldn't get my head around what was happening. Leon was still hunting Ronan. He didn't know he was dead. So I said nothing.

'Talk to me,' he said,

Still with my head buried in his shoulder, I shook my head. He laughed a little, tightened his embrace, and we stood together for a long time.

Eventually, he said, 'I'm sorry I'm cold and wet, but I've just rescued three idiots from a snowstorm at Stonehenge. I thought I'd just check in and make sure you made it back all right.'

Oh my God. Sometime last year, the three of us, Peterson, Markham and I had managed to lose ourselves in a blizzard. We'd been on the point of unconsciousness when Leon turned up and saved us all. He appeared out of nowhere, picked us up, dusted us off, pointed us in the right direction and disappeared. But not before telling me how much he'd missed me. Pondering this remark afterwards, I'd come to the conclusion I might have died. It had never occurred to me in a million years that he might be the one who'd died.

Still with my head buried in his chest, I nodded.

'Are you ever coming out?' And I could hear the smile in his voice.

Still with my head buried in his chest, I shook my head. He smelled of hot metal and sweat and Leon, and I was never going to let him go. I could feel the melting snow seeping through my T-shirt and clung more tightly. I had been convinced it was me who had died. It wasn't supposed to be Leon. It was never supposed to be Leon.

'I can't stay, Max. We're closing in on him. Any day now. His pod's shot and he must be nearly finished. We're all rendezvousing in an hour and then we'll make one final push to corner him. I just came to tell you – it's over. I'll be home by this time tomorrow.'

No, he wouldn't. He'd never come home again. Tomorrow they'd catch Ronan and he would kill them all. I clutched at him, gripping so tightly that it hurt my hands. Every part of me wanted to tell him not to go. And why. But I couldn't. In my personal timeline, it had already happened. And it was about to happen in his as well and there was nothing I could do about it. Not unless I wanted to bring catastrophe down upon us all.

I remember thinking it was such a good job he was already wet. He wouldn't feel my tears soaking through his clothing.

He was already picking up his pack. 'I have to go. I'm sorry, sweetheart. I shouldn't have come at all, but I wanted to let you know it's nearly over. I'm just going to stick my head around Matthew's door and then I'll be off.'

He gently moved my hands away and crossed to Matthew's room. He opened the door and looked in, stood still for a moment or two and then softly closed it again.

'How is he?'

I was proud of my voice. 'Absolutely fine. He rarely drinks from the toilet now. On the downside, he has taken to peeing in the shower.'

He laughed. 'There's always something, isn't there. Don't worry, I'll sort that out when I get back.'

He shouldered his pack and looked around. 'That dead dog on the wardrobe is going to have to go. I'm really not sure I can live with that.'

He was moving towards the door. He was leaving.

I ran after him and seized his arm. 'Leon …' and stopped. What could I say? What could I possibly say? If I threw myself into his arms, sobbing and begging him not to go, then he'd want to know why and I couldn't tell him. I mustn't do anything to change my past. His future. He was going to his death and I couldn't say a word.

This is the downside to time travel. Yes, you get to see wonderful things. But not all knowledge is good. Especially knowledge of events you can't change. Leon's death had already happened. There was no way I could save him. All I could do was ensure his last memories of me were happy ones. In that moment, it occurred to me that time travel was an absolute bitch.

He smiled and said, 'You have to let go of me so I can go. If I can't go then I can't come back again.'

I hung on even tighter.

'It's only one day, Max. Just twenty-four hours.' He put his hands over mine and gently pulled them away.

I could only hope he put my distress down to his imminent departure. 'Leon, please – you have to take care.'

'I always do,' he said, gently. 'I have a family to come

back to. Make sure you're both here when I do.'

I nodded.

He smiled down at me, his blue eyes very bright. 'This time tomorrow, Max. Be ready for me.'

Leon died thinking he'd be home this time tomorrow.

I found a dreadful cold strength from somewhere.

'I will,' I said, without a tremor. 'We'll have a quiet evening. Just the three of us. And a special dinner. With your favourite wine. And you'll be home again.'

He grinned at me. That's what I always remember. That last, tired, triumphant grin. He kissed me, oh so gently, and before I could say anything else, he was out of the door. I heard his footsteps clattering down the stairs.

The whole encounter had taken only a few minutes. No more. I'm still not entirely certain I didn't dream it.

For Leon, there was no tomorrow. He was already dead. I knew he was dead. I'd seen him die.

I spent the next day alone. I couldn't bear to have anyone near me. I sat in my room, straining my ears for his step on the stairs. In the evening, even though I knew it was futile, that there was no hope, that I was only hurting myself by doing this, I put Matthew to bed early. If there was even the slightest chance, then I was going to cling to it. Even though I knew that what I'd seen last night was little more than an echo, I showered and brushed my hair. I put clean sheets on the bed. I lit a few candles and then I sat down to wait.

He didn't come.

21

More time passed. I went into Rushford for my new glasses. I chose horn rims, telling Peterson they made me look both intelligent and sexy. He patted my shoulder and told me he'd always admired my capacity for self-delusion.

We had developed a routine to get us through the days. We would lunch together, just as we'd done last year, when he, Markham and I had got ourselves into a little trouble and been ostracised by the rest of the unit. The three of us had stuck together like glue – mostly because no one else would have us – and even after we were reinstated, we'd continued the tradition of eating together whenever we could. Now, with Markham dead, it was just the two of us.

We didn't do anything mawkish like always setting a third place at the table – Markham would have wet himself laughing over that one – but I don't think he was ever far away from our thoughts.

We worked closely together, in and out of each other's offices all day long. I tried hard to persuade him to swap Miss Lee for the lovely Mrs Shaw and all three of them shrieked with laughter over that one. He and Mrs Shaw adored each other. He gave her flowers and she brought him chocolate biscuits with his tea. They had the sort of relationship Miss Lee and I could only aspire to. Well, I could aspire. She couldn't bloody care less.

I was dictating one morning when I became aware she wasn't paying attention. She was staring out of the window. I opened my mouth to demand she do at least a little work before knocking off and going home when she said, 'I think the Time Police are here.'

'Why?'

'How should I know?'

A second later, my telephone rang.

Both Miss Lee and I looked at it.

'Well, answer it,' I said.

'It's your phone,' she said.

'It's your job,' I said.

'You're the closest,' she said.

'You're the assistant,' I said.

How long we could have gone on like that was anyone's guess. And it's not as if we didn't both know who would be answering the bloody thing no matter who had the last word. As it was, however, it stopped ringing. She fixed me with a look of triumph. I fixed her with the look of a defeated employer.

Dr Bairstow spoke in my ear. 'Dr Maxwell, are you in your office?'

'I am, sir.'

'You do not appear to be answering your telephone.'

'I was temporarily unable to do so,' I said. 'And my assistant was unable to recollect the series of actions needed to perform this complex function.'

Or indeed, any function at all.

'Please report to my office at your earliest convenience.'

'Yes, sir. Do I need to bring anything with me?' Which, I've discovered is a great way of asking what it's all about without actually asking what it's all about.

He said, 'The Time Police would like a word with you,' which was enough to wipe the smile off anyone's face.

Mrs Partridge was waiting for me. 'This way please, Dr Maxwell.'

Sitting at his briefing table were Dr Bairstow, Commander Hay and Captain Farenden. Again.

The Commander opened the batting. 'Dr Maxwell, may I express my regret over Chief Farrell's death. And that of Major Guthrie and Mr Markham.'

I nodded. 'Thank you. I'm sorry about Miss Van Owen.'

'Thank you. I know that it must feel as if your world has ended, and I am reluctant to seem to be adding to your difficulties, but there is an important matter I must discuss with you. I always intended to speak to you and your husband about this and then … well … Chief Farrell died and I wanted to give you some time before approaching you, but now I understand from Dr Bairstow that the question of Matthew's future is being considered, and I have a … a proposition to put to you. I do beg you will give me a hearing.'

I didn't like the sound of this.

'I should say now I don't expect you to make a decision today. Or in the near future either. Both I and Dr

Bairstow feel you should take all the time you need before making what is going to be a very difficult choice.'

What choice? What decision?

She appeared to take a very deep breath.

'Max, we at the Time Police have given this matter a great deal of thought. I would like you to consider what I am about to say very carefully. I am sure your first instinct will be to reject it out of hand, but I beg that you will take the time to think about it.'

Shit. I didn't like the sound of this at all.

'We propose that your son comes to live with us.'

She paused, as if bracing herself for a protest, but to tell the truth, I was too gobsmacked to speak.

'We have several reasons for proposing what to you must seem an impossible course of action, and in truth, I don't think we have any choice.'

I found a voice. 'Of course we have a choice. Ronan is gone – there is no reason why either Matthew or I shouldn't lead a normal life.'

I threw Dr Bairstow a look. Surely it was no coincidence that the Time Police were here with this ridiculous idea so soon after I had announced I was considering taking Matthew away from St Mary's.

He said gravely, 'I know what you are thinking, Max, but Commander Hay and I have been discussing her proposal for a little while now, and I am asking you, as a long-standing colleague and friend, to hear her out.'

I could do that. I could listen politely all the way to the end and then say no. I nodded.

She continued. 'Our plan is that Matthew comes to live with us. For him, the benefits will be enormous. We will

304

make ourselves responsible for his education and I guarantee it will be excellent. Under our care, he will be safe and secure. I categorically guarantee that. And, probably best of all, Max, he will be among people who understand who and what he is. He will never have to pretend or lie about his background. He can relax and be himself.'

'And what exactly do you think that is?'

She was silent for a while. 'I'll be honest, we're not sure. Oh please, don't misunderstand me. There's nothing wrong with him. He's a perfectly normal little boy. Yes, he has a few problems at the moment, but they're the result of his upbringing and can be dealt with.'

'So your interest in him is because…?'

'Is because he was born between times. Or out of time, if you like. Between one moment and the next.'

'Aren't we all?'

'Yes, we are, but Matthew, your son, was born in that split second when no time existed at all. Interesting, don't you think? We believe he might possess certain gifts relating to the reading of Time and it would seem that these talents have already begun to manifest themselves. For instance, I believe that you have given him the Time Map to play with.'

'Well, not *the* Time Map…' I said, not meeting Dr Bairstow's gaze.

'Of course not, but I believe he has already learned to manipulate the data.'

'Just randomly. He's too young to know what he's doing.'

'Of course,' she said again, 'but that's a gift that

should not be ignored.'

'And certainly not by the Time Police,' I said, brightly. She didn't rise to the bait.

'I understand this must be difficult for you. You lost your baby then he reappears as an eight-year-old boy.'

'And now you're proposing to take him away again,' I said, feeling that this had gone on long enough. 'Not going to happen.'

'No, no, Max. Please do not misunderstand me. There is absolutely no question of you never seeing him again. We would allow regular visits. Once a month at the very least. He can come to you at St Mary's or you can visit him to reassure yourself as to his living conditions. We are very conscious both of the need for him to form a good relationship with his mother, and of his need for safety and security which I think we can all, between us, provide. You would be able to see him at any time.'

'But as things stand at the moment, I can see him all the time.

'That is true, but…'

'And, just so everyone in this room is perfectly clear, because it would be a tragedy if anyone was labouring under any sort of misapprehension – *no one* has the authority to "allow" me to do anything pertaining to my son.'

I hadn't meant the words to ring around the room like that, but I was quite pleased with the effect.

'Of course not. I apologise if, in my haste to reassure you, I expressed myself badly.'

I let the silence hang around for a while. Just to let the guilt settle. She'd been clumsy. She knew it. The Time

Police were not noted for their subtlety. They'd handled the affair with Clive Ronan very badly. No need to mention that. It's always far more effective to let these things hang in the air, unspoken. I never say to Leon, 'Told you so.'

Said to Leon. I never *said* to Leon. No more present tense.

I stared down at my hands, shutting everyone out. One thought ran through everything. I won't lose Matthew again. I just won't.

Something of this must have shown in my face because she said gently, 'I do understand Max. We all do. This is not an easy decision for you to make.'

'I can't decide this now. I must talk to Matthew and hear what he has to say. I should tell you that if he doesn't want to go then that will be the end of it. And it won't be soon. He still doesn't know about … about his father.'

'I agree. I ask only that you allow me to speak to him as well, to make my own case.'

I hesitated.

'We've known each other a while now, Max. We sat down at the same table after the Battle of St Mary's and thrashed out the working agreement which has served us both so well. We trusted each other then. Can we not do so now?'

She was right. Yes, I was prejudiced against the Time Police and I had good reasons for that. They'd hunted Leon and me up and down the timeline, doing untold damage along the way – and everything that had happened to us recently – Helen, Ian, Markham, Leon – all those deaths were the direct result of their monumental cock-up over Clive Ronan. And now they wanted me to give up my son to them.

But, said the voice of reason, they're not all bad all the time. They saved you and Matthew when that bastard Ronan had marooned you in History. They took in Van Owen when she desperately needed a home and direction. You named Matthew after Captain Ellis. Commander Hay isn't Colonel Albay. They're not the same organisation they once were.

All this was true. Part of me argued it wouldn't take much for them to revert back to their old ways, but that's true of anyone. We all change to suit existing circumstances. We evolve.

She said gently, 'Perhaps you would find it reassuring to know we have several other youngsters in our care. In addition to all the benefits I have described, he would have the company of his contemporaries – people his own age around him.'

I drew a breath. 'I can't decide this now.'

'I understand. This is difficult for you. Take as much time as you need.'

Until he was eighteen years old would probably not be acceptable.

I said slowly, 'I would like to take advice on this.'

She inclined her head. 'Of course. And thank you for not rejecting this proposal out of hand.'

I shook my head. 'It's only fair I should tell you, Commander, that I am not inclined to accept. I can provide him with an education here. There's no need for the Time Police to be involved. And your other main point – that the Time Police can keep him safe – well, there's no need now, is there? Clive Ronan is dead. The threat is removed. There is no reason why Matthew shouldn't live a normal life. Here. With me.'

The silence went on just that little bit too long.

I didn't like this. I didn't like this at all.

I said sharply, 'Is there?'

She said, 'Of course not. But I had the feeling that wasn't what she had originally been going to say.

More time crept by. We worked our way through all the Beaurain, Bayeux, Stamford Bridge and Hastings data, and wrote the presentations. In the end, North, Sykes and Bashford took them to Thirsk. Lingoss went with them. The Chancellor received them kindly, they were on their best behaviour and everything went well which, according to Dr Bairstow, went a long way towards reconciling them to the cost of St Mary's restoration.

Of course, our supply of work dried up. The techies were the only people employed at the moment, busy rebuilding Hawking, repairing the pods that had survived and cannibalising the ones that hadn't.

SPOHB – the Society for the Preservation of Historical Buildings turned up, all of them wearing their traditional combination of drab knitwear and expressions of rigid disapproval. We continued the St Mary's tradition of ignoring them. They fired off a series of punitive memos, heading each one with their logo and the information that this communication had originated from the BDSM department. Everyone got really excited. Speculation was rife as to what they were wearing under those cardigans until we discovered the letters stood for Building Design and Site Management.

There wasn't anything for us historians to do. The more technically minded among us were allowed into Hawking in an unskilled capacity – holding tools, carrying stuff around, suffering the occasional mild electric shock, making tea. The rest of us assisted Dr Dowson to re-catalogue the Archive, or indulge in a little extreme gardening under the watchful eye of Mr Strong.

Months passed. Spring turned into summer and probably wished it hadn't bothered. I've never seen so much wind and rain. They had real problems getting the roof back on Hawking. Summer began to turn into autumn. Leaves fell early from the trees and lay in soggy piles everywhere. Mr Stone raked them away and then there were frosty cobwebs every morning. Leon had been gone for nearly six months. Matthew had almost stopped asking where he was. I concentrated on putting one foot in front of the other and just getting through each day and I wasn't the only one.

Morale was at an all-time low. We're St Mary's. We tend to be reasonably cheerful even when things aren't going well because things not going well is our default state. It wasn't that people were gloomy, but somehow, the spark had gone. Despite all our efforts, there were mutterings. I was concerned enough to mention it to Dr Bairstow, who said nothing, but looked thoughtful.

And then, one day, about a week later, he sent for me. I thought, initially, that he wanted to ask me again about my plans for the future – something he had heroically refrained from doing since our interview with the Time Police – but this was something completely different.

'Hello, Max. Come in and sit down.'

'Good afternoon, sir.'

'How are things out there?'

'Not too bad, sir. The Technical Section is working like stink and the rest of us are going slowly mad looking for something to do. I'm pleased to be able to report – possibly for the first time ever – that everyone's reports are written up, all filing up to date, the Archive re-catalogued, and all side-saddle hours completed and logged.'

'Yes,' he said thoughtfully, and then stopped.

I sat and waited. I had nowhere to go and nothing to do when I got there. That was my life now.

'I've been thinking, Max. I have an idea, which I'd like to run past you.'

'Yes, sir?'

'Out of respect, I have waited a while to say this, but I think the time has come for us to draw a line under past events. This does not mean we forget what has happened, or those who have gone, but I think it's time to move forwards again. The work in Hawking is nearly complete and we should have four, if not five, working pods very soon now. I have been thinking that, as a reward for everyone's hard work, we should have a small event to celebrate. Something for people to enjoy. I do not, however, wish to seem insensitive, and I would, therefore appreciate your thoughts.'

What did I think?

I sat quietly in that familiar room, looking at the patch of sunshine on the faded carpet. He'd had his clock repaired. The old familiar tick was back and in some small way, I felt comforted. I heard myself say, 'I think that's a good idea sir. You're right. It is time. Did you have anything specific in mind?'

He leaned forwards. 'Actually, yes. I am concerned at our current lack of impetus. What this unit needs is a little healthy competition. Nothing too strenuous, of course,' he said quickly, possibly remembering that the St Mary's response to anything even remotely competitive is to form the appropriate number of teams, spend ten minutes hurling insults around, and then knock seven bells out of each other. Quarter is neither expected nor given.

I ventured to express a few misgivings. 'An excellent suggestion, sir, but I can't help remembering last year's trebuchet versus ballista tournament, when Mr Keller broke his arm and we inadvertently demolished Mr Strong's potting shed. It was only due to the greatest good fortune and the call of nature that he wasn't in it at the time.'

He waved this aside as irrelevant. 'No one is more aware of the competitive nature of my unit than I, Dr Maxwell, but I hope to neutralise our more savage instincts by proposing a pleasant, gentlemanly game of croquet. In authentic costume, of course. To be followed by afternoon tea on the terrace.'

I blinked. 'Are you giving us the afternoon off, sir?'

'I believe that is what I said. Thursday next, I think, if the weather holds. See to it, Dr Maxwell.'

'Yes, sir.'

Obviously, despite his best intentions, it was never going to end well, but I don't think any of us realised

314

quite how bizarre the afternoon was going to be. Even by our standards. But I'm always being told off when I run ahead of myself.

I made sure I got to Wardrobe ahead of the crowd, snagging myself a rather pretty tea-gown in pale blue and turquoise. I didn't intend to play, but I didn't intend to burden myself with corsets either, and the loose tea-gown was perfect. Matthew immediately defected to the Security team, where they decked him out in knickerbockers and a cap. I wasn't sure whether his function was first reserve or mascot.

I'm not familiar with the rules of croquet – or indeed any game that involves hitting a ball with a stick. Golf, tennis, hockey, cricket – they all look the same to me. It's only the shape of the stick that's different. Unless you're the Queen of Hearts, of course, when you get to play with flamingos instead. Interesting idea, but difficult to organise at such short notice.

We set up tables and chairs along the terrace. A croquet … pitch? … court? …whatever … had been laid out. We had six teams and the smart money was on the Wardrobe Wanderers, who were generally reckoned to be unstoppable and led by Mrs Enderby herself, decked out in a high-necked blouse and long, full skirt. Her bustle was assumed to be weaponised and was being given a wide berth.

There would be a number of preliminary heats, then we'd pause for afternoon tea – the word sumptuous had been used several times – before the Grand Final. A small cup was to be presented to the winners by Dr Bairstow himself, stunningly attired in a crimson and cream striped blazer and crisp cream trousers. He sat with Mrs Partridge, who looked cool and elegant in white and carried a pink parasol.

Everyone, competitors and spectators alike, had made an effort with their costumes. I was wearing my pretty tea-gown with my hair coiled up in an elegant knot. And no corset. You can't eat afternoon tea in a corset.

Nearby, Miss Sykes wore a saintly expression and a pretty pink dress with more ruffles than was probably legal. Miss Lingoss, always different, had chosen a striking crimson affair, with her corset worn over the dress, which, I have to say, was a huge improvement on the way Victorian and Edwardian ladies wore them. Her hair was teased up to a height that Marge Simpson would envy. Even the men had shown willing, all of them in crisp white shirts and flannels, tied around the waist with old school ties. One or two souls not sensitive to public opinion wore straw boaters.

We arranged ourselves at the tables. I sat with Peterson, Lingoss and a blushing but delighted Dottle. We poured ourselves glasses of lemonade, made from an authentic recipe – Peterson surreptitiously added something from a small flask – and we watched the bloodbath begin. It was a knockout competition – sometimes quite literally – and the last two teams standing would slug it out on the green velvet perfection of Mr Strong's beloved South Lawn.

The History Department crashed out in the first round, but Miss Sykes's parting shot had led to Mr Evans staggering from the field, temporarily *hors de combat* and vowing future retribution, so we didn't feel all honour had been lost.

Peterson and I took advantage of the lull caused by the medical section getting people back on their feet again to take a walk around the lake. We paused by the willows and looked back at St Mary's. Just for once, it wasn't raining, the building glowed in the afternoon sunshine, the birds were singing, the swans were all safely at the other end of the lake. It was a lovely peaceful scene. Even the wounded had stopped bleeding.

'Enjoying yourself?' he said, as we slowly skirted the willows. In this dress, I had to do everything slowly.

'Yes,' I said, quite surprised to find I was. 'Are you?'

He nodded. 'It's good to do something just for fun, don't you think?'

'I do. I'd almost forgotten what fun is.'

'Me too. It's nice to see you smile again. Max, I wanted to ask you...' He stopped.

'Yes?'

'I wanted to ask if ... if you've made up your mind about letting the Time Police take Matthew.'

I wasn't sure that was what he had originally meant to say.

'No. I mean, no, I don't think so.'

'Do you mean you haven't made up your mind or you don't think you'll send him.'

'I don't know.' I tried to keep my voice steady. 'I honestly don't know. I only know he's all I have left of ... of Leon.'

'I understand,' he said, and we walked in silence for a while. 'On the other hand,' he continued, struggling for a

317

lighter tone, 'if you do send him then his drinking from the toilet will become someone else's problem. That's got to be a temptation.'

'It certainly is.'

He touched my hand. 'Is everything all right with you?'

'Yes,' I said, 'it is. Everything is absolutely fine.'

'Good. Now tell me the truth.'

We walked a little further. 'I'm not sure I can put it into words, Tim. When I first came to St Mary's, I was alone. A solitary unit – and happy to be so. And then, over the years, things got ... switched on. I learned to trust people. I met Leon. There was love. Marriage. Family. I was all set for a life I never thought would be mine, and I was right. Nothing ever came of any of it. Look what happened. Everything is gone. Just ripped away. But I can't go back to the way I was. I've opened myself up. Made myself vulnerable.' I swallowed. 'It's ... painful.'

'You still have Matthew.'

'But not for long, I suspect.'

'You don't have to do it. They can't take him against your wishes.'

'They'll give him an education. He'll be safe. He can be himself. He'll never have to pretend or lie. And he doesn't like me, Tim. Oh, he tolerates me and sometimes, in the evenings, we have a bit of a chat, but he's not warming to me. He probably never will and I don't know what to do about it. And the non-mother half of me says to let him go. He'll be happy. Even the mother half of me suspects it's a good idea.'

'But what do you *want* to do.'

'It's not what I want. That doesn't really come into it. I can't keep him here just to make me feel better.'

'What does he say?'

'I haven't asked him yet.'

'But you will.'

'Yes, I will. I promised I would. I'll have to pick a moment when he's not too displeased with me, otherwise it looks as if I'm sending him away out of spite. Sadly, those moments are few and far between.' I smiled a wobbly smile. 'I'm not a very good mother.'

'I don't agree,' he said. 'You're not a conventional mother but that's not to say you're a bad mother.' He stopped walking. 'Actually, Max, I was going to ask you if perhaps...' and he stopped, staring over my shoulder, apparently struggling for words. 'Bloody hellfire! ... What? ... *What?*'

Long dress notwithstanding, I swung around. Now what?

It takes a lot to catch St Mary's off balance. Over the years, we've been attacked, blown up, gassed – several times actually, because Professor Rapson just can't work out where he's going wrong – mobbed by swans, crushed and drowned by a runaway monolith, the list is long and we've risen above all of it. We're St Mary's, we say, and our proud boast is that we can handle anything, and that's true, but you can imagine my surprise and consternation when, out of the blue, a bloody great teapot materialised. Right in front of us. Right in the middle of the South Lawn and flattening a croquet hoop at the same time.

We're supposed to be a professional organisation. We're supposed to swing into action like a well-oiled ...

319

something or other, all ready to deal with whatever threat is presenting itself. We drew nearer for a better look. Yes, I know we should have let the Security Section deal with it but it was teapot, for crying out loud.

All conversation stopped dead. In itself a remarkable event. As a measure of our consternation, one or two people nearly put down their cups of tea. Apart from the distant sound of a car changing gear somewhere, there was complete silence. I'm sorry to say that far from springing into action like a well-oiled thingummy, we froze with our mouths open. Yes, I know, but you try having a giant teapot drop into your front garden and see how quickly you can get your mouth closed.

I stared at the … contraption. The word that sprang to mind was 'steampunk' and I don't even know what that means. If it means a twelve-feet-high precarious-looking structure, bulbously teapot in shape then yes – steampunk. An extrusion on one side looked like, but couldn't possibly be, a spout and a corresponding bulge on the other side resembled the handle. I had no idea what it could be made of, but I do know it was painted in shades of khaki and brown that were blistering and peeling away – where they weren't scraped off altogether – and with an amateurishly rendered Union Jack on the side. Significant dents and dints indicated some major collisions. It didn't appear to be making any sort of noise, but then in my experience, most teapots don't.

Not a solitary soul moved. Even the birds had shut up. I'll say it again. We had a twelve-foot-high teapot standing on our croquet lawn.

Anyway, while we were all sitting there, gaping like a

bunch of idiots, a hatch lifted up, and a head appeared out of the top, peering around, rather like a cross between a submarine periscope and a meerkat.

As Mr Evans said afterwards, all right, yes, he probably should have done something, but it's quite difficult to feel threatened by something that looked like a giant, patriotic, tea-dispensing appliance from his Great-Aunt Jemima's best dinner service.

The head looked around for a minute, caught sight of us, stared hard at our Victorian attire, and then said, 'Damn and blast.' Bending back down to address someone still inside the machine, he shouted, 'You'd better get up here, Mikey. We've gone wrong somewhere.'

Surveying us all, he cleared his throat and, enunciating carefully, said, 'Good afternoon. Er … jolly topping weather, what?'

'Oh, for God's sake,' muttered Peterson, 'Come on, Max. Let's go and see what's happened now, shall we?'

'Try keeping me away.'

We walked slowly towards the teapot, with Evans and the rest of the Security Section pulling themselves together and approaching from the other side. They might have looked more professional if they had put down their slices of Victoria sponge, although Evans and Cox had had the forethought to pick up their croquet mallets. Since the intruders were some ten or twelve feet off the ground, it was hard to know their intentions.

Peterson halted and looked up at them squinting into the sunshine. 'Identify yourselves.'

The head beamed. 'Um … well… I know you're not

going to believe this, but…' he paused impressively, and then announced sonorously, 'we're from … The Future.'

Somewhat taken aback by the lack of response, he continued valiantly. 'We come in peace. We mean you no harm.'

'Someone should explain it's likely to be the other way around,' I muttered. 'Do you think he'll ask to be taken to our leader?'

'Not if he's got any sense.'

'We're…' he paused even more impressively, obviously playing some sort of trumpet fanfare in his head, '… *Time Travellers*!'

'Yawn,' said Sykes, behind me.

Well, I suppose it had to happen sometime. According to the Time Police, the secret of time travel was – sorry, will be – public property, with amateurs zipping about all over the place trying to shoot Hitler, prevent the assassination of a US president – nine at the last count, and four in the last twenty years, so they're not doing that well – unexecute Mary Stuart, change the final score at Bosworth and now, apparently, visit St Mary's. You can see why, of course. St Mary's Institute of Historical Research. First and best. Where it all started. I stood with Peterson in the warm afternoon sunshine and we waited to see what would happen next.

'Er … my name's Adrian and this is…' another head popped up alongside, 'this is Mikey. We're awfully sorry, but we seem to be in the wrong place. We'll be off. So sorry to have disturbed you. Good afternoon.'

Well, they had lovely manners.

'Not so fast,' said Peterson. 'Get your arses down here

right now, the pair of you.'

'Well, that's not very Victorian,' said Mikey.

'Neither am I,' said Peterson. 'Get yourselves down here now before I have the pair of you shot.'

'Oh. OK then,' said Adrian, not particularly fazed by the threat. 'You might want to stand back a little.'

'Why?'

A heavy wooden ladder was heaved out of the hatch and thudded to the ground, missing his head by inches. By the time Peterson had recovered, Adrian was carefully climbing down, closely followed by Mikey.

Seen close up, they were much younger than I had first thought. Adrian was tall and gawky, wearing a long leather greatcoat. Mikey was smaller and wore what looked like a genuine WWII leather flying jacket. They both wore flying helmets and, for no discernible reason that I could see, goggles. I doubted either of them was out of their teens. Which wouldn't go down well with Dr Bairstow.

Men might be from Mars and women from Venus, but Dr Bairstow is from St Mary's, the centre of the universe and, as far as he's concerned, teenagers are from the other side of the Ort cloud. He has frequently been heard to express his astonishment that SETI are concentrating their search for extra-terrestrial life in space, when everyone can see there are several billion aliens (or teenagers as the rest of the world refers to them) already inhabiting Planet Earth.

The two of them stood in front of us, staring around in open curiosity.

'Where are we?'

'Where are you supposed to be?'

'St Mary's Institute. We wanted to see where it all started.'

'I don't believe this,' said Bashford. He glared accusingly at Evans. 'We're supposed to be a top-secret establishment and we're easier to get into than that new nightclub in Rushford.'

'Not the Golden Pussy?' said Keller.

'I think you mean the Black Cat.'

He grinned. 'I know what I mean.'

I cleared my throat. We were, to all intents and purposes being invaded by what looked like a collection of giant dustbins held together by a paperclip, and our Security Section was busy discussing Rushford's one and only nocturnal entertainment establishment. The Black Cat could supply the discerning patron with exorbitantly priced drinks, energetic young ladies and their poles, and gambling facilities for the inexperienced. The Security Section had taken out block membership. They thought Dr Bairstow didn't know.

'This is St Mary's,' said Peterson, because there was no point in denying it. For a start, there was a bloody great sign on the grass verge outside the gates.

They stared at us and our costumes. 'But…'

'Croquet tournament,' said Peterson, putting them out of their misery. 'Mr Evans, if you would be so good.'

He stepped forwards. 'OK guys – you probably know the drill. Assume the position. Are you armed?'

'Of course not,' said Adrian, indignantly, turning to face the teapot and raising his arms, obviously well acquainted with the procedure.

I found myself alongside an anxious looking Mikey. 'I'll do this one,' I said. 'Arms in the air. Anything in your pockets?'

'Um, a compass, some string, matches, my notebook, a small mirror, spare socks, two pens, my piece of cheese...'

'Cheese?'

'To replace the salt. Sometimes, after a jump, we feel a bit wobbly.'

'Oh?' said Peterson, sharply. 'How wobbly.'

'Just a bit sick, sometimes.'

I'd finished with Mikey. 'All clear.'

'Can I have my cheese back?'

'No,' I said, dropping it onto the grass. The ants could have it.

'My cheese,' cried Mikey, stricken.

'I'll get you another lump,' I said, feeling as if I'd just drowned someone's kitten. 'What are your feelings towards Double Gloucester?'

'Cheddar,' said Adrian, over his shoulder.

'Boring,' said Mikey. 'Wensleydale.'

I glanced towards Mrs Mack and she got up.

Peterson was talking to Dieter, who disappeared, signalling to several techies to follow him.

Adrian drew himself up. 'Take us to your leader.'

'Love to,' said Peterson. 'This way.'

As we set off, Dieter and his team passed us, clutching bits of technical equipment and a wand, which they began to wave around.

He looked at the ladder and then at Adrian. 'All right to go in? I'd really like to have a look inside.'

'Of course,' said Adrian amiably. 'Be our guest.'

I was torn between watching the enormous Dieter negotiate the ladder and then squeeze himself in through the hatch, or seeing what our two guests and Dr Bairstow made of each other. Dr Bairstow won. He always does.

I performed the introductions. 'Sir, may I introduce Adrian and Mikey. Adrian and Mikey, this is Dr Bairstow.'

They just stared at him, speechless, for once. Talk about shock and awe.

I think he completely took the wind out of their sails by asking them to join him for tea.

'Oh, wow!' said Mikey, staring around in amazement. 'Tea at St Mary's. With *Dr Bairstow*. Awesome! Thank you, sir.'

I could see Dr Bairstow thaw a little at this blatant admiration. He doesn't get a lot of that. On the other hand, of course, pants-wetting terror is usually his preferred effect.

'Max, Dr Peterson, would you care to join us?'

We settled ourselves down and continued with what was, according to Mrs Mack, the highlight of the afternoon. The tables were laden with four different types of sandwiches, scones with jam and cream, cheese scones with savoury butter, slices of quiche, Victoria sponge, Battenburg and jam tarts. All along the terrace, I could hear happy chatter and the chink of teaspoons in saucers. The English Tourist Board could have bottled us and sold us abroad and made a fortune. England at its most traditional.

Somewhat to our surprise, having loaded his plate with

as much as it could hold Adrian pulled out an old-fashioned alarm clock – the sort with the big double bell on the top – and set it on the table in front of him.

I have to say, they both of them looked pale and heavy-eyed so perhaps they needed help staying awake. Like the dormouse at the Mad Hatter's Tea Party. Please don't tell Dr Bairstow I referred to him as the Mad Hatter.

Tim was eyeing the clock. 'What's that for?'

'We only have two hours.'

'Until what?'

'Until the Time Police catch us. Sometimes a little longer – sometimes a little less – but usually about two hours. So we set the clock and when the alarm goes off – so do we. We have our own dedicated Time Police unit, you know. There's four of them after us. And they haven't caught us yet,' he added proudly, if a little thickly, because all teenagers can eat and talk at the same time. It's just a bit messy for everyone else. 'Sometimes,' he continued, 'we leave them a note telling them where we're going next and, every Christmas, we leave them a card with season's greetings, so they know we're thinking of them.'

I spared a moment to picture the Time Police reaction to this cheeky gesture of goodwill. Because if they were ever caught, it would no longer be a laughing matter … Not for these two, anyway. And they were so young.

'How do they find you?' persisted Peterson.

'We don't know,' said Mikey cheerfully, barely visible behind a plateful of sandwiches and jam tarts. I had the impression the abandoned lump of cheese now lying forlornly on the grass was less than a memory.

327

'I think I can answer that,' said Dieter, appearing as if by magic. No mean feat when you're that big. He was waving his wand around like a Teutonic Gandalf at Minas Tirith. 'You have a radiation leak.'

Dr Stone stood up, leaned over, and peered at the readings. 'Right, you two.'

They clutched at their plates, not moving.

He beamed. 'I've always wanted to say this: Come with me if you want to live.'

They picked up their plates, still stuffing sandwiches as fast as they could go. If they were permanently on the run from the Time Police, no wonder they were starving. Still, they seemed very cheerful about it. It was rather good to meet people for whom the Time Police held no fear.

'The resilience of youth,' said Peterson, watching them go. 'Remember that?'

'Not recently,' I said.

Dr Bairstow said, 'Mr Dieter, how bad is their leak? Should I be evacuating everyone?'

'Low level, sir, nothing for us to worry about, but prolonged contact is not doing them any good.'

'Can it be repaired?'

'I think so, sir. Can you keep them out of the way for an hour or so?'

Dr Bairstow picked up their alarm clock. 'You have forty-five minutes.'

'In that case, sir, if you will excuse me – I have a miracle to perform.'

He set off at a trot, closely followed by his team. They climbed into the teapot – and to this day I'm still not sure how they all got in, especially Dieter – and we could hear the sounds of metal hitting metal, together with a great deal of cursing, indicating that the Technical Section was at work.

I sat back to think. Adrian and Mikey – only a hop skip and a jump ahead of the people who would imprison them for the rest of their lives if they caught them. If they didn't shoot them first, of course. Never staying anywhere for longer than two hours. Trying to eat and sleep in two-hour bursts. Struggling to keep their teapot together. Yes, it was fun now, but what would it be in five years' time? Or ten? Would they still be enjoying themselves then? Because they could never stop. The minute they stood still, the Time Police would have them.

I looked across the table to Dr Bairstow and said, 'Sir…?'

He can add mindreading to his list of achievements. 'You may, Dr Maxwell. Go and organise something.'

I gathered up my dress in two big bunches and galloped off. I raced to Sick Bay where they were receiving – according to Dr Stone – Dr Stone's patented anti-radiation medication. I added a shower and having their clothes washed to the list of medical treatment they would receive.

And back out to Dieter, who had emerged from the teapot and was easing his back.

'Dieter – safety protocols?'

He said carefully, 'They don't appear to have any.'

'Really? Good.'

He sighed and rolled his eyes. 'Typical historian. Not good, Max. Not good in any way. Not good at all.'

'Yes, it is,' I said. 'It means they can still jump if I load them up with supplies.'

'You do realise that's one of the main reasons the Time Police are chasing them. Because they could, if they wanted, walk off with the 'Mona Lisa' while the paint is still wet.'

'But they haven't, have they? Plundered the past, I mean.'

'Not yet,' he said grimly, 'but they're only two skinny teenagers and this pod thing,' he gestured behind him, 'could be taken from them at any time and used by others for nefarious purposes.'

I was gathering up my skirts again, poised for departure.

'Nefarious?'

He beamed. 'The Technical Section's word of the day.'

'I thought you only understood words like hammer and thump and bro-ken.'

'Not at all,' he said looming over me. 'I also know words like cheeky and bug-ger and push off Maxwell and let us get on with saving their lives.'

I paused. 'That bad?'

'It would have been. Turning up here today has probably saved them.'

And back to the kitchen, where Mrs Mack was ahead of me.

'Care packages,' she said, nodding towards her staff stuffing compo rations into a box. 'And some fresh fruit. And chocolate. And a wheel of Wensleydale. They'll eat well for a week, anyway.'

I just had time for a cup of tea myself before Dr Stone brought them back, considerably cleaner and, presumably, radiation free. Each of them was clutching a little bag of medication. Each had a radiation badge pinned to their front. They were still eating and talking. Simultaneously. We should recruit them into St Mary's. They were certainly the Right Stuff.

We gathered outside their teapot.

'Listen to me,' said Dr Bairstow, and they did. 'If your badge turns red, return to St Mary's at once. If either of you are injured or sick, return to St Mary's at once. If, at any point, you are in trouble or in danger – or more trouble or danger than you feel you can cope with – return to St Mary's at once. We will do what we can for you. Now, your...' he glanced up at the teapot, appeared to select and reject various words, finally settling for, 'conveyance ... has been serviced. The radiation leak that would eventually have killed you has been repaired. A week's worth of rations has been loaded and you have been fed and watered. That should keep you out of trouble for the foreseeable future.'

They nodded, suddenly solemn. Adrian said, 'On behalf of Mikey and me, thank you, Dr Bairstow. We didn't know ... about the leak, I mean. Well, we did, but we didn't think it was that serious.'

Mikey nodded and beamed up at him. 'Thank you, Dr Bairstow. You've been very kind.'

I don't think anyone had ever accused him of kindness before. He put out his hand. 'Good luck to the pair of you.'

'Thank you, Dr Bairstow.'

'Don't thank me,' he said sternly. 'You're going to need it. However, remember what I said. You are not without a refuge.'

Somewhere in Mikey's capacious pocket, the alarm clock went off.

'Time to go,' said Adrian cheerily, and they climbed the ladder. Mikey hauled it up after them and they dropped it back into the teapot with a thud. Dieter winced.

They waved merrily and shouted goodbye and then the hatch closed. And opened again. 'You might want to stand back a bit,' shouted Mikey. And then the hatch closed again.

'I would certainly advise that,' said Dieter, ushering us all back to the terrace and the remains of our tea.

When we turned back – they were gone.

They'd cut it a bit fine, actually. I'd barely poured myself another cup of tea and picked up a salmon and cucumber sandwich when the Time Police turned up.

At least they'd learned not to come piling out of their pod, weapons raised, shouting at us to comply with a number of contradictory instructions.

We sat back and watched them cross the grass towards us. Mikey's cheese lay in their path and appeared to warrant a good deal of attention.

As Adrian had said, there were four of them and they opened the conversation by demanding to know where we were hiding them.

Dr Bairstow sat back, so I gathered it was up to me and Peterson.

'Who?'

'Those two.'

'Two who,' said Peterson unable to resist.

'Two renegades in a homemade pod.'

I was about to deny all knowledge when one of the cheese-fixated officers reported its radioactive qualities.

'That proves it.'

'Proves what?'

'That they were here. Their pod leaks radiation wherever it goes. This cheese is radioactive. Therefore, they were here.'

'Wow,' I said softly, just to wind them up a bit. 'This is advanced thinking for the Time Police.' Because angry people don't always think as clearly as they should.

Dr Bairstow decided to enter the fray.

'My dear sir, you are aware we recently sustained enormous damage when our hangar and pods were involved in an explosion? There is radiation everywhere.'

'Still?'

'Certainly. I do hope that those of you who have plans for imminent parenthood have donned the appropriate protective gear. Thank you for pointing that out to us, however.'

The officer had been looking around. 'Why is there a lump of cheese on the lawn at all?'

A good question, to which Dr Bairstow was more than equal. Raising his eyebrows, he said haughtily, 'Forgive me, I thought it was perfectly obvious that we were holding a croquet tournament.'

'So?'

'Is it possible that you are unaware of the significance of cheese in a croquet tournament?'

'It would appear they are, sir,' said Peterson, with his,

what idiots not to have guessed the significance of cheese in a croquet tournament expression. I have to say, that that one doesn't get a lot of use.

'But this cheese is radioactive.'

'Of course it is,' said Mrs Mack, standing up and entering the fray. 'It's a piece of the famous Rushfordshire Stinking Henry, a very old and famous cheese dating back to 1412. Legend says Henry V took vast quantities of it with him to France where the noxious fumes overcame all opposition and played no small part in his victory at Agincourt. Apparently the smell drove the horses insane with fear and they refused to approach the English lines resulting of course, in the famous English victory. As I'm sure you're aware.'

St Mary's sat, transfixed at this brilliance.

'But why is it radioactive?'

'If you'd been around since 1412 you'd be radioactive too.'

He looked around at the tranquil scene. St Mary's having afternoon tea on the terrace. The croquet rackets … clubs … bats … propped against the wall, our walking wounded sitting down and scoffing afternoon tea and, most importantly, the complete absence of giant teapots in the landscape.

Mrs Mack hadn't finished with him. 'Would you like some tea before you go?'

He shook his head wordlessly.

She beamed. 'Or a slice of cake?'

'No. Thank you.'

'Or we could make you up some sandwiches for the journey home.'

'No.'

'It's no trouble.'

'*No.*'

'We have plenty to go around.'

'Look, I said no. Are you deaf or what?'

Everything suddenly went very still and very quiet.

I stepped forwards. 'Silly me – where are our manners? I don't think we've been properly introduced, have we? You must allow me to present Theresa Mack, Kitchen Supremo and former urban guerrilla. Yes, that's right, *the* Theresa Mack. The one who led the resistance in London. The one who commanded the Battersea Barricades. The one who turned back the Fascist forces.'

I stepped even closer and lowered my voice. 'She could almost certainly kill all four of you where you stand, armed with nothing more than the sugar tongs too. So no sudden moves, eh?'

For a moment we all stared at each other. My back was to St Mary's, but I just knew people were reaching for butter knives, croquet clubs, hairpins, parasols, whatever. Major Guthrie always used to say that anything can be used as a weapon. Someone scraped a chair as people began to stand up. It really looked as if we were going to be able, legitimately, to kick seven shades of shit out of the Time Police. What a great day this was turning out to be. I was suddenly feeling better than I had for ages. Tim caught my eye and we grinned at each other. This was how our lives should be – enjoying ourselves at St Mary's and pissing off the Time Police.

Who were rapidly discovering that discretion was the better part of valour. No one wants death by sugar tongs at their post-mortem. They knew Adrian and Mikey had been here. Equally, they knew they'd missed them and they were long gone. And without leaving one of their famous notes, either. Their leader gave the word to withdraw. There were a lot of hard looks as they retreated back to their pod. Giving the cheese a wide berth, I was pleased to notice.

We smiled and waved as they left. Just to piss them off that little bit more, Evans instructed them to come back anytime and not to be strangers, do you hear?

Dr Bairstow sat back. 'That went well, I thought.'

His good mood was still in evidence the next morning. I'd brought the casualty list down from Dr Stone. This had been our doctor's first competitive event at St Mary's and he was still in a state of mild disbelief.

Dr Bairstow, on the other hand, was very nearly jovial. It wasn't every day he got to put one over on the Time Police.

'What's the damage, Max?'

'Well, sir, working my way down the accidental injury list...' I took a deep breath.

'One sprained wrist.

'One suspected case of tennis elbow.

'One suspected case of trigger finger. I've no idea, sir. Please don't ask me.

'Sundry bruised shins and ankles – mostly the result of poor aim or lack of coordination, but I suspect one or two old scores may have been settled.

'One suspected but very unlikely hernia.'

'One black eye.'

I swiped to the next page on my scratchpad.

'Working my way down the list of injuries incurred during disagreements over croquet protocols…

'A number of bruises and black eyes.'

'How many?'

'More than two but less than four, sir.'

He seemed impressed, but whether that was because the injuries were so many or so few remained unclear.

'Sundry lacerations.'

He nodded.

'Working my way down the list of miscellaneous injuries, sir…

'One case of mild sunburn.'

'In this country?'

'Apparently, sir.'

'Goodness gracious.'

'And um … one horse bite and some minor trampling.'

'I am almost afraid to ask.'

'Attempted retrieval of a lost ball sir. Turk took exception to Mr Bashford invading what he considers to be his personal space.'

'How much space can a horse consider to be personally his?'

'As far as I can ascertain, sir, an area covering most of Rushfordshire. There's also a small sprinkling of alcohol-related injuries, sir, including Mr Keller falling over as he tried to take off his boots. No concussion.'

He muttered something about Edward II sustaining fewer casualties at Bannockburn. And he'd lost. 'And damage to the building?'

'Relatively minor, sir. Mostly, but not necessarily

confined to, the occasional broken window.'

'And?'

'One or two items of furniture may have incurred minor damage during the action replays in the bar last night.'

'So yesterday went well then?'

'Indeed, sir. No one hospitalised, the building still standing, two charming new friends made, and the Time Police deceived.'

'And the final score?'

'The final result of the croquet match remains contested, sir, otherwise, St Mary's – one. Time Police – nil.'

'Have we learned anything from yesterday?'

'Well, I think Mr Evans has learned not to stand behind Miss Sykes when she has a croquet club in her hand. And Miss Lingoss's performance may have caused one or two people to revise their stereotypical opinion of the female inability to bowl overarm.'

'I am almost certain yesterday's game was croquet not cricket, Dr Maxwell.'

'A temporary confusion on Miss Lingoss's part, sir. Soon resolved and apparently no hard feelings afterwards.'

He sat quietly for a while, tapping his pen on his desk. I waited for what I knew was coming.

'They were delightful young people, weren't they?'

'They were sir. And, thanks to St Mary's, considerably less radioactive than they were this time yesterday.'

He leaned forward. 'Do you think Adrian knows Mikey is a girl?'

I grinned at him. 'I'd be surprised if Mikey knows Mikey is a girl, sir.'

One evening, about a week later, Peterson knocked on our door.

Usually, on Friday afternoons, while the Technical and Security Sections battered the hell out of each other in the name of football, I would go to his office with all my paperwork for him to sign. He would drop it all on the floor, yank open his bottom drawer and pull out a bottle of wine. I would put my feet up on his desk and we'd have a glass or two and a good old moan about the week. Sometimes, he would call by my rooms in the evening to help Matthew with his jigsaw, or even just to chat. I think he was lonely.

Anyway, this was obviously one of those evenings and I was pleased to see him. 'Come in.'

'What ho, Matthew.' He held up a bottle of wine. 'Have you got a minute, Max?'

'Of course I have. You're just the person I need.'

He looked uneasy. 'Why am I just the person you need?'

'Grab a seat. I need your advice.'

'On what?'

'You're a man, aren't you?'

'So it says on my documents,' he said.

'I wondered if you would have a word with the young master here about peeing in the shower.'

'For or against?'

'I can't believe you have to ask that, although given the number of things you've peed on over the years…'

'You never let that go, do you?'

'Unlike you who lets go all the time.'

'To the best of my knowledge I have never peed in your shower.'

'It would be nice if you could claim never to have peed in anyone's shower.'

He looked uneasy. 'How truthful do you want me to be?'

I got up to go and turn down Matthew's bed. 'I'll be back in a moment. I shall leave the pair of you to discuss improved flow control.'

'I really wouldn't bother Max. We're men. If there's running water and a drain, we just can't help ourselves. It's in our genes.'

'You are never setting foot in my bathroom again.'

'I've never set foot in your bathroom anyway.'

I returned to find Matthew grinning at Uncle Peterson and picking up tips on how to defy his mother.

I told him to go and get ready for bed.

'No', he said, obviously keen to put his newly acquired skills to good use.

'Now,' I said.

'Can't make me,' he said, well aware that corporal punishment was off the table.

'Want to bet?' I said

He folded his arms. My own eyes glared back at me.

'What can you do?'

'Nothing,' I said, rummaging for the corkscrew. 'Not now, that is.' I paused and pointed the corkscrew at him. 'But *tomorrow*, I shall wait until the entire Security Section is watching and then I shall put my arms around you, give you a huge wet kiss, and call you Mummy's Special Little Soldier.'

'Oh, I say,' said Peterson, shocked. 'Cruel and unusual punishment, Max.'

'Yeah,' I said, folding my own arms and glaring back at Matthew with his own eyes.

He stumped off to his room, muttering.

'Glad you're not my mother,' said Peterson.

'Please, that's not an image I want to carry with me. Open the wine.'

I don't know what Miss Lingoss and Professor Rapson had been doing to him that day, but ten minutes later Matthew was out like a light. He lay on his back, mouth slightly open, with a plastic T-rex clutched tightly in one hand, Miss Dottle's teddy in the other, and the Time Map whirling around his head. I shut it down and quietly closed his bedroom door so Peterson and I could talk in peace.

I poured the wine. 'Do you want some?'

'I don't know why you bother to ask.'

When I handed him his glass, he was stuffing a small piece of paper back in his pocket.

'What was that?'

'Oh – just something I found in my pocket.'

'So – what can I do for you?'

He didn't speak immediately, swirling his wine around

343

in the glass.

'What's the problem?'

'Nothing … Well, yes … but … There's something I want to talk to you about.'

He looked so serious that a sudden fear ran through me. 'You're not ill, are you?'

'No. Oh no. Nothing like that. Don't panic.'

'Well, what then?'

'I have something to say. To ask you, actually, and I'm worried it will lose me the best friend anyone could ever have.'

'If you mean me, dummy, I'm not going anywhere.'

'I wouldn't be too sure. You haven't heard what I have to say yet.'

'Am I in trouble?'

'Astonishingly, no. But I think I might be.'

'In what way? Are you sure you're not ill?'

'Quite sure. But I'm not fine.' He put down his wine, twisted around to face me and took both my hands.

'The thing is, Max … you and I are not the sort of people who … I'm not good at this … but OK … Here it is … I think I … I mean, I haven't said anything because … Well, I was worried it might be too soon … or that you might not … I mean … and then I said those stupid things … and I hope you know how sorry I am … but I was thinking that perhaps … Well, you know…'

He trailed to a halt, let go of my hands and took a gulp of his wine.

'I find it quite disturbing that I actually understood every word of that.'

'Well, thank God for that because I don't think I could

344

do it again. So what do you think?'

Good question. What did I think?

'Well, I think … I mean … it would be … Unless you thought…'

I stopped and took a gulp of my own wine.

There was a bit of a silence while the pair of us reassembled our capacity for coherent speech.

He said quietly, 'Max, I'm going to ask you a question. Please tell me the truth. Don't lie to me.'

I could feel my heart thumping with alarm. 'I never would. You know that.'

'How lonely are you?'

I thought I was all right. I thought I was fine. I had my job, my friends around me. I had Matthew, happily doing whatever it was eight-year-olds do. I had my painting and my books. I thought I had everything I needed but, with that one question, the whole empty, fragile framework that I had constructed on which to hang my life disintegrated around me and crashed to the ground in a shower of bittersweet memories, empty days and awful, aching, unacknowledged, lonely nights. For the first time, I opened my eyes to the hard road leading to a bleak and empty future and before I knew what was happening, two great fat tears rolled down my cheeks.

'Oh God, I'm sorry, Max. I didn't mean to make you cry.'

'I'm not crying for me,' I said, 'I'm crying because…' and was completely unable to put it into words.

We sat together on my sofa and I thought – this is Tim. Just tell him.

I sniffed a bit and then said, 'It's just … This sounds

stupid, but when did our lives become so dark, Tim? Do you remember the fun we used to have? When did everything become such a struggle? I know nobody sets out to have their life go wrong and I've always known mine would never be sunshine and roses, but I never thought it would be this bad. I thought I would have a little baby and he would love me and I would love him. I thought I could have both work and Matthew. I thought Leon would always be with me. I thought – oh so many things. How stupid am I? When did everything go so wrong?'

He sighed. 'When that bastard Ronan turned up. That's when things started to go pear-shaped. But he's gone now, Max. Yes, I know he took some good people with him, but if we allow that to darken our lives then he's still winning even after he's dead. And that's just plain wrong. We're still here. We still have a chance to bring some fun back into our lives. What do you say?'

I've been at St Mary's long enough for the kookaburra of caution to hover over my head occasionally.

'What did you have in mind?'

'Nothing onerous. I thought – if you don't object – we could just … go out … one evening.'

I smiled sadly. 'I'm not sure, Tim. When I think back on what's happened over this last year, I sometimes wonder if people like us aren't supposed to have normal relationships.'

He grinned at me, suddenly looking like a very young Tim Peterson on our first assignment together. To Westminster Abbey, when a socking great block of stone missed us by inches and he peed on me.

'Oh, come on, Max. Who wants a *normal* relationship?'

'Well, no one at St Mary's because they're certainly never going to get one.'

'Look, if it's too soon for you then I'll understand. I hope you'll say yes, but if you don't I don't want this to make any difference – to us – which is my main fear. So if you want to pretend this never happened, then just tell me, and I promise I won't mention it again.'

He peered at me hopefully.

I sought clarification. 'Is this a date?'

'No. Well yes, maybe. It's a kind of semi-date – just two old friends going out for a meal and a drink. Together,' he added, in case I was having problems with the concept.

I said more wistfully than I intended, 'I haven't been out for ages.'

'Well, there you are then,' he said, as if that clinched it. 'And it's not as if either of us has any unpleasant surprises for the other, Max. You're getting a man with only one working arm and poor bladder control and I'm getting a red-haired madwoman who triggers an apocalypse every time she walks into a room. Personally, I think we're perfect for each other.'

'I'm not sure I have anything decent to wear.'

'Doesn't matter. Casual is good. How do you fancy tapas?'

'Oh yes. I like exciting food.'

'Yes, because our lives are so dull. Is tomorrow good for you?'

'Yes,' I said, suddenly aware of a yawning pit of

inexperience. I would have to get to grips with babysitters. And make-up. And shoes that weren't boots. 'Although I'm not sure what I'll wear. I'm not sure I've even got anything appropriate. I mean, it's a long time since…' I petered out, adrift in a strange new sea.

'I'm sure you'll find something. I always liked that cream thing with the lace sleeves.'

My room was very quiet. The whole place was so quiet I could hear pipes ticking and the odd groan, which I hoped was just the building settling and not of human origin.

His face showed nothing but his usual lazy good humour, but I noticed his left foot jiggling away by itself. No matter how light-hearted his approach, this meant a lot to him.

I suddenly realised it meant a lot to me, as well.

I said, 'Are you sure?' because this was a big – a giant – leap for both of us, and he said, 'Oh yes, I think so, don't you?'

I was surprised to find that yes, I did think so too.

I nodded.

'Jolly good,' he said, getting to his feet. 'I shall suppress my inevitable misgivings about your appearance and present myself tomorrow at eight. See you then.'

As soon as he'd gone, I whipped open my wardrobe door and surveyed my options. That didn't take long.

I pulled out the cream top and slipped it on. It looked awful. I can honestly say it looked better on the hanger than it did on me. Actually, it looked better on the floor than it did on me.

I found a black thing I'd forgotten I had, and that

looked even worse. Everyone in the universe looks good in black except me. I sighed and tossed it onto the bed.

Next up was a nice, silky, pale green thing with slashed sleeves. On me it looked like a giant lump of snot.

Then there was the blue thing I'd never worn. I pulled it over my head and could see why.

Last up was a gold thing with a fringe. I don't know what I was thinking when I bought that. I didn't even bother trying it on. That went straight onto the floor.

I sighed and reached for the cream thing again. It looked no better the second time around. Sadly, neither did I. Even allowing for the distorting properties of my ancient mirror, was I really that shape? Did my hair really look that bad? Were my feet really that big?

Downstairs, Peterson would be happily watching TV or reading or something and not for one moment giving this sort of thing a second thought. All he had to do was find a clean shirt, put on his best jacket and comb his hair. Why was life so bloody unfair? You don't catch men trying on every single item of clothing they possess because they can't find anything that doesn't make them look like something the cat coughed up.

And I hadn't even started on my bottom half. Or shoes. Or lipstick. Why had I said I would do this? I had a demanding job and an even more demanding child. I couldn't afford to spend large chunks of my life staring at myself in a mirror. I needed help.

I went to Kal for advice. Her face filled my laptop screen.

'What's up?'

'I'm raging against humanity's injustices.'

She blinked. 'O … K. Any injustice in particular or is this an all-encompassing, one size fits everyone rage?'

'Why is everything always so much easier for men?'

'It's their outside plumbing.'

'What?'

'My theory is they wouldn't be half so light-hearted about everything if, every time they were caught short outdoors, they had peel off layers of clothing, squat and then wait for their shoes to dry out afterwards.'

I considered this. 'You could be right.'

'I'm always right. So what's brought this on?'

I explained about Peterson and my sartorial difficulties.

'Well, let's have a look then.'

I held up the black top.

'No.'

And the blue one.

'Really? No.'

And the third – the gold one.

'God, no. Good Grief, Max, you've really gone to pieces since I left, haven't you?'

'Well,' I said feebly, 'I've had a lot on and I haven't really felt much like clothes shopping.'

I don't know why I bothered. Kal does sympathy like Hitler did Stalingrad.

'What else have you got?'

I held up the green affair with slashed sleeves.

'Is that some sort of tea towel?'

I balled it up and threw it across the room. 'No.'

'Let's have a look at that other one. The cream one there. On the bed. Yes, that'll do nicely.'

'What about my hair. Up? Down?'

'In a loose ponytail tied with that black and cream scarf I gave you last Christmas. Let the ends hang over your shoulder. Those black trousers you have and black pumps. There. Done and dusted.'

It began to dawn on me her answers were suspiciously pat.

'Did you know about this?'

'Course I did. I've been waiting all evening to hear from you. What took you so long?'

'Did you know what he was going to ask me?'

She sighed heavily. 'I told him what to say.'

'What?'

'Well, I had to. He was useless. Gibbering like an idiot. So, in the end, I dictated. He wrote it down and learned it off by heart. How did he do?'

'How should I know? What was he supposed to say?'

She cleared her throat and said in a deep, gravelly voice. 'Max, I understand it may be a little soon to ask you this and if it makes you feel at all uncomfortable then of course, there's no more to be said, but I wanted to ask if you would do me the honour of allowing me to take you out one evening. We're old friends, you and I, and we enjoy each other's company. I don't want to put you under any sort of pressure and if you want some time to think about it then I shall quite understand. Is what he was supposed to say. How did he do?'

'He was spot on,' I said loyally. 'Almost word perfect. I was quite won over by his simple charm.'

'You're such a liar, Maxwell. Now, a few reminders because you won't have a bloody clue either. Remember

351

to wait for him to open doors for you. Abandon your feminist principles and let him pay. Don't talk about St Mary's.'

'But what will we talk about?'

'Books. Music. Politics.'

'OK.'

'Football, the latest holos, the weather.'

'Yes, OK.'

'Favourite food, wines, travel.'

'Yes, all right. For God's sake. Enough. What do you and Dieter usually talk about?'

'Who's turn it is to be on top. Good luck.'

And the screen went blank.

I opened the door to him. Just for a very brief moment, a flicker of relief flashed across his face. He hadn't been sure I would go through with it. Actually, neither had I. Especially after more last-minute doubts about the cream top.

'Well, what a pleasant surprise, Max. You don't look too bad at all. My worst fears have not been justified.'

'Thank you,' I said, closing the door behind me and heading towards the stairs, 'but I should warn you this is the only decent top I possess. If there's a second date, then I may have sartorial difficulties.'

'No need to panic. With luck this date will go so badly we'll never even speak to each other again, let alone achieve the giddy heights of a second date.'

'We can but hope,' I said gravely.

He smiled at me. 'I've been looking forward to this all day.'

I smiled back. 'Me too.'

He held out his arm and after only a moment's hesitation, I took it.

'Right,' he said, as we clattered down the stairs. 'Ground rules. No one talks about work. We're just two normal people looking for a normal night out.'

'Good idea,' I said, thinking that might be pushing our luck a little.

I was right. Just as we were crossing the hall, we were met by Mrs Partridge, emerging from the shadows. I don't know why, but I felt my heart sink.

She looked us up and down, noting Peterson's smart jacket, and my much tidier than usual hair, and said quietly. 'Dr Bairstow would like to see you.'

Peterson said, 'What? Both of us?'

She nodded.

'But we have a table booked. Won't tomorrow morning do?'

'No, I'm afraid not. Please follow me if you would be so good.'

'Has something happened?'

'Yes, it has. The Time Police want to see you, Dr Maxwell.'

People deal with different situations in different ways. Techies curse and reach for a screwdriver. Mrs Enderby has a wonderful repertoire of reproachful stares. The Security Section will probably shoot you. Historians panic. We're highly trained, lowly paid panickers.

I panicked now.

'Have they come for Matthew? They promised me time. Why are they here?'

Normally she just stares at me, effortlessly giving me to understand I am less than the dirt beneath her feet. On this occasion, to my surprise, she seemed genuinely distressed. My alarm increased. What could possibly distress Mrs Partridge?

'Mrs Partridge? What's happening? Please tell me.'

She said gently, 'I am unable to say,' but whether she couldn't or wouldn't say, remained unclear.

'Can't this wait? said Tim. 'We're on our way out.'

She said, almost with sympathy, 'I doubt, when you've heard what they have to say, that either of you will feel that an evening out is appropriate.'

I felt my stomach turn over.

Tim took my arm. 'Come on, Max, let's go and find out the worst. We can still go out afterwards.'

I looked at Mrs Partridge and the lack of expression on her face told me we wouldn't be going out afterwards.

I turned to him. 'Do you ever think we must be cursed?'

'All the time. Don't you?' he said cheerfully.

'What else could possibly go wrong?'

He shrugged. 'No idea, but this is St Mary's. Shall we go and find out?'

Commander Hay sat with Captain Ellis at the briefing table. Dr Bairstow stood by his desk, waiting. He too surveyed our unusually clean and tidy appearance. 'I am very sorry to have interrupted your evening but I think, when Commander Hay has explained, you will understand why this could not wait until morning.'

Explained what? Understand what?

'Please sit down. If you remember, at her request, I gave Commander Hay a copy of the footage from Hawking. Her people have spent some considerable time augmenting the tape and enhancing the quality. That done, they have subjected the improved tape to close analysis and scrutiny. And brought their findings for us to view this evening.'

'Have you discovered something?'

'We have.'

I looked at Dr Bairstow. 'What? What have they found?'

'I think you should sit down and see for yourself. I should warn you, you may find what you are about to see … unsettling.'

'In what way?'

Peterson said, 'Do you want me to remain, sir?'

'Yes, please. I would like both of you to see this and let me have your thoughts afterwards.'

I began to have a very bad feeling about this.

I sat at the table. Dr Bairstow activated the screen, and here were the familiar images, considerably enhanced this time. They'd split the screen and at one and the same time I saw myself in close up and far away. Dr Bairstow ran the footage at normal speed until Markham appeared, and then he slowed it down. Right down.

I watched Markham race slowly down the hangar, arms pumping. I saw him push me out of the way. Now Dr Bairstow minimised the second image, the distant one from the camera in Leon's office, and concentrated solely on the footage from the nearer camera.

I became aware my hands were clenched so tightly I was digging my nails into the palms of my hands. I looked down at the rows of little red crescents and made myself try to relax.

On screen, I had disappeared. It was just Ronan, Leon, Guthrie and Markham now. And, of course, the unseen Greta Van Owen.

Ronan stood in the doorway of his pod, just as I remembered.

Leon and Guthrie stood, guns raised, one or two paces from their own pod.

He slowed the film some more.

I saw Ronan bend his knees a little, preparing to hurl his bombs into the air.

Markham was closing but what could he do? If shooting Ronan was the answer, then Leon or Guthrie would already have done so.

357

Stupidly, I was holding my breath. As if that would make any difference. We all knew how this was going to end.

Beside me, Peterson stiffened and leaned forwards. A second later, I'd realised too. Markham wasn't heading for Ronan. He was running, flat out, towards Leon and Guthrie.

Ronan made his last, defiant gesture, bowing to the camera, and then he straightened his arms hurling two, small, black objects high up into the air.

They slowed the film again. Now it was clicking on. Almost frame by frame. The quality was deteriorating with each passing moment, but I saw Markham, still travelling at speed, crash headlong into Leon and Guthrie. The force of the collision and his momentum carried all three of them back towards their pod.

Dr Bairstow stopped the film.

I turned my head to look at him. My neck hurt when I moved. I hadn't realised I'd tensed every muscle.

He said, 'We shall split the screen again and play the two angles simultaneously. You will need to watch very carefully.'

He took up the remote and the film started up again, advancing, frame by frame. Click by click.

On the left-hand screen, the three of them, just a tangle of limbs and bodies, fall backwards.

On the right-hand screen, Ronan has released his bombs. He stands for a moment, arms above his head, looking up, following their trajectory. And then – something new – he steps back into his pod. He vanishes from sight. His door is closing.

On the left, almost inch by inch, they're falling. Falling back into the pod.

They say the onlooker sees most of the game. Had Markham, from far back in the hangar, realised what was about to happen? Was it possible that his objective was never Ronan, but Leon and Guthrie instead? He must have had less than a split second to make a decision and act on it. He gave his life trying to save them.

Click. They're almost through the door. Almost...

Click. On the other screen, Ronan's pod vanishes. He's gone. He got out before the blast. He's not dead. No time to think about that now.

Click. The other screen shows a dark hole which is the empty doorway. They're inside.

Then there's a huge white flash. Then nothing.

What?

I found I was gripping the edge of the table.

'Again,' said Dr Bairstow and, once again, there was Ronan's pod vanishing. He unsplit the screen. 'This is the best we can manage. Please watch very carefully.'

Peterson leaned forward. I pulled out my specs and practically climbed on the table.

Click. There's the open doorway.

Click. Still there.

Click. Still there.

Click. The dark shape has changed. It's smaller. The door is closing.

Click. Smaller still. But still not completely closed.

Click. Nearly. Nearly.

Click. Huge white flash.

Click. Picture gone.

I said hoarsely, 'Again.'

The open doorway.

The door closing.

Closing.

Closing.

Inch by inch.

And now I was leaning across the table, my nose practically on the screen.

Dr Bairstow paused the film and I squinted, blinked, and squinted again.

White flash.

'Go back!'

There was the door closing.

And there was the white flash.

But before that … just for a fraction of a second.

Without me asking, Dr Bairstow froze the screen.

And there it was. Or rather, there it wasn't.

Their pod was gone.

And then the white flash hurt my eyes.

But the pod was gone.

I sat back, thinking furiously.

The pod was gone. Before the explosion. But only very fractionally before the explosion. Was there a chance…?

I made myself take three long deep breaths before looking up to see everyone watching me.

Dr Bairstow said, 'It would appear there is a possibility – a small possibility – that their pod jumped away. Just a fraction of a second before the blast.'

No one spoke.

'However, it would also appear, on the face of it, that the door wasn't fully closed. Since, to my knowledge, a pod cannot jump with its door open, we are left with two conclusions.'

Still no one spoke.

'One – door status notwithstanding, they were able to jump away from the blast.'

I couldn't help looking at Commander Hay and her old/young face.

'Whether they would have survived such a manoeuvre is doubtful. Or two – the unclosed door means they weren't able to jump away from the blast and that our original hypothesis – that they were killed in the explosion – still stands.'

Silence.

So – the inescapable conclusion – either they were probably dead or they were certainly dead. Well, that was fractionally better than this time yesterday.

What now?

Commander Hay was talking. About the pod door, apparently. 'We're not sure if it was closed. Our best people have been over and over this footage and no one can definitely say yes or no. Let's say it was – because there's no point in speculating. If it wasn't – then they're all dead.

'Hey,' said Peterson, putting his hand on my shoulder.

'I'm sorry. I didn't mean to be so blunt. But the fact remains…'

No, she was right. If the door wasn't closed, then they were dead. Blasted into atoms. Or, if the door was closed but they were caught in the blast, then they were dead. But, if the door was closed and they somehow got away in time…

361

She was continuing.

'We're not sure what effect the explosion would have had on what was presumably an emergency extraction. We suspect that if they did survive, lacking any specific instructions to the contrary, the computer took them to their last known coordinates.'

'Which were?

'13th April, 1204.'

I felt my throat tighten. Fear clutched at me again. The unexpected joy of knowing that Leon and the others might still be alive was slipping away, to be replaced by something black and cold.

'Where?'

'Constantinople.'

Shit. Shit, shit, shit.

I heard Peterson swear softly to himself.

I stared at the table. One thought hammered through my head. Leon might be alive. They might all be alive. Suddenly, unexpectedly, out of the blue, I was being told that they might not have died in Hawking that day. That there was a chance they were still alive.

And then, in the next breath, I was being told they'd landed in one of the worst places in history. That even if they had survived the blast, or the possibility that the door might not be correctly engaged, or the crash landing, or whatever else had happened to them, then the chances were that they wouldn't survive for very long. Because they were in Constantinople on the 13th April, 1204.

I placed my elbows on the table, covered my face with my hands and let the tears fall, because I just couldn't hold it all back any longer.

They gave me two minutes. No more. Someone cleared their throat and I took my hands away to find Mrs Partridge handing me a cup of tea. Everyone politely murmured among themselves while I tried to pull myself together. Leon might be alive. Leon might actually still be alive. Why wasn't I more surprised? Deep down, had I always known? Was this why I'd never said anything to Matthew?

Don't get your hopes up, said a warning voice in my head. The blast – the crash – the landing – the terror of Constantinople on that day – any or all of those could have killed them. The odds against survival are very great. Don't allow yourself to hope.

Eventually, aware of the silence, I looked up.

Commander Hay clasped her hands on the table and leaned forward. 'I'm sorry, Max. You probably need time to process this, and you will have it, but not now. There is something else we must consider.'

I pushed thoughts of Leon to one side and croaked, 'What?'

'Yes, there is the possibility – a small one – that they weren't caught in the blast. But set against that is the certainty that neither was Ronan. And if he is still out there then all our previous arguments about Matthew's safety apply. We shall, of course, be staging a rescue mission to Constantinople.' She smiled faintly. 'We don't leave our people behind either. I am offering you a place on that mission, Max, but…' She paused. 'But, if you want to accompany us then I think you'll agree that Matthew should return with us to TPHQ. This is an excellent opportunity for this to come about quite naturally. You can leave him with us for safe-keeping. He can have a look around and decide what he thinks of us. You yourself can inspect our facilities, talk to people, whatever you need to do. Then, on your return…' she had the tact not to say with or without Leon, 'we can discuss something more permanent. If he wants to stay, of course. I think we agreed it would be up to Matthew to decide.'

I didn't think that was quite the agreement, but now was not the time and place. And she had a point. Ronan was still at large. If I was to go on this rescue – and I had a horrible feeling I was only being allowed to go because that would enable them to get their hands on Matthew – then it wasn't fair to expect others here to look after him. And Dr Bairstow's responsibility was to St Mary's. Lingoss had her own job to be getting on with. And Matthew had to start having a proper education sometime.

If I refused, then I wasn't sure whether I would be allowed to go and I had to. I just had to go. So – priorities. Get Leon first. Sort out Matthew later. And at least he would be safe at TPHQ while I was gone.

I nodded my agreement.

Afterwards, I found myself on the gallery, looking down at the deserted, dimly lit Hall. I leaned on the balustrade and tried to think. I heard someone approach and knew that Tim was standing behind me.

I turned to face him. He stood before me with his smart jacket and neatly combed hair. The expression on his face made me want to cry. I desperately wanted to put my arms around him and somehow make everything better for him, but that would not be a good idea for either of us.

I said, 'Tim…'

'Max, it's OK. I'm pleased for you. I really am.'

'Tim…'

'And if … well … you know, if things don't work out for … the best … then just remember I'm here … if you need me.'

I nodded, my eyes blurring with tears. 'You mustn't let go, Tim. You must hold on.'

His smile was crooked and bitter. 'I had hoped we would be able to hold on to each other.'

I couldn't speak.

He cleared his throat. 'You should get off now. Lots to do. You need to talk to Matthew as well. Anything I can do to help?'

I've known Tim Peterson for many years now and I could see how desperately he wanted to be alone. To absorb what had just happened. To come to terms with … events.

I pretended to think carefully. 'No, I think I'm OK, thanks very much. Are you around later if I think of anything?'

'Of course,' he said, backing away. 'Anytime. Just give me a shout.'

I nodded and somewhat blindly set out to find Matthew.

He and Lingoss were in R&D, building a dirigible. Of course they were. Just a small one, she reassured me.

'We're going to pilot it around the building,' she said,

forestalling my inevitable questions. 'There'll be a little basket underneath to hold files, scratchpads, memos, bacon butties – that sort of thing. People can use it to send things to each other. Like email, but with physical objects. It'll be really useful.'

There were so many things wrong with that statement that I never even bothered to start. I took her to one side and explained briefly.

She looked at me for a moment and said nothing. Today's hair made her look like Sideshow Bob, but underneath all that hair and make-up there's a very bright girl.

I took a chance. 'Can you do me a favour?'

'Of course.'

'I don't know how you'll manage it, but I don't think Peterson should be alone this evening. You're intelligent and resourceful without being obvious. Think of something.'

She nodded. 'I will, don't worry.'

'I knew you would. Go now.'

She disappeared.

I turned to Matthew, horribly dirty despite not having set foot out of doors all day. 'And now, young man, you and I are off on a trip.'

Back in our rooms, I pulled down my sports bag and, not without a great deal of deliberation on Matthew's part, packed three of his favourite toys. On top of those I hurled his sweatshirts, jeans and shirts. This not being bath or bedtime, he was wearing his precious trainers. I watched my hands folding and smoothing and, all the time, the same phrase was looping endlessly through my head – Leon might be alive. Leon might be alive.

I said nothing to Matthew. More than ever, I was glad I hadn't told him about his father.

I'd been told to bring only what I stood up in, but I wasn't going into battle in my only decent top, so I changed into blues. We were running down the stairs when he stopped dead and looked up at me.

'What?' I said.

'My teddy.'

I had forgotten all about it. It must have been buried under the clutter on his bed, but I could hear voices in the Hall. They were waiting for us.

'Sorry,' I said. 'I have to see Dr Bairstow. I'll get teddy for you later, I promise.'

He nodded. Sometimes his quiet acceptance of everything going on around him was quite worrying.

I called in to see the Boss. Time was short but there was something very important I had to say to him.

I sat Matthew down in Mrs Partridge's office and said, 'Wait here a minute.'

I left the two of them staring at each other with wary suspicion, but I didn't have the time – they'd just have to sort it out themselves.

The Boss was sitting behind his desk.

I couldn't think of any tactful way to put it, so I just came right out with it. Making sure the door was closed, I crossed his faded carpet and said, 'Sir, Ronan promised me he would kill everyone in my life. He's already killed Helen and probably Leon, Guthrie and Markham as well.'

I swallowed. 'Matthew will be safe at TPHQ, but I would be grateful if you could assure me that you have taken all steps necessary to protect yourself. I couldn't bear it if I got back and…'

He limped out from behind his desk and took my hand. 'I promise you, Max, when you return, I and Dr Peterson and everyone here will be safe and sound. You have my word.'

I nodded, unable to speak.

'I shall take advantage of this moment to demand that you also, Max, take every care. You are the spirit of St Mary's and we cannot do without you.'

'Yes, sir.' I turned to go and then looked back. 'Do *you* think they're still alive?'

'I am convinced of it, Max. Now, go and bring back our lost boys.'

I stood quietly at the back of the pod, holding Matthew's hand. He didn't seem particularly alarmed but that meant nothing. Captain Ellis was piloting the pod. He said cheerily, 'Hey, Matthew. Remember me?'

Matthew nodded, still not saying anything.

I squeezed his hand for reassurance although I should probably make it clear the reassurance was for me. We were jumping to the future – well, my future anyway – and that's enough to make anyone nervous. I'm an historian. I like to know when and where I'm jumping. I like to research the time period so I know what to expect. Jumping into the unknown makes me nervous. And I was jumping to TPHQ which would make anyone nervous at any point on the timeline. And I had no St Mary's team to back me up. It was just Matthew and me. It did cross my mind that this was all just an elaborate Time Police trap to get their hands on Matthew. I really do need to work on my paranoia issues.

Someone said, 'Commence jump procedures.'

'Commencing now.'

The world flickered.

That was it. Half of me was a little disappointed. Half of me was quite smug. St Mary's does it better.

My disappointment continued.

We began well, landing in any sinister organisation's mandatory underground bunker. I knew it was underground because I could hear the fresh-air blowers overhead. Under the pretence of straightening Matthew's perfectly straight hoodie, I tried, surreptitiously, to have a look around, getting only a very fleeting impression of rows of black pods stretching away into the darkness before a very large officer, deliberately or otherwise, blocked my view.

Matthew, perfectly aware he hadn't managed to disarrange his clothing in the four seconds between St Mary's and here, stared at me reproachfully.

We were escorted through the bunker, officers on either side of us. It smacked very much of prisoner and escort but I told myself they were the Time Police and probably didn't know any other way of doing things.

As far as sinister organisations go, however, it all went downhill from there. Once out of the bunker we were in a disappointingly normal corridor, clean and well lit, which ended in a disappointingly normal lift. Although it was circular – which did strike me as unusual.

Ellis grinned at me. 'You'll see.'

'See what?'

He just grinned again.

Once out of the lift, our escort peeled away – obviously we weren't going to be shot after all – leaving just Commander Hay, Ellis and Farenden, who was speaking into some sort of coms device.

'Our visitors' accommodation is ready, ma'am.'

Hay nodded and turned to us. 'We'll take you to your rooms in a moment, but first there's something I wanted to show you and, selfishly, I want to see your faces when you catch your first glimpse. This way.'

We entered a small room. I looked around. Desk. Chair. Filing cabinets. Shelves. Files. A couple of screens. Nothing out of the ordinary at all. Even more disappointment. Still, I should set an example to Matthew and be polite.

'Very ... nice,' I said.

Captain Farenden grinned. 'This is my office.'

'Mmmm,' I said, having run out of positive things to say.

He flung open a door with something of a flourish.

'And this is *my* office,' said Commander Hay, leading us into a large room. I'm sure there was the usual impressive commanding officer-style furniture scattered around, but I had eyes only for the enormous picture window behind her desk.

She gestured. 'And this is my view.'

Oh my God, I recognised this place. I knew where we were. So this was the legendary TPHQ. I couldn't help laughing.

She laughed too. 'Do you like it?'

'It's ... amazing. Of course I do.'

Now I knew why the lift was circular – because Time Police HQ was located inside and under the iconic Battersea Power Station and the lift must have been inside one of the four massive chimneys.

I couldn't get my head around it. For obvious reasons, St Mary's is almost as far from civilisation as it's possible

371

to get. This place was at the centre of the capital city. I remembered our recent explosion. If this place ever blew…

'We need to be a presence,'' she said, reading my mind. 'We need to be visible. Highly visible. A constant reminder of what will happen to anyone – and that ranges from an entire country down to a couple of bored teenagers too clever for their own good –' She shot me a look which I had no difficulty returning with blinding innocence. '– that *anyone* who takes it into their heads to nip up and down the timeline, will incur our displeasure. Our extreme displeasure.'

I made no comment. It seemed the safest thing to do. Instead, I peered out of the window. Just down there had been the famous Battersea Barricades. Where the resistance had made its final stand and, against all the odds, had prevailed. When the tide had finally turned. Where Mrs Mack had lost her husband. Somewhere down there had been – and maybe still was – the legendary Flying Duck pub, where Dr Bairstow had begun to assemble his people, prior to setting up St Mary's. I wondered if I'd have time to take a look. He'd like to know if it was still here.

We were high up, looking out over the Thames. I could see Barricade Bridge – the former Chelsea Bridge – painted in pink and yellow, like a huge slice of Mrs Mack's Battenburg cake.

London spread in front of me. Up and down river. It was an amazing view. I'm not hugely familiar with London even in my own time, but the city itself didn't look so different. There were the usual eccentrically shaped buildings – because every capital city in the world has to have a skyline like a mouth of broken teeth. I could recognise The Shard – now a national monument. And The Gherkin. And The Cheese Grater. To which we could now apparently add The Pack of Cards, The Folded Napkin and The Startled Hamster.

Except there was no traffic. There were almost no cars anywhere. There was a great deal of river and air traffic, but vehicles on the ground were few and far between. I stared in amazement, first at the crowded Thames and then at the slow-moving airships, the zipping drones, and the dirigibles either hovering, tethered to various buildings, or chugging majestically past on their way to somewhere else. For a brief moment I was completely disoriented. Now I knew how Matthew had felt in my world.

'This is typical of all major cities now,' she said. 'The ground is for people. Pedestrians, emergency vehicles or electric bikes only. Not so long ago, gridlock was common. Cities were dirty and polluted. In London, the air was generally considered to be worse than it was in the 19th century with its famous "pea-soupers". Something had to be done and then someone realised we had a major water system already in place and running right through the city. Canals were revived or rebuilt, new ones constructed, underground rivers uncovered, and now, as in medieval and Tudor times, people use water to get around. You travel up and down the rivers on public transportation, disembark at the stop nearest to your destination, and either take a bike or a dirigible the rest of the way. Clean, quick, non-polluting.'

'Dirigibles!' I said. Matthew and I looked at each other.

'Auntie Lingoss,' he said.

'You must tell her. She'll be thrilled.'

I craned my neck further. Oh. My. God. 'Jetpacks,' I said in huge excitement. 'Does everyone have their own jetpack? Can I have one?'

'No.'

More disappointment, but I rather thought I might have a word with Professor Rapson one day. I was certain he could knock something up.

'There are viewing windows all over the building,' said Captain Farenden. 'Please feel free to have a good stare whenever you like. Now, if you'd like to come with me, I'll show you to your accommodation. Max, there will be a briefing at 17:00 hours this evening. Captain Ellis will collect you. Would you like to come this way?'

Their visitors' accommodation was large and characterless. We had two small bedrooms, a bathroom between us, and a living room. Everything was painted in shades of beige or magnolia, with accents daringly picked out in cream. I bet some interior designer somewhere had an award for this. The walls were bare and crying out for a small historian and her paintbrush. Or her son and his crayons. But it was very clean, the furniture was much more comfortable than it looked, and the water was hot.

Matthew chose the right-hand bedroom. I was impatient for Ellis to appear, but I made myself slow down, because this was important, too. We unpacked his stuff and I let him choose where he wanted to put everything. I kept any comments to myself. I didn't want Commander Hay accusing me of undue influence. The priority now was Leon, Markham and Guthrie. I wasn't happy about leaving Matthew here but he would be safe, no doubt of that, and I could sort out his future later.

There were tea-making facilities but only six tea bags. What? Not even enough to see me through the next hour, let alone the rest of the day. I opened my mouth to complain.

'Rationed,' said Captain Farenden, before I could utter a word.

'What?'

'You won't know this, of course, but tea is rationed now.'

I was gobsmacked. We all imagine the future as being an improvement on the present. Things appeared to have gone full circle. When tea was first introduced to this country it was considered an exclusive luxury. For the upper classes only. 'Why?'

'Tax makes it too expensive for most people. Six of us gave up a precious tea bag so you could indulge in what is, today, almost a black-market vice.'

I felt rather ashamed and didn't know quite what to say. 'Please thank them and say how much I appreciate it.'

Our rooms were lower down than the commander's office. We had the same view out over the Thames, but being on a lower floor, we could see some rather pleasant public gardens between us and the river. Matthew and I stood at the window, watching people lying on the grass, chucking frisbees for their dogs, eating sandwiches and generally relaxing. I was surprised. I never really equate the Time Police with enjoyment. As I mentioned to Captain Ellis when he came to collect me.

'I thought the Time Police would be more comfortable with minefields and razor wire.'

'It's our public side,' he said. 'When Commander Hay took over, as part of her "The Time Police are really nice people, honestly" policy, she commissioned the gardens and opened them to the public. It was meant to be a nice gesture. We're encouraged to go down there occasionally, to eat our lunch and smile at the children.'

'And do you?'

'Good God, no. Nasty, sticky little things,' he said, grinning at Matthew who grinned back. I sighed. He really did like men better than women. And he liked everyone better than me.

Two officers, one male, one female, came to sit with Matthew. They didn't look much older than he was but, as I had to admit to myself, everyone was beginning to look young to me. They brought pizza and were armed with a box of goodies. I caught a glimpse of some sort of 3D jigsaw, some Harry Potter holos – both the classics and the new ones – toys full of flashing lights, and things that buzzed.

I thought he'd be thrilled and I would be able to slip away while he wasn't looking, but it didn't work like that. He looked at me over the box and I could see the questions in his eyes.

Normally, I'd make him speak, because it was important he communicated in words, not just grunts and gestures, but this wasn't the time. I said, 'Can you give us a minute, guys?' and they tactfully went off to cut up the pizza.

I sat him down and said, 'What's the problem?'

He simply looked around us and then back at me.

Like every parent on the planet, I considered lying to him because that was the easy way out, and then had second thoughts. This might be an opportunity to prepare him for bad news.

I didn't make the mistake of trying to take his hand or putting my arms around him, because he didn't like that sort of thing. Instead I said, 'We think Daddy might have hurt himself. We're going to look for him.'

He nodded but still said nothing.

'I've brought you here for these people to look after you while I'm gone.'

'Auntie Lingoss?'

'Is a little busy at the moment. You know we had a bit of an accident in Hawking and she's working hard to fix it.'

He nodded.

'I have to go for a minute now and talk to Captain Ellis and some other people. Will you be all right here with…' I paused.

They looked up. 'Trent and Parrish.'

'With Uncle Trent and Auntie Parrish,' I finished, which wiped the grins off their faces.

He stared at me for a moment, then nodded and began to rummage in the box of goodies.

I looked down at his dark hair, so like Leon's, stood up and headed for the door.

Just as I was leaving, he said, 'He's not with the others.'

I said, 'What did you say?' but he was already head down in his box. He had forgotten me.

Ellis and I set off for the briefing.

Which could have gone better.

It started well. I sat with thirty or so other people while Captain Ellis outlined the situation and briefed us on conditions in Constantinople and what we were about to encounter there.

Acting on the assumption that they were as badly injured as anyone could be without actually being dead, there would be four medical teams, each of three people, supported by four teams of four security guards. With Captain Ellis and me, that made a total of thirty people. Which was a lot. But, as Ellis pointed out, this wasn't a history-based assignment. This was a rescue mission.

I didn't argue. This was their way, not ours. Go in heavy – do the job – get out again. When I thought about it, I didn't have any problems with that at all.

We'd all go in their big hospital pod and I didn't have any problems with that either.

'We don't know what sort of condition they'll be in,' said Ellis. 'Or even whether they're alive at all.'

No one looked at me.

'Right then, people. Background. Constantinople in 1204 is a violent place. Everyone will be a threat to us. Invading crusaders are out for blood. Terror-stricken civilians will be desperate to escape and trampling anything in their path. There will be the elite troops, the

Varangian Guard, fighting a rearguard action. There will be toppling buildings and trampling horses. A lot of the city will be on fire. We'll be heavily armoured because on this occasion, historical accuracy is unimportant.'

Everyone looked at me. When did I get the reputation for being such a troublemaker? I'd barely been here ten minutes. For once, I agreed with them – historical accuracy was unimportant.

Unfortunately, that was as far as detente went. As usual, with the Time Police, things went tits-up fairly quickly.

Ellis had finished describing the conditions we could expect and was detailing the precautions to be taken. I had honestly intended to keep my head down and my mouth shut, but all I could hear was so much impatient, 'Yeah, yeah, yeah,' from the officers around me. I didn't think they were listening because this wasn't something they wanted to hear. Their attitude was very much, 'Can we stop talking and go and shoot someone now, please?' Shifting in my seat, I could see there were very few women present. Always a sign of an unenlightened organisation.

Eventually, I couldn't keep quiet any longer. Yes, I know but, honestly, this sea of testosterone was going to get us all killed. If Leon and the others were, by some miracle, still alive when we got there, I wasn't going to let these idiots blow our chances of getting them out safely. I raised my hand.

'Yes, Max?'

I did try. I tried, quietly and reasonably, to explain that shooting contemporaries, even in self-defence, would not

379

be a good idea. I tried to explain about History. I might as well have tried to explain evolution to a creationist. I was using words they simply didn't understand.

There was a certain amount of restless shifting in their seats and then someone said, 'It's going to be a slaughterhouse there. Are you saying we can't even defend ourselves?'

'It's a key point in History,' I said. 'We have to be really careful.'

I know – I can't believe I said that either. Two hours with the Time Police and my brain was already turning to yoghurt. I tried again. 'It's going to be tough enough without going in and deliberately asking for trouble.'

'We've never had any trouble before.'

'You were putting things right before. Righting wrongs. Repairing the timeline. As far as History is concerned, this will be just a bit of private enterprise. History isn't interested in rescues and noble causes and the like, and if you start mowing people down right left and centre then it will fight back.'

'That's no concern of ours.'

'It should be. There'll be enough going on around us without having to take on History as well.'

'Typical bloody St Mary's. It's a big boy's world out there, sweetheart, and if you can't hack it…'

'Hey, it wasn't St Mary's stupidity that caused all this to blow up in the first place.'

'It's your bloody boyfriend we're risking our lives for.'

'My bloody *husband* kicked your arse and don't you forget it.'

'Listen, sister…'

'Enough,' said Ellis sharply and we subsided. 'Our mission is to locate three St Mary's personnel – two of whom were working with us to assist with the apprehension of Clive Ronan – together with one of our own, and bring them home. They were working together in a common cause and so are we. We go in and we get them out. Sonic weapons. Low charge. For defence only – and only then as a last resort. The medical teams will do their job and the security forces will do theirs. This is new style policing. Minimum impact. Is everyone clear?'

There was some muttering and I began to suspect that Commander Hay might have more of a problem on her hands than I'd realised.

We went to get kitted out.

I liked their armour. It was a matt black, flexible and light – far better than anything St Mary's had – and, as far as I could see, capable of keeping out everything from a charging rhino to a small thermo-nuclear device. They issued me with a sonic gun. A very small one. I'd rather hoped I'd get one of the big ones and I'd look really cool, but no. I also picked up a small med-kit and a helmet. I thought I looked just like a real Time Police officer, but apparently I was in a minority of one on that one.

We assembled outside their hospital pod. Blacker and more sinister than your average medical facility, but with a big, red reassuring H painted on every side. And, presumably, the roof.

Inside, they'd set up four stations, each bed surrounded

381

by banks of equipment. A medical team stood by each one. Two pilots sat at the enormous console. I was impressed. Standing quietly against the wall, well out of the way, I looked around me. Everyone was armoured, even the medical teams. Their names were stencilled across the helmets, together with the red cross, the red crescent and every other medical aid symbol I knew. And a few I didn't. Faces were grim. Weapons ready. We were set to go.

For the first time since being caught up in events only a few hours ago, and whirled here almost without having time to think, I took a moment to consider the implications. Not just for me, but for everyone. They might not be dead. There was only the faintest chance, but they might not be dead. Ronan was almost certainly still alive, so why not Leon and the others? They were three tough professional men. And Van Owen was no slouch when it came to looking after herself, either. If anyone stood a chance of survival it would be those four. They could have done it. They could have survived. For the first time since I heard the news, I felt almost optimistic.

Until we got there and I saw for myself what we were dealing with.

As I've said on many occasions, we're historians. History is our business. Show me any major historical event and I'll point to a couple of badly-dressed misfits muttering to themselves and slowly rotating through 360 degrees in an effort to get everything safely recorded before being trampled, shot, covered in boiling oil, executed as spies, or catching something unpleasant. You may not have noticed, but although we do have an enormous amount of enthusiasm for our job, sometimes things don't go quite according to plan.

This doesn't mean, that our enthusiasm encompasses all of History. While we all have our wish lists, many of us have whatever the opposite of a wish list is. Things, people, places we definitely don't want to see.

For Peterson, it's the execution of Charles I. He gets very upset about it. No one knows why. Dr Bairstow respects this and should we ever jump to that particular event, it is clearly understood that Peterson will not be included.

I myself have two events on my list. The first is the murder of the scholar Hypatia, mathematician and philosopher. She was head of the Neoplatonic School of Alexandria. Dragged from her chariot, she was stripped and flayed alive by Christian zealots – an unfortunate victim of the power struggle between Orestes, Prefect of Egypt, and Cyril, Bishop of Alexandria. It is argued that her death marked the end of classical antiquity.

The second event is the Fourth Crusade. The Sack of Constantinople, April 1204. If our people were indeed here, then they were in some very serious trouble. It's well known that the Crusaders fell on the city, looting, burning, raping and murdering. Over three days, they stripped the city of everything of value – that's how the famous bronze horses ended up in St Mark's Square, Venice. Countless irreplaceable treasures were broken up or melted down only for their material worth. The wonderful statue of Heracles, made by the court sculptor of Alexander the Great, Lysippos himself, was melted down for its bronze. The Library was burned. Sanctuaries looted. Nuns raped. Thousands upon thousands of people were killed, raped or mutilated. For three days, the Frankish Crusaders, mad for blood and gold, and having, as they thought, a free pass from the Pope to do as they pleased, turned the city into a living hell. The Crusaders' treatment of Constantinople and its people would shatter the Christian church. The Greek Orthodox and the Roman Catholic churches were irrevocably sundered. The city would never recover its former glory.

And somewhere, in all this maelstrom of fire and blood, death and destruction was one small pod and its probably critically injured crew. Even if they'd survived the blast (which they probably hadn't), and the crash landing (which they probably hadn't), they'd be in no state to defend themselves against whatever was going on around them.

We could only hope we got to them before the invading Crusaders did.

I know we landed in the vicinity of the church of Hagia Sofia because the coordinates said so but visibility was so poor we could have been anywhere.

We were in an open space at the end of a narrow street with tiny houses on either side. This must be an area of small artisans. Each little house had a let-down front on which goods could be displayed. Normally, this street would be bustling with people going about their business: women shopping, men sitting outside their shops talking to each other, mothers shouting for or at their children, dogs sniffing around – all the sights and sounds of everyday life.

Today, that life was gone; for many people, gone for ever. It looked as if a tornado had been through the place. Gone were the carpenters, bread makers, tanners and leather workers, the metal workers, the masons. Broken pottery lay everywhere. A hand spindle lay abandoned nearby, still with tufts of sheep's wool. Looters had already been through the place. Overturned wicker baskets spilled their contents across the street. The table fronts on which the traders would display their wares were broken off, or hanging at crazy angles. There were signs that people's pathetic possessions had been dragged out into the street, kicked around for anything of value and then abandoned.

The air was so thick with smoke from burning buildings that even the looming presence of Hagia Sofia was lost in the murk. And given what the Crusaders were getting up to inside, it wasn't a place where anyone sensible would want to be.

In addition to the big screen over the console, this pod had screens on every wall, all of them showing different viewpoints, and none of them good. Even as I stared at the one closest to me, a group of people burst from the smoke, scorched, choking, dishevelled and desperate, running for their lives. They streamed past the pod, so terrified, so frantic, that I doubt they even saw us. Their open mouths showed red in their smoke-blackened faces. Lost children screamed in fear and panic, holding out their arms to be picked up and comforted. By anyone.

Moments later, in hot pursuit, half a dozen men, their armour splattered with blood, swords drawn, erupted from the same smoke.

They talk about crowd mentality. How – as part of a crowd – people will do things they wouldn't dream of normally. Terrible things. Looting. Rape. Torture. Murder. Things they would never have thought themselves capable of. Often, afterwards, they are horrified at their actions. They can't believe what they've done. They're distraught and ashamed. But here's the thing. That's afterwards. No matter how sorry they are afterwards, somehow it never stops them committing those atrocities in the first place.

They fell upon the fleeing people, most of whom were only women and children and all unarmed. They just hacked them into pieces. Not one swift, sure, almost merciful stroke. They fell upon them in a frenzy, hacking them apart. Limbs flew through the air, trailing arcs of scarlet blood. The man closest to us stabbed wildly into the tightly packed throng and, somehow, a bone must have locked on his sword. He tugged and tugged but to no avail. He shouted for help. Two others came to assist, laughing and tugging with him. His victim – a little boy of about ten – dead already, thank God, jerked like a hideous puppet as they pulled and pushed. It was a great game. Eventually, they had to use their own swords, hacking the body into pieces until finally the knight was able to wrench back his weapon. He aimed a final kick at something that really wasn't recognisable any longer and followed his comrades back into the smoke.

We watched all that in silence.

I thought – that could have been Matthew. That could have been my own little boy. Where was his mother? Was she watching in anguish, unable to protect her own child? Or, more likely, was she already dead?

Under the guise of passing me my helmet, captain Ellis said softly, 'Don't look, Max. I know what you're thinking, but for your own sanity, don't look.'

I did look of course. I had to. It's my job. Someone has to bear witness. I've seen brutality. I was up with the archers at Agincourt as the French cavalry crushed itself underfoot and drowned in the mud. I saw the Persian revenge on the Spartans who dared stand in their way at Thermopylae. I've seen Joan of Arc burn. I thought I'd seen it all, but I've never seen anything like the ferocity with which Christian fell upon Christian this day. It was beyond violent. Beyond brutal. The events of these three days would cast long, dark shadows over the next eight hundred years. Popes would apologise to Patriarchs but the Venetians still have the famous horses. Millions of tourists gawp at them every year and have no idea of the price paid for them.

Ellis turned to the woman in the right-hand seat. 'How long have we got?'

She swiped a few screens on the console, bringing up maps and figures. 'We have seventeen minutes before their estimated time of arrival.' She enlarged a display. 'Look for them in a north-easterly direction from this pod. Approximately five hundred yards. In about seventeen minutes. I'm sorry I can't be more precise.'

'No, good job. Listen up everyone. Everyone stays in their teams. One security detail to each medical team. One medical team to each casualty.' He turned to the driver. 'Get that ramp up as soon as we're gone and be ready to have it back down again in double time. We do not want to hang around here. Max, you will stay with me at all times. Ready everyone? On three.' He flipped down his visor. 'Good luck, everyone.'

The ramp came down and we moved out, plunging ever deeper into the artisan quarter. The narrow streets were like a maze. Some were no wider than the width of a skinny donkey. There were ankle-twisting steps up and down, or right-angled bends appearing out of nowhere. Sometimes we had to squeeze between two buildings. There were doorways and alleyways leading in all directions. It was almost impossible to take a direct path. Sometimes we were beaten back by flames, or the narrow streets were so choked with rubble we had no choice but to go back the way we'd come and find another way.

Wooden balconies, burning thatch and roof tiles fell on us from above. I had thought our main problem would be avoiding the gangs of Crusaders roaming the streets, drunk on blood and lust and stolen wine, but actually we were in more danger from the inhabitants themselves, so blind with terror that they would run straight over the top of anyone or anything in their way.

I caught a flicker of movement in the corner of my eye. A leather curtain hanging across an open doorway twitched. Someone wanted to see us without us seeing them. I guessed the family was still inside. They would remain there until the very last moment because no matter how dangerous it was to remain in a burning house, it wasn't half as dangerous as being out on the streets. As we were.

I've never seen so many people in so many tiny spaces. They were everywhere, lugging useless household possessions, trying to drive terrified goats or sheep. They surged first one way, and then discovering they couldn't get out, would attempt to turn back the way they'd come, only to become inextricably entangled with those desperately pushing from behind. We were continually buffeted by people who never even saw us, so desperate were they to get away. I saw people lying pinned under rubble, feebly calling for help, struggling to get free before they were trampled. Or burned. Or fell victim to the Crusaders working their way through the city. And there were dead people everywhere.

There was no order. No one was in control. I knew that the army had fled. The Varangian Guard, the elite, would hold their ground and fight, but they were hopelessly outnumbered. And they were a long way off by now. They would be guarding what was left of the churches, the monasteries, the palaces. This was one of the poorer parts of the city. The people here were on their own.

The real downside, as if there weren't enough of those already, was that because there was nothing of value here, those roaming these streets would probably not be Crusader knights at all, but the very worst kind of soldier. If they could be dignified with the name. Most of these men were not wearing the traditional white surcoat emblazoned with the red cross. Many wore no uniform at all. Some wore workmanlike leather tunics and boots and carried professional-looking weapons. They were mercenaries, maybe – here only because they were paid to be, and eager to enrich themselves with as much treasure as they could carry, and woe betide anyone who got in their way.

The very worst of them were covered only in rags and carried sticks with a stone lashed to the end. These men weren't even the jackals snapping around the edges. These were the utter dregs, here only to rape and kill. They had papal dispensation for any acts committed on a crusade and they intended to take full advantage of it.

The emperor, Alexios V, had abandoned his city and his people to the invaders and there was nothing and no one to stand in their way. Every soul here was doomed.

Whichever way we went, we always seemed to be swimming against the flow. Everyone else was always running in the other direction. We closed ranks and barged our way through, knocking people aside. The noise was tremendous. Thousands and thousands of people – all shouting and screaming as they fought to escape the burning city.

Away in the distance, I could hear the clatter of horses' hooves, but these streets were too narrow and too filled with obstacles. No horses could get down here. And why would they? There was nothing of value here. No churches full of gold and jewels. No fine buildings. No palaces. Just ordinary little homes and the people who lived in them. The defenceless people who lived in them. There was no one here who could put up any sort of fight. A few men had picked up pieces of wood but what use would they be against broadswords wielded by men with nothing on their mind but treasure and slaughter?

I remember the heat. The heat prickling the backs of my hands and coming up through the soles of my boots. The perspiration running down my face and making my eyes sting.

I also remember the isolation. I was alone inside my helmet. I could hear my own breathing rasping in my ears. I could hear other people's voices, clear but tinny and remote. I could also hear roaring flames, crashing buildings and screaming people. Biometric readouts flashed before my eyes and there seemed to be some sort of sit-rep trickle down. Red and green symbols and figures clustered at the edges of my vision. I had no idea what they meant and neither did I care. I ignored them.

I remember the piles of bodies lying everywhere like discarded dolls. Some of them were small enough to be discarded dolls. They lay half in and half out of doorways. Whether fleeing the burning building or seeking shelter from the slaughter, we'll never know. They lay heaped against the walls against which they'd huddled. Men lay in front of the families they had tried and failed to save. Dead women curled protectively around dead infants.

But mostly I remember the blood. Everything was red with it. We ran through sticky pools of it. I gave thanks for the breathing filters in my helmet. That I didn't have to breathe that distinctive copper smell or taste the metal in the back of my throat.

Everything around us was being destroyed. Flames licked around roofs and billowed from doors and tiny windows. And it wasn't just this street or a few streets around us. A whole city was burning. Constantinople – the queen of cities – was being devastated. Churches, palaces, monasteries – ancient and beautiful buildings were being torn apart for the treasures they contained.

The same went for the people. They too were torn apart for the treasures they carried. Necklaces were ripped from dead necks. Arms were hacked off for the bracelets and armbands they wore. Hands were chopped off living people and thrust into a bag because there was no time to prise the rings loose now. That was for later. Later – three endless days later – when some semblance of sanity would return to the invaders, they would find a skin of wine and a quiet corner, and rummage through the stinking, fly-swarmed bags for the treasures therein. I saw a woman standing motionless in shock, handless arms held rigid in front of her, screaming a long, high, thin scream as she watched her life blood arc through the air.

So I ignored Captain Ellis's well-meant advice and I looked. I saw it all. It was far worse than anything I had ever seen and I've seen a lot. This wasn't a battle between more or less equal forces with some rough sort of soldiers' code – this was armed men, blind with lust and greed, pitted against an unarmed, abandoned population.

Ellis kept us moving. Emerging from a dank, dark alleyway, we found ourselves in a small square. On another day, this would have been a pleasant place. Someone had placed a bench against a sunny wall. A few pots of herbs stood nearby. On another day, their scent would have filled the air. But not today. Today, something bad was happening here. A group of about twenty people mostly women and old people were grouped against a wall. They were surrounded by a group of laughing men, their swords drawn. A small pile of probably valueless trinkets lay on the ground in front of them, and even as we watched, a few coins were tossed down as well. Were they trying to buy their safety?

Satisfied they had extorted everything of value, the group of men lifted their swords. It was obvious what was going to happen next. Women screamed and cowered against the wall while one of the old men made useless appeals for mercy. At the same time, another man appeared at the other end of the square. A Crusader, it seemed, wearing the traditional long white surcoat emblazoned with the red cross – although the cross was no redder than the wet blood streaked around his hem. He was helmeted but his visor was raised. Shouting, he strode forwards, gesturing the men to keep away.

Reluctantly, they obeyed him. It was obvious this man held authority. Still shouting, he placed himself between the helpless civilians, many of whom were crying and wailing hysterically.

The mercenaries paused. I imagine greed was warring with discipline, but eventually their leader, a big man in a leather jerkin, bareheaded but wearing a breastplate, nodded. He stepped back, motioning to his men to do the same. It seemed this lucky group of people might be allowed to live after all.

Satisfied, the Crusader sheathed his own sword and turned away. They let him take three, maybe four paces before someone shouted. He wheeled around and the big man stabbed him in the face. He fell to the ground. He was probably dead already, but two men leaped on him, and while the leader stabbed him repeatedly, the others men fell on the screaming civilians.

Within half a minute, everyone was dead. The bench had been overturned, the pretty pots smashed, and the little square was running with blood. I watched it twist across the paving, seeping through gaps in the stones, mixing with the dirt, shit, straw and scummy water, and turning everything a bright, brilliant red. It was hard to imagine that anyone would ever again sit in this little square, feeling the sun on their face or smelling the herbs.

I stared at the dead Crusader, lying in his own blood. At some point his helmet had come off. His face was gone. A good man who had tried to do a good thing on this very bad day.

I dragged my eyes away. I wasn't here for this. I was here for my boys.

Ellis motioned us back the way we had come.

Bearing in mind my own advice about not interfering in any way, I stayed at his shoulder and concentrated on keeping my feet as we picked our way through rubble-strewn streets.

In my ear, a female voice said, 'Two minutes. Estimated landing site one hundred yards to your right. Remain where you are. Maintain safe distance.'

'Copy that,' said Ellis.

We stood in our teams, backs against a solid wall for protection. I was looking all around me. Where were they? Where would they appear?

I had forgotten to count down the seconds in my head and the two minutes seemed a very long time. Were their calculations wrong? Had we missed them somehow? I took a pace forwards to see what was happening around me and Ellis pulled me back against the wall. Something dropped from above, missing us by inches and shattering on the ground at our feet, but he still wouldn't let me move.

I was turning my head, trying to see everything at once, worried I wouldn't be looking in the right direction when the pod materialised. Straining my eyes for a familiar tiny flicker in all this noise and movement.

It wasn't like that at all. I don't know why I worried I would miss them. You would have had to have been dead to have missed them.

From nowhere, there came a great rushing wind. A roaring wind that picked up thatch, wool, dust, splinters of wood, and left them all whirling in its wake. Something blurred past like an express train, destroying the wall opposite, bringing down the house behind it and the one behind that and so on, shattering everything in its path, right across the city. Like a runaway express train. New fires bloomed in its wake.

Everyone else did the sensible thing. They screamed and ran away. Everyone ran. Crusaders, mercenaries, the local inhabitants. Rubble, timbers, thatch, stonework were all exploding into the air and, then, as is usual in the scheme of things, dropping heavily back to earth again.

We did the unsensible thing. We ran towards. We followed the trail of destruction. We scrambled through unsafe buildings, clambered over smoking debris, fought our way through people so terrified that nothing we could do could possibly make things any worse. We followed – for want of a better expression – the skidmarks.

I thought we'd find the pod at the end of the burning trail. Like a pot of gold at the end of the rainbow. But there was nothing. No pod anywhere. But I couldn't see any sort of crater either, so it hadn't exploded on impact. It just wasn't here.

I stared around, bewildered. Pods are designed to put up with a lot. Fire, explosions, impact – they're supposed to be almost indestructible. Dieter and I dropped one off a cliff once, and we survived. Professor Penrose and I found ourselves in a place so far away that time didn't even exist, and apart from minor melting of the casing, we survived that as well. On the other hand, they're not designed to be blasted out of existence at one end of the jump and crash land into an entire city at the other. Because no, it hadn't exploded. Worse – it had disintegrated. It had just fallen apart. Now that my eyes were becoming accustomed, I could see a piece of the console. And a bent and twisted locker door. And over there was part of the toilet door hanging from a hinge.

And there was the main part of the pod – what was left of it – lying on its side, half buried under a demolished building and with black smoke pouring from the remains of the console. But there was no fire.

'Spread out,' said Ellis. 'Search pattern alpha. Activate your tag readers. One security team with one medical team. You all know what to do. Eyes open everyone.'

At least we didn't have to worry about the locals. They'd long since gone and even the Crusaders had sensibly decided this was a good time to rape and pillage somewhere else.

I stayed with Ellis as the teams scattered, tag readers bleeping.

They found Markham first.

A shout went up and I could see a group of them bending over something I couldn't see.

I scrambled over ruined buildings and kicked aside burning timbers, hearing my own heart thump inside my head, terrified of what I might see.

He lay, face down, half buried under a pile of rubble. Not moving. Broken and covered in blood. He was burned in places. He hadn't been wearing armour and most of his clothing had been torn away. I could see white bone.

A medical team shouldered everyone out of the way and began unpacking their kit. Their security people formed a protective ring around them.

'How is he?' I said, preparing myself for the worst.

They were all too busy to talk.

Ellis took my arm. 'Let them do their job.'

'But I don't even know if he's alive or dead.'

'He's alive.'

'How do you know that?'

'They're working on him. They wouldn't do that if he was dead. Come on. Three more to find.'

He'd barely finished speaking when another shout went up.

'Van Owen. Over here. I've found her.'

I went to join the medics as they crowded around her, but at the same moment, another shout went up, indicating they'd found Guthrie.

It wasn't good.

He was still in the remains of the pod. Unlike the others, he hadn't been thrown clear. I didn't see how he could possibly still be alive. He lay, impaled on a jagged piece of metal, the end of which was piercing his shoulder. His helmet had been torn off and his whole face was a mask of blood. I could only see one eye. Astoundingly, he was not only alive, he was conscious – or seemed to be. His eye was half open, although I don't think he was seeing anything. He was in shock, shaking, white-faced, teeth clenched against the pain.

There was something else. What was it? What wasn't right? A silly voice in my head said, 'What is wrong with this picture?'

I couldn't take it in. It just didn't register. Guthrie was here. His leg was over there. How could that be? Why was his leg all the way over there? I could see it quite clearly. Quite intact. Boot, armour, all there, just a nasty ribbon of flesh and torn skin dangling from the end. For one stupid, stupid moment, I wondered if he had three legs. Had he brought a spare? And then, of course, I realised. He'd lost his leg. My dear friend Ian had lost his leg.

I threw myself to the ground beside him, hardly aware of the pain in my knees.

'Ian. Ian, it's Max. We're here. We've got you. Can you hear me?'

His eye flickered towards me. He grunted, 'Max,' and then as if that had opened the floodgates of pain, he began to scream.

I was shouldered aside by another medical team. Smoothly, they split themselves into two teams. One for Guthrie and one for his leg. Ellis yanked me to my feet and pulled me out of the way.

I stood watching them work. Not daring to look around me. After seeing Guthrie and Markham, I had no hope left. How could Leon possibly be alive?

'Guthrie's still alive,' said Ellis, reading my mind. 'His armour and helmet went a long way towards protecting him. Markham survived and he wasn't wearing any at all. Leon will have been protected too.'

Protected against what? Against being blown up by a madman? Against being hurled through time and space in a disintegrating pod? Against crashing into half a city on landing? Against having his pod break up around him?

'The other three are still alive,' said Ellis softly. 'He will be, too.'

He might have been right, but we couldn't find him.

We walked a spiral pattern, covering every inch, everyone staring at the ground. No one spoke. I wondered if they were looking for body parts rather than an actual body. Ellis was consulting others, as they tried to get consistent readings from their instruments. And all the time the smoke billowed, hampering all our efforts, and the distant screaming never went away.

My fear was that Leon was completely buried and it would be beyond our resources to dig him out. That they would have to leave him. Of course they would. They'd want to get the other three back for life-saving treatment as soon as possible. Especially Guthrie. A limb is only viable for so long. Yes, they were searching for Leon – and very diligently too – but the time would come when a good commander – and Captain Ellis was a very good commander – would give the order to withdraw. I didn't blame him. In his position I would probably do the same.

Except that it was Leon and the chances of me going back with them and leaving him here were nil. They couldn't force me to go. They couldn't use Matthew against me and, let's face it, most of them would probably be quite happy to leave me here for ever anyway.

I climbed to the top of what might, two days ago, have been a public oven and looked around me. I could mark the pod's progress by the deep, burning groove through shattered walls and houses. I could see where it had broken up, hurling out Markham, and Van Owen more or less in the same spot. I could see the Time Police, turning over rubble and timbers, kicking open sagging doors, sticking their heads through holes in walls, waving their tag readers around, all of them doing everything they possibly could, and still not finding Leon. Who could be trapped, dreadfully injured but still alive, as the flames drew ever closer to him. I saw pictures in my head. Leon burning to death. Bleeding to death. Stabbed to death. Trampled to death. Dying alone. He could be only yards away and I'd never know. He might actually be able to see me and couldn't call out. He might be dying now and I'd never know.

The sudden rush of panic made my head spin. I bent and put my hands on my knees, fighting off feelings of being trapped for ever in this bloody helmet.

I had a sudden memory of Matthew's dark head, bent over his box of new toys. Well, he wouldn't miss me. He would probably settle at TPHQ very well. The place was full of men and they had the definitive Time Map. He'd like it there.

'He's not with the others.'

Who had said that?

Matthew had said that. He had said, 'He's not with the others.'

I didn't stop to question how he could know such a thing. I was prepared to seize any straw. He'd been right. Leon wasn't with the others. I didn't know or care how Matthew could possibly know or that he hadn't also told me where Leon actually was. I had come to find Leon and that's what I was going to do. To find Leon and bring him home.

I turned and stared in the direction diametrically opposed to where we'd found the others. The remains of a high wall – none too safe by the looks of it – would be a good starting point. From there I could work my way back towards the med teams, still frantically working.

I scrambled over rubble, feeling it shift under my feet, burning my hands a couple of times and wishing I'd thought to wear gloves. Close up, the wall looked even more precarious than it had from fifty feet away. If Leon was anywhere near it then we would both be in trouble.

Several black figures were making their way towards me.

'What are you doing over here?' asked Ellis.

I took a deep breath and told the truth. 'Matthew said he wouldn't be with the others.'

He looked at me for very long moment and then said, 'Did he indeed? Well, I think that's worth investigating, don't you? See what you can find, guys.' They consulted their tag readers, muttered to each other, and moved away.

We stood in silence and then he looked at his watch and said, 'Max...'

'I know,' I said. 'You must do what you need to do,' and tried not to think about how I would feel as their pod blinked away and I was alone in all this destruction.

And then a voice spoke very quietly.

'We've found him.'

I peered through the drifting smoke. About twenty yards away, an officer had raised his arm. Another crouched over something. The remaining medical team was scrambling towards them, but carefully. The remains of the high wall hung over them. Given the amount of stonework and timber, I wondered if this had been a church. It was certainly substantial enough to have brought a runaway pod to a halt, but whatever it was, having performed this useful function, had then collapsed, leaving just this one precarious-looking section still standing.

Ellis took my hand. 'Come on, Max. Let's go and see.'

And – now that the moment had come – I wasn't sure I wanted to know. If I remained here then there was a chance Leon could still be alive, but if I went and looked then I would know for certain. I remembered Leon's voice from long ago, telling me about Schrödinger's Cat. Two possibilities. The cat is alive. The cat is dead. And only when you open the box to look do the realities collide and you know, one way or the other, whether the cat is alive or the cat is dead. But so long as I stood over here, there would always be the hope that Leon could be alive.

'Max?'

'I'm sorry. I was thinking about Schrödinger's Cat.'

Staggeringly, he understood. 'Well, let's go and see, shall we?'

The only thing that stopped me falling apart completely was that Leon's visor was down and I couldn't see his face. I told myself it was some other man who lay at my feet.

We couldn't get to him. He was buried under a criss-cross of burning timbers. I remember thinking it looked like that child's game where you have to pick up a coloured stick without disturbing any of the others – I couldn't remember what it was called.

We heaved and strained at the beams but it wasn't easy. Every time we pulled at one, something moved somewhere else. It was a giant cat's cradle of heavy wood.

In the end, Ellis stood back, directing operations, instructing us to lift this end, pull that bit free, hold that one up, slide this one out. It all took time. Too much time. Every now and then he tilted his head and I knew he was listening on his private link. I could guess what they were telling him.

I left them to get on with it, because I was less worried about the timbers under which Leon was pinned and more about the very, very unstable wall towering above us all. Captain Ellis followed my gaze. 'Keep an eye on that for me, will you, Max. I'm concentrating on getting Chief Farrell free.'

I nodded gratefully, not for one moment taking my gaze from the wall, which gave me an excellent excuse for not seeing what they were doing to Leon. Because I couldn't even think about it. That he would come so far, survive so much, only to die now, within sight of rescue. And there was nothing I could do. I stared at the wall as if, by sheer strength of will, I could stop it toppling on us all.

Their talk was all of the job in hand. Quiet instructions were issued and carried out without fuss. The medical team had set up drips and were still monitoring his readings – so he was still alive. I stared at the crumbling brickwork. Somewhere out there, a city was dying, but I have no memory of the shouts, the screams, the flames. I watched the wall. There's an old smuggling saying:

Watch the wall my darling, as the gentlemen go by.

And I did. I watched that wall to within an inch of its life.

And then, suddenly, everything happened at once. The last few timbers were lifted and tossed aside. Whether, in some way, the timbers had been supporting the wall, or whether it was just its time to fall, I don't know. The wall moved. It leaned. A stream of dust fell down upon us. Small stones rattled down; the precursors of the bigger stuff to come.

I opened my mouth to shout a warning but it was too late.

I had the briefest glimpse of Leon, visor up, white

406

faced, among a throng of Time Police, and then the wall sagged.

Two men seized Leon by the straps on his armour and dragged him out of the way, bumping him over the rough ground. The medical team threw themselves sideways. Captain Ellis lost his balance and fell. Without even thinking – I have to stop doing that – I threw myself over his upper body.

I don't know what hit me. I only know that it was heavy. Wood or stone – something struck me a massive blow between my shoulder blades, driving all the breath from my body.

I lay, face down over Matthew Ellis, completely unable to move. Frightened thoughts scampered through my brain. Was I paralysed? Had I sustained some dreadful injury to my spine?

A muffled voice said, 'You just can't stop saving my life, can you?

Someone shouted. The weight was lifted. Someone gently rolled me over. I remember I cried out in pain.

There was a babble of voices.

'We need to get out of here now. The whole lot could come down at any moment.'

'Stretcher. Bring up another stretcher.'

'We only have four, sir.'

'Well, we can't leave her here and she can't walk so think of something.'

At that moment, I couldn't have cared less if they'd gone off and left me. I was in so much pain I could hardly think straight. I tried to tell myself this was a good thing. The pain showed that things were still working. Just a

407

little less pain would have been good though. Everything hurt. My ribs, my back, my front, my inside, my outside. Everything. A thick, hot, never-ending pain radiated outwards, sitting heavily over my heart like a lump of red-hot lead. I had no idea about broken bones but I certainly had extensive soft-tissue trauma. My back felt as if it was on fire and I had pins and needles in my hands and feet. I wondered whether, if I hadn't been wearing armour, I would be dead.

Someone said, 'Can she stand?'

'Not a chance.'

They were fitting me with a neck brace and, from what I could see at ground level, they were improvising a stretcher from a broken door. Everyone worked quickly and efficiently. I felt comforted.

We set off for the pod. I assumed the others had gone on ahead with Leon and I still didn't know if he was alive or dead. Then there was Guthrie, with his terrible wounds, and Markham, covered in blood. And I hadn't even seen Van Owen.

I lay on my side and tried to grip the edge of the door, feeling it tip and tilt as they scrambled over the uneven surfaces, up and down steps, around corners. I lay still, lost in my own little pile of pain

I was pleased to see everyone else had proper stretchers – canvas between light tubular poles. The poor sods with my heavy wooden door had definitely drawn the short straw. I had a horrible feeling the officer on the front right-hand corner was the one whose thumb I'd dislocated last year. It was probably best not to mention that now.

The journey back seemed endless although they told me afterwards that our return trip was considerably quicker than our outgoing trip. Everyone just put their heads down and ran. The security teams ranged around us, shouting and waving their guns at anyone stupid enough to get close to us. Not many did. There was enough going on in Constantinople that day without taking on nausea-inducing black-clad strangers as well.

They did their best, but speed does not mean comfort. I think the others were unconscious, but I was wide awake for every bone-jolting moment of it. Ellis ran alongside, saying, 'Sorry, Max. Just hang on,' every now and then. They were all doing their best, so I stifled my groans, did as I was told, and hung on.

And then, just as I thought we'd made it – just when we were within sight of the pod, I heard a shout and my team ground to a halt.

One or two men appeared from a wrecked building. I could hear more men shouting and laughing. Someone inside was screaming. My group was at the rear of our column, moving slowly and awkwardly. The door was heavy and so was I. No one had an arm free. Even more men poured out of the door, swords in hand.

I was lying on my left side. I had a tiny sonic weapon clapped to the sticky patch on my leg, but the officer on the right-hand corner had a much bigger effort in a holster on his hip. I reached over, doing myself an enormous amount of hurt, pulled it free, aimed, and fired past him.

I heard nothing but something certainly happened.

The leaders stopped and staggered. One put his hands on his knees and began to vomit. Red wine by the looks of

409

it. The others appeared to lose their balance and sat down suddenly. One turned and ran full tilt into the door jamb, hitting it so hard that he knocked himself unconscious and brought a hail of dust and small stones down on top of him.

'Nice,' said the Time Police officer appreciatively. 'Tell me again about treating hostile contemporaries like fragile flowers.'

It hurt to speak, but in a low drone between short, shallow breaths, I told him to go forth and multiply.

We ditched my door outside the pod and thundered up the ramp which hissed shut behind us, shutting out the noise of a dying city. They lowered me gently and covered me with a blanket. I stretched out on the cold floor and tried to see what was going on.

There were only people's boots. I could hear the medical teams, urgent but calm. Requests for drugs, instruments, readings. Bloody swabs fell to the floor like a colourful blizzard. The occasional instrument tinkled.

Ellis was demanding to know when we could jump.

'In a moment,' said a deep voice. 'Nurse…'

'Got it,' said someone quietly.

The bustle continued.

I plucked at Ellis's leg. 'What's … happening? Why … aren't we … jumping?'

He crouched at my side. 'We're stabilising them. In case of a rough landing. Don't worry, this is a portable hospital, they're being well taken care of. This is standard procedure. And they're all still alive. They have to be. We're not allowed to die in here. It leads to additional paperwork and it makes the med team grumpy. Well, grumpier. They were grumpy when they got here.'

'Leon?'

'They're all still alive. We're working hard to keep them that way.'

My entire body was just one mass of pain, radiating out from my heart.

'Am I ... having ... a heart attack?'

'No, it just seems that way.'

I tried to look around him. To see what was going on.

'Keep still, Max,' he said sharply, pulling the blanket up to my chin. 'Don't try to move at all. We don't yet know the extent of your injuries.'

'Tell me ... about Ian.'

'We were able to retrieve his leg. It's been preserved and we're taking it back, but I'm making no promises. And there's some damage to his eyes as well.'

I heard someone say, 'Team Three – ready.'

'Team Two – ready.'

'Team Four – ready.'

Silence.

'Team One?'

'Just a minute.' Another long pause. Team One was Leon. 'OK. Team One – ready.'

'Commence jump procedures.'

The world flickered.

Still disappointing.

We didn't disembark immediately. From floor level I watched other people's boots moving backwards and forwards. I lay very still, trying to hear what was going on. The ramp was down and medical people moved in and

411

out, wheeling equipment around.

Worryingly, they moved Leon first. I watched his wheels disappear from my narrow view. Then Markham. Then Van Owen.

Guthrie had a huge number of medical personnel around him, but eventually, he too was wheeled away.

That left me, still lying on the floor. I opened my eyes to find I was surrounded by a number of Time Police boots. You would have thought that would have brought me to my feet but, somehow, I just couldn't bring myself to care. I could hear disjointed phrases. 'Blow to her spine … rib contusions … intercostals … damage … fractures.' None of that sounded too serious. A little less pain would be good, though. A figure crouched alongside, syringe in hand, and smiled in what she probably thought was a reassuring manner.

It seemed I was about to get my wish.

I lay in a Time Police bed, wearing a Time Police hospital gown, staring up at a Time Police ceiling. I was experiencing difficulty in breathing. And standing. And sitting. And lying. And living. My ribs ached. It hurt to move. And it hurt not to move. Massive painkillers made me woozy.

I should have been panicking. What was happening with Leon and the others? How much damage had I sustained? Would I ever walk again? But the medication took care of all that. Which was probably their plan.

A deep-voiced doctor swam into view again.

I croaked, 'Leon?'

'No, I'm a doctor. Just lie still, please.'

There's only one thing worse than a doctor without a sense of humour and that's one with.

'Is he dead?'

'No. And before you ask, you're not going to die, either. You have a bruise the size of a kitchen table all over your back and your bottom looks as if you've sat in a plate of blackberries.'

I wasn't sure how comfortable I was with the Time Police peering at my bottom.

'Will I walk again?'

'Yes.'

'You're sure?'

'Pretty sure, yes.' He still hadn't looked at me. 'We don't have any particular treatment for you. Not that we're just going to let you lie here and do nothing, of course. We'll let you drift off into merciful, pain-free oblivion and then we'll wake you up and make you take some deep breaths. Which will hurt. Then we'll make you cough. Which will be excruciating. We need to keep your lungs working and prevent infection. We'll keep at it until you either die or get better. We're the Time Police, you know – this isn't some girlie St Mary's where you wake up between clean sheets and look forward to a happy ending.'

He lifted his eyes from his medical gizmo to look at me, which was probably a cardinal sin in the Time Police doctor/patient etiquette rules. Never look at the patient. It only encourages them to think they matter.

'Where is Leon?'

'Safe.'

'But where?'

'Here.'

For God's sake … I was instantly suspicious. What was he hiding from me?

'Tell me the truth. Will he die?'

He said very quietly, 'I'm honestly not sure yet. But he's still with us so try not to worry too much.'

'Guthrie?'

He hesitated. 'We have re-attached the lower part of his leg. Not sure yet how that's going to turn out, but I'm reasonably optimistic. He has lost the sight of one eye.'

I closed my eyes. Ian, my friend…

'And Van Owen?'

'Pretty smashed up.'

'That's a medical term, is it?'

'We tend to dumb things down for St Mary's, but she's stable. The other one, however…'

I panicked. 'You mean Markham?' I saw him again. Lying in the rubble. Broken, bloody … 'What does "however" mean?'

'Awake and talking.'

'*What*?'

I forgot my ribs and tried to sit up and even the medication couldn't cope with that.

'For heaven's sake,' he said. 'I know you're from St Mary's but do the words *just lie still* not mean anything to you?'

'He's awake?'

'He is.'

'He's talking?'

'Well, his mouth is opening and closing but he's not actually making any sense at the moment.'

'No, that's quite normal.'

'Well, that's a relief. We're not sure he's much aware of what's going on around him, which means he probably won't know about the enormous sexual harassment suit coming his way from at least three of my nurses. One of whom is male.'

'He can't help himself,' I said. 'I recommend you put something in his tea to calm him down.'

'We can do better than that. We've sent for a…' He consulted his gizmo again. '… Nurse Hunter, who is, I

415

believe, his significant other.'

Peterson would want me to ask. 'Do you mean his wife?'

He started bashing his gizmo again. 'Is he married?'

'Don't you know?'

'Well, if you don't know then how should I?'

Good point, I suppose.

'Dr Bairstow will also be here sometime this afternoon, together with Dr Stone who will form his own assessment of the situation with a view to shipping you all back to St Mary's and out of my medical centre as soon as possible.'

'Thank you for making us feel so welcome.'

He flashed me a brief smile. 'Not at all, Dr Maxwell. Would you like to give me a gentle cough now?'

I closed my eyes. Doctors. I hate them.

Leon remained unconscious. I spent as much time with him as they would allow me. He hadn't woken up next to me for a long time and I was determined I would be there when he eventually opened his eyes. He lay motionless, barely visible through all the equipment surrounding him. Occasionally he seemed to sigh. I held his hand and waited.

Two days later they told me I was much better. I could barely move and barely breathe so this was obviously some Time Police definition of the word better – as in 'not actually dead'. I was commanded to exercise and there was no arguing with them, so twice a day I allowed myself to be pried away from Leon's bedside to roam the corridors, keeping my eyes peeled in case I came across anything that could be used against them in the future. Because, of course, they were just the sort of organisation to leave top-secret stuff lying around where any prying historian could get her hands on it, weren't they?

Anyway, I was shuffling painfully down yet another anonymous beige corridor, worrying about Leon, when two officers appeared, walking towards me. The corridor wasn't wide enough for all three of us abreast and since it was obvious I had the manoeuvrability of a super-tanker with the handbrake on, they were going to have to step aside for me.

As I limped past, I heard one of them say, 'Bloody St Mary's – they think they own the place.'

I stopped dead.

There are those who say that violence is never the answer. Apparently, having a massive punch-up is not the mature way forward. The response to any sort of conflict, they say, is a fair-minded discussion in which both sides are able to state their grievances in an attitude of tolerance and non-judgmental what-not. All parties are supposed to discuss their feelings and agree a solution. According to these people – who, let's face it, are not normal – conflict resolution should proceed thusly:

Giant, scarred, muscle-bound Time Police officer: I am upset that so many St Mary's personnel are currently in our building. It makes me feel threatened and afraid.

Small and only slightly less scarred St Mary's historian: I recognise and understand your feelings. I am upset that my husband is possibly dying and your hostility makes me feel vulnerable.

TP: I regret my attitude has caused you to react in this manner. Your feelings are understandable and I will endeavour to keep my insecurities in check.

St Mary's: I am grateful for your endeavours. I accept the validity of your feelings and will keep my appearances to a minimum. Perhaps later we could embark together upon a session of meditation and relaxation to embrace feelings of mutual tolerance and respect.

TP: I endorse your suggestion and would like to offer you this small phial of lavender and tea-tree oil which I find to be extremely beneficial in times of stress. I am also in possession of a mantra which, when chanted regularly, induces feelings of great calm and tranquillity.

St Mary's: I am most grateful for this show of understanding and pleased that a resolution to this conflict has been proposed. I look forward to joining you later.

TP: Would you like to borrow my leg-warmers?

St Mary's: What a kind thought. Which way is the bar?

And then, of course, there's the proper way of doing things.

I spun – well, lurched – around and was in his face, demanding to know what his problem was.

He replied that I, along with every other member of St Mary's, was his problem and that every time he turned around there was another of us scuttling along the corridor. Like rats.

I replied that we were here only because the Time Police make such a piss-boiling cock-up of everything they touch that they need St Mary's to sort it all out for them.

Any reservations he might have had about thumping

418

an injured historian went straight out of the window. They were closely followed by any sensible qualms I might have had about taking on two enormous, state-sponsored bullies while in less than perfect health myself. We squared up to each other. I was all set to go. My boys were upstairs in pieces, and now the god of historians had presented me with two of the people responsible for that, an empty corridor, and just the sort of mood to do some damage. I take back everything I've ever said about the god of historians. As deities go – top banana!

Fortunately for all of us, at that moment the lift door opened revealing Captain Ellis on the threshold with Matthew at his side.

Damn and blast. Obviously, I didn't want Matthew to see his mother brawling in public. We all stepped back, held a small competition to see who could summon the falsest smile, while making it absolutely clear that hostilities had only ceased because of the presence of a senior officer and a small boy, and began to edge past each other.

'Are they going to shoot Mummy again?' piped Matthew. I thought I detected a slight note of anticipation.

'No one's shooting anyone,' said Ellis reassuringly, and stared across at his men, who said nothing but managed to convey their disappointment at this sad state of affairs.

'Where are you off to?' I said, donning my mother hat.

'Time Map,' said Matthew simply, obviously losing interest now he'd ascertained no one was about to shoot Mummy.

Ellis just grinned. They disappeared around a corner,

the officers cast me unloving looks, and I pushed off while I still could.

Obviously someone had a word with Commander Hay. I suspect she had a word with Dr Bairstow. Who turned up to have a word with me. Apparently, we were all to be shipped back to St Mary's. Even the still unconscious Leon. I think it was felt that relations between our two organisations would be immeasurably improved if we saw much less of each other for a while. A bit like marriage, I suppose. Anyway, mutual relief at seeing the back of each other caused us all to be quite civil to each other and, by the end of the week, we were back at St Mary's. I felt better at once, although Dr Bairstow warned me that any fighting in the corridors would result in his extreme displeasure. I was so happy to be home that I was easily able to ignore the injustice of his comments and just smiled and nodded.

I wasn't around when Hunter and Markham were reunited, but I was sitting with Guthrie when Peterson and Grey turned up.

'Just like old times again,' slurred Markham from beneath his mass of flexi-bandages and tubes. Very little of him was visible, which Peterson said was a huge improvement, and had he considered making this his permanent look.

I thought he looked like a badly wrapped Egyptian mummy, and Guthrie, speaking in a painful whisper, likened him to one of those adverts for toilet paper, except the puppy did it better.

Peterson was pinning a sign above Guthrie's bed.

Here lies One-eyed Guthrie, twinned with Cyclops, Nick Fury, Mad-Eye Moody, Rooster Cogburn, Odin and Horatio Nelson.

When he was satisfied it was level, he climbed down off the chair, put a very brief hand on Guthrie's shoulder, and went off to sit with Markham.

Grey, confronted with the wreck that was Guthrie, sat wordless, silent tears pouring down her cheeks. If – *when* – Leon ever opened his eyes, I was going to be at least as bad. I felt so sorry for her, but any sympathy would just push her right over the edge. And maybe the rest of us, too. Guthrie looked at me through his bandages, appealing for help.

I nodded.

'I know why you're here,' he said to her, carefully not noticing her tears. He had to turn his head to see me as well. 'I'm less clear about you, but that just about sums up our working relationship.'

I beamed at him. 'I'm visiting the sick.'

He nodded over to Leon, still asleep in his cubicle and still surrounded by medical machinery. 'Don't you have your own sick to visit?'

'He's not awake yet.'

'He's not stupid, is he? If I'd known that I would find you crouched at my bedside, then I wouldn't have woken up either.'

'Hey, I'm sick too, you know.'

'That is pretty much the consensus. Both here and at Time Police HQ.'

'Aren't sick people supposed to be saintly and patient?

421

That's where the word comes from.'

'I've worked with you for more years than I care to remember. On at least three separate occasions that I can remember, I have had to exercise the greatest self-control to refrain from shooting you. I have also not stabbed you, poisoned you, drowned you, or pushed you out of a window. And don't think that last one wasn't a struggle. I have, at all times, conducted myself with the greatest professional decorum. I've never even boxed your ears and I can't begin to describe what a temptation that's been. So yes, saintly exactly describes me.'

'Actually, I meant the word patient.'

'I work with historians. Patience is a given.'

'Hey,' said Grey, who had used the time to get herself under control and wipe her eyes. 'I'm an historian too, you know.'

He took her hand. 'One makes allowances for the woman one loves.'

She smiled mistily at him. He smiled back.

I told them I was departing in search of a sick bag and struggled to get up.

'Need a hand?' said Peterson.

'I'm fine. I can do it.'

'You should let others help,' said Markham, veteran of more than his fair share of hospital treatment. 'No man is an island.'

Peterson wheeled around to face him. 'When did you read John Donne?'

'Just now,' he said, nodding at the small leatherbound book on his bedside table.

'No,' said Peterson, firmly. 'That's it. I've had enough.

Where were you educated?'

'School – same as everyone else.'

'And then?'

'More bloody school,' Markham said feelingly. 'I mean – it just went on and on.'

'Which school?'

He shifted in his bed, radiating all the righteous discomfort of one who nearly died for the cause and is determined to cash in on that. 'Oh, all sorts. Can't remember the names of most of them. I think you should all go away now. I'm feeling rather weak, you know.'

'Tell me the truth and I will,' said Peterson commandingly. 'Are you married or not?'

'He's married?' said Grey in astonishment, twisting in her chair to look at him. 'To whom?'

'Hunter,' I said.

'You're kidding. Although actually, now I come to think of it…' She paused, considering.

'If you say our children will be both smart and beautiful then I won't be responsible for my actions,' warned Markham.

'You're not responsible for your actions anyway,' said Peterson scathingly. 'Max, we're going to get to the bottom of this. You hold him down and I'll punch his head.'

Markham painfully pulled the bedclothes up to his chin. 'Why is it so dark? Am I slipping away? Is that you, mother?'

'What's going on?' demanded Hunter from the doorway. Dr Stone stood with her. I had a nasty feeling they'd been there for some time. Certainly long enough to

423

hear Peterson threaten one of their patients with violence.

Markham reached out a trembling hand to her. 'Save me.'

'You're never going to believe this, but Max was about to beat up a helpless patient,' said Peterson, displaying the qualities that would take him to the very top of the management tree. Along with all the other monkeys.

'I am frequently appalled at the horrifying levels of violence displayed at St Mary's,' said Dr Stone. 'Everyone who isn't a patient should leave now. That includes you, Maxwell.'

'I'm a patient,' I said, miffed at my loss of status.

'You're only a former patient,' said Dr Stone to me. 'You've been downgraded to convalescent. Go away and stop harassing the sick people.'

'You can't harass Markham – it's not possible. We're just trying to find out if he's married to Hunter or not.'

Hunter wheeled on him. 'You're telling people we're married?'

'I really don't feel at all well. I think I may have been overdoing things. I'm quite badly injured, you know.'

She was glaring at him, hands on hips.

'Why are you telling people we're married?'

'Note,' whispered Peterson to me. 'She's not denying it. A little courage and strength of purpose and we'll finally get to the bottom of this, Max. Take your cue from me.'

She swung around to him. 'Why are you still here?'

He quailed. 'I – er – um – we…'

'Don't you *want* to be married to me?' quavered

Markham, piteously.

Heads swung back to Hunter. Who paused.

Markham was grinning at her over the bedclothes.

She glared back at him and he just grinned some more. Asking for trouble.

'You can wipe that stupid smile off your face right now.'

'Go on then, tell them we're not married.'

She went to speak, paused and looked at him.

He returned her stare in what he probably thought was a beguiling manner.

Apart from Leon's machines, the ward was very quiet.

She folded her arms. 'I'm not saying anything about marriage, but I'll tell you this for nothing – our child *is* going to be both smart and beautiful.'

'Well, of course it will be,' he said smugly, and then stopped.

I saw the exact moment realisation dawned. 'Wait. What? What did you say?'

He tried to sit up, hurt himself and fell back on his pillows again with a cry of pain. I thought everyone would rush to help, but no one was looking at him. For some reason, everyone was staring over my shoulder. At the same time, one of Leon's many machines began to beep. For a second, I didn't get it. And then I did.

I turned slowly, half in hope, half in fear. It was Schrödinger's Cat all over again. I remember I moved very slowly. Everything was happening very slowly. I looked at Leon. Waiting for the realities to collide. To know … I was trembling all over. I remember someone putting their arms around me to hold me up. My legs were going. I couldn't take it in. Because suddenly, I did know.

Leon had opened his eyes.

THE END

ACKNOWLEDGMENTS

Grateful thanks to Dr Alan Greaves BA MA PhD from the University of Liverpool for his company over lunch and for allowing me to pick his brains concerning buried artefacts. Any mistakes are all mine.

And to Sian Grzeszczyk who so graciously allowed me to use her surname as an inspiration for Max's eye test.

More thanks to Jan and Mike for their hospitality.

Thanks to the world's newest superhero, Editwoman, who patiently answers questions ranging from the use of coffins at funerals, to how to spell the plural of willy, where the hyphen goes in baboon-buggering son, and the difference between otic conflagration and aural conflagration. Not a lot of people know that. I certainly didn't.

The Nothing Girl

Getting a life isn't always easy. And hanging on to it is even harder.

Known as The Nothing Girl because of her stutter, disregarded by her family, isolated and alone, Jenny Dove's life is magically transformed by the appearance of Thomas, a mystical golden horse only she can see. Under his loving guidance, Jenny acquires a husband – the charming and chaotic Russell Checkland – together with an omnivorous donkey and The Cat From Hell.

Jenny's life will never be the same again, but a series of 'accidents' leads her to wonder for how long she will be allowed to enjoy it.

Hailed as a fairy tale for adults, Jodi Taylor brings all her comic writing skills to a heart-warming and delightful story.